Incendiary

THE PREMONITION SERIES
VOLUME 4

AMY A. BARTOL

Also By Amy A. Bartol
Inescapable: The Premonition Series Volume 1
Intuition: The Premonition Series Volume 2
Indebted: The Premonition Series Volume 3

ISBN: 1479207128
ISBN-13: 9781479207121
Library of Congress Control Number: 2012917672
CreateSpace Independent Publishing Platform
North Charleston, South Carolina

For my dad, John Lutz. I love you.

Contents

Evie

CHAPTER 1

The Moon

Opening my eyes in the darkness of the bedroom, the sheer canopy surrounding the bed sparkles with frost. I sit up against the pillows, allowing the silken sheet to slip from me. Reed, sleeping soundly next to me, looks so peaceful...angelic. His dark brown hair is falling over his brow in messy wisps. Reaching out, I smooth his hair lightly away from his face, feeling his warm skin beneath my fingertips. His charcoal-colored angel wing slips forward a little, brushing against my thigh. It, too, is warm against my frigid skin.

Something's wrong, I shiver, exhaling a breath and seeing it curl into a white current in front of me, as wintery air will do. It's too cold...Goose bumps rise on my arms as dread runs like icy water through me. Zephyr's island is located in the South Pacific; it never gets this cold here.

I toss my long, auburn hair over my shoulder and wrap the white sheet securely around my body. I put my bare feet on the teak floorboards, feeling them crackle with cold beneath me. Frosty condensation covers everything in the room, causing surfaces to sparkle eerily in the hazy moonlight from the half-shuttered windows.

Walking slowly to the bedroom door, I turn and go to the front door of our small, beach bungalow. As I open it, black clouds roll and boil toward the cove of Zephyr's island paradise. My hand clutches the doorframe, watching the ominous storm blowing in. The wind whistles against the feathers of my crimson wings, causing them to ruffle. The palm trees that line the beach are swaying in the breeze as the whitecap water churns against the white sand.

I hear cracking sounds, like someone is walking on ice too thin to sustain weight. A dark figure strides beneath the storm clouds toward me out on the open water. A thin layer of ice forms beneath his feet with each step he takes. Coming closer, the wind carries his sweet, sticky scent to me, covering me like it's marking me as his. A terrible kind of love swells in my heart—painful and raw—enslaving and cruel.

With slow, obedient steps, I walk toward the water's edge, feeling powdery, icy sand between my toes. Frigid water laps against my feet, wetting the bottom of my sheet, as I wait for Brennus to come to me. Wearing a dark, perfectly tailored suit, he appears outwardly calm. His steps are unmeasured, strolling over the ice as it continually branches out ahead of each of his strides beneath the wicked sky.

Stopping in front of me, only a breath away, Brennus smiles. He scans every inch of me with his assessing gaze. His black hair, which contrasts starkly with his pale, white skin in the moonlight, doesn't hide his eyes as they darken with pleasure. "*Mo chroí*," he breathes, calling me "my heart." "Ye seem ta have escaped da fallen *aingeals* quite well."

I nod numbly, whispering, "You survived, too, I see." There is fear and relief in my tone, betraying my feelings for him. Looking into his light green eyes, they're registering his relief at finding me.

Brennus shrugs. "I'm a good swimmer, so I survived da spell ye cast ta scatter da fallen *aingeals* and wi'out Casimir ta lead dem, da Fallen lost deir focus and began ta recognize dat dey were losing da battle," Brennus replies with an angelic expression on his beautiful face.

Seeing him smiling, it's hard for me to remember that he's truly a killer—a lethal predator. It's difficult for me to think of Brennus as evil now because he protected me, not only from the Ifrit, Valentine, who would've killed me, but also from the army of fallen angels who stalk me still. But, he had also enslaved me, keeping me from everyone that I love so that he could make me his queen: a queen to reside over the Gancanagh—his race of undead, magical Faeries with enthralling, toxic skin.

Brennus adds, "I tought dat ye were taken by da fallen *aingeals*. Dat's where we've been looking for ye."

His words evoke images of the last time I saw him a few weeks ago. Casimir and his army of fallen angels had cornered us at Brennus' estate in Ireland. I had used magic to save us by summoning the sea and drenching us all in a churning, swirl of ocean water. It had separated me from Brennus, washing me away from him and into Casimir's control.

"How's Molly? Finn? Declan?" I ask, not able to stop myself from inquiring about Brennus' brother, Finn, and my Gancanagh body-guard, Declan...my prison guards.

"Molly is grand. Finn is better. 'Twas Declan dat we were all worried about. He took losing ye very hard. He improved a wee bit when we found Casimir's corpse in pieces on the lawn of da estate. Was dat ye who killed him?" he asks with approval.

I shake my head, "No. Reed killed him," I reply, seeing a flicker of jealousy enter Brennus' eyes at the mention of Reed's name. He warned me never to speak my angel's name in his presence, so I try to cover my slip by asking, "How did you find me?"

"Ye took me blade wi' ye. 'Tis moin...it calls for me, jus as ye do, but ye do na know dat, do ye?" he replies. I close my eyes, feeling my heart begin to race as I think of the knife I'd taken and shoved into my boot when we were escaping from the army of fallen angels. "Come, we'll find a way for ye ta leave dis island now. Yer family misses ye. I miss ye," Brennus says softly. "'Tis time we had ye home."

Opening my eyes and staring into his, they reflect absolute certainty that I'll follow his orders and return with him. As his captive for the last few months, I had done my best to act like I was one of them, a Gancanagh, in order to survive. But now, I'm no longer his hostage. Now, I have a chance of staying with Reed, my love. Moistening my lips that have become very dry, I say, "I can't come with you, Brennus. I'm sorry."

"Why na?" he asks me patiently, like he has all the time in the world to sort this out.

"Because my family needs me and I need them," I reply, seeing his brows turn down as his mouth slants into a frown.

"We are yer family, *mo chroí*. Ye're our queen," he says calmly enough, but his pale face looks stern. "I am yer king."

I shake my head at him, taking a step back from the edge of the water and from his outstretched hand. My heart is beating so fast now that it's pounding in my ears. "I belong here, with them...with him," I say quietly, watching Brennus' frown turn into the darkest anger. A click sounds from Brennus as his retractable fangs shoot forward in his mouth and he bares their razor-sharp points menacingly.

"Ye would leave me alone wi' whah I feel for ye? I would die for ye. Is dat na enough for ye ta see dat I love ye?" he asks, sounding wounded and hurt.

"I know that you love me, Brennus. I even know that you would protect me with your life if I'd let you, but I can't let you. I can't be with you," I say, feeling tears coming to my eyes.

"Ye can and ye will," he retorts, reaching out to take my arm. His fingers pass right through me, leaving a frigid gust of air where his hand had been. Amazed, I look at his face, seeing his frustration.

"You're a clone...a spell," I breathe, looking at him. "You're not really here!"

"Ye're surprised?" he asks, losing a little of his anger as he sees my astonished expression. "Ye live wi' an extraordinary craitur, such as yerself, for long enough, ye learn a ting or two. 'Tis a spell, Genevieve. I liked whah ye can do wi' yer clones...da images of yerself dat ye create. I tought I would try it meself. Do ye want ta see more?" he asks, but he doesn't wait for me to answer as he casts his hands in waves about us.

A rippling echo of energy billows out around us. Murky forms of Gancanagh begin emerging from the depths of the sea and striking out in legions onto the beach. These undead Faeries swarm around us, looking very real beneath the light of the moon. Fear and anger sweep through me, seeing the army he would bring down upon me, but I try to hide it as I say, "They're not here either."

"Na yet," he replies darkly. "Do na make me bring dem ta fetch ye back ta me. I tought we had gotten past dis. Chasing ye is beginning ta take a toll on me, *mo chroí*. I do na know how ta make ye understand dat ye are me heart. Wi'out ye I do na exist...and wi'out me, ye will na exist."

"So you're saying that if I don't come back to you, you'll kill me?" I ask him, feeling cold inside.

"I will bleed ye dry," he threatens, showing me his gleaming, white fangs. His image leans closer to my neck, allowing icy air to radiate near me. Remembering the gut-wrenching pain of being bitten by him, I cringe.

"If you bite me, you'll have nothing," I retort, feeling betrayed by him. "I won't drink your blood and become one of you."

"I have nuting now! When I bite ye, ye'll be Gancanagh," he counters. "Me true queen. Ye'll be unable to resist me blood."

"No," I reply, shaking my head. "I'll refuse," I say bravely, trying to mean every word.

Anger makes him sneer, "Ye may, and ye may na. I'm willing ta take dat chance."

"Are you?" I ask, feeling like every word he ever spoke to me was a lie.

"I am," he affirms, staring back at me with a predatory gaze.

"You'd give my soul to Sheol? To those monsters for eternity?" I ask him, feeling crushed. If I do drink his blood, then my soul will be surrendered to Sheol, to the fallen angels for eternity. I'll die and be reborn an evil, undead creature…like him.

"If ye make me, I will," he replies without a hint of doubt.

Russell's voice interrupts us as he nears. "Brrrr, you feel that, Red? Now that's cold," Russell says, swinging his five-iron to dispel the imaginary Gancanagh that Brennus has conjured on the beach.

As their sinister images ripple and fade away, Russell rests the golf club on his shoulder. When his tall frame towers over me, he doesn't hesitate, but drops his club and engulfs me in his arms. Picking me up off my feet, he gives me a bone-crushing hug that takes my breath away.

"Russell," his name escapes me like a prayer as I look into his chocolate-brown eyes. His tawny hair looks almost golden in the moonlight.

Russell grins broadly at me. "Ah, you know I've been wantin' to do that for so long, it hurts," he admits, loosening his grip on me, but not putting me back on my feet. "Am I interruptin' somethin'?" he asks, looking at Brennus' livid face. "Ah, it's the stalker again. I should've known, but your stink is not so bad out here…maybe all y'all should move somewhere tropical," he suggests in a smart-ass tone. Seeing Brennus' eyebrows draw together, he adds, "I'm just sayin'."

"Da other, I—" Brennus begins, using the name he has attached to Russell. Brennus calls Russell "the other" because Russell is the only other being just like me: a human-angel hybrid. He could also mean the other half of my soul, since Russell is my human soul mate.

Russell holds up his hand. "Just one second, Brennus, you total freak," Russell says insultingly. "I just gotta get a little smackerel from my girl."

Russell's hand snakes up to weave in my hair at the base of my neck, while his lips press firmly to mine, kissing me with an intensity and longing that I'm not expecting. A low growl comes from Brennus, and an instant later, another growl answers his from Reed. Reed directed it at Brennus, I'm sure, but I push against Russell anyway, trying to make him stop kissing me. However, Russell is really freaking strong now, stronger than me, so I can't budge him an inch.

When Russell ends the kiss, he looks into my eyes, like we're alone and says, "I missed you, Red."

I touch my fingertips to my lips, feeling confused and overwhelmed. "I missed you, too," I respond softly. We haven't had much time alone together since I'd been rescued from Brennus' estate in Ireland. Most of my time has been spent with Reed. There is still a lot left unsaid between my soul mate and me.

"You still here, Brennus?" Russell asks, not looking at him, but just at me. "Why don't you give up now? Go on and find someone else to haunt, ya creepy, dead bastard."

"I will enjoy killing ye," Brennus says intently.

"Well, that's really easy to say, when you're not really here, isn't it?" Russell replies, smiling into my eyes, like it's a private joke between us. "Next time, you should come in person…you get more respect that way."

"What are you doing," I whisper to Russell, feeling fear wash over me at his provoking words.

"I'm pickin' a fight I know I can win," he replies with a cocky grin.

Looking at Brennus' face and smiling unabashedly, Russell's crimson, Seraphim wings stretch out menacingly from his body. They remind me of the fierce strength that Casimir showed with his.

Brennus turns his eyes to mine. "Do na hide from me, *mo chroí*, and do na make me come ta ye. I do na want ta make ye beg," he says, ignoring both Reed and Russell as they growl at him.

My skin pales, feeling like my whole world is caving in on me. I feel as bad as I did in the cell in Houghton—when Brennus first tried to turn me into an undead monster like him. No, I feel worse. I hated Brennus then. He was never my friend then. Now…it's like Freddie all over again. I let him into my heart and he's tearing it apart.

"Why are you such a major tool, Brennus?" Russell asks, scowling as he puts me back on my feet.

"He can't help himself, Russell," Reed replies, holding his hand out for me to take. Taking it and holding it tight, I feel Russell reach out and take my other hand.

"Red," Russell says, using his nickname for me, "just tell him that things weren't working out, that he's a really bad boyfriend. Tell him that it's definitely not you—it's him," Russell says, smirking at Brennus' image.

The air around us is growing colder. I can feel it and see it as my breath makes smoky plumes.

"Open up yer eyes, *mo shíorghrá*," Brennus warns me. "I'm coming closer and ye know whah I can do. When I find ye, ye had better be ready ta submit ta yer true family. Do ye need more tellin'?"

My hands are shaking, like he's really here. Both Reed and Russell tighten their grip, feeling my fear.

"Come and die, Brennus," Reed says, stepping between Brennus and me.

Brennus sizes up Reed, saying "I have one ting ta say ta ye. *Cogadh.*"

I pale at the word. It means "war."

"*Tuigim,* Brennus," Reed replies casually, saying "I understand."

"*Póg mo thóin,*" Russell grins, telling Brennus to kiss his ass. "Now run along. I wanna talk to my girl."

"Carnage. I like it," Zephyr says from behind us, making me jump. I hadn't heard the stealthy way my Power angel mentor had approached us. "When will you get here? I grow tired of waiting." Zephyr asks as the light-brown feathers of his angel wings ruffle in the ocean breeze.

"Soon," Brennus replies coolly to Zephyr, not taking his light green eyes from mine.

"Don't do this. Please," I whisper to Brennus.

Brennus' image nears me and it feels just like he's here. "Ye're such pretty pain, Genevieve. Beautiful poison." he says as his eyes fill with the bitterest regret.

"Then let me go," I beg him as a pain in my chest begins to ache.

"Why would I do dat when I enjoy pain...all types of pain?" he asks as his eyebrow rises in question. "Ye'll be my lover and ye'll learn all about pain, I promise ye."

Russell growls. "Look at the dead guy trippin', Zee," Russell says with an undercurrent of menace in his tone "He must not know that we have more game than Mattel."

"I was going to crash your party as soon as I found you, Brennus. Consider yourself invited to ours, if it's more convenient," Reed says lightly. "Just make it soon."

"I will, *aingeal,*" Brennus replies to Reed, trying to keep his cool.

Gazing at me, the light from the moon causes Brennus' black hair to shine with a silvery glow. "Ye were right...ye did end up doing me wrong. I gave ye everyting. Ye'll spend eternity making dis up ta me," Brennus whispers in my ear with the harshness of betrayal.

Turning, Brennus' image begins walking away, back over the sea and into the frightening, black-cloud horizon. As he retreats across the frozen waves, one thing is clear to me: I believe him. Touching the onyx locket hanging from my neck with trembling fingers, I whisper, "He's coming. We have to leave."

Reed's gentle voice interrupts my panicked thoughts as he says softly, "I will never let him have you again."

The murky clouds roll back, receding and uncovering the night sky speckled with pinpoints of fire. Russell and Zephyr come nearer to us, lending me their support with their presence.

Shivering in Reed's arms, I drop Russell's hand and huddle nearer to Reed, while the moon casts its light upon us.

"Still…we should go," I reply with my hands shaking.

"We expected him to find us," Reed remarks softly, stroking my wings. "You have his knife—"

"You knew he'd find me!" I frown, pulling back from him so that I can see his eyes.

"Yes," Reed answers honestly. "The only thing I regret is that he didn't really come here tonight. I would've felt him if he had, but since I'm not affected by his magic, I did not sense his shadowy presence. We put Russell on point to detect Brennus' magic."

"I felt that cold freak all the way over on the other side of the island," Russell says grimly.

"Why didn't you tell me that his knife would lead him to me?" I ask Reed, feeling like I have just attended my own funeral.

Reed's eyebrows draw together over his lovely green eyes. "I didn't want to worry you, Evie," Reed says with concern in his tone. "You have been through so much—"

"Yeah," Russell chimes in. "We'll take it from here." He points his chin toward Reed and Zephyr.

"You don't know Brennus, Russell," I warn. "He'll destroy himself to get me back."

"Good!" Russell shoots back. "It'll be his funeral—we're ready for him and his army to come. I like the way you stood up to him, though, tellin' him you weren't goin' with him. I thought maybe he still had you wrapped 'round his finger—"

"I'm not his slave," I interject defensively.

"The last few weeks you were with him, you acted like one of them," Russell counters quietly. "I was afraid they might own you now."

"I had to act like one of them," I reply, truly beginning to shake now. The breeze is becoming gentle with only the scent of salt and tropical flowers woven within the balmy heat. "But I always wanted to come home."

"Shh," Reed hushes me in a soothing tone. "Of course you did," he agrees as he shoots Russell a look full of censure.

"You have a plan and you haven't told me about it?" I ask, before piercing each one of them with my narrowing eyes.

Zephyr's light-brown wings twitch as he replies, "We were waiting until you fully recovered from your captivity."

"When did you think that was going to happen?" I counter, annoyed that they're keeping things from me again.

Zephyr's eyebrow arches over his ice blue eye as he smiles, "I believe that you just proved that you are ready," he replies.

"Okay," I breathe, trying hard to slow the pounding of my heart. "So, what's the plan?" I ask, needing something to concentrate on other than Brennus' inevitable arrival here.

Reed's shoulders cave in around me protectively. "Zephyr, would you please go and wake Buns and Brownie? We will meet at the big house to discuss the plan with Evie." I look toward the huge, plantation-style house on the ridge above the beach. Zephyr and my Reaper angel friends, Buns and Brownie, have been staying in that house on and off for the past few months while they were trying to figure out where I was, and then how to free me from the Gancanagh.

Zephyr nods to Reed before he steps forward, placing a gentle kiss on the top of my head. "I am glad you are back," he says, treating me like a little sister.

"Me, too," I reply. Zephyr nods toward Russell before he leaves in the direction of the big house. Russell looks reluctant to leave me, knowing that I'm still scared. "I'm fine, Russell," I assure him.

"Naw, you're not," he replies in a discerning way, "but you will be after we kill Brennus." Russell can always read me like a book. He's my soul mate and the sum of all our lifetimes together stretches back thousands of years. He remembers them all, but I can't remember any of my past lifetimes as a human.

"Brennus is already dead, Russell," I frown, thinking of Brennus' beautiful, cold skin against mine. I shiver.

"Semantics, Red. He's not dead if he's walkin' 'round," he replies.

"No, he's undead with magical powers that can crush you and me," I counter hollowly.

Reed smiles reassuringly. "His magic can't hurt me, therefore, I'll take down Brennus and his fake empire," Reed says quietly. Gancanagh magic has no effect on angels, like Reed and Zephyr, but since Russell and I are human-angel hybrids, faerie magic can bury us. However, the toxic skin of the Gancanagh can enthrall angels like junkies to a powerful drug, whereas Russell and I are immune to the Gancanagh touch.

My heart beats harder in my chest at Reed's words. My need to be with Reed is what gave me the strength to survive my captivity with the Gancanagh. Without that, I would have succumbed to the gnawing need to feed on Brennus' blood after he had bitten me. I can't lose him now, when I only just got him back.

"Let's run," I whisper in Reed's ear. "We can hide again," I plead.

"You haven't even heard our plan, Evie," Reed says softly, hugging me tighter to him.

"If it involves you getting close to Brennus, then I'm against it." I say as my stomach twists at the thought of Brennus using his thrall to control Reed.

"Shh, Evie," Reed says, smoothing back my hair as he listens to the pounding of my heart. "Now that your life is no longer bound to Brennus' life, I can kill him without any repercussions. The magical contract he made with you that tied you to him is the only reason he's still alive. Without it, he would already cease to be. I have had so many opportunities to kill him, but I couldn't do it without killing you, too. But, Brennus broke the contract, so he's as good as dead when I see him."

I pale. "Reed, he has an army," I argue.

"You'll never be his slave again. I promise you," Reed breathes in my ear, and I want so badly to believe him. "Let me explain our plan to you. You'll see."

Gently, Reed leads me towards our bungalow on the beach. Hesitantly, I look over at Russell who's watching me walking away with Reed. Pain is in his eyes, seeing me with Reed. I've always been Russell's love in every one of our lifetimes together…except for this one. This one's different. I'm no longer just human anymore, I'm also angelic and the angel part of me really loves Reed—needs him. But, my soul…my soul will always love Russell—he's my best friend.

"Are you coming, Russ?" I ask him over my shoulder.

"Naw," he says, softly swinging his golf club against the sand at his feet. "I already know the plan. We can talk on the beach tomorrow when we train together."

"Okay," I agree, not knowing what else to say. I know that my love for Reed is torturing Russell, but I don't know how to fix it. If there's a solution, I don't know what it is. I watch as Russell walks away from me, back towards the other end of the island…as far away from Reed and me as possible.

CHAPTER 2

Infighting

"Concentrate, Red, shoot...you're all over the place," Russell breathes, sitting cross-legged next to me on the beach. He directs his clone's image in front of us to pick up my clone from her feet and slam her to the ground, dissipating her like a small, mushroom cloud.

"Russ-ell," I breathe in a frustrated tone. "Stop killing my clones."

"But you make it so easy..." he trails off with a smirk until I elbow him hard in the arm. He's as tough as a mountain now; nothing short of everything I have would hurt him.

I fall back on the sand, putting my arm over my eyes to block out the intense sunlight above us. It is so physically draining to create these mirror images of me—my clones. Russell can do it now with no problem. Each of his clones look and act like his twin. He can sit next to me on the sandy beach and make the image of himself do whatever he's thinking, like his mind is within the spirit-like body, carrying his consciousness.

Then there's me. My whole world spins like I'm on the teacup ride at Disneyland just getting my clone to appear. Directing it and trying to see what she sees is like looking at everything underwater or through someone else's eyeglasses: everything is distorted and blurry.

Russell pulls my arm back from my eyes as he kneels over me, blotting out the sunlight with his huge six foot five inch frame. "We have time for one more clone..." he trails off again as he looks at my face. "Ah shoot, Red, I'm sorry," he says in a gruff voice.

Leaning back he pulls a tissue from the pocket of his board shorts, dabbing it at my nose gently.

"Another nose bleed?" I ask tiredly, taking the tissue from his hand and holding it to my nose.

"You have to tell me when you're gettin' to that point," Russell says, sounding guilty. He puts his arm around my shoulder, making me sit up so he can look in my eyes. "How many of me are you seein'?"

"Three...no, four...and all of you should get a haircut," I reply, trying to minimize the fact that I'm disoriented. He lets go of my shoulder to run his hand through his tawny hair that has been bleached in blond streaks from the sun. Then he has to quickly catch me as I begin to topple over onto his chest.

"Whoa!" he says, before pulling me against his bare chest and letting me rest my head while he strokes my back soothingly. His impressive, crimson wings shoot from the camouflage of his back as he holds me in his arms, making him look every inch the lethal, Seraphim angel that he is now. "Ahh, I hate when my wings do that!" Russell admits with irritation in his voice.

"I know," I agree, seeing exactly what he means. "It embarrasses me when mine do that on their own."

"I keep wonderin' if it would've been easier if we were entirely angelic...you know? Does this kind of stuff happen just 'cuz we're part human, too?" he asks, sounding frustrated.

"You mean...if we weren't half-breeds, would we have more control over the angelic part of our nature...like our wings?" I ask for clarity. Closing my eyes, I find that it doesn't help the dizziness, so I open them again quickly.

"Yeah, that's exactly what I meant," Russell says, giving me a quick squeeze.

"Reed said it's normal. Emotions seem to trigger them. I think age helps. You're only, what, twenty now?" I ask, knowing he had a birthday in August that I missed. I close my eyes again, not wanting to think of where he had been on his birthday, but goose bumps run the length of my body anyway, thinking of the church in the Ukraine where he'd been held and tortured by a sadistic Ifrit.

"Yeah...that birthday was a little dark," he mutters, his hair rising on his arms as his wings move agitatedly behind him, kicking up sand. He takes a quick breath, attempting to calm his heart that I can hear pounding in his chest. "I hope I'll be able to control my wings completely in the next century or two," he says with a wry smile.

"I bet it'll be much sooner than that. You seem to master everything so quickly," I reply honestly. "There's only one thing you're going to struggle with, Russell."

"What's that?" he asks with a smile in his voice.

"I don't think you're ever going to be able to detach and become emotionless like the Seraphim I've seen. You're too human for that... it's not in your nature," I reply.

"You only ever met one Seraphim, Casimir, and he was a fallen freak, Red," he replies. "They can't all be like him...cold and hard—completely evil."

"My father is one and he...well, I don't know what he's like because I've never met him, but I imagine he's a lot like Casimir," I reply, feeling some of that hardness inside of me when I think of him.

"Ah, you don't know that...he's a divine angel and you don't know his circumstances—"

"I don't want to know his circumstances, Russell," I snap.

"You always were a daddy's girl—in just about every lifetime I had with you...'cept when you were a mama's boy," he laughs.

I roll my eyes and then have to hold on to him tighter as it makes me dizzier. "I wish I could remember all of our lives together. I'm sure you were very interesting as a girl. Were you ever a girlie girl?" I ask. His knowledge of all of our past lifetimes together as my soul mate is as irritating to me as it is fascinating. Just imagining myself as his love for a past eternity is a complete, mind-blowing trip.

"You always thought I was hot," Russell smirks, not as freaked out as he used to be about remembering our past lifetimes when he was the female.

"It's impossible for me to picture you as a girl, Russell," I reply, smelling his masculine scent that's so attractive, just like him.

"Good, since this is probably the last form I'm ever gonna take, I prefer to be the man...the angel...the man angel...ahhhh...we should come up for a name for what we are now. How do you like 'mangels?' Or, what 'bout 'Sera-mans?'" he asks me in his gentle, chiding way.

I groan at his attempt to humor me. "That's awful. I definitely prefer to be called a 'half-breed' or the 'half-humans,'" I say, pushing away from his chest so I can look in his brown eyes.

"We're gonna hear that a lot from now on. We might as well get used to it," he says in a cheery voice.

"That doesn't bother you?" I ask, wiping my nose and seeing that it has finally stopped bleeding.

"Naw, I mean, it's just jealousy. They all wanna be me," he replies, looking in my eyes and checking to see if I can focus on him.

"Jealousy?" My eyebrows rise incredulously.

"Yeah," he smiles slowly. "There's somethin' 'bout me havin' a soul that makes all the angels I've met wanna be me. 'Course, it helped that I took on the biggest angel I could find when I first met the Power angels from Dominion," he says, loosening his grip on me a little to see if I topple over again. I manage to hold my balance, but he doesn't let me go completely.

"What?" I ask.

"Yeah...I hadn't met Preben or I would've punched him first, just 'cuz he's the biggest Power I've ever seen. Naw, I hit what's his name?" Russell asks, snapping his fingers as he thinks. "Tycho—I think that was his name. Anyway, I had to let them see that I wasn't puttin' up with their shen."

"What happened?" I ask, my eyes growing wide at this new information.

"Ahh, they let us fight for a while before Zee stepped in and broke it up. I was holdin' my own and that freaked them out a little, since they know I'm only twenty years old and they're all like a billion in dog years," he grins. "They don't fight like I've been trained to fight...when I was a soldier...when I was just a man. They fight like angels and they expect certain things to happen."

"Like what?" I wonder aloud, not knowing how he and I differ from them.

"They read body language. They expect to know what you're gonna do before you do it 'cuz a lot of them have tells. But, I'm part human...I wasn't raised with them. I didn't get their angel imprinting branded on me. They can't read me yet," he explains.

"So...it made Tycho almost blind when he was fighting you?" I ask, trying to understand.

Russell nods. "But, he still had a wicked right cross," he says, rubbing his chin as if remembering the pain.

"That was stupid, Russell. He could've killed you. You're not even fully evolved yet," I say, growing white thinking about what could've happened.

"I had a lot of rage at that moment, Red," Russell says, looking away from my eyes. "I fluctuated between pretendin' Tycho was that Ifrit, Valentine, to pretendin' he was Brennus." I flinch, hearing Russell say Brennus' name. "I'm sorry...I didn't mean to use the vampire's name in front of you," Russell says in a low tone, brushing his fingers in my hair soothingly.

"He's not a vampire, Russell," I reply, trying to be normal as my hand shakes a little. "He's an undead Faerie."

"He's gonna be an all-dead Faerie when I see him again," Russell states, sweeping a stray hair back from my face.

Gripping Russell's arm, I look into his eyes. "Russell, you need to be really cautious around him."

Russell's face relaxes. "His skin doesn't work on me. He can touch me and I won't go all zombie and do everything he tells me to do, like the angels will if he touches them," Russell replies. "That makes me the perfect candidate to take him on."

I frown at his obvious disregard of my warning. "No, it doesn't," I say.

Russell's eyebrows pull together in anger. "He wants to see you on your knees, crawlin' back to him. He's gonna kill you for sure if he gets you back and you'll be his ice-cold, undead…" he trails off.

"Gancanagh lover…his queen," I finish for him.

Russell's expression darkens. "I'm not gonna let him do that to you. I'm not gonna let him send your soul to Sheol for eternity, not for those fallen monsters in Hell to torment," he says, his face flushed with anger. "Why hasn't he come yet? He said he was comin' soon. It's been a couple of weeks! He should've made his move by now."

"He's really intelligent, Russell. He's been around forever—he doesn't act until he has the advantage—the entire advantage," I explain, knowing just how Brennus operates because I'd spent the last few months as his captive queen. "Then, when he does act, it's like a snake striking…it's so fast, you almost never see it coming."

"He's bitter, Red," Russell says softly. "It may cause him to make mistakes."

I shake my head. "Don't count on it. He knows almost everything there is to know about me. He got in my head and crawled around… he knows everything about us. He studied me," I whisper, feeling like I have a rope around my neck, choking me.

"We studied them, too. While you were his pet," Russell replies. "Let him think that I have the power of a wet firecracker being lit by a flint. He's gonna underestimate me and then he's gonna die."

"He knows what you are to me, Russell," I say, feeling panicked.

"Really, Red, and what's that? What am I to you?" Russell asks, and I can hear the undertone of bitterness in his voice.

"You're my soul mate…my best friend…" I trail off, biting my lip as I see sorrow in his eyes.

"Best friend…" he says, hanging his head. "I am that, Red, if nothin' else; I am that. But, I remember so many, many lifetimes when I was everythin' to you—all you needed."

"I need him," I whisper, not wanting to try again to explain my intense love for Reed. But, looking at Russell, I feel an unbelievable ache in my chest for him that won't go away. He's been my lover in every lifetime but this one and my soul knows him as its match. "I'm bound to Reed for eternity. I swore a vow to him. He's my *aspire* and its irrevocable."

"Well, we were married in just 'bout every lifetime we had together and I've heard that being a soul mate is pretty much irrevocable, too," he replies softly.

A crack of thunder makes us both look over at the horizon as dark, rolling storm clouds gather offshore. I pale, seeing the azure sea darkening underneath them. "It's supposed to rain today," Russell assures me softly in my ear. I can't stop the shiver of dread that courses through me, remembering how the sky had been even darker than that when Brennus had found me here. "Don't worry… it's not Brennus."

I nod, trying to hide my fear. "What are the odds of us not training with Reed and Zephyr after lunch if it rains?" I ask, turning to look at him again and hoping desperately that he'll let me change the subject.

"Vegas wouldn't bet on it," Russell replies, getting to his feet. He reaches down, extending his hand to me to help me up. "C'mon, we better go eat somethin' before the angels start poundin' on us and call it trainin'."

"Thanks," I say with relief, allowing him to steady me on my feet as we walk hand-in-hand to Zephyr's huge plantation house on the hill for lunch.

When we arrive at the house, he leads me through the elegant, winding halls to the ornate dining room. The white, plantation shutters have been closed over the open windows, but they are open enough to allow the breeze in to cool the house. Walking with me to the table, Russell holds out a chair for me next to Reed. He then seats himself in the empty chair next to mine.

"Thanks, Russell," I murmur as I attempt to look normal. I don't want Reed to know that I'm still a little dizzy because he'll want to examine me himself and I'd rather not go through a battery of tests now.

"We were just about to discuss security," Buns says, directing her attention to Russell and me. She nudges a heaping basket of rolls in my direction, eyeing me closely. "You look tired, sweetie," Buns comments with a frown.

"I'm fine," I assure her hurriedly, taking a roll and putting it on my plate.

Selecting white fish from the myriad of entrées in the center of the table, I listen while Buns, Brownie, and Zephyr continue discussing recent intel from the Reaper angels stationed on the outlying islands. They haven't seen any activity from the Gancanagh yet.

Feeling Reed's eyes on me, I'm not very surprised when he says, "You look pale." His strong fingers brush against mine as they rest on the table.

Smiling at him, I reply, "I'm a redhead, remember? We're supposed to be pale, but I prefer the term 'pigmently challenged.'"

Reed's eyes soften at my comment and his perfect face makes my cheeks flood with color and my pulse quicken. "There…that's better," Reed breathes near my ear.

"She had another series of nose bleeds," Russell says to Reed as he watches my face.

Reed's eyes darken as his eyebrows pull together. "Evie, you're working too hard. You need to find a balance—" he starts, but I interrupt him.

"I will—I just didn't realize it until it was too late. I'll work on toning it down," I say in a placating tone, while stepping hard on Russell's foot beneath the table for ratting me out to Reed. Russell ignores my feeble attempt to hurt him, smiling at me angelically.

"Maybe you shouldn't train this afternoon," Reed says seriously, setting his fork down near his plate.

"I'm fine, really," I reply with indifference, because if I look too anxious, he'll make sure I rest and I don't want to rest. When I try to relax, all I can think about is Brennus and his promise to teach me all about pain when he gets me back.

I touch the onyx locket around my neck, feeling the smooth, opal moon affixed to the surface of it. It's really a portal, a transport to another place far from here. I know exactly where it goes, and so does Reed. I plan to use it if I have to escape the Gancanagh. Our portals, Reed's and mine, will go to the same place. Zephyr's and Buns's portal's will arrive at a different location from ours. We'll have to meet up with them, which we plan to do by using the Internet. Russell and Brownie are paired together again, which makes me extremely nervous, knowing that they had been captured and nearly killed the last time they were left alone to fend for themselves.

"You should prepare to get wet," Reed says, looking out the open windows. Sheets of rain are falling on the tropical paradise of Zee's island.

"Sweet," I say sarcastically. "I better hurry up and eat before it becomes a monsoon."

༄

Standing in the heavy downpour on the beach, I let rivulets of water stream down my face, dripping in torrents from my bottom jaw. I angle my chin downward and slightly to the left so that I can see any movement Reed might make toward me.

Th-thump…th-thump…th-thump…my heart wants to increase its beat, but I'm trying to control it as I wait like a statue for him to make a move. The clang of swords being clashed together near me fades to the background because I know the lethal threat is the one just ahead of me. My fingers twitch on the long-handled dagger in my left hand while my hand tightens on the sword hilt in my right.

I take a deep breath, and as I begin to exhale Reed makes his move, instantly cutting in half the distance between us. I tense for a millisecond, waiting for him to get closer before I spring forward, running at him with all my speed. I jump up and over the swing of the sword in his right hand, planting one foot on his arm. I feel the whistle of air from the dagger in his left hand blow upward, inches from my cheek as my other foot steps on his shoulder. I launch into the air, using my planted foot to kick off from his shoulder, and hopefully, knock him off balance. Stretching my crimson wings out and gliding back to the sand, I spin around, facing my opponent again.

As I stare into Reed's dark green eyes, a slow smile twitches on the corners of his lips, causing me to narrow my eyes at him. Then, I feel the severed left strap of my tank top slip from my shoulder. The fabric of my shirt slouches over, but still clings to my wet body. Looking at it, my eyes narrow more before I lift them to Reed's face again. Both his eyebrows rise quickly before he lets them fall, making his face go blank.

I wait a half a second, and then, as if on cue, the front pocket of his t-shirt droops over and falls to the ground at his feet. Reed looks down at it and then over at me. I lift my eyebrows quickly before letting them both fall.

Reed's charcoal-gray wings unfold from his back menacingly, as a frown touches his lips. Tensing, I wait for him to make another move toward me. In an instant, he shoots straight up in the air and seems to dematerialize. Turning in circles, my heartbeat kicks up as I try to see where he went, and more importantly, from which direction he's going to pounce. Pulling energy to me rapidly, I whisper words quickly, erecting a transparent wall of energy around me as a shield, I feel safe for maybe a millisecond. Then, warm arms wrap around my waist, startling a scream from me as Reed comes from behind me, pulling me against his chest. Shifting in his arms, he grins down at me in triumph before leaning down and kissing my lips.

"How did you get through my shield?" I ask breathlessly, feeling my heartbeat increase as his warm lips trail lower.

"I was already here by the time you employed it," he says, reaching out and tapping on the invisible energy field around us. "But, it was impressive, nonetheless."

I drop my weapons to the sand, putting my arms around Reed's neck lightly and touching his dark brown hair. It's dripping wet from the rain. "I should've built a wall around you instead," I whisper, brushing my lips against his jaw and over his cheek to his lips, tasting the salty water on his skin.

"That would've been a better strategy," he agrees, his fingers tracing a path from my waist up my side. "One I would've had to outrun."

"As if you could outrun my magic," I reply sarcastically, kissing his lips gently.

"As if I could," he agrees, deepening our kiss.

*Tap, tap, tap...*Knocks sound on the invisible barrier surrounding us, startling me. I look over to see water dripping from Zephyr's disapproving face staring down on us. His startling-blue eyes narrow as my cheeks redden.

"It does not appear to be dinner time, yet," he says, showing us his watch and reminding us that we have more training time left before Reed and I can have some private time together.

"Uh...sorry," I mutter, pulling energy back to me so that the shield I erected around us melts away to nothingness.

"We are switching partners," Zephyr says sternly to Reed as I pick up my weapons from the sand. "You go train with Russell," he orders Reed, while his light brown wings unfold in agitation.

"Naw, Zee, I'll train with Evie," Russell says from behind him, his face growing dark.

"That will not work, since I want the two of you to learn how angels fight," Zephyr argues. "I want you to study what to look for in an angelic opponent. You cannot learn that from Evie."

"C'mon, Zee," Russell says, scowling at Zephyr.

"We need to bring Evie up to your level, Russell," Zephyr explains. "She had no real training in fighting while she was with the Gancanagh."

"Uh...I trained a little..." I trail off when I see the frown on Zephyr's face.

"They trained you to fight like a Faerie. We will have to break you of all the bad habits they taught you," Zephyr replies, sounding superior. He lifts his wicked broad sword and looks down the hilt of it as he points it at me. "You cannot concentrate with your current partner."

Looking at Reed, he gives me a sensual smile. I lose my train of thought for a second as my mind wanders to the way he kissed me just a few seconds ago. In the next moment, I am jolted out of my revelry by Zephyr again. "Did you hear what I said?" he asks.

"Uh...bad Faerie habits?" I ask, looking as his eyebrows draw together, indicating he probably said something I completely missed.

"Reed," Zephyr says in a stern tone as water drips from his brown hair.

Reed steps reluctantly forward, putting his arms around me and hugging me to his chest. "We'll have time alone together tonight, love," he whispers in my ear, and I nod.

As Reed walks over to Russell, each of them begins sizing the other one up. They haven't been training together, not really. They barely speak to one another, as the bond between them that had formed when I was a captive of the Gancanagh keeps dissolving by the day. Brownie and Buns have both noticed it. We've discussed it a few times when I took my flying lessons with them in the evenings after dinner. It worries me to see them spar now, like this is a real battle over a coveted prize.

"Zee," I murmur, watching Russell's sword cut dangerously close to Reed's neck. "Is this a good idea?"

"Time will tell," he replies, picking a position on the beach in which to start instructing me on using the broad sword he holds. I'm having a hard time focusing on anything he's telling me, since my eyes keep drifting to the intense fighting taking place between Russell and Reed.

"That's not—sshheeeeze," I inhale between clenched teeth, seeing Russell's sword cut a thin line in Reed's cheek. I make a move toward them, but Zephyr grabs my upper arm, holding me back.

"Do not even think about getting in the middle of that fight, Evie," Zephyr says. "It has been coming for too long now and there needs to be some lines drawn."

"What lines?" I ask numbly, trying to make him let go of my arm.

"Dark, thick ones with pain and menace," he replies. "Perhaps you should go now—you do not need to see this."

"See what? What are you talking about, Zee?" I ask, fear oozing into my tone. I glance over to see Reed's sword cut a large gash in Russell's upper arm, causing blood to course from it in rivets with the rain.

"REED!" I shout, feeling Zephyr's arms go around me to lift me off my feet so that I can't run to them. Reed ignores me as his features remain blank, not giving away any of what he's thinking.

In an instant, Russell begins to morph, his bright red wings being replaced by the orange and black stripes of a jungle tiger as he springs toward Reed, his jaws going for Reed's throat. Reed manages to avoid being bitten by the tiger's fierce teeth, but he doesn't avoid the sharp claws that dig into his back, dragging jagged lines of blood into his flesh. A millisecond later, Reed morphs into a panther, pouncing on the tiger as they roll around on the shore.

"THEY CAN'T DO THIS, ZEE!" I plead, trying to make him let me go, but he just shakes his head. Picking me up, he tosses me over his shoulder, hauling me off the beach in a blink of an eye. He runs through the lush foliage of his South Pacific island toward his sprawling plantation house.

Crossing the sweeping veranda and entering the house, Zee says, "Buns."

In less than a few seconds, Buns enters the foyer. Seeing me dripping wet, slung over Zee's shoulder, Buns says, "What's up, sweetie?"

"Buns, tell Zee to put me down! I have to go stop Russell and Reed from killing each other," I explain frantically, not being able to really see her because Zee is holding me upside down by my feet. I catch a glimpse of her honey blond hair as she turns to Zephyr.

"Oh…Brownie," Buns calls out. She puts her hands on her hips as she narrows her cornflower-blue eyes. "They couldn't do this on the DL, Zee?" Brownie appears instantly at Buns's side, looking at us curiously.

Zee shrugs, "It was coming…he's really powerful now, Reed knew it would come to this."

"Reed knew it would come to what?" I ask, paling.

"Reed knew it would be a fight for you sooner or later," Zephyr replies.

"BUT, THAT'S RIDICULOUS, ZEE!" I shout, not being able to contain my anxiety. "Reed doesn't have to fight for me!"

"Tell that to Russell. He's as much an alpha male as Reed and he wants you just as much as Reed does," Zephyr replies.

I cringe, feeling ill. "Fine, put me down and I'll go tell him," I growl.

"No," Zephyr replies. "You have to stay here. I will go and make sure that they do not really harm each other. I just need to make sure you will not interfere."

"Why?" I ask, not understanding why I can't break up the stupidest fight in the history of fights.

"Because you will make it worse, Evie, trust me," he says with absolutely no doubt in his tone.

"Here, Zee, put her down. I'll take care of her while you go referee. Make sure they both stay in one piece," Buns states, taking charge of the situation. "We need them."

The blood drains from my face. Zephyr says, "I will go referee if Evie promises to stay here until it's over."

"Sweetie, tell Zee you'll stay with us and he'll help," Buns urges.

I pause, not wanting to promise because I'm not convinced that they won't listen to me if I go down there. Zephyr says, "Every moment you make me stay here, they are alone together."

I groan before saying, "Okay, I promise."

Zephyr sets me on my feet and is gone before I gain my balance.

"You're dripping wet, Evie," Brownie says, putting her arm around my shoulders.

"What's going to happen, Brownie?" I ask as she leads me up the grand staircase that seems like something out of a Civil War novel. Buns follows behind us looking a little worried.

"I don't think Zee will let them go too far," Brownie says, leading me to her suite of rooms on the second floor. She brings me to her bathroom, turning on the shower.

"How far is not too far?" I ask, refusing to go any further until my question is answered.

"Reed and Russell both know that we need them to fight the Gancanagh. They're probably just trying to establish dominance..." she trails off, seeing me blush. "They're male and they both have angel DNA. It was going to happen," she says, testing the shower to see if it's warm enough.

"Why is everything so complicated, Brownie?" I ask, closing my eyes and putting my hands over my face.

"Because it is," she replies. "Take a shower. We'll bring dinner up here."

We eat dinner in Brownie's lavish room. Buns tries to distract me from watching the old pendulum clock on the mantel slowly tick out the seconds. Hours pass and there is no word from the beach. The rain falls steadily outside, bringing with it loud claps of thunder and brilliant displays of lightning.

"I'm not down for flying lessons in this weather. Are you, Brownie?" Buns asks, sipping a cup of tea by the fire, her golden, butterfly-like angel wings resting comfortably behind her as she sits on the chaise lounge.

"Nope...let's do something fun," Brownie says, looking at me from her seat on the bed as her copper, butterfly-like wings float gracefully behind her.

"Like what?" I ask listlessly from my position on the window seat. I pull at a crimson feather of my wing, straining my ears to hear anything from the total idiots on the beach.

"There's an old jukebox down in the ballroom. Let's go see what it has in it!" Brownie says, getting to her feet and smoothing her perfectly quaffed platinum blond hair as her blue eyes sparkle.

Buns joins her instantly, looking excited. "Sweetie, we learned some amazing dance moves in London, while we were trying to figure out a way to get rid of the Dominion Power angels."

"OH!" Brownie chimes in. "You need to see this! C'mon, Evie!"

Brownie grasps my wrist, hauling me out of my seat, because although she's a Reaper angel, like Buns, she's strong, much stronger than a human. "Okay," I mutter, feeling like I have to do something before I start crawling up the wall, which I can actually do now.

Brownie leads the way down the hall. The ballroom is located in the back of the house. Entering the large, gilded room, Brownie flips on the light switch to the rows of crystal chandeliers overhead. Beautiful, whitewashed, wood paneled walls with gilded, beveled edges face the opposing wall of French doors that runs the length of the room. Hardwood floors reflect the light almost as much as the gilt-framed mirrors that adorn the walls. Coven ceilings with painted frescos depicting angels at peace tower over our heads. Buns laces her arm through mine and walks with me to the other side of the room.

"It's so beautiful in here," I breathe, while she depresses a hidden panel insert in the back wall. A hidden door opens. Folding it back, it exposes a room filled with the most lavish items I've ever seen. An old phonograph stands on an antique table next to a not so ancient jukebox.

Looking further back in the room, I spy dresses of every cut, color, and style dating back at least a couple of centuries. Most of them are swathed in clear garment bags hanging along the walls.

"This dress would look so good on you, Evie," Brownie says, picking up a silver flapper-style dress that looks like it's straight out of the roaring 20's. "It would go well with your gray eyes. How tall are you?" she asks, holding it up to me.

"Uh...five-nine," I reply absently, still looking around at the trunks that line the walls, but I'm distracted from opening any of them when Buns gives a little squeal of pleasure next to me.

Coming closer to the jukebox, I peer through the glass front, seeing an eclectic selection of music from classical to solid gold oldies. "Zee said he hasn't really used this house since the sixties...I think it shows. Oh! Look! Jerry Lee Lewis—Great Balls of Fire!" she squeals, plugging in the jukebox and watching it light up. Pressing buttons, the arm of the jukebox moves and a record drops. The pounding lyrics of the song belts out something about nerves shaking and brains rattling.

"SOCK HOP!" Buns says, grabbing my hand and pulling me towards the ballroom floor. Showing me dances that she must have learned in the fifties, I grin as Brownie joins in selecting songs by Elvis and 'The Big Bopper,' whoever that may be.

After dancing for an hour, I go to the French doors, opening all of them to get the cool breeze to filter in. Looking out at the dark sky I close my eyes, breathing in the damp, tropical air as the rain continues to pour down outside. Hearing another record drop, I wait to hear what Buns will select next. The haunting strains of a song I've never heard before begins to fill the room. Feeling butterflies taking flight in my abdomen, I know that it's Reed who just wrapped his arms around my waist.

"Will you do me the honor of a dance?" Reed asks in a sexy tone that makes my heartbeat pick up.

"I don't know...I'm angry with you," I reply, turning around and looking at his perfect face that is now marred by a cut on his cheek and a split lip. Biting my own lip at seeing the marks on him, I raise my fingers gently to his cheek. He closes his eyes briefly as I rest my hand on his face. Then, taking my hand in his, he leads me to the middle of the ballroom floor. Feeling his hand rest gently on the small of my back, he begins to lead me confidently around the dance floor.

I follow him, surprised at how easy it is to dance with him to the soft, rhythmic music floating around us. It's effortless...like a dream. "What's this song called?" I ask, enthralled by the soulful, romantic melody.

"Pavane. It's by a composer named Gabriel Faure," he replies, gazing into my eyes. "It reminds me of you...beautiful and haunting, filled with grace and elegance…and a hint of sadness…longing…" he breathes near my ear, causing a tumult of desire to rush through me. His masculine cheek brushes against mine, sparking every fiber in me to attune to him.

"Is that how you see me, Reed?" I ask, continuing to follow his elegant movements around the floor.

"You have so many facets, Evie," he replies, his eyes growing dark with desire as he lifts his head to look at me. "I thought that I could never love you more than when you were a fragile, brave girl just beginning to change into an angel. You were so courageous then, you took my breath away," he says, gently steering me in the hypnotic dance. "But then you began to change and with that evolution came power…power like I never expected…strength and intelligence… flawless beauty…" he smiles, his eyes seeming to touch every inch of my face. "In all the years that I have lived, the time that I have spent with you has been the most exquisite…and this moment, our first dance, I will never forget if I live forever."

"I still can't believe you're real," I whisper, leaning my face against his shoulder, hearing his heart beating strongly in his chest. "I love you."

"And I, you," Reed whispers back as the final strains of the song fade to silence.

Lifting my head as we come to a stop in the middle of the room, I smile while the breeze lifts my hair and pushes it toward my face. Another record drops as my eyes widen in reaction to the sweet, sticky scent that assails my nose.

CHAPTER 3

Nicolas And Simone

Tensing in fear, a growl escapes me as I react to the scent of the Gancanagh carried to me on the tropical breeze. Reed's charcoal-colored wings shoot out of his back, tearing his white Oxford shirt away as he steps in front of me, shielding me from the French doors. My eyes go wide, seeing the lacerations on Reed's back. He has at least two, huge, black bruises on his ribs, multiple contusions and that's just what I can see from this angle.

"Eaves," a familiar feminine voice calls from somewhere outside in the darkness. "It's me. Don't freak out—"

"Molly?" I breathe, trying to step around Reed, but he continues to block any attempt I make at getting a clear view of what's beyond the French doors.

"You move and you die," Zephyr growls from the darkness.

"Whatever you say, *aingeal*," Molly replies, and I can hear the cheeky grin in her tone. "I just have some intel to impart to my friend and then I'm out. Nice place you got here. I'd ask you if it's been on MTV's Cribs, but I doubt you'd get it."

"Molly," I say again, closing my eyes and trying to calm my racing heart. "It's okay, Zee. She won't hurt us."

"No, it's not okay, Zee." Reed says, still in a defensive posture. "This is the friend that helped lure Evie away from us in China."

"I remember you," Zephyr says in a growling tone.

"'Twas me all right," Molly replies, parodying the accent of the Gancanagh. "But, I've since had a reversal of fortune, ye might say. 'Twould seem dat wi' Evie on da outs, I'm deir number one pawn ta get her back...except I'm no one's pawn."

"It wants pity, Reed," Zephyr says, sounding disgusted.

Molly hisses, "Don't make me have to touch you, angel, because I'd enjoy having you as my slave." She sounds like she's close to losing it. "Evie has been my friend since second grade—she's the only family I have left and I'm not going to let them change her into a Gancanagh if she doesn't want to be changed. So you can either let me talk to her or you and I can get better acquainted."

Low growls sound from Zephyr and Buns. "ZEE! Please don't hurt her—Molly, please don't threaten the seriously lethal angels—everybody be cool!" I say, putting both my arms out, motioning to Buns to stay back because I can see that she didn't appreciate Molly's threat to her angel.

"IT shouldn't have any problems keeping cool," Zephyr replies, referring to the fact that Molly's basically undead and therefore ice-cold to the touch.

"That's original," Molly says, and I can hear her rolling her eyes in her tone. "I'm cold and smelly. I've heard that before so maybe you should get a new playlist of insults."

"Reed, please let her in. I need to hear what she has to tell me," I plead, feeling overwhelming sadness for Molly.

Brennus had found Molly after I escaped him in Houghton. He had Finn, his brother, change Molly from a human girl into a Gancanagh by biting her and then sharing his blood with her. They wanted Molly to use as a pawn to make me come back to them, banking on the fact that I would try to help my childhood friend. But, there is nothing I could do to help her. She is a Gancanagh with a thirst for blood, and toxic skin, which she uses to control the will of her victims. Anyone she touches will become her slave—anyone but Russell and I. We are immune to the touch of the Gancanagh. It is one of the reasons why Brennus finds me so appealing. He can touch me and I won't become his slave who will follow any order he gives me.

"Evie," Reed says, shaking his head sadly, "she's not your friend anymore."

Putting my hand on his arm, I manage to get him to look at me. "Listen to me. Molly offered to bite me, to break Brennus' contract and set me free just after the Werree attacked me."

Both his hands go to my upper arms as he straightens his posture and looks into my eyes. "Why didn't you let her do it?" he asks, looking outwardly calm, but I can tell that there is a fire being lit inside of him, knowing I could've returned to him sooner.

"Because Brennus would've killed her if she did. He promised to torture and kill anyone who bit me and freed me from his magical contract," I reply.

"She is evil now," he says without a hint of doubt.

"She's always been like a sister to me and that is just as strong in her," I reply, watching his brow pull down in a frown. "Please, hear her out."

Reed pauses, looking reluctant. "Molly...please come in," he says, not taking his eyes from mine.

"Awesome," Molly says, before strolling into the ballroom. "Nice pad, Eaves."

She's dripping wet from the rain, leaving a trail of water as she stops several feet away from any of us. Buns and Brownie stay well back from her as Zephyr trails her in, training a seriously hostile automatic weapon on her.

"Thanks," I say, trying to take a step toward Molly and not being able to budge because Reed is still holding both my arms. "Reed," I murmur.

"You can hear her from here," he replies calmly.

"What happened to him?" Molly asks, pointing at Reed.

Looking back in Reed's direction, I pale, seeing his chest for the first time. He has a deep, claw mark running from his left shoulder to his right hip and a definite bite mark from a tiger etched into his side. It's healing, but it still looks painful.

My eyes drift to his face, which flushes with color as he mumbles, "You should see him."

"Forget it, I don't really want to know about your kinky, angel things," Molly says, waving her hand as if to erase the last exchange. "I'm here to let you know that Brennus has gone off the deep end. It's lunatic fringe time," she says, looking at my face. "Finn has been filling me in when he can, but I haven't been able to see him in a few days."

"What do you mean, Mols?" I ask. "Aren't you with them?"

Shaking her head, she says, "Finn sent me away from the estate before you opened the compact that Casimir gave you. He knew that the Fallen would retaliate, succeed or fail, and he wanted to protect me. He also knew that if the angels succeeded in getting you back, I'd be toast. Finn knew they kidnapped Leif so he would bite you to break the contract. That put my life in jeopardy," she says. "Brennus wouldn't hesitate to torture me in front of you to make you do whatever he wants you to do, but I'm not gonna let him do that to us."

"But...Finn loves you! Brennus couldn't do that to his brother..." I trail off, watching her shake her head.

"He's too obsessed to let you go, Eaves. He is insane now. I hope he never gets you back because...it'll be gruesome. He was never such a tyrant before, not like he is now. He'll kill anything that shows the least resistance to his will, now. Finn and I won't be seeing each other for a while after this…not until it's over," she says, looking like she's in pain. "So, I'm on my own…well, not really, I'm as rich as sin now, thanks to Finn. He said he'll find me when this is resolved."

"I'm so sorry…" I trail off when she holds up her hand.

"Don't say you're sorry. You never had a chance…not after Alfred gave Brennus the portrait." I cringe, thinking of the portrait painted of me depicting the Goddess Persephone.

Russell was against me modeling for it. I should've listened to him.

"When will they mount their attack?" Reed asks, trying to get specifics.

"I don't know, but it'll be soon. Brennus is as impatient and demanding as a two-year-old. I do know a few things, though. Don't expect them to go easy on you, Eaves. Playtime is over. All the fellas know that they're allowed to bite you. Brennus thinks that it will help to subdue you because he is aware of how powerful you're becoming. He said if you're trippin', then you're less of a threat."

"But that's a huge risk for him…someone like Eion has a hard time stopping once he bites…he could drain me before Brennus can stop him," I say, feeling ill remembering how I felt the last time I was bitten.

A gnawing ache of hunger begins and if I can't find any animal blood to satisfy the blood lust, the horrific hallucinations follow soon after. Anyone else bitten by the Gancanagh wouldn't feel this type of pain, because the Gancanagh's skin drugs him. Only Russell and I would feel the pain intensely.

"Well, I guess that's the risk he's willing to take. He did warn them not to share their blood with you. He wants you as his *sclábhaí*, his slave. No one else will be your *máistir* but him," she says as she shivers. "But he's not sure he wants that anymore. He swings between killing you slowly, refusing to turn you as you die by degrees, and waiting until the last possible moment to turn you, if you beg him and tell him you love him."

My legs feel numb with fear, hearing the plans Brennus has for me. If one of his men bites me, but doesn't turn me, I will be in so much pain I will be praying for death to arrive…but it won't. It will just be intense pain, unless I beg Brennus to end that pain for me… to share his blood with me. He may even refuse me at that point. He may just leave me in intense pain—forever.

How long will I have to endure that kind of pain? I wonder, feeling like everything is coming to an end. All my hopes of staying with Reed seem so feeble and naïve.

"Tell us about their forces, weapons, how will they strike?" Reed asks, his face going blank. He's in war mode now.

"They're having problems…" Molly trails off, and I can see that this is difficult for her. Her loyalties are divided. What she tells us can ultimately harm Finn. "Your angel army has been wreaking havoc on the Gancanagh forces. They're actively hunting all of us now…them and your buddies, the Fallen."

"He made you targets," Zephyr says, referring to Brennus.

"You think?" Molly replies sarcastically. "But, it's okay…I've actually acquired a taste for fallen angels. I figure they have it coming, since they have my soul."

"Brennus is having a hard time mobilizing his forces. Moving them without detection is difficult, even with money," Reed says in a meditative way. "A surgical strike would be easier and quicker. Grab and go."

"Or bite and go," Molly replies. "But, I wouldn't count on Evie being the only objective. He wants revenge. He wants blood and retribution. You took something that belongs to him and no one gets away with that in our world."

"What are you saying?" I ask, feeling nauseous.

"I'm saying you can't be a martyr in this one, Eaves. Don't even think about going to him," she says, watching my face and reading it like a book. "You can't barter yourself for them—or me. Those days are over. The only way your friends will be safe is if he's ended. Even if he makes you his queen, and that's a big if, they all die."

Zephyr scoffs, like the threat of the Gancanagh getting him is minimal. "He is deranged."

"Now you're getting it," Molly replies, checking her fingernails.

"Will he send his men or will he be comin' himself? Do we need to start huntin' him?" Russell asks quietly, from the doorway of the ballroom. Startled by how stealthily he came in, I glance at him and my jaw falls open. His face is bruised and swollen from his fight with Reed; one eye is almost completely closed.

"Russell," his name escapes my lips as my stomach clenches. He ignores me, watching Molly.

"I don't know. Maybe you should get some more men…unless this isn't the position you intend to defend," she says, tilting her head like she's assessing us all. "You don't seem like you plan on being here when he makes his move."

"How old are you?" Zephyr asks suspiciously.

"Nineteen and a half, but I had brothers growing up and they played every combat game known to man," Molly replies. "It was kinda freaking me out that you allowed me to get this close to you. I was thinking that this was amateur hour with a neon sign that blinks: VICTIMS HERE. But, you're not lame, are you?"

"Oh, there's zero lameness here, sweetie," Buns replies, smiling derisively at Molly.

"Epic, do me a huge favor and kill him for me. I can't be with Finn as long as Brennus lives so he has to be ended," she replies, showing a cold, calculating ulterior motive for coming here. "I don't think we'll be seeing each other for a while, Eaves," Molly says, backing toward the doors.

"Molly, wait!" I say, my heart twisting in my chest as I pull against Reed's grasp on my arm. "Remember me and I'll remember you—remember...crawling out of your bathroom window so we could look at the stars and talk all night. No matter how old we get, we'll be under those same stars."

"I won't forget," she says softly. "Maybe you'll think of me now, when it rains, too. May the road rise up to greet you, Eaves."

"May the wind be always at your back, Mols," I choke as tears fall from my eyes. She backs away from us to the door, watching Zephyr suspiciously as he continues to train his weapon on her. The instant she hits the cover of darkness, she turns and runs from the house.

"She's onto the plan," Russell says softly, not moving from the doorway of the ballroom. "We should probably go and take care of her."

"Nobody touches her," I state numbly. "She wants Brennus dead. She won't tell them anything."

"She might tell her boy to keep him from comin' here, knowin' that's what we want them to do. If Finn doesn't come, chances are he'll keep his brother from comin', too," he replies, wanting me to see that the plan has a loose end now. "They'll just send their men."

"I don't care," I reply, refusing to see it any other way but that she stays unharmed. "Anyway, good luck finding her now. She's probably twenty leagues under the sea as we speak," I say, hoping I'm not bluffing. "The beauty of our plan is that it only, really, needs one person to be here when the fellas arrive and that has to be me, since I'm the one they're the most focused on. You guys should leave now. I can execute the plan and escape through my portal when it's done."

I touch the moon-shaped locket on my neck, making sure it's still with me.

Every face in the room frowns at me. "Were you listening to Molly?" Reed asks, still holding my arms that are now beginning to shake as the numbness in me is wearing off. "She said you couldn't martyr any of us out of this. They want revenge. They will hunt us all until we kill them."

"I heard that...so I will kill them all," I reply, looking into his eyes. "They don't get to hurt my family."

"She's back!" Zephyr grins, looking at me proudly. "Welcome home, Evie."

"Sweetie!" Buns cheers as she and Brownie both run to me and hug me, forcing Reed to let me go. "We thought we lost a part of you to them, but it's back!"

"I learn from my mistakes, Buns," I say, allowing them to hug me as I look over their heads at Reed. Wondering briefly if he can see the pain inside of me, I continue, "You're never going to be safe while they survive...so they have to be ended."

My heart contracts in pain like I've just lost something, something that I love. There are fragmented pieces inside of me that no longer fit where they once did. I feel betrayed by them—by Brennus. He told me that he loved me, but his version of love is not my version of it.

"No one expects you to do it, Evie," Reed says. "I'll be the one. It's my mission."

"Naw, that stone-cold freak is mine," Russell counters in a menacing voice, while walking into the room. As the light of the chandelier touches his face, I cringe, seeing his broken nose that is now beginning to heal.

Approaching Russell, Zephyr says, "Hold still." He places his thumbs on either side of Russell's nose and straightens it for him with a loud *crack*.

"Thanks," Russell says, not even flinching.

"I'm her *aspire*," Reed says in a quiet tone, facing Russell.

"Well, I'm her soul mate," Russell replies. "Brennus is gonna suffer for tryin' to make my girl grovel."

"And making him grovel in return is my right. Didn't we just establish that she's not your girl?" Reed asks, his brows drawing together.

"She'll always be my girl. She may be your angel...but she'll always be my girl," Russell replies, crossing his arms over his chest.

"She's made her choice. It's time for you to begin to accept it," Reed counters in a cool tone, his fingers touching my arm as he trails them gently down to hold my hand.

"Someone always tries to come between us, but they don't last long...we always end up together, sooner or later," Russell replies with a certainty that makes me frown.

Seeing Reed's brows begin to knit together again, my eyes shoot to Russell. "Can I talk to you, Russ?" I ask, not waiting for him to answer. I let go of Reed's hand and walk to Russell, trying to pull him with me toward the door.

"Sure," Russell says, "we can talk at my villa."

"We should remain in the big house for now," Zephyr says, stopping us. "You can collect your gear in the morning and move it to a room here. I believe it is time to make this headquarters. No one wanders around alone."

"Alright, Red, do you wanna be my buddy so that I can go to the kitchen and get some food? I'm starvin'," Russell asks, tucking my arm in his, like nothing out of the ordinary has happened. I frown at him, showing him my irritation with his behavior.

"Fine," I say to Russell, then I frown at Reed "Don't think you're off the hook, Reed. We'll talk later."

He looks surprised by the edge in my voice, until he sees that I'm going with Russell. "Evie," he says as he begins to look deadly.

"We'll talk later," I reply, trying to ignore how sexy Reed looks when he narrows his eyes at me like that.

"Yes, we will," he agrees with an equal amount of edginess in his tone.

I follow Russell to the kitchen. We pass through the arching doorway that looks like something out of a designer home magazine. The enormous area is lit by firelight from a stone hearth, reflecting on the glass doors that lead to a stone terrace dining area outside. The doors are closed now against the pouring rain. Russell lets go of me, turning on the lights that hang directly over the stone countertop island. I go to the stainless steel refrigerator, scanning the contents to see what's in it.

"There's left over fried chicken," I say over my shoulder, "or that barbeque from last night?"

"Yes," Russell says, joining me at the door and pulling out both the chicken and pork. "Are there anymore of those muffins left?" he asks, loading his arms with food and hauling it with him to the barstools by the counter.

"Let me check," I say, opening the storage container where Hati, the head chef, keeps all the fresh baked breads. "Cranberry or mandarin?"

"Uh huh," he replies. I roll my eyes, taking several muffins out of the bin. I bring the muffins to him, placing them on a napkin.

Pouring myself a glass of orange juice, I sit on the stool next to Russell, toying with the glass in my hand while he eats. "Don't worry 'bout it, Red," Russell says when I glance at his face. "I should be purdy again in a couple of hours."

"You were never pretty, so I wouldn't count on it. That's not what I'm worried about, Russell," I sigh, not looking up from my glass. "I'm worried about why you and Reed are fighting."

"Just checkin' the barometer," he replies.

My brow wrinkles as I ask, "Am I supposed to know what that means?"

"Reed is the epitome of strength and agility. I needed to know where I measure up on the scale," he says quietly, before taking a bite of chicken.

"Why not fight Zee then?" I ask, knowing that there's more to their fight than he wants me to know.

"Reed is the best fighter, even Zee admits that and that's sayin' a lot," Russell replies grudgingly.

"And what did the barometer tell you?" I ask.

"I'm gettin' there," he answers with a small smile.

"Getting where, Russell?" I press him.

"Where I need to be," he replies.

"If you're fighting because of me, then please stop," I say quietly.

"I can't stop when it comes to you," he replies, looking stubborn as his jaw sets. "It's my eternal flaw."

"You can't fight for me," I say, looking back at my glass.

"That's not entirely true," Russell replies before taking a bite of muffin. "Normally, you'd be right, with you bound to Reed, there'd be no way...but there are special circumstances here. Reed didn't exactly follow all the rules when he bound his life to yours—"

"What are you talking about?" I ask, feeling tense.

Russell finishes chewing before he says, "Number one, you were under duress when you bound yourself to him—"

"I was not under duress. I knew exactly what I was doing," I say, refuting his point. "I'd never have done it, if I hadn't wanted to be with Reed for eternity."

"Red, you're basically nineteen," he says, like he's not hearing me. "You have no idea what kind of time you promised him."

"And you do?" I ask, "You're only twenty."

A slow, rueful smile spreads across his lips as he says, "I'm thousands of years old, 'cuz unlike you, I remember every lifetime I've had on earth and most of those moments I spent with you...or dreamin' 'bout you—"

"Then you should know me well enough to know that I wouldn't have promised Reed anything if I didn't intend to honor every single word I spoke to him," I reply. Getting up from my chair, I take my glass to the sink, rinsing it out. I close my eyes with my back to Russell as I continue, "So…whatever you're fighting for is pointless."

"Number two," Russell says, sounding angry and hurt, "you never asked me for my permission to bind with him."

I pause in what I'm doing. "What?" I ask. Setting down my glass, I turn to face him, feeling my heart begin to beat faster.

"You're supposed to ask me if you want to bind to someone. I'm your soul mate. I'm supposed to be able to say no if I object," he says, looking bitter.

"How do you know all of this?" I ask, feeling my pulse racing.

"Zee and Buns told me," he says.

"When?" I ask.

"Just before I left and went home," he replies. "They had to tell me 'bout what you did 'cuz you were gone with Brennus and the other vampires…Reed was a mess. How did you think I found out 'bout it?" he asks accusingly. "You should've told me."

"I never wanted you to find out from anyone but me," I reply, not answering his question. "When was I going to tell you? On the phone?"

"It's probably better that Zee told me instead of you. I didn't take it well," he replies, getting up from his seat and taking his plate to the sink. I move around the counter away from him, feeling awkward and sad.

"Russell, I wasn't getting out of Dominion's chateau without Reed. I made a lot of enemies when I went there. They would've found a way to kill me," I say, trying to explain.

"Yeah, I know. I got that part: your life was threatened—that's what duress means," he says.

"I know what duress means. I'm trying to tell you that maybe that's why no one told me I had to ask you for permission," I say with exasperation.

"No, Zee said they didn't ask me because they were afraid I'd say no," he replies.

"What?" I ask, not sure I heard him right.

"Yeah, he said that he and Buns were holdin' their breath 'cuz without my permission, it shouldn't have worked," he says with reluctance.

"But it did work," I reply absently, touching my shirt where the mark of Reed's wings lies above my heart—a brand that looks like the image of his wings appeared on my skin after we swore our vow to be united for eternity.

"Yeah," Russell says quietly, "but it may not be irrevocable. I still have at least an equal claim to you."

"And where am I in all of this?" I ask, watching him rinse his dish and put it in the dishwasher. "Don't you think you should ask me what I want?"

"What I'm sayin' is that you still have time to figure that out, Red," he replies.

"I don't need time to figure it out. I love him," I say, feeling my throat closing. I struggle to keep the emotions I'm feeling from showing because it's killing me to have this conversation with Russell. The last thing I want to do is hurt him. I love Russell. I love him with a certainty that I'll never know a better soul than his, but he has to know that Reed is my angel—my *aspire*. "Do you...do you ever wonder why we're here?" I ask.

He laughs, but not with humor. "All the time," he says, leaning against the counter and crossing his arms over his chest. "Why? Has Reed told you his theory?"

"Reed has a theory about why we're here?" I counter, feeling confused. "What did he say?"

"He hasn't told you?" he asks, looking a little surprised.

I shake my head. "What...what is it?" I ask timidly, not sure I'm ready to hear this theory.

"When he came to get me...after I went home," he says, "Reed might've mentioned to me somethin' 'bout why he thought you chose this mission—to be the first half-breed angel with a soul."

"He thinks I chose this?" I ask, feeling my anxiety increase because Reed has never mentioned anything to me about it.

"He asked me what I did to make you accept a mission like this one...one that not many souls would volunteer for 'cuz there are so many ways to lose your soul to Sheol for it," he replies, and I shiver.

I close my eyes, rubbing my hand over them. "Uhh, this is a nightmare," I say under my breath. "I'm sure it wasn't anything you did."

"He said somethin' to me though. I can't seem to get rid of it. Reed asked me how it was possible for him to come between two soul mates. He seemed confused by it," Russell says, watching my reaction.

"I'm part angel now," I point out. "Maybe if I was still entirely human, then it would be different."

"But, that still doesn't account for you takin' this mission," he says.

"I wish I knew, Russell, but I'm in the dark just as much as you are," I reply.

"I just…if I did somethin' to you…somethin' that made you have to get away…I'm sorry," Russell says, his voice sounding strained.

"Don't…we don't know what happened. I'm sure it's not you—it couldn't be you," I say, feeling awful.

"I don't remember anythin' 'bout Paradise…I remember the life before this one," he says.

"You do?" I ask, seeing the lightning outside illuminate his face. He's starting to look a little better, not as swollen as he was earlier.

"Uh huh, it was sorta tragic…we were French," he says with a grin.

"Oh yeah?" I ask, smiling at his remark. "Don't tell me that we went to the guillotine together," I add, playing along.

"Naw…I'm not sure what happened to you…I was a soldier…I swear, I've spent most of my lives fightin'," he says with a sad twist of his lips. "I was young—twenty-one and World War One was eruptin' in Europe. It was the summer of nineteen fourteen. I'd been in love with you since the first time I saw you. You were a few years younger than me. Your brother, Michel, introduced us when I came home with him for a holiday from University the year before," he says distantly, his slow smile at the memory brings lightness to his face. "The first time I saw you, you were sittin' in the music room of your house, playin' the piano for a room full of your beaus…you were awful, the worst Bach I had ever heard," he grins, his brown eyes dancing.

"Nice to know that nothing has changed," I reply with a smirk.

"Naw, nothin' has changed, 'cuz it was all an act," he smiles, shaking his head. "You could play flawlessly and when they all left and you thought you were alone, you played like you wrote the piece yourself."

"That does kind of sound like me," I say, smiling. "Did you tell me I should join a band?" I ask, knowing what a smartass he can be.

"Standin' in the doorway of the room, I asked you how you managed to enchant the very air around you with just the soft touch of your fingers," he says as the lightning illuminates one side of his face. "But, to be honest, it wasn't just the music…it was seein' you that took my breath away."

"So, what happened?" I ask, not being able to help myself.

"Well, when I went back to school, I lived for the letters you sent me," he admits, glancing at me with a touch of embarrassment coloring his cheeks. "I married you in the spring of nineteen fourteen. It was a smaller wedding than you should've had…you were the daughter of a prominent lawyer in your town," he says, "but everythin' was bein' hoarded at that time so it was hard to get anythin'."

"What was your name?" I ask, trying to picture the life he's describing.

"Nicolas...Pierpont and you were Simone...Vassar," he says, the names rolling off his tongue as if a true Frenchman spoke them. "You were...Lord, I can't even describe you 'cuz there aren't words for your kind of beauty. I guess you're just gonna have to look in the mirror. You were a little different...smaller...with hair the color of chocolate and your eyes were dark...smoky...but you look the same somehow—same face."

"Simone," I whisper the name, closing my eyes and trying to see if I can remember being her.

"We didn't have enough time together before I had to leave you," he says, the look of pain on his face makes me aware that he's seeing it all again.

"Did you die...in the war?" I ask when he doesn't continue.

"Yeah...the last thing I remember was bein' in a trench near the Belgium border. We were gettin' pounded by the kr—uh...the Germans," he says, watching my face and seeing my confusion. "We had been there for weeks. It was miserable, 'cuz guys were dyin' all 'round us from bein' shot, but the medics were havin' a hard time gettin' to our position at the front. I had a picture of you...it was spattered with mud and grime. I was holdin' it, when the clouds came rollin' in..." he trails off, looking pale.

"Clouds?" I ask, confused.

"Some kinda gas...chlorine maybe...the first hint of it smelled like a swimmin' pool, but then it was..." he shakes his head, running his hand through his hair like he does when he's upset. "The next thing I can remember after that is being mad at my little sister, Scarlet, for knocking over my green, plastic army men I had set up in the backyard. I was about six...in this lifetime," he says, looking at my face across the island between us. "So when you asked me before, 'bout why I think I'm here...I'm sure that it's 'bout you... 'cuz it's always 'bout you."

Listening to the rain softly hitting the panes of glass outside, I can see the pain that I'm causing Russell because of my love for Reed. "Russell...I'm not sure why we're here, but there's one thing that I do know: no one is safe around me."

"You think I care 'bout that?" he asks calmly. "I've died so many times in so many ways...but I think there's only one way to destroy me...so I'm gonna fight for you, 'cuz that's all I got, Red."

"Russell," I say, bursting into tears and covering my face with my hands. "You don't understand…you're fighting for a time bomb! I'm going to blow up in your face! It will be worse than chlorine gas…it will be Hell."

Coming quickly around the counter, Russell puts his arms around me, hugging me to his body. "Shh…ahh, c'mon now…don't cry," he whispers, kissing the top of my head.

"I'm sorry," I whisper back. "I don't know what happened between us, but things are different now. Can't you feel it? Just because I've been the only one for you forever, doesn't mean that things can't change. Look at us…we're not the same, not now. We have wings, we can fly—conjure fire and make it rain…" I trail off, sniffling.

"And we can love eternally," he replies, leaning down like he will kiss me.

Pulling back from Russell, I say, "You want to know why I think I'm here?" I ask, not waiting for him to answer, I go on, "It has to be because of Reed. I know now that I'd risk anything, everything, to be with him. So stop fighting for me, please."

Letting his hands drop away from me, I see the tragic twist of his mouth, while his brown eyes scan my face. Looking away from me, he pauses, before turning and walking slowly toward the door of the kitchen.

Stopping at the threshold, he doesn't turn around as he says, "Eternity is a very long time, Red. You should be sure that you're makin' the right decision before you push me away."

As he leaves the room, I can feel something inside of me recoiling and urging me to go after him—to beg him to stay with me—to love me. It's my soul letting me know that I still love him, even if I can't remember the echoes of time between us.

CHAPTER 4

Rude Car

I watch the rain falling outside through the glass doors of the kitchen before opening them wide and feeling the cool breeze rush in. As I step outside, I cross the shelter of the stone porch and begin to walk in the rain. The water falls on my face and mixes with my tears. Sitting down on the stone steps of the terrace, I put my face in my hands. In minutes, I'm completely soaked. Silently, Reed appears next to me and picks me up, cradling me to him. My arms wrap around the back of his neck as I rest my cheek against his chest. Not saying a word, he carries me through the house and upstairs to a room on the opposite wing from Brownie's and Buns's rooms. Placing me beside the crackling fire, Reed enters the bathroom, returning with a huge towel. After wrapping it around me, he pulls me against him, holding me to his chest.

I let the towel fall from my shoulders to puddle at my feet. Pulling back from Reed, I gaze into his dark green eyes, seeing raw emotion in them. He knows that I'm in pain and my pain causes him pain. In a fraction of a second, it has become simple again. When I'm with Reed, it all fits. What I want is right in front of me. All I have to do is reach out and take it.

Slowly, I reach my hand out to him, resting my fingertips against his damp t-shirt. Trailing them down to the hem, I curl my fingers around it. Instantly, his wings shoot from his back, tearing through his shirt and leaving it shredded in my grasp. I let his shirt fall from my hands. My fingers go to the bottom button of my blouse, toying with it as I watch Reed's eyes zero in. His eyes grow darker as I pull the button through the eyelet, exposing my navel.

Heat from the fire touches my skin as my fingers work the next button, pushing it through the eyelet to expose more of my abdomen.

Watching his respiration increase, I feel a flush of warmth dance over my skin. Reed reaches out, but I step back teasingly, not allowing him to touch me. Slowly, he moves forward a step, beginning to stalk me while I take another step back, working on the next button and pushing it through the eyelet, exposing my ribcage and just the rounded edge of my lacy bra.

As my knees back up to the bed, a smile forms on my lips, knowing Reed is steering me in the direction he wants me to go. Sitting on the bed, I fall back onto it, letting my arms stretch out. The mattress moves as Reed places his hands on the bed. Leaning down, his lips touch my skin near my naval, making my muscles contract as his face tickles me. If I could see my heart, I'm sure that it would be glowing at this moment.

Reed trails kisses upward over my abdomen, traversing the linen of my blouse to return to the skin at the column of my neck. Putting my hand on his cheek, I touch the other to his hair, teasing a wet curl by his temple. Gazing into his eyes, I whisper, "All I want is you."

"Evie," my name is barely audible as he touches his lips to mine. His fingers finish opening the buttons of my blouse. The fabric slips from my arms, exposing my bare shoulders. Reed trails kisses over the curve of my shoulder to the hollow of my throat, causing his name to slip from me. No more words are spoken between us, but we make promises to each other that words can't communicate.

⁓

As I lie in Reed's arms, my fingertip skims over the healing tracks of claw marks etched in his chest. "I want you to stop fighting with Russell," I say, before placing my lips tenderly to the scratch.

Lifting my fingers to his lips, he kisses them before saying, "No."

I search his eyes, "Why not?"

"I will handle it," he replies softly.

I frown, "This is between Russell and me. I had a conversation with him tonight. I asked him to stop fighting you for me because I've already chosen you."

"You think that will work?" he asks, looking into my eyes.

Biting my lip, I lower my gaze from his. "Maybe...but, you don't have to worry about it because I'll handle it," I reply.

"Love," Reed sighs. "You are a frustrating creature." He frowns.

"What?" I ask, startled by his comment.

"It's my right to fight him for you. Don't interfere," he replies, pulling me closer to him.

"Explain," I demand.

"He has to go through me to get to you. Since we are bound to each other, he can only court you if I'm defeated by him," he says.

"Defeated how?" I murmur with growing panic.

"If he can dominate me, then he could open the door between you both. Since he is your soul mate, he has an equal bond with you," Reed admits in an even tone. "It's an equal claim to you. I'm not going to just step aside and allow that to happen, so don't ask it of me. I will fight for you whether it angers you or not."

"You're saying I'm intruding on some male ritual between the two of you?" I ask.

"Yes," he replies, frowning.

"But, that's—why can't I just tell everyone who I want?" I ask in frustration.

"Because you may change your mind when you see how powerful one is verses the other," he replies. "I'll never give him the upper hand. I'll never let him defeat me. When I'm challenged, I'll accept it and I won't lose."

"Brennus is right, I am pretty poison," I mutter, pulling away from Reed's chest and lying back on a pillow.

"He's wrong. His words were spoken in the bitterness of jealousy and loss. He knows what you are. It's why he cannot let you go," Reed says.

"What am I?" I ask.

"Unforgettable," Reed replies. "You're art that cannot be concealed…danger that cannot be tamed…love that cannot be measured…a new law that denies a probable outcome."

"And you're my heart," I whisper.

Reaching over, Reed pulls me back to his chest. "I want to discuss something with you, Evie," Reed says, toying with a strand of my hair.

"Hmm?" I manage to reply.

"I had some intel from Dominion," he says. "Molly was truthful when she said that Dominion has been engaging the Gancanagh."

"Did you tell them where we are?" I ask, knowing that Dominion has not been let in on our location because they want to seize control of Russell. He is a fascinating weapon to them. He attracts evil to him, just as I do, and they want to use him to lure the Fallen and any other prey they want to snare.

"I haven't given up our location. We don't want them here, but there's a complication…they have something we want," Reed says.

I become alert, sitting up against the pillow, I ask, "What?"

"Tau has arrived at Dominion," he states.

"He's at the chateau? My father is at their chateau?" I ask for clarity.

"It would seem," he replies.

"Why?" I wonder.

"He's looking for you," Reed says softly.

My eyebrows pull together. "He's a little late, wouldn't you say?" I ask sarcastically, feeling the heat of anger creep to my cheeks.

"No, I'd say he's right on time," Reed counters.

My eyes widen at him. "You think this is good news," I say accusingly.

"Yes," Reed replies.

"How do you know he's not here to rip out my evil heart?" I ask, crossing my arms over my chest.

"Your heart is not evil," Reed says, frowning. "And I know because he just about tore down the walls of the place looking for you."

"That doesn't prove anything other than he wants me for some reason," I counter.

"He demanded his daughter," Reed says calmly.

"Oh, so because he's claiming me as his daughter, you think that means he's on my side?" I ask, narrowing my eyes at him as I bound out of the bed and begin pacing in front of the fire. "Maybe he just heard I was there and felt curious—"

"No one storms in and threatens to annihilate an entire city of angels if they don't produce his daughter out of mere curiosity," Reed says, sitting forward on the bed and watching my every move before the fireplace like a cat watching a mouse. A slow, sensual smile forms at the corners of his mouth, and I swear, if he had a tail, it would be swishing. "When he heard that the war council put you on trial for your life, he challenged each of them to combat."

I stop dead. "He did?" I breathe, feeling a deeper blush rush to my face.

"He did," Reed nods.

"Oh," I murmur, feeling confused. I turn toward the fire and my wings move in agitation. A groan sounds from the bed behind me. Looking over my shoulder at Reed, my eyebrow rises in question.

"I'm trying to have a serious conversation with you, Evie, but it's really difficult when you look so tempting…" he says, holding up his hand to indicate me in front of the fire, completely naked.

"Oh!" I say, startled. I move to the bed, pulling the sheet from it and wrapping it around me.

"Better?" I ask as I cover up.

Shaking his head, he says, "Not really, but it will have to do."

A reluctant smile touches my lips, before I ask, "Who did you talk to at Dominion?"

"Preben, but our conversation was interrupted when Tau learned that he was speaking to me," Reed explains.

"You spoke to Tau?" I ask with my voice becoming breathless.

"Yes, he was uncharacteristically agitated for a Seraph," he smiles.

"What do you mean?" I ask.

"Seraphim are known for their cool demeanor. Tau threatened to shred me if I didn't let him talk to you," he replies.

My eyes go wide, "What did you say to that?" I ask.

"I told him I'd tell you and if you want to speak to him, you'll call him back," he replies, watching me and assessing my body language. "I have his number."

"What does he want?" I sit down on the edge of the bed. Reed reaches out and takes my hand.

"You," he replies, rubbing his thumb over my skin.

"Why?" I watch Reed's expression soften.

"I don't know...maybe it's because you're his daughter," he murmurs.

"What do you think I should do?" My unoccupied hand toys with the end of my sheet.

"Call him," he says without hesitation.

My throat becomes tight. "Why?" I pull my hand from his.

"He might have the answers we need regarding why you're here— your mission. He is also a great angel. His prowess is legendary. We could learn many things from him..." he trails off when he sees my scowl.

"You respect him?" I ask, not being able to contain the edge in my voice.

"Of course. He is one of the most courageous angels to have ever been created, Evie. When there is a parley between Sheol and Paradise, it is often Tau who is sent to speak to the Fallen...alone... in Sheol," he replies.

"So, he's a good communicator. Bravo for him," I say sourly.

"It takes more than communication skills to enter Sheol. You know that. It takes the kind of courage that not many possess. You should not judge him until you have the facts, and you cannot get the facts until you speak to him," Reed says, leaning to me and stroking my hair.

"Well, if you're going to be all rational about it," I mumble sullenly, still picking at the sheet.

"You could call him now," Reed says, taking me in his arms and pulling me back to his chest.

"No, I'm tired now...maybe later," I say, resting my head against Reed's chest again, watching the fire dance.

"Then rest, love," Reed says, continuing to stroke my hair until I fall asleep in his arms.

૭✑

I awake to shafts of sunlight casting a glow over my bed. Stirring, I lift my head, seeing Reed sitting next to me reading an old, worn book. Smiling sleepily, I sigh almost inaudibly the word, "Hungry," as I stretch out my limbs.

Tossing his book on the bedside table, Reed says, "Me, too," and begins nibbling on my neck. Squirming as his mouth tickles me, I laugh and pull him closer.

"Who needs food?" I ask, nipping gently at the skin of his shoulder. Reed makes love to me again in the shafts of sunlight of the perfect morning. Sometime later, while lying in Reed's arms, my stomach growls noisily.

My eyes grow wide as Reed's face hovers above mine. "I am starving you," he says contritely.

"Yes, you are," I agree, not making any excuses for him.

"Then, let's go eat," he says, getting up and going to the closet near the bathroom.

"I need to take a shower," I reply, hurrying to the bathroom and turning on the water. Brushing my teeth after my shower, I shamelessly watch Reed in the mirror as he shrugs into a pair of board shorts and a t-shirt. Smiling to myself, I walk to the closet, finding my clothes that have been brought here from our bungalow on the beach. Choosing a pair of denim shorts and a nearly backless top that ties at the neck, I push my feet into a pair of chic sandals.

"Ready?" I ask Reed and see him smile as he grasps my hand and walks with me out of our room. "Are we training today?" I ask, because everything seems to be different now after the visit from Molly.

"Zephyr and I discussed it. We'll stay near the house. We can train in the ballroom or on the patio by the kitchen after the staff leaves. They should only be here to drop off supplies. The boat will take them back to the other island. We ordered food for a few weeks because we will be suspending the staff visits from now on…so, how good are you in the kitchen?" he inquires with a smile.

"I make a mean PB and J," I reply, "a decent lasagna, and some killer scrambled eggs.

"Good. Zee said Hati is putting together recipes that we just need to follow," he informs me.

"That shouldn't be too hard. I can't wait to see you in an apron," I tease him, trying to picture him cooking anything.

"I have prepared food before, but it's been awhile," he says, smiling at me.

"When was the last time?" I ask.

He looks up at the ceiling, "A few decades ago…more or less," he replies.

"Ah…before refrigeration or after?" I ask, hiding my smile.

"Hmm, before…I believe…" he says seriously, and when I burst out laughing, he grins at my response. "What?" he asks as I shake my head, "I said it's been awhile."

"You can help me make some breakfast…it'll be fun," I say, squeezing his hand and looking up into his brilliant green eyes. Entering the kitchen, I go directly to the sink and wash my hands. Reed follows me, washing his hands beside me. As I walk to the refrigerator, I open it and scan its contents. "Eggs?" I ask, glancing over my shoulder to see Reed watching me.

"Yes," he replies, coming closer, resting his arm on the open refrigerator door in a sexy way. A slow blush begins in me as our eyes meet, making me have to look away.

Pulling out the carton of eggs, milk, and butter, I carry them to the counter. "Do you like cheese?" I ask, glancing up to see Reed nod.

After retrieving the cheese, I go to the cabinet. On my tiptoes, I attempt to get a bowl down from one of the higher shelves. Reed steps behind me, wrapping his arm around my waist; he leans in and presses a sultry kiss to my neck while reaching up and grasping a bowl from the shelf with his other hand. I bite my lip as my entire body reacts to his touch.

"Thank you," I breathe, taking the bowl from him.

"You're welcome," he answers in a low tone, before nuzzling my ear lobe, sending shivers of desire through me.

I exhale the word, "Okay."

Reed's hand on my waist falls away as I move toward the counter where I had put the eggs. Heat is rushing to my cheeks as I set the bowl on the counter. I pick up an egg and crack it against the counter before pouring it in the bowl. Several more eggs go in after it before I look at Reed's face to see him leaning against the counter with his eyes training on me.

Finding a whisk in a drawer, I put it in the bowl before handing the bowl to Reed. "Stir this, please," I order, before hunting for a frying pan. Putting the pan on the stove, I turn on the burner, melting the butter in the pan. Looking at Reed, he hasn't moved, but continues to watch me. I raise my eyebrow and nod toward the bowl. He looks down at it for a second before he seems to realize that he's not doing what I asked. Setting the bowl down on the counter, he begins to stir it like a five-year-old would: in circles.

Smiling, I walk over and place my hand on his, showing him how to fold the eggs with the whisk. "Ah, there is a technique," he says, grinning at me and causing my heart to speed up.

"Don't tell me that I finally found something that I know more about than you do," I say. Picking up the bowl, I bring it to the stove and pour the contents in the pan, hearing the eggs sizzle. Using a spatula, I stir the eggs, adding some cheese.

"You've just introduced a whole new world to me, Evie. We should always do this. It's very…intimate," he says, watching my reaction to his words.

"This is just eggs, Reed. You should see lasagna," I tease.

"I don't know if I can handle lasagna…what will you be wearing when you make it?" he asks, putting his arms around my waist and hugging me from behind.

"Plates, please," I order, pulling the pan off the heat and turning off the stove. Reed reluctantly lets me go to get the plates. I serve the eggs, placing the plates on the island in front of the barstools. As we sit next to each other, eating our eggs, a kinetic energy seems to pass between us. Picking up my empty plate, Reed takes it to the sink and begins rinsing it off for me while I clean up our mess.

As he wipes his hands on a towel, he moves to me where I'm leaning against the counter watching him. Picking me up in his arms, he seats me on the countertop, kissing me with the pent-up heat that has been building between us throughout the entire meal.

A consuming passion overwhelms me, but it's cut short by confusion as Reed ends our kiss abruptly. The world whirls around me as I'm moved through the air in a fraction of a second to a position behind his back. His wings are already arching out, shielding me from whatever it is that's making Reed adopt a defensive posture in front of me. Instinctually, my wings shoot out of my back as I try to see around Reed.

Reed growls and a few seconds later, Zephyr and Russell appear in the doorway to the kitchen. They halt just inside it, staring at the open glass doors that lead to the patio. Stepping to Reed's side, I still, seeing Hati, the head chef and her staff, standing outside. They all look pale and zombie-like with blood trailing from puncture wounds in various areas of their flesh.

Hati stumbles into the kitchen, looking only at me as she comes closer. Her face is old and weathered, not at all the normal prey of the Gancanagh, but one chosen because she is familiar to me. The bite wounds on her neck look particularly deep, continuing to ooze blood ceaselessly.

Hati's eyes dart around as she shifts from foot to foot like a junkie in need of a fix. "My master commands me to give you a message," Hati hisses with her thick, South Pacific accent. Seeing her like this is making my skin crawl because I know she is under the thrall of the Gancanagh and unable to resist their will. "Brennus says he will hold you in his arms while you beg for the death of your heart and you will know that this is all of your own making. He will kill your lover—your angel, and his death will be on you...all on you. He draws closer—closer now. Can you feel him? He is coming and with him the pain he will bring will have no end," she breathes, while she produces a knife from her pocket.

"No! Please," I whisper, feeling the blood draining from my face. I watch as she plunges her knife into her own chest, twisting it with a satisfied smile before she falls limply to the kitchen floor. Looking outside, the rest of Zephyr's staff has followed suit, stabbing themselves to death in front of us.

My mind wants to pretend that this is all make-believe, but I know that I'm just waking up. Everything I thought was Brennus was make-believe and this is reality. Tears of regret fill my eyes because he has opened them and I want to go back into the dark. He knows what terrifies me; he has been privy to my deepest fears. When I had asked him before about what would destroy me, he had said, "*Tristitiae*," meaning, "sorrow." Losing Reed would be the death of my heart, more so than if Brennus stopped my own from beating and he knows that, too.

"Evie...love," Reed says gently, holding my chin and trying to get me to look at him instead of Hati's inert body. "It's psychological warfare...he will try to erode your defenses by causing fear."

"Spider..." I say numbly.

"What, love?" he asks, searching my face.

"He's a spider...he enjoys it when I struggle in his web. It makes him want me more," I reply, feeling cold in the heat.

"Your heart is too pure for him to hold onto," Reed says. "It has broken free of his web and he cries for the death of his own heart. It's here; in the rage he's showing us. We will end him soon and this will all be over."

"He's so depraved, Reed," I say, feeling tears falling from my eyes. "I didn't know—I couldn't see, I..." Reed pulls me against his chest.

"Souls," Buns says, entering the kitchen. Zephyr holds her back near the door as she and Brownie try to go to the bodies sprawled in front of us.

"Stay," Zephyr warns Buns, creeping forward stealthily and investigating the patio. Taking flight outside, he sweeps the immediate area. Russell follows close behind him, scanning for Gancanagh.

Buns and Brownie both kneel by Hati. "What happened?" Brownie asks Reed.

"They were all under the thrall of the Gancanagh," Reed answers.

"You need to get Evie and Russell out of here. Hide them until we can negotiate for the souls," Brownie says in a commanding tone, rising from Hati's side.

"You have to do that now?" Reed asks, while stroking my hair.

"Of course," Brownie says.

"It's our job, sweetie," Buns replies. "We're Reapers."

Reed frowns. "Yes, but this is a volatile situation. We didn't intend to complicate our position with the presence of the Fallen. Is it possible to just...claim them for Paradise without summoning a fallen Reaper?" Reed asks, looking concerned.

"Ah, no," Brownie says swiftly, not even considering going that route. "We enjoy breathing."

"What's the worst that can happen if you just gave the humans a bye?" Russell asks curiously, entering with Zephyr from outside.

"The best thing that can happen is they just shred us," Brownie replies. "And that's the Thrones or the Cherubim in Paradise. We don't even want to think about what Sheol would do to us."

"We can't wait much longer—we have to release them from their bodies. They will find a way to escape them on their own, if we do not. Once that happens, the Fallen will come," Buns says in agitation.

"It's chill. The half-breeds will find a place to hide out until this is over," Russell says, holding out his hand to me. "C'mon, Red, let's go before the fallen freaks come and find out we're here."

Reed's arms tighten around me protectively. "I'll stay with you both. Zephyr, you watch the Reapers," he says over the top of my head. To Brownie and Buns, Reed says, "Take nothing for granted. This is a calculated move by Brennus. We don't know if the Fallen are in league with the Gancanagh, now that we have Evie back. If the fallen Reaper does anything untoward, do not hesitate to end him, Zee."

"You can't do that, Zee," Buns says with growing panic. "Even if it's sabotage, you run the risk of throwing things off balance."

"Things are already off balance, Buns," Zephyr replies, spreading his hands wide at the carnage on the ground.

"Just let Brownie and me handle this. We're professionals," Buns says, sounding like she's trying to reason with a child. "You go with the others. The humans were under a thrall. They may not remember what just happened and therefore they won't be able to speak of why they came here and did the things that they did. It will look suspicious if we have a Power hanging around with us."

"That is unfortunate, but it cannot be helped," Zephyr responds, crossing his arms in complete disregard of what she just said. "I prefer that to the alternative."

"We'll be fine, sweetie," Buns assures him, smiling a little at Zephyr's stern face.

"You will be because I am not leaving," Zephyr replies. Looking over Buns's head at Reed, he adds, "Take them. I will remain."

"Zee—" Buns begins.

Zephyr takes Buns in his arms and kisses her. He breaks off the kiss only after Reed clears his throat. "Staying," Zephyr murmurs. Not looking away from Buns, Zephyr says to Reed, "The weapons room is a decent position."

"Agreed," Reed says, guiding me to the kitchen door. With his eyes on Russell, Reed nods in the direction of the door, indicating he should come with us.

"How do y'all say, 'hoorah' in Angel?" Russell asks Zephyr.

Grinning, Zephyr says a word in Angel that sounds like "rude car."

"Well…'rude car,' Zee," Russell replies, putting up his knuckles.

Knocking them back, Zephyr advises, "Keep your eyes open."

"Knowin' those stinky devils, it's not my eyes that'll smell them comin'," Russell counters.

Reed says something to Zephyr, Buns, and Brownie in Angel. They all nod as Brownie and Buns touch their portal necklaces nervously.

"What did you say?" I ask, letting Reed lead me from the room and making sure that Russell is following close behind us.

"Roughly, I wished them the absence of fear and Godspeed on their mission," Reed replies. Walking with me down the hall, we just make it to the gallery when the first tripwire on the island activates, causing all hell to break loose.

CHAPTER 5

Elevation

"Here we go," Reed says in a quiet tone beside me, squeezing my hand as it begins to tremble in his. "Russell, stay close. That sounded like the incendiary in our bungalow. If they were following Evie's scent, then they would've been drawn there first."

"I hate this," I whisper, following Reed down the hall that leads to the library on one side and the weapons room on the other.

"Why?" Reed asks, a sexy smile on his face. He looks absolutely relaxed.

"Because they're coming," I answer, feeling my heartbeat drumming hard against the walls of my chest.

"Yes," he says, "they're coming and I can kill them without any repercussions—no worry for the consequences of what could happen to you if I do." The look of pure satisfaction crosses his face, making me lose some of the fear I'm feeling for a moment.

Turning into the weapons room, Reed goes straight to the vault. Opening secret panels in the wall, he unlocks an array of badness that I can't even begin to describe. "What looks good?" Reed asks, glancing at Russell.

"Machine gun—broad sword—throwin' stars—percussion grenades," Russell barks out, strapping weapons to his body as fast as Reed is handing them to him. "You feel that, Red?" Russell asks, looking over as electricity begins to build around me, prickling my skin.

"Yeah, someone's divining for us…that's annoying," I reply, wrinkling my nose as my hair stands on end. "Let's see if they like being shocked," I mutter, closing my eyes and pulling energy to me, I feel it dancing over my skin. Expelling it from me in a pulse, it shatters the windows as it exits the house.

"That was a bit more than a shock," Reed grins, seeing the shower of shattered glass lying on the floor.

"Oops," I shrug sarcastically, causing the smile to go all the way to his eyes. "I'll take the daggers and a battle-axe." Leaning over, I strap the daggers on my thighs, looking up to see both Reed and Russell checking out my butt. Straightening, I clear my throat, narrowing my eyes at them. Reed is trying really hard not to smile. "Shouldn't you be concentrating," I scold them both.

"Just gettin' the proper motivation for a fight. It's more fun when you know what you're protectin'," Russell says, grinning.

"Just make sure you protect your own butt, Russell. I'll worry about mine," I reply, reaching for the axe and testing its weight and balance. Reed puts on his protective gear to cover his skin. It will help shield him from the touch of the Gancanagh, should he need it. He doesn't draw the hood up over his head, leaving his face exposed.

"Get ready to test that theory, Red," Russell says, all signs of humor are gone as he stares over my head towards the outer wall with the shattered windows. Dark, ominous storm clouds are billowing up outside, carrying on the frigid wind a sweet, sticky scent.

Smelling the scent of the Gancanagh is having a debilitating affect on me. It's almost like a learned helplessness reaction—like struggling is a futile effort. Reed wraps his arms around me and holds me to him. "You need not stay for this, love," he says softly in my ear. "You've already done your part. They're here. Leave now and I'll join you when it's done."

My fear increases instead of lessening at his suggestion. "No! I'm staying—we go together…or not at all."

"Love, they won't touch me," he says with a radiating confidence. "Use your portal and I'll follow you after—"

"I'm staying. I'll have your back," I reply, feeling a creeping chill blowing in the windows. "Can you feel that?" I ask Reed, a shiver passing through me as icy currents begin collecting around us.

"Feel what?" Reed counters, looking at me with concern.

"BRRR," Russell says next to us. "The temperature just dropped 20 degrees."

"I can't feel it," Reed says, watching the goose bumps rising on my arms. "Their magic doesn't affect me."

"Well, I'm feelin' pretty damn affected," Russell mutters, showing us the hair on his arms standing straight up.

"Push back," Reed says, frowning. "Don't let them take control of your environment. You own it, Russell, you keep it—defend it."

"Right, Red, help me," Russell says. Pulling me out of Reed's arms and into his own he sweeps my hair back from my forehead, gazing into my eyes. "Start pulling energy—let's heat it up."

"What do you have in mind?" I ask, pulling energy to me.

"How about we roll out the carpet for them," Russell replies, concentrating.

Reaching out to Reed next to me, I pull him into our circle, saying, "We're kinda loose cannons at this point, Reed. It's best to stay close when we go off."

"Noted," Reed says, resting his hand on my hip.

Feeling energy burning me, I say, "Okay Russell, say the words."

Russell mumbles something under his breath. When he squeezes my arm, I turn the energy outward. It releases from us in a mass of billowing heat. Fire erupts in the room while a river of flames snakes and weaves away from us, blowing a gaping hole in the side of the house and continuing on toward the beach.

"Russell," I murmur, staring out of the gaping hole in the wall in disbelief. Gancanagh that I've never seen before are walking through the burning river of fire from the beach, like we extended a red carpet for them.

Russell scowls, "Not quite the effect I was goin' for." He lets go of me and pulls the machine gun up from its place on his back.

"Finally," Reed breathes, pulling me back behind him, he moves forward, his sword grasped casually in his fist.

Panic begins to choke me as my wings move in agitation. Taking flight, I hover in mid-air in the middle of the room. Gancanagh soldiers branch out, moving in groups of twos and threes. Whispering words to myself, I pull energy to me, feeling cold fellas fighting me for control of it. Releasing energy, I form a shield over the flaming opening in the wall, forcing them to enter through the broken windows.

As the first wave of Gancanagh enter the house, they spider over the walls with the supernatural speed of the undead. Reed doesn't hesitate, moving to them with a dizzying speed, hacking their limbs from them with the brutal force of an avenging angel.

"Where is your king?" Reed grits out, not letting the soldier answer him before slicing through cartilage and sinew, causing blood to seep in coagulating dollops from his severed head.

Rapid gunfire punctures the air from Russell's gun as 40 caliber rounds burst forth, riddling the chest of several Gancanagh who keep moving toward him, smiling the eerie smiles of the blissfully dead.

But, Russell doesn't get a chance to use his sword on them before Reed falls upon them, cutting them down before they can exhale. Reed manages to kill every one of them in the space of a few seconds.

"Hey, those were mine," Russell accuses.

"Sorry," Reed says, shrugging. "There will be more."

Zephyr bursts through the door of the room, carrying Buns under one arm and Brownie under the other. Setting them on their feet, he asks, "What did I miss?"

"Just the warm-up," Reed replies with a grin.

"Ugh, you guys are completely insane," Buns says, straightening her top.

"How'd the negotiations go?" Russell asks, not looking at Buns or Brownie, but scanning the exterior of the house, waiting for more undead to drop in.

"I'll tell you how they went, Russell. They went bad. Very, very, bad," Brownie replies with her brows drawn together, while moving to the vault and plucking a crossbow off the rack on the wall. Loading it and strapping a quiver of steel-tipped arrows to her she continues. "We sorta ran into an impasse when Zee here hacked the fallen Reaper's head off!" She extends her hand to Zephyr who grins broadly.

"I did not like the look of him," Zephyr shrugs, checking his sword and the menagerie of knives he has strapped to him. "He was hiding something."

"Let me skool you, Zee. They're all hiding something. All of them. No exceptions. Ohhh, we're so dead! You filleted him," she says, rubbing her forehead. She then shrugs into her protective clothing, covering her skin from the Gancanagh's touch.

"He had nothing on those souls. He was stalling. You could see it when he started sweating," Zephyr counters, donning his armor.

"Sweetie, maybe you staring at him was making him sweaty. You're kinda scary," Buns says, catching the bow that Brownie tosses to her with one hand, plucking the tension of the string while narrowing her eyes as she looks through the sight window.

"You think I'm scary?" Zephyr asks, his amazing blue eyes shining.

"Uh huh," Buns says, nodding her honey-blond head, "Super scary."

"Alright, save the bedroom talk for later," Brownie says, rolling her eyes.

"Don't be a hater," Zephyr grins at Brownie, before winking at Buns as she slips into her armor. "I can feel the Fallen. They are here—on my island—without my permission. That Reaper was gathering intel. He was a scout, but a very bad one. Why do they employ the tragically lame?" Zephyr asks derisively, looking at Reed. "The pizza man has more game."

"The Reaper didn't expect you to be with them, Zee," Reed counters.

"No, he did not," he agrees. "I found this on him." Zephyr tosses a small buttonhole camera to Reed. Reed holds it in the palm of his hand, crushing it into dust and letting it fall to the ground.

"You're off the hook, Brownie," he says, sniffing the air. "Zee's right. Fallen are stalking us."

"That doesn't make us off the hook. They don't care if Sheol is stalking us. No one gets a bye," Brownie states emphatically, pointing up. "They'll send Cherubim—a Throne at the very least."

"Shit's about to blow up," Russell breaks in. "You feel that, Red," he asks quickly.

"Yeah," I nod, landing on the ground near him and placing my hand on his arm.

"What?" Zephyr sniffs.

"It feels like…a wrinkle in the air…like someone touched the air with his finger and it sent out ripples—like in water," I try to explain the waves of energy hitting us.

"They're rampin' up!" Russell says through his gritted teeth, as the waves become shockwaves pounding us. Then, one huge wave hits us. Lifting us both off our feet, it throws Russell and me back into the far wall, before dropping us to the floor in a heap.

"That completely blows," Russell gasps, holding his side.

Reed is at my side immediately, having not been affected at all from the magic swirling all around us. "It's time to pull the plug on you two," Reed says while his hands rove over my body, checking for injury. "Use your portals now, I'll follow you soon."

"No, I'm staying," I reply stubbornly, trying to stand, but Reed has his hand on my shoulder keeping me down.

"Time's up, Evie," Reed orders, while his hand moves to my necklace. I quickly cover his hand with mine as it rests on the onyx moon around my neck.

"Please, let me stay with you," I plead, tasting blood in my mouth.

"No," Reed replies grimly. "This whole place is wired. All we need to do is draw them in. They won't know you've gone. Your mission is done. When they come, I'll incinerate them and join you." He holds up the detonator that triggers all the C-4 on the island. It will be raining pieces of Gancanagh for days.

"Reed," Zephyr says in a stiff voice.

Looking up, the sky outside grows dark as swarms of angels gather in the skies above the big house. "Holy. Freakin'. Hell!" Russell says next to me. Windows in other parts of the house begin shattering, announcing the arrival of our evil guests.

"I didn't know it was my birthday!" Zephyr grins, like the Fallen amassing all around us is a gift to him. "Time for you to go, Buns and Brownie, this is our party," he says, nodding toward Reed.

"Stay-ing," Buns replies in a singsong voice.

"Ah, you are so cute, come here," Zephyr says. Striding to Buns, he takes her in his arms, kissing her. Drawing back, he breathes, "Bye," as he pulls the portal of her necklace open, while stepping back from her.

Instantly, Buns seems to fold and contort into the small opening of her sun necklace. I pale, knowing that she is being squeezed through space to another destination. I remember what that feels like and I'm not in any hurry to relive the experience. Her necklace falls to the floor, pulling the furniture toward it. Zephyr manages to pick the necklace up, his hand distorting and twisting before he snaps it closed, smashing the necklace into dust, so no one can follow Buns through her portal.

"Oh, you are so dead, Zee," Brownie says, a smile forming on her lips. "I'm not even gonna help you out on that one. I'm just gonna sit back and watch her tear you apart."

"Brownie, can you give me a hand," Russell groans, looking like he's having trouble standing.

Brownie shifts her gaze from Zephyr to Russell. "Are you okay?" Brownie asks, her eyes going wide while hurrying to Russell's side and crouching down near him.

"Yeah—sorry," he says, reaching up and flipping her star necklace open. Brownie folds too, twisting into her necklace as it drops to the ground in what feels like slow motion. Russell deftly closes Brownie's portal, smashing it in his palm.

I knock Reed's hand away from my necklace while he is distracted by what Russell just did. "No way," I say, grasping the moon around my neck in my fist. "I'm staying."

"Evie," Reed says in a stern tone, but he can't argue with me as a voice from behind him distracts us.

"OY! GENEVIEVE! Ye really did it dis time," Eion says, walking through the gaping hole in the wall that's no longer being blocked by my magic. "Ye broke his heart, now ye had better fix it, if ye know whah's good for ye."

"Eion," I reply, getting to my feet, "have you ever known me to do what's good for me?"

"I have na," he replies, seeing me behind Reed. "Ye are a confusing, delicious craitur, but I do na mind ye, 'cuz now, I get ta taste ye and 'tis worth all da sleepless nights I've spent dreamin' about ye."

"Eion, you never sleep...or dream," I reply coolly, scanning his Gancanagh army and seeing many familiar faces behind him. Brennus is not here, nor are Finn, Faolan or Declan. My heart twists in frustration, knowing Brennus is avoiding our trap. "Where is my king?" I ask, trying to appear calm.

"He could na make it," Eion replies, allowing Ninian, Eibhear, Goban, Keefe, and Torin to enter the room ahead of him. Russell gets to his feet beside me, pulling out the sword that he had strapped to his back and grasping it casually in his hands. "He sent me instead. Ye'll be seeing him soon, but only after I taste ye."

"If any of you make it back to Brennus, give him a message for me," I announce, ignoring Eion. "Please tell him that he is not my king. He failed to come here himself. That makes him a coward and I bear no allegiance to a coward and neither should any of you," I add, raising my chin a notch and scanning their faces.

"Maybe ye do na mean as much ta him as ye tink ye do, Genevieve," Eion replies, a sneer twisting his lips.

"Then, why are you here, Eion?" I ask, tilting my head to the side while blowing a hole in his theory.

The doors behind us swing open admitting a score or more fallen angels with more behind them. Their stench fills the room, making me shudder as my eyes widen. "It *is* my birthday," Zephyr breathes, looking elated. He speaks in Angel to the big fallen Power in the front of the pack, drawing the evil one's eyes from me to him. Watching the angel's eyes narrow on Zephyr, I can tell that Zephyr is trash talking him, but it sounds like lovely music all the same.

"Go now, Evie," Reed whispers to me, looking calm and relaxed as he does before every conflict.

"I will, I just have to face the Gancanagh. I have to show them that I'm not afraid of them—that I'm not putting up with any of their shen," I say, raising my axe in Eion's direction. That is all it takes for the Gancanagh to scatter like roaches, running at the walls and using inertia to scale them.

Launching upward and flying to a position in the center of the room, Russell follows me, taking a position at my back. Ninian springs at me first, trying to grab onto me as he rockets through the air. I grasp him by his wrist, spinning him around in the air to gain momentum and tossing him directly into Goban as he pitches toward me. They collide in midair, falling to the floor beneath us where Reed steps on their necks, slicing off their heads.

A hoard of Fallen engage Reed and Zephyr in a battle below. I can hardly follow them with my eyes, not only because I'm fighting with the Gancanagh, but also because angels are so incredibly fast. There are too many Fallen, even if Reed and Zephyr are the best at what they do, they will soon be overwhelmed.

Russell is hacking at the Gancanagh that are lurching at him from the walls. "Russell, we have to go," I call out, putting my hand out and pushing energy outward to deflect the elf darts that Torin is throwing at Russell and me. The fireballs ricochet off the shield, showering ribbons of sparks and flames down on the heads of the fallen angels hacking at Reed.

"No shit! I'm with you, Red," Russell calls back, getting pounded by a shadowy nevarache, conjured by Eion. The nevarache's black, spiky tail snakes around Russell's body while it tries to dig its sharp, ferocious claws into his neck. I pull energy away from Eion, making his nevarache fade, bleeding away like a falling star.

"EVIE!" Reed shouts, spinning away from the attack from fallen angels on the ground and taking flight near us. "GO NOW!" he orders, catching the arm of a fallen angel who is about to cleave me in two with his axe. Reed struggles with him, forcing him back into the wall and embedding the axe in the fallen's chest.

Closing my eyes, I pull all the energy in the room to me. I whisper words to myself, before forcing the power from my body. Icicles run the length of the walls, coursing down it and branching out, freezing everything in its path. Missing Zephyr by mere inches, the burgeoning ice flow encompasses many of the fallen angels near the doors, continuing out into the hallway beyond this room. Zephyr swings his sword at a frozen fallen angel, creating long, web-like cracks that rip through the tragic figure, shattering the fallen Power like glass.

Satisfied that I've done all I can to help, I reach for my necklace, signaling to Russell that we need to go. My gaze turns to Reed, winking at him as I touch my necklace, feeling the smooth onyx beneath my fingertips. Catching the clasp, the necklace springs open. The expression on Reed's face changes from relief to wide-eyed horror. An instant later, Eion pounces on me, wrapping his legs around my waist and hugging his body to mine like a serpent. Pressing his cool lips against my neck, his sharp fangs bite into my flesh just as we're stretched and pulled together into my portal.

CHAPTER 6

Anya

Crashing onto a hard floor in a magnificent bedroom, my mouth opens wide in utter agony before my teeth clench together in pain. Eion is beneath me; his legs are still wrapped around me like a clamp as he continues to tear and suck the rapidly flowing blood from my neck. Struggling to break away from him, my vision slips out of focus as stabbing pain tears through me. It feels like Eion is collapsing a chamber within my heart as he greedily draws more and more blood from me.

Straining, I reach back, clawing at his eyes with my fingernails. He has to pull his teeth out of me to avoid me gouging his eyes out. Panting like he's run a race, Eion speaks behind me, "Ye are incredible, Genevieve."

I pick my head up, and then drive it back hard into his face, hearing a crack of cartilage as I break his nose. His legs loosen on my waist and I try to stand, but I fall forward instead. I crawl toward the bedroom door, kicking my feet at Eion who groans and tries to grab me again.

Eion holds my leg, pulling himself up; he bares his teeth again, driving them into my thigh. As he feeds on me again, a scream of agony rips from me. I grasp his hair, pulling out a fistful of it and dislodging him from me. Kicking him in the face, I turn again, crawling again toward the door. Almost gaining my feet, I sway, falling over as dizziness overwhelms me.

"Dis is so much better den da mindless compliance from da wans," Eion says behind me, referring to the enthralled women who cannot fight back. "'Tis no wonder why he can na live wi' out ye. 'Tis so sexy when ye struggle…I can taste da fire in yer blood—or maybe dat is whah ye always taste like."

Standing over me, Eion looks drunk; he sways a little before catching himself against the post of the enormous bed. "I need ta know whah it feels like when ye struggle as I bury meself in ye…can ye do dat for me, *aingeal*…will ye struggle for me while I make luv ta ye?" he asks, scooping me up off the floor and carrying me towards the bed.

"Eion—don't," I say weakly, seeing his intent.

"Struggle for me, Genevieve, and I will share me blood wi' ye. Ye'll be me *sclábhaí*, me slave, and I will kill Brennus for ye," he promises, kissing my temple.

"You're insane. He'll destroy you, Eion," I counter, feeling the soft mattress beneath me. "My blood is making you drunk—"

"'Tis, Genevieve, and now dat I've tasted it, I'll die before I give ye ta another," he replies. Wrapping his fist in my hair he brings his face to within mere inches of mine, his brows draw down in a fierce scowl as he says, "Now…struggle!"

Pulling my hair back and making my neck arch up, Eion bites into my neck again, causing unbelievable pain to run like poison through my veins. Reaching down, I pull one of the daggers from my thigh holster. Turning the knife in my hand, I drive it into Eion's side, twisting it before his teeth come out of me again. His hand covers mine, knocking my hand away from him. Pushing Eion away from me with my foot, I pull the other dagger from my thigh holster, swiping the air between us to make him stay back from me.

I list to the other side of the bed and manage to crawl off it, putting it between Eion and me. Hunger pains gnaw at me as the scent of Eion's blood, seeping from his side, floats to me.

"Ye smell me, do ye na?" Eion smiles, his fangs still dripping with my blood. "Ye can taste me, Genevieve. I want ye…I've always wanted ye. I can na live wi'out ye now. Join me…we'll conquer dis world."

"Eion, you repulse me," I say, but the urge to pounce on him and drink his blood makes me sweat.

"Dat will change. I can make ye want me," he smiles, using the knife I had left in his side to cut his wrist, letting his blood well up and seep out.

I put one of my arms up to try to cover my nose and mouth from the scent of him. My stomach twists in a knot from hunger as I whimper and clutch my abdomen.

Bright red wings catch my eye then, as Russell skids past me, bouncing and tumbling over the floor with a pale, undead fella attached to him. Russell rises to his feet with Keefe on his back. He ducks down, pulling Keefe over the top of him like a ragdoll. Grasping Keefe's neck in his hands, Russell snaps his neck with a loud crack before dropping Keefe's listless body to the floor.

"AHHHH, THAT FREAKY ANIMAL BIT ME!" Russell shouts angrily, looking like a raging bull before whirling and seeing Eion. "WHERE IS SHE?" he shouts at Eion, his wings arching out while striding menacingly toward him. Eion lifts the dagger in his hand to ward off Russell, but Russell lunges at him, taking the dagger right out of Eion's hand and turning it on him.

"She's there," Eion says, pointing in my direction. Looking at me, Russell's whole face changes from anger to raging insanity. My bloody appearance distracts Russell, allowing Eion the opportunity to sink his fangs into Russell's arm. He clamps down hard, drawing Russell's blood from him.

"YOU NASTY PARASITE!" Russell rages, picking Eion up by the throat with his other hand and tearing him off of his arm. Russell extends his arm, crushing Eion's neck with just one hand.

"Russell!" I say breathlessly, watching him drop Eion's corpse on the floor. "How?" I ask, not understanding how he has come to be here. He is supposed to be with Brownie. Their portals are paired as Zephyr and Buns are paired. Reed is supposed to be with me in this safe house.

"Ahhh, those bites burn! LORD THAT SUCKS!" Russell rants, shaking the arm that Eion preyed upon.

"How many bites do you have?" I ask weakly, leaning against the wall behind me.

"I don't know," Russell says, and then he sways on his feet. Dropping his hands and bracing himself against the bed, I can count at least five or six bite marks on his chest that are oozing trails of blood.

"Turn around, Russell," I murmur. As he turns around I gasp, seeing at least ten more bites covering his back beneath his wings. "What happened?" I ask, adrenaline kicking in so that I'm becoming more alert.

"When Eion grabbed you, Reed tossed the detonator to me, and then he tried to follow you. He activated his portal," Russell says, looking down.

Gazing around frantically, I stagger toward the bedroom door, searching for where Reed could be in the house. I haven't heard him. He could need our help on another floor.

"He's not here, Red," Russell says, looking guilty.

"Where is he?" I ask, feeling my world spinning around and leaning at odd angles.

"I switched our portals a couple of days ago. I wasn't just gonna roll over and let Reed take you away from me, so I switched his watch with mine when y'all were swimmin'. When Reed left the fight on the island just now, he went to Brownie's safe house with my watch," Russell explains quickly.

"Oh my God, Russell! He's going to kill you!" I breathe, staggering to a chair by the fireplace. Grasping the back of it, I try to stay on my feet. "What happened next?" I ask, not wanting to think about what Reed will do to Russell when he finds us.

"Well, I couldn't leave to help you because I had the detonator. I got jumped by a couple of stinky devils who thought I tasted like 'Heaven,'" he explains, his voice sounding strained and raspy as he swipes his hand through his hair. "Zee got to me, knockin' the bastards off of me. He took the detonator and told me to go, so I went. He planned to blow the island and leap into his portal. That one hitched a ride when I was leavin'," Russell groans, gesturing to Keefe's body. "What is that smell?" he demands, doubling over like his stomach aches.

"That's Eion...and probably Keefe...their blood," I answer, panting. "It smells..."

"Delicious," Russell finishes for me.

"We gotta go, Russell, before we try to eat them," I gasp, feeling a bead of sweat drip down the side of my face. "We need to find clean blood...animal blood to curb the bloodlust."

"I remember...I just didn't know...this is..." he strains to stand.

"Agony," I finish for him, gritting my teeth and pushing myself away from the chair.

"Yeah," he agrees, "I think I'm startin' to trip, Red," Russell says, swatting at something he's seeing in the empty air. "Or is this place crawlin' with mosquitoes the size of Krispy Kremes?" Russell asks, ducking his head.

"No, you're hallucinating," I reply, feeling choked up because I can hardly move. "You have so many bites, Russell."

Terror creeps up my spine, knowing that I'm going to have to try to help Russell before he completely freaks out. Once he loses all sense of reality, I'll probably look like the enemy to him. He could kill me without even knowing it's me...and I could kill him.

Trying to think, I say, "Russell, take off all of your weapons and throw them away."

"Why?" Russell says, not doing what I told him.

"Because, we're going to be each other's worst nightmares soon and I don't want to get my head hacked off by your broad sword," I retort.

"Oh...good point," he replies, taking off all his weapons and tossing them near the window. I do the same, tossing mine into the fireplace.

"Okay, now…we have to leave. We have to get as far away from the blood of the Gancanagh as we can," I say, while my mouth begins to water.

"It's snowin' outside, Red," Russell says, gazing out the window at the snowy night sky.

"Maybe Reed has clothes," I say, lifting my hand listlessly toward an elegant wardrobe. The room is beautiful, with stucco, arabesque molding and baroque architecture. It is the most elegant room I've ever been in.

"It won't matter, Red," Russell replies, staggering toward me instead. "There's no way I'm gettin' my wings to retract. I can't even put a coat on." Grasping me by my upper arm, he steers me towards the bedroom door. "Do you know where we are?"

"Torun, Poland," I reply.

"No kiddin'?" Russell asks, a small smile forming in the corners of his mouth.

"No, why?" I counter, leaning against him.

"'Cuz I've been here before…'bout six hundred years ago, more or less—I was the daughter of one of the town's merchants."

Entering the hall, Russell sways on his feet, crashing into the wall. I grab onto the banister looking over the landing and seeing that we're three stories up in an elegant town house. The spiraling staircase is ornate, with oak spindles in the form of angels, running the breath of the staircase.

Placing his hands on the wall, Russell leaves huge, bloody handprints on it as he gains his balance. "Sorry, Red." Russell groans.

"S'kay," I slur, feeling him take my arm again and lead me to the stairs.

"I'm startin' to suspect that nothin's a coincidence, Red," Russell says, sitting down on the top step and pulling me down next to him. He scoots down a step, the way a toddler would to descend the stairs, pulling me along with him. "Are them angels on the railin' cryin', Red?" he asks, shying away a little from the balustrades.

I scrutinize the carved banister as it shivers and melts. "No," I answer. "Do you see any tiny, evil-looking sprites chewing on bat wings?" I mutter, sliding my butt down to the next stair.

"Naw," he answers, looking around in shock.

"No? No sharp-teeth little creatures dressed sorta like Santa's elves?" I ask again warily, as a ferocious sprite eyes me from his position flying above my head.

"Naw," Russell shakes his head. "How prepared would you say Reed is?" Russell asks, pulling me faster down the steps.

"Uh…Reed? He makes the boy scouts look like loafers," I reply, bumping down the stairs.

"And he's super paranoid where you're concerned," Russell adds.

"Protective," I agree.

Russell drags me faster down the remaining stairs. At the bottom, Russell gets to his feet. I try to stand, but I can't. Toppling over on the ground, I lie there looking up at him.

"Which way would you say it is to the kitchen?" Russell asks grimly.

When I shrug, Russell grasps my hand and drags me across the floor. Pulling me from room to room, he finally locates what he's looking for—the kitchen. He drops my arm and it falls across my chest. Staggering forward, Russell opens the refrigerator.

He laughs before he shouts, "RUDE CAR, RED!" Holding up a large, glass jar, it looks like blood that has separated. Shaking it, Russell mixes it together in the jar, making it look more like blood. Peering back into the refrigerator, he frowns. "Damn!" he says.

"What?" I ask, pulling myself to a sitting position against the wall.

"This is it," he says. It's about a quart of blood…enough for one of us. "Here," Russell says, extending the jar in his hand as he walks toward me.

"No," I croak, putting up my hand so he won't come near me. "Don't let me smell it. I might—I might try to fight you for it." I cover my nose and mouth with my hand.

"We could share it—" Russell says, and I shake my head.

"It's not enough for both of us. You should drink it—" I begin.

"Naw," Russell says, a fierce scowl transforming his face. "It's yours!"

"Think about it, Russell," I say, feeling really ill. "You're stronger… if I drink it and you keep hallucinating, you'll probably end up killing me, even if I manage to bring back blood for you. You just said you've been here before—"

"THAT WAS SIX HUNDRED YEARS AGO! THE PLACE HAS PROBABLY CHANGED!" Russell shouts at me.

"Russell, I'm so weak that I can't even stand up. I think Eion might've drained half my blood supply. That blood is yours because you can go out and get more and…I'll wait here for you," I say listlessly, feeling like I'm going to burst into tears at any second.

"NO!" Russell shouts stubbornly.

"YES!" I snap back. "And tie me up, so I don't stagger away or try to hurt myself…or you. Use your belt—tie me to a chair—one of those kitchen chairs will be okay."

"Naw! I'll take you with me," he counters with pain in his eyes.

"Yeah, it won't look weird that you're carrying an angel through town looking for blood. What if a Fallen spots us?" I ask. Russell groans in indecision, so I press my advantage. "Hurry, Russell. I'm not getting any better while you're sitting around on your ASS!"

"ASS KICKER!" Russell spits out between his teeth. "You're the most difficult—irritatin'—stubborn—it's always gotta be your way!" he says, before twisting the lid off the jar and putting it to his lips, downing half the blood in a few gulps. My mouth waters along with my eyes watching him. Digging my nails into my palms, I glance away so I won't get up and try to take it from him.

When he finishes the blood, I stagger to my feet, using the wall to get to one of the kitchen chairs. Sitting in it, I pant, "Now tie me up."

"Red—" Russell starts to say.

"When you're done, knock the chair back, so I can't walk around. HURRY!" I order, feeling like I'm going to attack him at any second and try to rip the blood out of him. Taking off his belt, he winds it through the back of the chair and around my hands while I make a concerted effort not to move.

Russell walks around to the front of the chair. He eases it back so that I'm resting on my arms. "Don't die, Red," Russell pleads softly. "Promise."

"I won't," I say weakly, trying to smile, but I can't see his face through my tears. "I promise."

Russell leaps away then and is gone from the house with the banging of a door several rooms away. I close my eyes. The house takes on the silence of a tomb; the only sound becomes my ragged breath as it passes over my dry lips. The silence grows as my breathing begins to slow and wheeze out the name, "Reed...Reed...Reed..."

As if in answer to my mantra, whispering hisses assail me from all the corners of the kitchen, *Genevieve...struggle now...it makes us want you more.* Opening my eyes again, shadows flitter and scurry, beetling along the walls like gruesome Werree monsters.

"Not here...YOU'RE NOT HERE!" I scream at them with tears sliding down my cheeks as my breathing becomes erratic once more.

The smell of Eion's blood drifts to me from the floors above, causing my eyes to roll in agony. I strain forward, struggling against the leather belt binding my hands, wanting to go to him—to feed on his dead corpse. Bashing my head hard against the back of the chair a couple of times, I try to knock myself out so that I won't move from here. My head feels sticky, like I might've cut it open as disorientation makes me rest it against the seat back again.

A noise from the hallway outside the kitchen makes me cringe as I imagine every type of monster that I have met being the source of it. I groan while I try to lift my head so that I can see the doorway.

The golden glint of a tip of an arrow breaks the plane of the door-frame. My eyes widen, following the shaft of the arrow back to delicate-looking fingertips, pulling the string of the bow taut.

A deep, quivering exhale comes from me as a beautiful, pale face of a feminine angel turns her green-eyed gaze on me through the sight window of her bow. Her inky black wings rise threateningly and her eyes narrow as she stares back at me with a grim expression. Taking a step into the kitchen, she doesn't lower her bow, but draws her arm back a little more, ratcheting the arrow tighter on the string.

"You're not real," I mumble to her, staring back at the ceiling and waiting to see if she'll morph into something else or just disappear.

Sweet, soft music tumbles from her lips, sounding like she's speaking to me in Angel. But, if she's really here, the derisive expression on her face is letting me know that she's not friendly.

"Blah, blah, blah," I mutter feebly. "You're my hallucination. You should know that I don't speak Angel."

She approaches me then, peering down on me. Using her foot, she catches the base of my chair, tipping it up abruptly. She bends down so that we're at eye level. Her black hair falls forward as she speaks in Angel again. The tip of her arrow arches close to my head.

"Okay," I murmur, moistening my lips, "that seems a little more real."

With a scowl on her face, the black-winged angel puts her foot on my chair again. Kicking the bottom of it, my chair slides back across the floor, crashing into the wall behind me and crushing my arms painfully.

"Bitch!" I cringe, my wings moving painfully, trying to get me to fight back, but my hands are still locked behind me.

Again, beautiful music tumbles from her mouth.

"I DON'T SPEAK ANGEL!" I shout back at her, straining my hands to get free. Her fingers relax then, releasing the string and sending her arrow spiraling toward me at a deadly velocity. Throwing my body to the left, I pitch the chair over, avoiding the arrow aimed at my heart. It embeds in the wall behind me. Hitting the floor, the chair breaks, releasing my hands.

"RUSE-EL," she shouts, pulling another arrow from the quiver strapped to her side. She looks like a trained assassin; her tight black outfit hugs her every curve so that no one can grab any loose fabric to use against her in a fight.

"Wait," I say, stumbling to my feet and rubbing my numb hands together. Dizziness overcomes me and I fall back against the wall, sliding to the floor again.

"Ruse-el," she snarls between her teeth, easing the string of her bow back and aiming another golden arrow at my head.

"RED! I FOUND BLOOD!" I hear Russell shout as he bangs open the front door of the town house, pounding down the hallway toward the kitchen.

"RUSSELL, NO!" I shout. The black-winged angel turns when she hears Russell's voice, lowering her bow to her side.

Entering the kitchen, Russell's face goes from relief to confusion as he freezes, taking in the situation before him. "Sheeee-it, Red," Russell breathes, seeing the angel in the middle of the room. His hand goes to his stomach, touching it lightly. He turns his eyes on me, seeing me sitting listlessly on the floor.

"Russell," I whisper. "Run."

Russell

CHAPTER 7

Don't Wake Me

Scannin' the broken kitchen chair next to Red, my eyes quickly go to her pale face before they shift, restin' on the black-winged angel between us. I touch my stomach again, it's flutterin' and jumpin' like it's filled with thousands of crickets. My face darkens. Slowly, I set the canister in my hand down by the wall. Then, my wings emerge from my back, archin' out like thick, blazin' banners. It had been a huge effort to get my wings to go back in, but it's a relief to have them out now.

"Red, who's this?" I ask, takin' a cautious step toward her position on the floor by the far wall.

The black wings of the other angel spread out wide in front of me, blockin' my view of Red behind their long, elegant expanse. I scan her face; her beautiful, green eyes follow my every move. Her wings twitch agitatedly, movin' her long, thick, black hair.

"I don't know," Red whispers, "but, she's not friendly. You need to go now." Splinterin' pain creeps into her voice. I know the pain she's in now. It probably feels like her veins are turnin' to stone.

"Yeah...that's not gonna happen," I whisper back, feelin' like I should be sweatin', but I'm cold, like I'll never be warm again. "What do you want?" I demand of the stranger in the kitchen. My hands feel weak and I want to drop them to my sides, but I don't.

Tiltin' her head to the side, she gazes at my face. Her flawless skin flushes, a soft blush spreadin' over her cheeks. Then, her eyes rest on my neck, and her brows shoot together in a scowl. Beautiful music falls from her lips in a rapid flow of Angelic words. It's like how Buns sounds when she's talkin' to Zephyr in Angel. She moves toward me, and I take a guarded step back from her.

She stops talkin' and just looks at me. There is a long pause before she says somethin' else. Her eyes look strange, like she's expectin' a different reaction from me. My eyes follow hers and I see that she's lookin' at my chest, seein' blood oozin' from the Gancanagh bites that aren't healin'.

I touch my neck lightly, "Yeah...the blood suckers got me," I admit softly. "They got my girl, too. I need to give her some blood... so she won't be hurtin' so bad," I try to explain, gesturin' toward Red on the floor behind her. I pick up the canister I had brought and try again to inch around the seriously sexy angel in front of me.

She steps in front of me again, and raisin' her bow, she points her gold-tipped arrow at me. "Okay, listen," I exhale, puttin' out both of my hands to stop her from shootin' me. "This is blood," I say, shakin' the canister demonstratively, "I need to give it to her. You'd never believe it, but the butcher shop that was here six hundred years ago still exists." I inch another step toward Red, continuin' to talk like everythin' isn't completely effed up and out of control. "Coincidence you might say, but I'm thinkin' that this was all in some huge play-book and I already studied the play—I just need to execute it."

More music spills from her lips as she looks through the sight window of her bow. Takin' a breath, I say, "Well, that sounds seri-ous...and I can see that you mean everythin' that you're tellin' me, but you gotta get outta my way now 'cuz I'm fixin' to go mental if you don't let me give this to my girl."

I brush past the black-winged angel to kneel down by Red. Openin' the lid to the canister, I lift Red's head, cradlin' it while puttin' the rim of the canister to her lips. Red drinks the thick, coag-ulatin' liquid as bloody trails drip down her cheek, fallin' onto her little halter tank top.

"That's it, Red, keep drinkin' it, sweetheart," I whisper to her, seein' her eyes open a little at my words. Liftin' her hands to the canister, she holds it to her mouth, drinkin' in large gulps like she's dyin' of thirst.

The angel behind me growls, makin' me stiffen. I say over my shoulder, "Just a second...I'll get to you." Usin' my hand to smooth Red's hair back from her face, I murmur "It's gonna be all right, Red. I won't leave you again."

Instantly, I feel somethin' hit the back of my head, causin' me to reach up and touch my neck. Dark spots swim in my vision as eve-rythin' begins to sound like it's comin' from far away. Another swat to the back of my head makes me drop Red as I fall on her, while everythin' goes dark.

Wakin' up, my vision blurs as whistlin' blares from nearby. My head feels like it's *seis de Mayo* and I had been up doin' tequila shots all night with the *señoritas*. Shiftin' my head toward the sound, I see a kettle on the kitchen stove emittin' a stream of steam from its spout. Tryin' to move, I find that it's impossible. Thick chains are wrapped around my waist, holdin' me to a chair in the kitchen. My hands are bound behind my back with the same type of chains.

Glancin' over, I see Red is in a similar position, chained to a chair next to me. Her chin is slumped forward on her chest, but she looks like she's still breathin'. Strugglin', the chains rattle loudly behind me. The pot on the stove continues to boil until the lithe figure of a beautiful, young woman enters the kitchen and takes it from the burner. Her wings are in now, and she's put her hair up in a sleek ponytail, but I still recognize her as the angel with the black wings.

She takes a couple of mugs down from the cupboard and pours hot water into one, droppin' a tea bag in it to steep. Pickin' up a bottle of whiskey from the counter, she pours a generous amount into the other mug. She glances over her shoulder at me and her eyes catch mine. Keepin' her features blank, she turns, bringin' the mug of whiskey to me and settin' it on the table. Then, she reaches out and touches a lock of my hair, brushin' it back tenderly from my face.

"You changed. Is that one of Reed's sweaters?" I ask, my voice sounds rough. Her eyebrows soften as she touches my cheek, runnin' her slender fingers over it. Her scent drifts to me and somethin' flitters through my mind like a whisper, tormentin' me with a stab of... yearnin'.

I swallow hard against the unexpected tightening of my throat. "You wanna let me go here? 'Cuz you're totally startin' to freak me out," I say honestly, tryin' to get my hands loose from the chains bindin' them. "Don't get me wrong, this is strangely excitin' and under different circumstances I'd probably find it sorta hot...but right now, I gotta say, it's really just shady." I flex my arms again, tryin' to pull my chest away from the chair, but my shoulders are bound to it.

A cooin' sound comes from the strange angel as she puts her finger to my lips, tracin' them gracefully and makin' me shiver. She bends down so that we are eye to eye before she says, "Ruse-el..." then she shifts to her Angelic language, speakin' with a look of concern on her face. She lightly touches my chest where I'm still bleedin' from

Keefe's bites. She pulls her fingers away, showin' me the blood on their tips.

"Yeah, I know I'm bleedin'," I reply, lookin' in her eyes again. "Let me go and I'll call my friends—they'll know what I need to do to stop it."

She frowns. Lookin' down at the table, she picks up the mug, bringin' it to my lips. "Whoa, wait! Hold up!" I sputter, movin' my head and not lettin' her make me drink it. She pulls the mug back, frownin' at me.

"That's straight whiskey! I'm not gonna be able to stand up if I drink all that," I explain quickly. She shoves it back in my face, puttin' it to my lips again. Forcin' some in my mouth, I spit it out at her, scowlin'. "I'm not drinkin' that!" I retort between my teeth.

Angrily, she puts the mug down on the table, wipin' away the whiskey I've spit at her on the sleeve of her sweater. In a blur of angelic speed, she goes to the counter and back. Wieldin' a very sharp knife in her hand, she lifts Red's head by her hair, holdin' the knife to her neck as she watches my reaction.

I 'bout lose my mind, goin' wild and strainin' against the chains. I feel 'em cut into my wrists. When I exhaust myself, I sit pantin', scowlin' at her as I'm fantasizin' 'bout ways to kill her slowly.

Easin' the knife from Red's neck, she puts it down on the table before pickin' up the mug of whiskey again. She puts the cup gently to my lips, tippin' it so I'll take a sip. I refuse again, lettin' it drip down my face as I glare into her eyes.

She pulls the mug back from my lips. Lookin' at the mug almost desperately, she puts it to her own lips, takin' a huge swallow of it. Immediately, she coughs and sputters, her eyes waterin' from the effects of the strong alcohol. After she recovers a little, she sets the mug on the table again. She picks up the knife, takin' it back with her to the stove. She lays the knife on one of the burners, turnin' on the gas. Flames leap up around the blade of the knife. She doesn't look at me at all while the knife heats on the stove; she hangs her head, like she's in pain.

In a few minutes, she lifts the glowing-hot knife from the stove. My nostrils flare in fear. "Ah, c'mon...what are you doin' now?" I ask in a strained voice.

She squares her shoulders, steppin' towards me.

"You don't need to do this...why are you doin' this?" I ask her, seein' the knife's dull-orange cast. I strain hard against the chains and struggle as if I'm down in the basement of the evil church again. Drool and sweat course down my chin in equal measure.

She walks behind me. Then, the beautiful siren with green eyes presses the hot knife to my back, causin' my muscles to contract. I close my eyes, shoutin' in pain. Pantin' and tryin' not to pass out, I feel her pull it from my back as the scent of burnin' skin enters my nostrils. It takes me right back to the altar of the evil church and Valentine's torture. Grittin' my teeth, I shout, "YOU'RE DEAD! I'M GONNA KILL YOU! YOU'RE GONNA WISH YOU NEVER MET ME!"

She lays the blade on my back again in a different spot. Searin' pain erupts, causin' me to arch my back and I cry out again. She leaves me to reheat the knife and she doesn't make eye contact with me as she comes back, repeatin' the process over and over again. When she moves on to my chest, I lash out at her, tryin' to knock her away from me with my head, but now I'm so weak I can hardly hold my head up.

She catches my head, wrappin' her arm around it and pullin' it to the side of hers. She holds my cheek to her cheek, whisperin' raspy words that don't sound very musical now. As I strain against her, she refuses to let me go, holdin' me in place for several minutes. When I don't move, she lets me go. She walks back to the stove and begins heatin' the knife again. My chin rests on my chest, waitin' to fight until she comes back.

She's back without me hearin' her, but she doesn't have the knife, she lays a cold cloth on my back rubbin' it over the burns. I cringe at first, until she just leaves it there, steppin' back and lettin' the coolness of it ease some of the pain.

I open my eyes, seein' her approachin' me. She kneels beside me, puttin' her hand on my chest to keep me from movin' forward. She lifts her knife, I watch her place it on a bleedin' bite mark, searin' it. As she does, her teeth clench, makin' her delicate jaw strain. Her dark, arcin' eyebrows draw together while she angles her head away, like she's forcin' herself to watch my skin sizzle. Her nostrils flare when the smell of my flesh rises up, lookin' like it's chokin' her.

"You're tryin' to help me," I croak, feelin' like I'm gonna puke at any second. She touches me again, placin' her hand on my cheek. As she continues to scald the bites, my body trembles and begins to become numb. But, when she moves on to my neck, I strain against the chains again, while groanin' and tryin' to pull away from her.

At last, she steps away from me. My head slumps weakly on my chest while I watch her walk to the counter. Placin' both her hands on it, she hangs her head. Then takin' out a soft cloth from a drawer, she submerges it in the teacup she had made earlier. She wrings it out a little as she goes to the freezer. Pullin' out some ice, she wraps the cubes in the tea cloth and walks back to me, holdin' the cloth to my neck where she had burned me.

"What's your name?" I ask, feelin' dizzy and sick.

Silence meets my question as she continues to soothe the burns. Steppin' in front of me, she kneels so that our faces are on the same level. She wipes my face, her fingers movin' to my hair and tuckin' it back behind my ear. "Your name, what is it?" I ask again, tryin' to make eye contact with her. She pauses, before sayin' somethin' in Angel.

"I'm Russell. What's your name?" I repeat.

"Ruse-el," she says, givin' me a grim smile.

"Yeah, that's me…Ruse-el," I agree, mimickin' her pronunciation of my name. "What do I call you?" I ask, pointin' my chin at her.

Her face changes then as her eyes scan mine. She looks so sad. Holdin' both her hands to her chest, she whispers, "Anya."

"Anna?" I ask, and she shakes her head, tears fillin' her eyes.

Clearin' her throat and lookin' away, she says, "An-ya."

"An-ya?" I repeat to her and she nods, not lookin' at me. Gettin' up off her knees, she walks behind me. My chains rattle and loosen before they drop from my wrists.

Quickly, Anya moves away from me, back to the counter of the kitchen. She picks up the knife again, holdin' it in front of her like she's protectin' herself from me. With my hands free, I wrestle the rest of the chain off of me that had bound me to the chair. Leanin' forward, I rub my wrists, tryin' to get the circulation back in them.

"You missed a spot," I say grimly, holdin' up my wrist to show Anya the bite from Eion on my arm.

She closes her eyes briefly, seein' the blood oozin' from my flesh. Turnin', she puts the knife back on the burner.

When the knife is hot again, she picks it up off the stove. Slowly, she comes towards me, watchin' my face. I lean forward, layin' my wrist on the table calmly. Seein' the mug of whiskey sittin' next to it, I pick it up with the other hand and drain the mug in a couple of swallows. The burnin' of the liquor makes my eyes tear a little. Anya stands next to me, tryin' to hand me the hilt of the knife so that I can take care of this one myself.

I shake my head. "Ah c'mon, you're not gonna stop now, are you? You already burned the tar outta me. You might as well finish the job," I say, givin' her an ironic smile. She hesitates, but then she leans over my arm. Her hand shakes when she presses the knife to my wrist, burning away all the traces of Gancanagh from me. My fist flexes as I close my eyes, tryin' not to move my wrist at all. In a few moments, it's over. Anya pulls the knife from me, throwin' it hard; it sticks in the far wall.

"Thank you, Anya," I say grimly, openin' my eyes.

She sinks to her knees in front of me, restin' her head on my legs. Hearin' a sob comin' from her, her body shakes as tears drip off her cheeks. In confusion, I rest my hand on her head, slowly strokin' her hair as she continues to weep like her best friend died or somethin'.

"Shh," I murmur, tryin' to soothe her. "It's all right. Now, we have to take care of my girl, Evie," I say, lookin' over at Evie. She's still unconscious, bound to her chair.

Anya lifts her head slowly from my lap, her eyes narrowin' as she wipes the back of her hands over her face to dry her tears. "NO EV-IE," she seethes between her teeth.

"What?" I ask, confused by the anger I see in her eyes.

"NO E-VEE," she repeats, gesturin' to Evie again. Then, she breaks into Angel again, and she really looks like she's tellin' me off.

Holdin' my hands out, I say, "Okay, okay—what the—why are you freakin' out at me?"

Takin' off her sweater, she tosses it away, leavin' just an oversized t-shirt that has to be Reed's, too. Pullin' down the crewneck of the shirt, she exposes a tattoo above her heart. It's the image of deep red Seraphim wings emboldened on her delicate skin—a binding mark. Pointin' at the mark, she leans forward, lettin' me see it up close. Then, she reaches out, strokin' the feathers of my wing. My eyes follow her hand, seein' the crimson of my feathers.

"Ruse-el ANYA *aspire*...NO E-VEE," she sneers. Pointin' at Evie, she says, "Ruse-el soul mate." Then, pickin' up my hand and placin' it on her heart, she says, "Ruse-el *aspire*."

I pull my hand back from her, feelin' like she burned me again. "What are you talkin' 'bout, Anya? I don't even know you! I've never seen you before in my life!" Lookin' around in confusion, I stare at my chest, seein' nothin' branded to it—no binding mark, like the one Anya is sportin'. "I think you have the wrong guy, 'cuz I'm not wearin' a ring," I explain, pointin' to my chest.

She frowns, bitin' her bottom lip. Shakin' her head, she says adamantly, "Ruse-el *aspire*."

"I don't know you," I reply, feelin' irritated and sick. My head is poundin' and all I want to do is lie on the kitchen floor, but I can't 'cuz Red still needs my help. Standin' up, I almost fall back down. I grasp the table in front of me for support, lettin' the dizziness pass. I straighten, walkin' to the far wall. Pullin' the knife out of it, I take it to the sink and clean it off. Then, I set it on the burner, heatin' it up to use on Red.

Grimly, I walk back to Evie, brushin' her hair back from her face. "Red? Can you hear me?" I ask. Out of the corner of my eye, I see Anya walkin' to the door of the kitchen. She doesn't look at me, but just leaves with her shoulders hunched and her arms huggin' her body. Somethin' in my heart twists, like it's breakin' inside of me.

"Anya, wait!" I call to her, but she doesn't come back. In seconds, the flutterin' feelin' of crickets in my stomach is gone, makin' me feel worse than I did before.

"Evie," I nudge her gently, before cuppin' her cheeks and tryin' to get her to wake up. She groans, not openin' her eyes. "Evie, I'm gonna take care of your bites now. Maybe it's better that you're not awake for this." I fetch the knife off the stove. Spottin' the whiskey bottle on the counter, I pick it up, takin' a huge sip of it and wipin' my mouth on the back of my hand.

Seein' the blood seepin' from her thigh, I start there, pressin' the knife to her wound. Evie's eyes flare open as a hoarse scream tears from her lips. Lookin' at me with a wild expression, Red yells, "RUSSELL! YOU TOTAL A-HOLE! STOP!" I pull the knife back, smellin' her burnin' skin.

"I'd love to stop, Red," I mutter wearily, watchin' her body recoil from me. "I promise I'll stop when you do."

"Ah crap, Russell!" she says, pantin' from the pain. "I hate this part! God, I hate this part!"

"Is this how they did it last time? When you were bitten by Brennus?" I ask, takin' another swig of whiskey.

She nods, eyein' the whiskey bottle in my hand. "Here, give me some of that," she whispers, pointin' her chin at the bottle. Carefully, I place the bottle to her lips, givin' her a generous taste of it.

Coughin' and sputterin' she manages to catch her breath before she nods at me. "Okay, how many more bites do I have?" she asks me grimly.

"You got two on your neck that I can see," I assess, lookin' her over. "That might be it."

"Okay," she says with a stoic expression. "I'm ready."

"You sure?" I ask, feelin' awed by her.

She nods and she closes her eyes right before I put the knife to one of her wounds. Pantin' and grittin' her teeth, she unleashes a torrent of bad words on me, the likes of which would rival anythin' I've ever heard in the locker room. Despite everythin', I crack a smile.

Openin' her eyes and seein' me smilin', she scowls at me. "Having fun?" she asks.

"Yeah, this is truly awesome," I reply with sarcasm. "Maybe we can build a summer house here. Let's come back in the spring, when it's warmer." Holdin' the whiskey to her lips again, I say, "One more, then it's over."

"Do it," she replies in a raspy voice.

I burn the last one, seein' her bite her lip so that she won't scream again.

"Overachiever," I mutter under my breath, pullin' the knife back from her and gettin' up. Findin' a key on the table, I unlock her chains, releasin' her from the chair. Catchin' her quickly before she topples to the floor, I pick her up in my arms, walkin' to the front room.

I lay her on the elegant sofa and locate a blanket on the arm of the chair, puttin' it on her gently. Sittin' on the other sofa, I rest my head on the arm of it. "Russell?" Evie asks weakly.

"Yeah?" I ask, closin' my eyes.

"What happened to that angel?" she whispers.

"I don't know," I reply in exhaustion. "She...I don't know."

"I thought she was going to kill me," Red says, her voice soft.

"Me, too," I reply.

"Throne—black wings...she was a Throne...karma," Red murmurs, trailin' off.

"She karmaed me, all right. She burned the snot outta me," I say softly.

"She fixed you?" Evie asks sleepily.

"Uh, yeah, I guess..." I say in confusion.

"Why?" Evie asks.

"I don't know," I reply, feelin' somethin' in my heart contract painfully. I open my eyes again, lookin' at Red.

"She just left...after she fixed you?" Evie asks, turnin' toward me.

"I think—I think I hurt her," I say in a low tone.

"How? Do you think she'll come back?" Red asks nervously, lookin' toward the door.

"I don't know," I reply wearily, lettin' my eyes close again.

"But—" Red starts to say, ready to pick the scab off this one.

"Shhh," I hiss with irritation in my tone. "My head's poundin'. Can you be quiet for a second? I feel like I just got roasted on a spit at a family reunion. I need a second, okay?"

"Okay," she agrees, ignorin' my tone.

Feelin' like I'm floatin' on an ocean, my body just gives out on me and I fall asleep with my arm over my eyes.

A while later, stranglin' pressure on my neck makes my eyes pop open as Reed lifts me off the sofa. He holds me off the ground with one arm. My hands go immediately to his, tryin' to pry his hand from my throat.

"Give me one reason why I shouldn't kill you, Russell, and don't say it's because Evie will be mad because that no longer matters to me," Reed hisses in a deadly calm voice.

CHAPTER 8

You're What?

I'm pretty sure Reed doesn't want me to answer him, 'cuz the pressure on my neck increases and there's no way I can speak. With my feet danglin' off the ground, a chokin' sound comes from me. But, a second later, somethin' crashes into the room, hittin' Reed like a defensive end blindsidin' a quarterback.

I tumble to the ground, which is good for me, 'cuz it allows me to take a gaspin' breath. The blur of angels locked together in a fierce fight flashes in front of me. Furniture topples over and splinters as their wings crash into everythin' around them.

Reed must've gotten the upper hand, 'cuz the beautiful, black-winged angel is thrown against the far wall. Slidin' down it, she looks stunned for just a split second before she growls. Risin' to her feet, she rushes Reed again. Evie springs up, hearin' the growl and the chaos. Seein' Reed gettin' pounded by Anya, Evie's eyes narrow as her wings spread out around her.

Growlin' at Anya, Evie lunges forward, but I catch her 'round the waist, haulin' her back from the fray. "REED! STOP!" I shout at him, seein' him pick Anya up off her feet again and toss her back into the same wall.

Reed takes a defensive position between Anya and us, speakin' to her in a rapid flow of Angel. Clutchin' her ribs, Anya doesn't rise this time; she just sits on the floor pantin' while glarin' at Reed.

Seein' a bag by the door, dropped in haste, I let go of Red. Walkin' to the door, I pick it up. It's filled with bread and cheese. I turn back and go to Anya's side. When I reach her, I slide down the wall to sit next to her. Her eyes register pain as I hand her the bag.

Reed has Evie in his arms, holdin' her to his side as he's strokin' her wing. But, his eyes are on Anya and me, lookin' puzzled and upset. "Who is this, Russell?" Reed asks.

"I don't know. She said her name was Anya, but I don't think she speaks any uh…human," I reply, feelin' my stomach flutterin' wildly again.

Reed speaks again in Angel to Anya. She lifts her chin a notch, but she doesn't reply to whatever he's askin' her. Reed narrows his eyes at her, lettin' go of Evie, he moves forward, producin' a knife from somewhere and tiltin' his head to the side, lookin' deadly.

"What are you doin'?" I ask Reed, feelin' like I need to step between them before somethin' really bad happens.

"She's not answering my questions, Russell," Reed says softly. "That's unacceptable. I'm simply going to make her find her voice."

"WAIT! HOLD UP!" I yell, 'cuz everythin' is so outta control. "I think she was gettin' my back. She came in and you were—she probably thought you were killin' me."

"I was killing you, Russell," Reed replies in a calm tone. "I was just doing it slowly."

"Reed!" Evie says behind him, soundin' offended.

"Who is she, Russell?" Reed asks again.

"I DON'T KNOW!" I shout back, ready to pounce on him if he gets any closer to her. "But…" I hesitate, glancin' at Anya, "she's got a…a…" I trail off.

"She has a what, Russell?" Reed glowers.

"She has a tattoo thingy…on her heart," I reply in confusion.

"A binding vow emblem?" Reed asks, his brows unknittin'.

"Yeah, one of them," I say, pointin' to Reed like he hit the nail on the head.

Reed speaks again to Anya and she narrows her eyes before replyin' to Reed.

Reed says, "She doesn't trust me."

"Maybe it's 'cuz you just tried to kill her," I mutter with sarcasm. "What'd she say?"

"Basically, she told me to get stuffed and go to Sheol where I belong," Reed replies grimly.

"Is that all?" I ask, fightin' the urge to grin.

"Not quite. She says she is going to personally see to it that every Throne hears about me and puts me on their karma payroll," he frowns.

"Is that bad?" I ask.

"It's not good, Russell," Reed replies dryly. "She thinks that I'm here to hurt you. We need to assure her that I'm not going to kill you."

"How do we do that?" I ask.

"Why don't we all sit down in the kitchen?" Reed says in a calm tone, easin' back a step and straightenin' up.

"Kitchen's no good. We broke most of the chairs," I reply.

Lookin' 'round, Reed says, "Well, the parlor is destroyed. Maybe upstairs?"

"Dead guys on the third floor," I state.

"How about the dining room on the second floor?" Reed asks civilly.

"Should be thumbs up," I answer.

"Fine, I'll escort Evie, and you take Anya," he says. Reed takes her in his arms, his eyes travelin' over every inch of her face.

I rise and offer my hand to Anya, hopin' she'll take it so Reed doesn't try to hurt her again. She tentatively puts her hand in mine, lettin' me help her up. She holds her arm to her ribs, like they're botherin' her. An instant later, her wings retract into her back, makin' her look almost human. She opens the bag and extracts a t-shirt from it. She pulls it on over her tight, black outfit. Then, she glances up at me.

Slowly, I slip my arm through hers, leadin' her toward the staircase. She brings her bag with her. As we walk together, her eyes scan my face, like she's memorizin' every line of it. Enterin' a regal room on the second floor, I pull out a posh chair for Anya to sit in.

Once she is seated, I take the chair next to hers. Reed and Evie take seats on the other side of the table facin' us. Lookin' 'round the room, there are several windows linin' the wall behind Reed and Evie. The dark sky outside is alive with softly fallin' snow.

Reed speaks to Anya in Angel, attemptin' a smile, but she frowns before answerin' him. Pointin' to the window behind him, Anya waits until Reed and Evie both glance over their shoulders before she swipes a candlestick from the table. Pullin' it into her lap under the table, she stills when they turn back 'round.

"Did she just take a candlestick?" Reed asks me.

"Yup," I reply. "What did she say to get you to turn away?" I inquire.

"I asked her if she had just arrived on Earth. She said she had and that she's not used to the cold or the snow," Reed replies.

A small smile creeps to the corners of my mouth, until I think that she might be afraid and that's why she took the candlestick. Maybe she's thinkin' 'bout usin' it as a weapon to defend herself. Impulsively, I reach for her hand beneath the table. Startled, she flinches a little, her face palin' before she realizes what I'm doin'.

Her cold fingers squeeze mine tight, and I feel her hand tremble a little.

"Maybe this would be better if it seems like I'm askin' the questions and you're translatin' it," I say, lookin' at Anya and seein' her green eyes watchin' me.

Reed says somethin' to her in Angel and Anya nods, turnin' her attention to me. As I study her green eyes, they soften. "Uhh," I say, findin' it hard to think with her starin' at me, "why are you here?"

Reed translates this for Anya. She listens and then she shrugs. Her voice is gentle as she answers, like she's speakin' just to me.

Reed says, "She said she had to come—she was worried about you."

My eyebrows rise in question.

Reed listens to Anya as she speaks again.

"She said that she wasn't supposed to be involved, but she has friends that heard some very disturbing things, so...she had to come," Reed says with some surprise.

I frown. "Do you know what she's talkin' about, Reed?" I ask in confusion. "She's havin' me watched?"

"Yes," Reed says, sittin' back and lookin' really interested now. "We should ask her what she heard about you."

"Okay, ask," I agree.

Reed asks the question in Angel.

Anya answers him.

Reed's expression turns incredulous. "She said you didn't come back. You were supposed to come back, but you didn't," he murmurs.

"When was I supposed to come back?" I ask, seein' pain in Anya's eyes.

Watchin' Anya's face, it falls when Reed poses the question. She glances back at me and says, "Ruse-el stay Ev-ie. Very cry."

Reed says somethin' to her.

"Very sad," she amends.

Reed leans forward then, speakin' in a torrent of Angelic words, his face intense.

Anya replies and Reed leans back in his chair, like he's shocked.

Reed says, "You were supposed to die, Russell...in the convenience store in Crestwood. That was your plan."

"WHAT!" I shout at him.

"Everything shifted when Evie healed you...when you agreed to stay," Reed says, lookin' at me and somethin' in me knows he's as freaked out as I am.

"Anya," Reed says, speakin' to her in Angel. Hearin' her respond to Reed's questions, he has a "holy crap" look on his face. "She's not supposed to be here, Russell," he says.

"Whaddaya mean, like here in Torun or like here here...on Earth?" I question.

"Here here," Reed replies. "She heard bad things...she heard about the Gancanagh. She was afraid that they would force you to give up your soul and then you would never come back...to her."

"Come back to her?" I ask. Adrenaline courses through me. "Why would I come back to her?" I look at Evie to see how she's takin' all this. She's absolutely still, but all the hair is standin' straight up on her arms. "Is she really my *aspire*?" I ask Reed. His face goes blank, just like it does when he's goin' into battle.

"What did you say, Russell?" Reed murmurs, like he's sure that he didn't hear me.

"Ask her if she's my *aspire*," I say, tryin' not to freak out.

Reed poses the question to Anya.

We watch as she pulls aside her t-shirt and then the black bodysuit, exposin' a bindin' mark above her heart that looks a lot like my wings. Reed reaches for the other candlestick on the table. He crushes it into a pebble in a fraction of a second. Then, Reed begins laughin' like it's the best joke he's ever heard.

Reed kisses Red's forehead, before turnin' to me and sayin', "Russell, meet your *aspire*, Anya!"

"HOW?" I shout at him, feelin' off-kilter and strangely hurt. "I don't have any marks on me."

"You wouldn't, would you?" Reed asks, grinnin'. "You're on a mission and you were reborn as Russell. Russell is human—you have always been human. Anya," he says, speakin' to Anya in Angel.

She replies to his question.

Reed nods, grinnin'. "Anya said her mark was different; it used to reflect the image of your soul, but when you changed, it changed, too."

"And I don't have one 'cuz I'm on a mission?" I ask quickly, tryin' to understand.

His brows knit together as he processes my question. He speaks to Anya.

Her eyes cloud with worry and she looks really sad as she answers him.

Reed frowns. "Maybe," Reed says. "Nothing is certain, Anya said. This is a mission that's is ever evolving. If you were to lose your soul to

Sheol, she would be released from the vow. That was the stipulation you made before coming here."

"AHH, HELL, REED!" I yell at him, boltin' to my feet and puttin' my hand through my hair. "IS IT POSSIBLE TO HAVE JUST ONE THING MAKE SENSE IN ALL THIS?"

"It sounds like you, Russell," Evie says quietly from her seat.

I turn on her in anger. "What sounds like me? Throwin' aside the love of ALL my lives for someone else? Or marryin' someone and not comin' back to her?" I seethe, lettin' Red have it.

Red doesn't flinch. "Accepting a mission to protect me, staying to protect me even though you planned to go back, and worrying more about having someone you love suffer because you might not be able to come back to her so you gave her an out, just in case…it sounds like you, Russell," she says again quietly.

Anya speaks then to Reed, her voice completely unmusical. Gesturin' to Evie, with a flick of her wrist she scowls at her like she hates her. Evie, not understandin' much more than me, sits back a little in her seat. Reed's face is blank again, but he's listenin' to Anya like she spillin' the secrets of the universe.

"What?" I ask, leanin' both my fists on the table when Anya is done talkin'.

Reed looks grim, and he's not answerin' me. Gettin' up from his seat, Reed says quietly, "I'll go take care of the corpses upstairs. There are bedrooms on this floor, if you want to clean up and rest. Love," he adds, takin' Evie's hand, he gestures toward the door, "you should lie down. You look pale."

"I'm fine. What did Anya say?" Evie asks, lookin' concerned and not gettin' up from her seat.

Reed's jaw tenses; he looks like someone punched him in the stomach. "She's upset. She just transitioned from Paradise. She needs our support…she's like a child here…she doesn't know how things work."

"Tell her to leave, Reed," I say in a quiet tone. "She's not supposed to be here, so tell her to go back."

"I can't," Reed says, watchin' me.

I scowl. "What do you mean you can't?" I ask, feelin' anger risin' in me again.

"She can't, I should say," he replies. "She left on her own. She'll have to be called back, just like the rest of us, Russell."

"So, why haven't they called her back?" I ask.

"Maybe they approve. She has a right to protect her *aspire*. Maybe they believe she can help us," he says softly.

"Or maybe, it will just get her killed," I reply. "She doesn't have a soul—no do overs for her. She's not trained to fight like you, is she? That makes her a liability, not an asset."

"Yes," Reed agrees, watchin' me close.

"WHAT ARE YOU WAITIN' FOR ME TO DO, REED?" I shout at him. Evie, jumps, lookin' stressed 'cuz I'm yellin' at him.

"I'm waiting for some spark of recognition from you," Reed replies. "Something that will assure me that what Anya believes is wrong."

"What does she believe?" I counter, rubbin' my brow wearily.

"She thinks that Evie agreed to this mission to tear you away from Anya…to get you back," he replies coldly.

Feelin' elated and pissed off at the same time, I sit back down in my seat, puttin' my face in my hands. "She thinks that?" I mumble.

"That's what she said," Reed replies.

"Can we trust what she says?" I ask, glancin' at Anya and seein' her still glarin' at Evie across the table.

"She's not Fallen, Russell," Reed replies, watchin' Anya, too. "She seems to believe what she's saying, but…none of us are infallible." Reed speaks to her again and Anya's eyes shoot to his, scowlin'.

"What did you just say to her?" I ask.

"I simply told her that if she harms Evie, I will kill her," Reed says in a low tone.

"Reed—" Evie starts to say.

"Love, she thinks that you are coming between her and her mate," Reed says softly, not takin' his eyes off of Anya. "She will defend what is hers. She's a Throne, you are Seraphim, it is nearly equal ground, but I can still defend you." Pullin' aside the shirt he's wearin', he leans closer to Anya, showin' her his bindin' mark.

Anya smiles then, her whole face lightin' up, like Reed has just given her the keys to Paradise. She speaks rapidly to Reed, pullin' on his arm and makin' him lean closer to her so she can see his mark of Evie's wings better. He smiles, too, answerin' back after streams of music come from her.

Lookin' at Red, I say softly, "It's like listenin' to a symphony of fallin' snow—their voices…like they have the power to change our world."

"They do, Russell," Red replies, watchin' me across the small space. Red's words hit me and my throat feels tight, like I can hardly breathe. Glancin' out the window at the fallin' snow, a shadow moves along the window ledge.

"GET DOWN!" I yell, springin' up and tacklin' Reed and Anya, just as bullets explode the window behind us. Fallin' on the floor beneath the window, Reed pushes me off of him, lungin' to Red's chair and pullin' her from it to the ground with us. Anya's eyes squeeze shut as glass and fabric from the curtains fall on us.

As I look up, the toe of a boot drifts over the edge of the sill. Reachin' up, I grasp the ankle attached to the foot, twistin' and hearin' it *crack* as I break it. I push the leg backward and hear a scream as he falls out the window toward the street below.

Reed holds up the phone from his pocket, usin' the reflective surface to scan the outside. "Gancanagh—do you sense any magic, Russell?" Reed asks grimly.

"Naw, not yet…let me do some recon," I say, closin' my eyes and concentratin'. The world 'round me starts to do back flips as I force a clone out of me. Anya, seein' my clone, gasps before reachin' out her hand to try and keep it from movin' away from us. "Reed, explain what's happenin' to Anya."

"I'm going with you," Red says, makin' her clone appear beside mine.

"Yeah, okay," I agree, directin' my clone up onto the window ledge. Automatic gunfire pulses right through my clone and I grin at the stinky freak in the window of the townhouse directly across the street from us. I spread out my clone's wings, just for fun, and watch the frustration mount on the cold creepy one's face when none of his bullets affect me.

Watchin' Red's clone frown at my clone, I ask, "What?" Ignorin' me, she directs her clone to fly across the street and mine follows hers.

When we near the Gancanagh with the automatic, I ask, "Friend of yours?"

"No, I don't know him," Red answers, movin' 'round and scannin' the area. "Two more in the bedroom. They're speaking Polish, I think," she informs me. "How do you say 'Kiss my ass' in Polish?"

"*Pocałuj mnie w dupę*," I reply, grinnin' as one of the cold ones takes a swing at my clone and his arm slips right through me. I add, "*Twoja matka to bajki.*"

"What's that mean?" she asks, wrinklin' her clone's nose at me, not even tryin' to avoid the spiky spear the Gancanagh thrust toward her from behind.

Shruggin', I say, "It means, 'Your mother is a Faerie.' Well, three here. We should check the other levels across the street."

"Okay," Red's clone says, disappearin'. I let my clone speed back to my body, too. Returnin' to my normal consciousness, I report, "Three across the street—banjax charmed weapons, not a big arsenal—couple of gats and some smokies—oh, and those long spiky spears."

"Thanks, Russell," Reed says, "I'll be right back." In a fraction of a second, Reed is gone from beneath the window.

Gunshots ring out from the house across the street, while one of the cold freaks screams, "*Gdzie poszedł?*"

"What did he say, Russ?" Evie asks nervously.

"He just screamed 'Where did he go?'" I grin, knowin' that Reed is scarin' the crap out of them before he kills them. He's mean like that when it comes to protectin' Red. Glancin' next to me, Anya's lookin' at me like she's seen a ghost…well, maybe not like that 'cuz she's probably seen plenty of ghosts, but she's as pale as one anyway.

Walkin' in from the landin' that leads downstairs, Reed says, "I'm fairly certain that's all of them. They must have tracked Eion, or the other one—"

"Keefe," Evie and me say in unison.

Lookin' between Evie and me, Reed frowns, "Right—making our position volatile."

I rise cautiously from the floor and shake the broken glass from my hair. Evie, lookin' shaky, goes immediately to Reed's side. Scoopin' Red up off her feet, Reed says, "I have to clean up here—get rid of the corpses. While I do that, I want you to shower and change. We leave in twenty minutes." Turnin' to me, Reed asks, "Can you be ready by then?"

"Yeah. I need to borrow some clothes," I reply.

"There are bedrooms equipped with bathrooms on this floor. Check the closets. There may be something you can squeeze into," Reed says, and he leaves the room with Evie in his arms.

As I glance back to Anya, I see she hasn't moved to get up. She is curled in a ball with her eyes squeezed shut and her hands tremblin'. Crouchin' down, I touch her shoulder, sayin', "Anya…"

Springin' from the floor, Anya wraps her arms around my neck. Her whole body trembles as her shallow breathin' tickles my neck. "Hey…that was just a little gun fight, Anya. If you're gonna hang with us, it's gonna get a lot worse than that. Maybe there's somewhere else you can go? Do you have friends here?" I ask, gently rubbin' her back to try to calm her down. She doesn't answer me, so I sigh, "You don't understand a word I'm sayin', do you? No? Okay, let's get you cleaned up and we'll figure it out later."

CHAPTER 9

Miss Me Dearly

Takin' Anya in my arms, mainly 'cuz I can't get her to let go of my neck, I scout the second floor of Reed's townhouse. A bedroom down the hall presents itself as a good enough place to get cleaned up, so I go directly to the attached bathroom. Its small, like most everythin' in Poland…that I can remember 'cuz technically, I've never been here when I was this tall…or male.

Turnin' on the small shower, I look down at Anya and feel a blush creepin' up my neck. I clear my throat and say, "Uh…Anya? We're fixin' to leave as fast as we can so we need to shower and change into clothes that are less…well, that blend in more with the locals."

She lifts her head from my shoulder and waves of her beautiful dark hair tumble off my arm. I can tell she's still freaked 'bout what just happened with the Gancanagh. "Ruse-*el leh-chi lit…*" she breathes.

"Huh?" I ask, testin' the water to see if it's too hot.

"*Leh-chi lit,*" she says again, touchin' the feathers of my wings gently.

My eyes widen. "That sounds…are you speakin' Navajo?" I ask in surprise. "Did you just call me 'red smoke?'" I ask her, wonderin' if she's referrin' to my clone.

"Ruse-el *a-tkel-el-ini,*" she says, pointin' at my chest.

"Troublemaker, huh?" I ask, smilin'. "Damn…what do I remember 'bout Navajo…*to-altseh-hogan*—this is a temporary place—camp. We have to move to avoid another *khac-da*…another ambush." Seein' her eyes go round in fear, I frown before saying in a soft voice, "Russell *yah-a-da-hal-yon-ih* Anya…I'll take care of you," while strokin' her hair.

"Anya *yah-a-da-hal-yon-ih* Russ-el," she breathes, tellin' me that she'll take care of me, before touchin' her lips to mine.

"Anya…" I murmur, turnin' my face and tryin' to avoid her kisses.

"*O-zhi*, Russ-el," Anya says against my cheek, tellin' me she missed me.

With my brows pullin' together, I reply, "I don't remember you."

"Russ-el, *na-ne-klah*," she says softly, callin' me "difficult" while brushin' her incredible lips over mine. Feelin' somethin' in me explode, like her lips set me on fire, I press her back into the glass shower door, kissin' her like somethin' in me is achin'—has been achin' for a very long time.

Hearin' her groan in pleasure, I reach over, tearin' her shirt off of her and pressin' my lips to her neck. Her skin is warm and smells like flowers I've only sensed in dreams. Reality hits me then and makes me pull back and look at the beautiful creature in my arms. Anya's perfect. Her face is exquisite—her long, black lashes are hooded over green eyes that I've only seen cats possess. Her archin' eyebrows are black, like her hair…and her body, good Lord; her body is made for the sweetest sin.

"Whoa," I murmur, pressin' my forehead to Anya's, tryin' to think. "We gotta stop now," I say pantin'. "*Ji-din-nes-chanh*," I mutter, meanin' "retreat."

Anya, pullin' on my neck breathes, "*Na-dzah*," meanin' "return." "Russ-el *to-ho-ne*." She just said I'm sufferin'.

I groan. "Yeah, I'm sufferin' all right," I agree with her last statement. My lips twist in a grim smile. She has me fightin' for air, feelin' her soft skin pressin' against me. Puttin' her on her feet, I turn her, scootin' her toward the shower.

"*Nil-ta*," she says, callin' me "stubborn." Not turnin' around, she removes the rest of her clothes. I feel heat ball up in the pit of my stomach, makin' me have to turn away from her.

"I'll go hunt for clothes," I say, fleein' from the bathroom 'cuz if I start kissin' her again, I might not stop. I have to stop, 'cuz I can tell that whatever would happen next would have a different meanin' for her than it does for me.

Runnin' upstairs, I knock on the door of the master bedroom. Reed comes to the door, openin' it and lettin' me in. He has already cleaned up the dead corpses from the floor, burnin' them in the fireplace. They burn well, but it smells like someone lit candy on fire.

"Problem?" Reed asks in his clipped, military way.

"Girl clothes," I reply. "We need passports, too."

"Clothes I have now—we worry about documents later," he says, going to the wardrobe and pullin' out an armload of girl clothes that he probably bought for Evie. Handin' them to me, he goes to another closet, pullin' out some clothes I might fit into.

"Thanks," I say.

"How's Anya?" he asks, his face blank.

"She speaks a little Navajo...not very much, a few words," I say. "Can I ask you somethin'?"

Lookin' curious, Reed says, "Yes."

"Those butterfly things...that you feel when you're near Evie...does it feel like...crickets jumpin' 'round inside your stomach?" I inquire.

A slow grin spreads over Reed's face. "Yes, Russell, that's exactly what it feels like."

"What do you think that means," I ask.

"It would be one way to...recognize someone, even if you cannot remember her," Reed replies, lookin' happier than I have ever seen him.

"Yeah, but...does it make you want to tear her clothes off?" I ask, feelin' irritated.

"Yes, it does," Reed affirms, lookin' even more stoked.

"Okay...good talk," I say awkwardly, feelin' even more confused than before.

"Very good talk," Reed agrees, watchin' me leave.

Runnin' back down the stairs, I walk into the bedroom again, tossin' the clothes on the bed. I search the closet and find a small suitcase. Puttin' it on the bed too, I stop, seein' Anya walk out of the bathroom drippin' wet and completely naked. "*Tkoh*," she says the word for water, indicatin' with a gesture that it's drippin' off of her.

"Good Lord! What are you doin' to me?" I breathe, lookin' at her standin' there all wet. It feels like someone aimed a flamethrower at me. "You're not shy, I'll say that for you."

Starin' at her and seein' her teeth chatterin', she says, "*Tkin*," which means "ice."

I quickly step past her to the bathroom, findin' a towel. I cover her with it. "Here," I say, "Get dressed while I shower. We have to leave, uh...*da-de-yah*...we have to 'depart.'"

She nods, and then she walks slowly toward the bed, pickin' up clothes and lookin' at them critically. Sighin', I turn and close the bathroom door. In the shower, I wash quickly. Grabbin' a towel and wrappin' it around my hips, I run my hands through my hair, while walkin' back into the bedroom.

Anya is by the foot of the bed, slidin' a pair of jeans over her lacy underwear, makin' me stumble to a halt. Her wings are in now, and she figured out what the bra is for, but it's a little small on her.

"I should've taken a cold shower," I mumble to myself, avoidin' lookin' at Anya again as I sift through the clothes on the bed.

Finding a cable knit sweater that fits me okay, I shrug into it, but the pants are all too small. Lookin' in the closet in this room, I locate more clothes. Pullin' out jeans that are designed to be loose, I put them on and they fit me except they're a little short.

Sittin' on the edge of the bed, I fall back on it, holdin' my arm over my eyes. I feel like I've been run over by a truck, picked up and tossed down a ditch, rolled over and doused in gasoline, and then lit on fire—in that order. I know I should be hungry, starvin', but I'm not.

"Russ-el *tso*," Anya says, climbin' up on the bed next to me and snugglin' into my side.

I smile, despite how bad I'm feelin', hearin' Anya call me "big." "Yeah, Russell *tso*."

"Russell," Evie says, comin' in the room. "Oh, I'm sorry..." she stammers, turnin' and leavin', lookin' embarrassed.

"NO! Red, don't go!" I order, sittin' up. "Are we leavin'?"

"Uh, yeah...if you're ready," Red says, blushin' and avertin' her eyes from us.

"Is this ass awkward, or is it me?" I ask, sittin' up and rubbin' my eyes.

"No, no...it's ass awkward," she agrees, lookin' as grim as I feel. "She hates me, Russell," Red says in a whisper, lookin' at Anya who now looks like she's gettin' ready to pounce on her.

"That's the same look Reed is always givin' me," I reply, indicatin' Anya's scowl.

"Ugh, what do I do?" she asks, whisperin' again.

"I think you can stop whisperin', for one. It seems to be botherin' her and she can't understand you so there's really no point," I reply.

"This is worse than Candace," she says. "At least Candace couldn't shred me."

"Red, you're pretty strong and wily. She'd have a hard time gettin' the jump on you," I reply.

"Is she really your *aspire*, Russell?" Evie asks, lookin' pale.

Shruggin' I say, "I have no idea, Red. At this point, anythin' is possible."

"She's really pretty," Red points out, lookin' at Anya, who's runnin' her hands through her hair to try to get the tangles out of it. Evie goes quickly to the bathroom, bringin' back a hairbrush for Anya.

Tentatively, Anya takes the brush from Evie, still watchin' Red like she'd like to break her in two. Anya is more than pretty...she's sexy. Even wearin' a shirt and a sweater, they can't hide her curves. Just rememberin' her naked is returnin' the heat to the pit of my stomach.

"Yeah…she's pretty," I agree.

"What are you going to do?" Red asks, watchin' Anya brush her long, black hair.

"I don't know—maybe we should go and pick out china," I say sarcastically.

"Okay—so you have no plan yet?" she asks, frownin'.

"There should be a plan, Red? Really? Like what?" I counter, rubbin' my eyes. "I've never been in this situation before. I could use a hand."

"Exactly. We need Brownie and Buns," she agrees, like I wasn't just bein' totally sarcastic.

Anya growls and immediately Reed is in the doorway, speakin' to her. Listenin' to them talkin', it looks like they're discussin' some sinister plot. Then, Reed smiles at Anya and his head nods slowly as he looks between Evie and me.

"What, Reed?" I ask, wonderin' what they're discussin'.

"Anya asked me how I can stand watchin' your souls interact. It disturbs her, how intimate you are with one another," Reed replies.

"WHAT!" Evie and I say in unison.

"I've long ago decided that you two don't realize that you have auras that entwine whenever you are near one another. Therefore, I ignore it, but Anya finds it irritating," Reed replies, smilin' again at Anya.

Anya speaks to Reed again and he listens intently before answerin' her.

"What did she say," I ask.

"She said that you and Evie are very dangerous, makin' you targets. She wants to know what I'm doing to protect you and what she needs to do to help me," he replies.

"Did you tell her that we're pretty good at protectin' ourselves now?" I respond stiltedly.

"I told her we have friends that help and I promised her that she will meet them soon," Reed replies, ignorin' my comment.

"You shouldn't be promisin' her that. You should be tellin' her to go home," I reply.

"And I already told you that she can't go home," Reed counters.

"Then tell her that she should find a safe place and stay there 'til this is over, Reed," I say in frustration.

"When will that be, Russell?" he asks.

"I don't know," I answer. "But hangin' with us is dangerous. Too dangerous for someone like Anya."

"It's her choice, Russell. She came all the way from Paradise for you. Do you know what a sacrifice that is?" Reed asks, lookin' stunned.

"I didn't ask her to come," I point out.

"And, yet, she came anyway," Reed says. "If courage has any weight with you, she has it."

My eyebrows pull together. "She's gonna need courage, isn't she, Reed?" I ask him rhetorically, gettin' up from the bed. I don't even know why I feel so angry, but I do. Anya is an angel and she can probably take care of herself fairly well. She's also probably super old—old enough to make her own decisions. So, why is it that I already feel responsible for her?

"Let's discuss it somewhere else," Reed says, frownin'. "I found this while I was tying up the loose ends. Is it yours?" he asks, holdin' up a cell phone.

"Naw...shit!" I say, scramblin' off the bed. "How much time do we have?"

"Minutes," Reed says, graspin' Evie's hand and leadin' her down the stairs. I take Anya's hand, pullin' her along with me.

"Do you think Brennus tracked the cell?" I ask. "Do you think he sent the Polish freaks to stall us?"

Red gasps.

"Let's count on it," Reed replies. "He must not have realized right away that we didn't die on the island or he would've been here hours ago. He knows now. He's coming."

"You have a car here?" I ask hopefully.

"Yes, but we leave it," he says, tossin' coats to us from the front closet before leadin' us to the back, through the kitchen. Anya, seein' her bow and quiver on the table, snatches them up, strappin' them to her back before puttin' her coat on over them.

"Where are we goin'?" I ask Reed, takin' a knife from him and puttin' on the coat he had handed me.

"I was about to ask you that, Russell," Reed replies, watchin' me.

"Huh?" I ask, used to him barkin' out the orders.

"I need your help. I'm too predictable for Brennus," Reed replies. "I act with supernatural instincts and training. My instincts tell me that we should fly from here, but somehow I know that's wrong."

"You think they're out there?" I ask, feelin' my skin crawl.

"Yes," Reed admits. "Can you do some more recon?" he asks.

"Yeah," I reply, not waitin' for direction, but makin' my clone jet out of my body and leave through the back door of the house.

It creeps up along the drainpipe to the rooftop, keepin' to the really dark part of the eaves. In the moonlight across the street, I see what looks like humans stirrin', watchin' Reed's house. Doin' a sweep of the area, my clone nears the rooftop of the house next door. The garbled voices of inhuman body snatchers drift to me on the muffled snowy air. Next to them, three fallen freaks are just standin' 'round out in the open.

If they're not even hidin' that means there are more of them 'round, I think, and that knowledge causes chaos to reign inside of me.

Jettin' back to my body, I report, "We're in trouble. It's those things that make all the hair on my arms stand straight up."

"Kevev?" Reed asks.

"Naw, the other ones—the ones that are all moldy dead and walkin' 'round like zombies, but when they're after you, they run like dogs—super fast on all fours. They talk like they have water in their mouths," I describe, feelin' adrenaline runnin' through me.

"Inikwi," Red and Reed say together.

I point my finger. "That's them—I counted thirteen. Five across the street four on each roof flankin' this place," I assess. "And three Fallen, not even tryin' to be covert."

"Ready to jump on us if we try to fly," Reed says absently. "Evie, we need to leave here without being seen. Can you think of a spell that will shroud us?" he asks, rubbin' her arms.

"Why haven't they attacked us?" Evie asks.

"They're making sure we don't leave. Brennus is coming here," Reed says, and Red looks like she might faint.

"How long do I need to hold the spell?" she asks, lookin' tired and scared.

"Where are we going, Russell?" Reed asks me over his shoulder.

"Just down the block. Then we cut over a couple of blocks. There's a pub," I say.

"Why there?" Reed asks, frownin'.

"'Cuz it's the last place you'd go, especially now," I reply. "If the Inikwi are here, then we can assume that they're coverin' the railway, the roads, and the river. Let's go have a pint. They'll think we slipped through and they'll leave."

Rubbin' his eyes, like he thinks I'm completely out of my mind, Reed mutters, "You're the most human and you're right, it is the last place I'd go right now."

"You'll like it, Reed. I'll buy you a beer," I say, tryin' to grin.

"You ready, love?" Reed asks Red softly.

"Uh huh, tell Anya the plan," Red nods.

Reed speaks quickly to Anya, and although she seems to lose color in an instant, to her credit, she merely nods.

I gather energy to me, then I turn it outward, pushin' it towards Red as she mumbles her spell. As Red releases energy slowly, she disappears from my sight along with Reed and Anya.

"Please tell me you're still here," I whisper, holdin' out my hands and feelin' Anya next to me. I trail my fingertips down her arm, findin' her hand.

"Yes," Reed and Red both say.

"My turn then," I say grimly. "Red, you take Anya's other hand and Reed's hand. It's just like kindergarten again, we're gonna daisy chain. Reed, since you're the caboose, it's your job to make sure our tracks are covered in the snow."

"Okay," Reed's voice answers me.

"Here we go—no talkin' in the halls," I order.

Leadin' the way outside, I move slowly, cautious not to make a sound. When we make it to the sidewalk, I freeze. Several Inikwi are standin' across the street from us. They're not speakin', but just starin' at the house while their bodies twitch oddly—flares of unintentional muscle movements course through them sporadically, makin' them twitchy.

One of the Inikwi sniffs the air loudly, mutterin' somethin' in his garbled tongue to his buddies. This one robbed a grave and snatched his body for sure, 'cuz his skin is blue and his eyes are no longer moist, but dried beads in his eye sockets. Springin' forward on all fours, the Inikwi pounds across the street toward us.

My breath sticks in my throat, not knowin' if I should break cover and take him out or stay where I am and wait. The wind shifts then, blowin' toward us. He halts, sniffin' the air again, lookin' confused as he crouches like a dog in the middle of the street.

Anya's hand squeezes mine tighter, makin' me inch away from the creature that's causin' my skin to crawl. With my heart poundin' in my chest, I take slow, patient steps, easin' down the sidewalk. When we make it to the corner, I immediately turn down the next street, increasin' my speed. Hearin' Red gasp behind me, I feel the rest of the energy she was holdin' flow out of her. We all become instantly visible again.

"Sorry," Red whispers, soundin' weak.

"Naw, it's cool, Red. We're almost there," I whisper back, wrappin' my arm 'round Anya's shoulder and usherin' her quicker up the street, so we don't draw attention to ourselves by holdin' hands.

Hearin' singin' and the comfortin' sound of human voices, I open the door of the pub, feelin' warm air tumblin' out. I hold the door for them and follow them in, headin' down the stairs to the club below. Located in old town, this club is built in a cellar, consisting of three large rooms. Two rooms have rounded sofas and private alcoves. A third room is set up for dancin' with a bar in it that is hoppin'.

Reed moves to one of the private alcoves. He leans down and speaks to the people seated there and they all immediately get up from their loungin' positions on the sofa, vacating their seats without a word. Knowin' that he just used his power of persuasion to make the humans leave, I grin at him.

I usher Anya to sit and I sit beside her on the soft sofa. As I take off my coat, I say, "Reed, remind me to bring you with me to the next keg party. You can clear the line for us."

"Now what, Russell?" Reed asks, lookin' across the table at me from his seat on the opposite sofa.

"Now we chill," I reply, watchin' Reed pull Evie against his side and feelin' the familiar flare of jealousy that he's touchin' her.

"That's it?" he asks, lookin' frustrated.

"Listen, the plan is to keep it simple—be human," I reply. "I've been a sailor in a few of my lives. I've learned that sometimes it's better to drop the anchor when you can't steer. We act human. We find out where the youth hostel is and we get a few beds for the night. We stay away from all the transportation in the area. Brennus is gonna put his feelers out and he's gonna come up with nothin' 'cuz he won't be askin' the right people. Just make sure Red doesn't cut herself and we'll be fine."

"We avoid youth hostels, Russell," Evie says, lookin' grim. "The Gancanagh frequent them like diners. Young women traveling abroad are…tasty."

"Ah, that's awful," I say, my brows drawin' together. "Where should we go then?" I ask her.

"Did you happen to see any furniture stores?" she counters.

"Why?" I wonder aloud.

"They have the softest beds on display…maybe a mattress carnival?" she asks with a small smile.

I grunt, my lips twistin' into a grudgin' smile as I remember bein' with her in Houghton before we even knew Gancanagh existed. "Y'all hungry?" I ask, lookin' at Anya for the first time. She's starin' at everythin' 'round her like a tourist and smilin' as she's runnin' her fingers over the danglin' crystal fringe hangin' off the candlestick in the center of the table.

"Yes," Reed says, holdin' a menu out to me. Orderin' food and drinks, we eat quietly, while the club-goers pour in around us. Reed and I take turns checkin' our position, covertly tryin' to maintain recon on the freaks only blocks away.

Comin' back from checkin' the door, I stumble to a halt by the archway that leads to the room with the DJ and dance floor. The party is in full swing as mad beats pulse from the sound system, but it is seein' Anya near the dance floor that makes me stop. She's holdin' on to her glass of water, watchin' a crowd of young dancers movin' to the music.

She's not goin' unnoticed. She's drawin' a small crowd of her own as men have definitely taken notice of her. One in particular is circlin' her, signalin' his buddies 'bout how hot she is behind her back and indicatin' that she's his. Feelin' anger flare up in me, I change my direction, enterin' the bar room instead of headin' back to the table. I begin stalkin' the silly boy who's stalkin' my—

"Russell," Reed says behind me, "what's the status?"

"Huh?" I reply, stoppin', but not takin' my eyes off Anya. Freak boy has made contact with her, leanin' close to her and sayin' somethin' in her ear as his eyes rove over her body. Feelin' my neck gettin' hot, I run my hand through my hair.

"Did you see anything upstairs?" Reed asks, followin' my eyes to Anya.

"Naw," I murmur distractedly. "It's all good. Where's Evie?" I ask.

"Bathroom," he replies. As if on cue, Red appears by Anya's side. Now, every male in the place has their eyes on my girls.

As if in slow motion, the guy talkin' to Anya, moves his hand, brushin' it over the curve of her breast. A fraction of a second after that, Reed's arms go around me as I tense to spring in the direction of the unfortunate man touchin' Anya.

When I try to throw Reed off of me, he says in my ear, "You can't kill him, Russell. And look—"

Tensin', I watch as Anya grasps the human by his little finger, bendin' it back so that he falls on his knees at her feet. She smiles down at him, waggin' the index finger of her other hand in his face before lettin' him go.

Breathin' hard, I relax a little, feelin' Reed's grasp on me loosen, but he's not lettin' me go completely.

"What was that?" I ask, feelin' like I need to break somethin'.

"Instinct," Reed replies calmly.

"What?" I ask.

"You're Seraphim. You'll protect what's yours," he explains.

I begin to argue, "Reed, she's not mine—"

"She's yours—she's definitely yours. Some part of you remembers her, or you wouldn't be ready to kill that boy," he replies, noddin' toward the boy gettin' up from his knees.

"I still want to kill him," I admit, grindin' my teeth.

"Here," Reed says, handin' me an empty wine bottle from a table. Crushin' it in my hands, it pours like sand to the floor.

"Thanks," I mutter.

"Are you in control now?" Reed asks.

"Yeah...maybe...I don't know," I reply, and Reed lets me go, but he's still watchin' me. "Let's go scare them away."

Reed grins. "Okay," he agrees, walkin' by my side. Comin' up on the men eyein' Anya and Evie, I tower over them, scowlin' and invadin' the personal space of a few of them. They retreat from me, turnin' and headin' toward the bar.

Musical laughter sounds behind me. I turn to see Anya grinnin' at me. Somethin' in my chest twists, and my knees feel a little weak. "What?" I ask, pretendin' innocence.

Approachin' me slowly, Anya's hand rests on my chest. She gazes up at me and her eyebrow quirks as she says, "*Ne-ol.*" The word means "storm."

"Yeah, somethin' is goin' on in there and it ain't pretty," I agree, watchin' as she trails her finger down my sweater. Heat coils in me again and I stop her, coverin' her hand with mine.

"They're closing soon," Red says next to us. "What should we do?"

"Nothin'," I reply. "We stay here. Reed, persuade the staff that we don't exist. We can sleep on the couches. The sun will be up soon. I say we stay here durin' the day. When it gets dark again, we'll move out."

Reed smiles at me again, noddin'. "I located a computer in the office. I'll work on finding Brownie, Zee, and Buns while you and Evie sleep. You two look exhausted."

"I'm walkin' wounded," I mutter, rubbin' my eyes again.

Reed then talks to Anya, and she immediately takes my hand, leadin' me back to the couches. Movin' our coats, she gestures for me to sit down on a long couch. I sink into the seat and she gently nudges me to lie down. She covers me with my coat, and then sits across from me. Takin' out a gold-tipped arrow from her quiver stashed under her coat, she notches it in her bow and places them in her lap. She shrouds the weapon from view with Reed's coat over her lap. She's guardin' me.

I raise my eyebrow in question as I look at her face.

With a determined look, she says, "Anya *yah-a-da-hal-yon-ih* Russell," tellin' me that she'll take care of me.

Evie

CHAPTER 10

Bow To The Champion

I awake and stare at the fake-crystal chandelier over my head while the scent of stale cigarette smoke clings to my clothes and my hair. Russell's long body is stretched out on the couch across from me, asleep. Rubbing my eyes and wishing I had a toothbrush, I sit up on the couch. We're still in the basement club a few blocks from Reed's house in Torun. The place is completely empty, but I have no idea what time it is because there are no windows down here.

Glancing at the chair next to me, I startle, seeing Anya studying me with a blank expression. "Hah," I gasp, feeling as if I've just been performing for an audience of one. "You scared me, Anya." Her expression doesn't change, so I ask, "Is it me, or do you feel like everything is being written in reverse?" Her green eyes scan me as if she's picking out all of my weaknesses. I run my fingers through my hair, trying to smooth the tangles.

When she tilts her head, like she's trying to understand me, I mutter under my breath, "Never mind." Rising from the plush sofa, I ask, "Do you know where Reed is?"

She growls low and instantly Reed appears next to me. Not taking her intense eyes off me, she says, "Reed."

"Uh…thanks, Anya," I say, seeing the confused look on Reed's face. "Hi," I smile at him, walking into the curve in his side and feeling his arms instantly hug me. "What did I miss?" I ask, cognizant that I still need that toothbrush.

"The news conference, Mrs. de Graham," Reed says with an ironic expression on his face.

My eyebrow lifts in question. "Huh?"

"Yeah, what's that supposed to mean?" Russell asks, sitting up and rubbing a hand over his face.

"Brennus—he's in Poland," Reed replies.

"How do you know that? What's the vampire doin'?" Russell asks as he rises from the couch looking rumpled from sleep.

"He's looking for us," Reed informs, motioning toward the flat-screens mounted around the bar. Switching all of them on with a push of a button, he uses the remote to turn up the volume. "He's employing the haystack to find the needle."

On every screen in the bar, a doctored photograph of me in a wedding dress standing next to Brennus appears along with a local phone number. "How very human of him," I choke, feeling scared. "What are they saying?" I ask with goose bumps rising on my forearms.

Reed rubs my arms soothingly and says, "They're saying that you're Brennus' wife—kidnapped from your home in Ireland. They're asking that if anyone has information on your location that they call the number on the screen...for a substantial reward."

A photograph of Reed at Crestwood flashes on the screen next. "What are they saying now?" I ask with my heart in my throat.

Russell answers, "They're describin' Reed as a stalker who has been harassin' you. They're sayin' he's a person of interest in this case and offerin' a reward for any information on his location, too. Ahh! You've gotta be kiddin' me..." Russell trails off, listening to the newscaster as his football picture encompasses the news item box at the left of the screen.

"What do we do?" I ask. "We can't leave here without someone seeing us." The wedding photo of me pops back up on the screen and I make a derisive sound, gesturing to it. "Please! Like I'd even be caught undead in that wedding dress!"

Russell, smirks, "Just when you think that maybe Brennus is runnin' out of crazy, he shows up with a brand new can of it...economy size."

"So now every human will be looking for us, too," I say with a sinking feeling in my stomach. "How are we going to avoid being seen?"

"We're not, love," Reed answers in a gentle tone. "We need help. I contacted Dominion—"

"Dominion! We can't do that! What about Russell?" I interrupt, feeling panic threading through me.

"Russell has an *aspire*—a Throne that outranks even the highest level Power. Anya can take care of Russell so that they don't take him as their weapon," Reed replies candidly.

"Oh," I murmur, reading Russell's confused expression. "You already contacted them?" I ask for clarity.

"Yes," Reed says with his eyes shifting away from me.

My eyebrow lifts. "What?" My voice is suspicious, seeing his guilty expression. "Did you talk to Preben?"

"No," Reed replies, watching our pictures on the screen.

I frown. "The war council?" I try again.

"No," Reed shakes his head as he avoids looking at me, and when I gasp, he cringes a little.

"YOU SPOKE TO MY FATHER!" I yell at him while a blush stains my cheeks and my body becomes rigid.

Reed turns and looks in my eyes. "Tau is a master at strategy and tactics. He's bringing an army to ensure that nothing happens to you. He may be able to catch Brennus here before he has a chance to hide again," he explains.

"You didn't even ask me what I thought about that plan," I say softly, feeling a stab of pain.

"You were asleep," Reed replies in a low tone.

"You mean you waited until I was asleep," I accuse.

His eyes narrow. "It was necessary to call for an extraction," Reed says in a military tone. "I couldn't call Zephyr. There are now hundreds of Fallen crawling around this city. The Inikwi are everywhere as well and…" he hesitates.

"And," I ask with a lift of my eyebrow.

With reluctance, he adds, "And, I spotted Werree just a few hours ago."

A shiver of dread goes through me at the thought of the Werree being nearby. "Brennus is allowing the Werree to hunt for me? Even after they killed Lachlan?" I ask, feeling numb from shock.

"Casimir is no longer pulling strings with the Werree, so they have naturally shifted back to their old alliance with the Gancanagh," Reed says, like it's to be expected—a foregone conclusion. But, Reed wasn't in the hall when the Werree attacked us. He didn't witness them kill Lachlan while Lachlan tried to defend me. I can still see the Werrees' shadowy figures beetling over the walls and ceilings, trying to get to me so they could take pieces of my body for their flesh suits.

My throat constricts. "How can Declan and Faolan go along with that?" I ask in a shallow voice, remembering my Gancanagh bodyguards who fought with me. "What is wrong with everyone?" My eyes fill up with tears. "I don't understand! How can they just let those THINGS hunt ME! HOW CAN THEY DO THAT?" Betrayal stabs me like never before.

"I saved them from the Werree and now they're going to let the Werree kill me?"

Reed frowns. "Evil is—"

I hold up my hand to him. "NO! I know you don't understand this, but they were my FRIENDS!" I explain, feeling myself truly beginning to freak out as tears stream down my face. "DECLAN AND FAOLAN WERE MY FRIENDS!"

"Just like Eion was your friend?" Reed asks in a quiet tone. "But I just burned his body a few hours ago because he fed on you like you were a snack."

I wave my hand. "That was Eion. He always lacked control," I reply dismissively, wiping my tears on my arm.

"No, that is their hallmark, Evie. They'll consume you until there is nothing left of you and then they'll destroy you," he replies. "I know you need time to figure all of this out—"

"There's no time to figure it out, Reed. There's never any time," I whisper, before walking away in the direction of the bathroom.

Reed calls to me, "He saw his entire future with you. When you left Brennus, Evie, he..." Reed's voice is rough, and I pause, listening. "He was left with just his life as it was before you came into it and he...he realized that there is no life without you—nothing matters. You stole his life from him and it slowly began to take him apart. Everything else is the same, but it takes on such...drabness...you have no idea." Reed gives a humorless laugh. "He can still taste you on his lips, smell your scent in his memory, remember when you smiled just for him, and the thought of never having that again is...harrowing. So, he's willing to hurt you because he's focusing on the pain to try to kill everything that you were to him...so that he can survive it."

A tear runs a path down my cheek. An instant later, Reed's arms wrap around me and pull me to his chest. "I'm so sorry I did that to you," I croak.

"Shh," he hushes me. "All that went away when you came back to me."

"I never—"

"I know," Reed replies, rubbing my back. "And sometime soon, when this is all over, we're going to have all the time we need. I promise you that we will."

"My father is coming here," I say in a small voice. "What am I going to say to him?"

"Well, I never had a father so...I," he stammers.

Russell says, "You won't need to say anythin'. He'll like you no matter what."

"How do you know?" I ask, sniffling. "We're kind of freaks, remember?"

"Yeah, but you're his freak. His little baby strange," Russell says, grinning.

Frowning, Reed says, "Tau is also an angel, Evie. He might not be like you expect him to be."

My brow furls. "What do you mean?" I ask.

"He's not human, so don't expect him to behave like one," Reed says. "He's never had a model either—he's never had a father in the sense that you're accustomed to with your Uncle Jim."

"Oh," I murmur. "So you're saying he may not like me."

"No, I'm saying you may not like him," he replies worriedly.

"This is not how I planned on meeting him," I mutter, looking down at myself. "Does anyone have a toothbrush?" I ask, feeling like I might cry again.

"I think that there's an unopened one in the office…" Reed trails off, looking at the T.V. screen again. Brennus' face is on every one of them.

"Turn it up," Russell says, looking intense.

Reed uses the remote. "Genevieve is da light of our family," Brennus says, his expression grim. He looks calm and regal in a dark suit with his dark hair slicked back in corporate elegance. "She is… irreplaceable." His voice is like silk, drawing in the female reporter who is all but touching him now. He is one of the most beautiful and poised men I have ever seen, but he's not a man. He looks colder now; he's more like a statue: hard and untouchable.

"Do you believe she is now with either this Reed Wellington or Russell Marx?" an interviewer asks Brennus in English.

"I do. We believe dat she's being held against her will by both men," he says, looking like he's truly in pain as his light green eyes show his misery.

Russell wrinkles his nose. "Ahh, you creepy, cold freak!" he says next to me, while running his hand through his tawny hair. "It's gonna feel so good knockin' your head off!"

As I listen again to the television, Brennus says, "'Tis our understanding dat Genevieve was last seen in Torun. Any information from yer viewers would be a great help ta us in da investigation. We can na even begin ta put a price on whah dat kind of information would mean ta us. Yer viewers will have ta decide whah is a fair reward for it."

"Why not just put a bounty on our heads, Brenn?" I ask the T.V. screen.

"He just did," Reed replies, his green eyes looking even darker.

"Did he get a spray tan?" Russell asks incredulously next to me.

"I think so…I suggested that. It looks good," I say absently. Russell turns his brown eyes on me like I've lost my mind. "What? I'm just saying…it makes him look less, you know, dead."

Russell scowls. "He looks orange to me," he says, and I shrug guiltily.

"What would you like our viewers to know about Genevieve?" the interviewer asks Brennus, probably trying to push the human-interest angle of the story.

Giving the female interviewer a small, alluring smile, Brennus replies, "She's jus very…sweet…"

"Tastin'," Russell interjects.

"And naïve," Brennus continues. "She's too trusting—'tis her only flaw. She's always ready ta champion a lost cause. It may sound like I have a callous heart…"

"You mean the one that's not beatin'?" Russell says sarcastically to the television.

"But, I've suffered since I've lost her," Brennus continues, looking wrecked.

Russell growls, "You're gonna suffer more, freak."

"And if you could say something to her now—if she was listening, what would that be?" the interviewer asks Brennus in a soft, reverent tone.

Brennus' nostrils flare as he tries to suppress the violent emotions he's feeling just below the surface. "Together we were invincible…we will be again," he says in a raw voice.

"And to her captors?" the interviewer asks.

A surge of adrenaline pulses through me, awaiting his answer. Watching Brennus, he pauses, before frowning. Then he pulls his phone from his pocket. He scans its display before a small smile creeps over his face. Reaching up, Brennus unclips the microphone on his collar, pulling off the receiver on his back.

"Mr. de Graham?" the interviewer asks in a startled voice, but Brennus simply walks off the set, leaving the interviewer to awkwardly try to deal with the aftermath of his unexpected departure from her interview.

"Uh…that's not good," I murmur, turning to look at Reed, my eyes wide.

"Ahh…shit, Red! You feel that?" Russell asks as a ripple of energy passes over my skin, causing the fine hairs to rise.

"RUSSELL!" I shout, feeling panic hitting me as I try to pull all of that energy that I can to me. "WE NEED A—"

In an instant, my world explodes. I lift off the ground and spin in midair like a tornado. The entire room cascades and whirls around me while I hover above the ground.

"DO SOMETHING, RUSSELL!" Reed shouts, flying to me and trying to hold on to me. He extends his wings and attempts to stop me from spinning, but it causes him to whirl with me.

"OY, RUSSELL, WHAH ARE YE GONNA DO?" Lonan calls from the stairs, having blown the doors off the hinges in a cascading flurry of splintering wood. Alastar and Cavan are by his side and the wind carries their heavy scent to us.

In the next instant, I stop spinning, but I feel like I'm a penny in the path of an electromagnet. The only thing holding me back from streaking across the room, straight into Lonan's arms, are Reed's arms around me.

"Ughh," I groan, feeling like my insides are going to spill out of me. "Shield," I whisper weakly.

"Where's Brennus?" Russell calls to the Gancanagh, scowling as he watches Reed struggle to keep me in his arms.

"He's on da way," Lonan replies smugly.

An antagonistic scowl crosses Russell's lips. "Why does he keep sendin' the B-Team? Is he afraid to face me?"

Lonan playfully replies, "We requested da honor o' meetin' ye now, da other. Do ye remember Ultan?" Beneath Lonan's archness, he's seething with a desire for revenge.

Russell lifts his eyebrow. "You mean Zoltan? Yeah, I remember him. He was the first vampire I ever made really dead," he smirks.

"He was Gancanagh! Me brother," Lonan snarls with loathing.

"Really? I can't tell, 'cuz all y'all look the same to me," Russell replies, shrugging.

Cavan grinds his teeth. Winding back his hand, Cavan throws an elf dart at Russell. The fiery ball swirls and hisses through the air like a teardrop from a melting star.

Raising his hand, Russell whispers words that cause the flaming ball of fire to reverse course, plowing back towards Cavan. Cavan dodges the inferno by mere centimeters, lunging to his side and falling into Alastar. His eyes go wide in shock at Russell's ability to manipulate his spell.

"Y'all wouldn't last a second in MLB," Russell heckles them.

"Russell, block their spell on Evie," Reed demands, straining to keep me with him.

Russell scowls seeing me lurch forward as Reed's grip slips a little. He pulls energy in the room to him and whispers words I can't hear. The brief silence gives way to a trembling vibration as an incredibly loud hum erupts from Russell's chest. The vibration moves the very air like a woofer trembles with sound in an amp. A wavering bubble of low frequency waves swirls out around us like steel-gray water in a pool. The tremor shudders the cellar as it pulses forward. I flinch in agony at the noise, grateful that I'm behind the sound, not in front of it. The thunderous roar from the deep-frequency noise shakes the ground as the tempest cracks the floors and surges ahead. The sound collides with chairs and tables in its path, disintegrating them into poofs of splintering wreckage. Disbelief shutters over Lonan's features. When it reaches the fellas, it blasts Lonan off his feet, hurdling him back outside along with Alastar and Cavan.

Lonan's pull on me severs and I hug Reed to me. "We need a shield, Russell," I manage to say. Reed lands with me on the floor by Russell and Anya.

"Okay," Russell replies. Immediately, he forms a wall of energy in front of us.

"Uhh," I groan, gripping my head in my hands. My universe is still spinning.

"Somethin's comin', Red," Russell warns, while crouching in a defensive posture. "Reed, tell Anya to get behind me."

At the doors at the top of the stairs, shadowy figures creep around the doorframe, moving down the walls of the stairwell. "Werree," I shiver, taking a step back and feeling an eerie chill. Shadows move between the crevices as the disembodied demons stalk us. They're not alone because a wave of Inikwi have joined them, speaking in garbled voices as they cautiously climb down the stairs on all fours.

Reed's need to protect me shows as he inches in front of me, cutting off any direct line to my position. "Light—" Reed says, "we need light to kill the Werree, love." He assesses the windowless walls. "I can kill Inikwi. You focus on the Werree."

I nod, hoping the room stops spinning for me soon.

Inikwi group together in a pack like wolves. Moldering skin and the scent of mildew-decomposition makes the windowless cellar musty and nauseating, but it's their absolute contrast to each other that makes them eerie as well. If they were "normal" humans, they probably wouldn't be together. An elderly woman with a lime green headscarf covering her wiry gray hair shifts agilely to the right, her white orthopedic shoes make no noise on the stone steps. The extremely tall, middle-aged man, who must have died from the gaping slash across the base of his throat, accompanies this lady. A twenty-something hipster inikwi with skinny jeans goes left, his once cunning scarf frayed and dragging behind him. He's followed by a grizzled, ancient-looking corpse in a brown nylon suit.

In the center of the inikwi, a thirty-something female corpse with wheat-colored hair and unnaturally milky-blue eyes gives the others a garbled-voiced command. One of her cheekbones has been crushed in and discolored. Black liquid mold slips from the corners of her mouth to speckle and mar her ivory coat. A second later, she breaks from their ranks, running straight at Reed while the other four try to flank us on all fours like dogs.

Reed speaks to Anya in Angel, giving her some kind of order. Anya notches a gold-tipped arrow in her bow before lifting it and letting it fly. It strikes; the arrow pierces the charging inikwi in the chest, spewing silver blood in a growing circle on the ivory fabric of her coat.

The blond inikwi's head shifts forward while her hair obscures her face. The host carcass crumples to her knees, and then she tumbles backward to the floor. A thick, snake-like creature begins wiggling out of the dead woman's gaping mouth. It almost looks like her large intestine is trying to liberate itself from her body. Crrcrrack, her jawbone breaks apart as the wet tail slides over her teeth. Anya's second arrow punctures the slimy flesh of the silvery inikwi, tearing a hole through it.

As I look away from the gruesome scene, I see Reed already tearing the hipster inikwi apart, cutting it off before it could coordinate an attack with its nylon-suited partner. Having been distracted by the Inikwi, I completely miss the Werree coming at me from above.

A shadowy werree notches an inky arrow that is really an extension of itself. It lets the arrow fly at me. The projectile pierces my side, propelling me backward from the force of the strike. The dark arrow melts into me and is absorbed into my skin. Frigid poison corrodes up my side and down my leg.

I let out a whimper of pain, trying to grasp the shaft and pull it out of me, but it's not solid and the poison continues to seep into my side. "Russell!" I grit my teeth.

Russell growls as his face becomes a mask of indecision. Instantly, he crouches at my side, asking, "How do you get this out, Red?"

My teeth chatter from a growing coldness bleeding through me. "I dddon't know," I whimper, and I close my eyes to think. When I open them again, I scream, "Russ—behind you!" I warn, pushing Russell aside to focus on a group of werree above us. I lift one hand

and murmur through gritted teeth, "Darkness hides the light. Light destroys the night," while all of the energy I collected flows from my body.

A beam of white-hot energy bursts forth from me, shining directly on the Werree. The light licks at them as if it were orange embers destroying decaying brown leaves; it causes them to fall from the ceiling and writhe in agony as they turn to ash and smoke. The Werree that remain change direction then, slinking backward away from us—retreating to the stairway and out of the bar.

Russell's expression is anxious. "Red, you're wounded," he states, hovering near me.

"I'm…not…" I murmur, running my hand along my side and feeling for the arrow, but it's not there anymore. "But, I was."

"What'd you do? Heal yourself or somthin'?" Russell breathes, seeing that I'm no longer bleeding as he lifts my shirt to help. A red scratch is all that is left from the Werree's black, shadowy arrow. "How'd you do that?"

"Maybe it was the light?" I ask. Then, I witness two inikwi knock Anya down. One is stomping on her chest, while the other is easing around toward her head.

Russell sees it too and moves fast, plucking an inikwi off of Anya's chest and hurling it into its buddy. The creatures fall back into the wall. Russell follows them, picking one up in each hand; he bashes them together like he's pounding dirt off the bottoms of a pair of shoes. Silvery blood oozes out of their mouths, a sure sign that whatever was in them is definitely dead now, but Russell doesn't stop pounding them.

It's quiet; the only sound now comes from Russell beating the dead inikwi. Reed has already killed the rest of the inikwi and is now crouching over Anya, helping her to sit so that he can check her wounds.

"Russell," I say, but he's not hearing me; he's still beating on the clearly dead inikwi. I put my hand on Russell's arm to stop him.

Russell's face is growing pale. "Is she all right?" he asks with fear in his tone, like he's afraid to turn around and see for himself.

I glance at Anya. "Reed, how is she?"

Reed tears a white tablecloth into strips and starts wrapping Anya's ribs. "She has two broken ribs and a laceration on her forearm. She should heal quickly," he reports.

"She's going to be okay," I say to Russell, touching his arm and indicating that he should drop the Inikwi in his hands. He does, turning slowly to look at Anya. "She's an ass kicker," I comment, watching her cringe as Reed pulls the binding tighter on her ribs.

"I should've had her back," Russell says with stiff remorse.

"You just did, Russ," I say, indicating the pulverized corpses on the floor.

Russell's expression darkens again. "She shouldn't be here," Russell says, turning on me ominously. "We have to make her go home."

"She doesn't look like she wants to go, Russell."

His frown deepens. "Then we gotta make her go somehow," he replies with a grim twist of his lips.

"How?" I ask in confusion.

"I don't know how, but I can't keep track of both of y'all," he replies angrily.

I frown. "But, what if—"

"Naw, Red! Don't argue with me! You made me stay here, so now you gotta help me!" he counters in a tense tone of intimidation, his brown eyes stormy. Stabbing his finger in Anya's direction, he says, "I don't know exactly what she is to me, but she's somethin' and I...you just gotta help," he says between clenched teeth.

"Okay," I agree, feeling a wave of guilt hit me because I did make him stay here with me when I healed him. "But, first we have to get out of here."

"I'll go do some recon," Russell says, instantly sending out his clone. His body sags and I catch it before it falls on the ground. Gently pulling Russell to the floor with me, I hold him as his consciousness travels with his clone.

The instant Russell returns, I know it because he lurches forward out of my arms, saying stonily, "We're not goin' anywhere."

"Why," I ask, feeling Reed standing by our side.

"You ever see that old movie—the one with all the black birds?" Russell asks, his hair standing up like wires on his arms. "Hitchcock?"

"The Birds?" I whisper.

"That's the one. Well, it's kinda like that out there, 'cept instead of birds lurkin' 'round, we've got fallen angels and Gancanagh linin' the pitched rooftops, waitin' for us to come out," Russell reports, looking pale. "It's just gettin' dark and the Fallen are flyin' 'round like they could give a crap that they're among humans."

"We're dead," I choke, feeling oddly calm about it.

"No, we're in a good position," Reed disagrees, crouching down to look in our eyes. "Russell, you did a good job picking this bar. It's an underground fortress with only one access point. It's hollowed out of stone—lacking incendiary properties. Even if they try to burn us out, you and Evie can bring the rain and extinguish it. We are the bait now and the trap is set." Reed gives us a smug smile, his green eyes shining with anticipation.

"Tau," I say, feeling scared and hopeful all at the same time.

"He's going to bring a reign of terror on them the likes of which they've never seen," Reed says, studying the clock on the wall as if calculating when the reign will begin. "Zephyr is going to be disappointed."

"When is Tau gettin' here?" Russell asks, but the phone behind the bar begins ringing, causing me to jump at it's shrill tone.

Wetting my lips, I glance at Reed, asking, "Tau?"

"I gave Tau my private number," Reed replies, letting the phone continue to ring.

"Well, maybe—" I say, watching Reed shake his head slowly.

"No, that's Brennus," Reed says. Walking toward the phone, Reed crushes it, silencing it in mid-ring.

"What do you think he wants?" I ask with a cold shiver.

"You," Reed replies. "Russell, can you handle the door while I contact Tau?"

"I'll growl if there's any movement," Russell replies.

"Do you want to speak to Tau?" Reed asks, moving to me and cupping my cheek.

"No, I'm going to clean myself up, then I'll help guard the door," I reply, feeling adrenaline burst through me again.

"I'll be right here," Reed says, kissing my forehead before letting me go.

Quickly I go to the bathroom, cleaning myself the best that I can in the sink. I glance in the mirror and notice that I'm really pale. It's probably from being bitten; my blood hasn't had a chance to fully replenish. I still feel really weak. Brennus' magic could snap me in two right now and I'd barely be able to fight back.

When I return to the room, Russell is behind the bar, wiping his dripping hands and face on a towel. As he comes around from the bar, he carries a bag of pretzels and water with him. Tossing me a bottle of water, he sits next to Anya on an elegant couch and offers her some pretzels. She snuggles into his side, resting her head on his chest and he doesn't seem to mind having her there as he watches the entrance ahead of him.

"*Lei-cha-ih-yil-knee-ih il-day,*" Russell says to Anya, "*be-al-doh-tso-lani al-tah-je-jay* Gancanagh." He strokes her hair soothingly.

I sit down by them on an adjacent sofa. "What did you tell her?" I ask.

"I said 'the army will arrive—many big guns to attack the Gancanagh,'" Russell replies.

"*Ne-tah*," Anya says with the intimacy of a secret.

Russell squeezes her to him and smiles cunningly. "That's right, we'll fool them, Anya" he replies.

"What language is that?" I ask, taking a handful of pretzels when he turns the bag toward me.

"Navajo," Russell says, munching on his pretzels. "We were Apache, but we traded with the Navajo once in a while," he adds, and then he gives me a crooked, little smile. "You were a purdy squaw."

Lifting a pretzel to my lips, my hands shake. I show them to Russell and say in a self-effacing way, "You'd think that I'd be used to this by now."

Anya studies my hands, and then she lifts her trembling ones, saying, "*Toh-bah-ha-zsid.*"

"What did she say?" I ask, feeling relief that she's not scowling at me now.

"She said she's afraid, too" Russell answers with a grim frown, clearly bothered by the last exchange.

Anya's deep green eyes hold mine and I want to tell her I'm sorry, but I'm not sure exactly for what. However, in the next moment, a prickling cold touches my skin. Swirling patterns of frost form on the walls beyond Anya, running up over the ceiling to crystallize the glass chandeliers. My breath comes out of my mouth in hazy clouds as the temperature in the room drops severely. Russell, Anya, and I stand up at once. Reed instantly appears by my side again, taking my hand casually in his. Hearing the sound of cracking, like thin ice when someone walks on it, Brennus appears at the doorway of the pub.

Still in his dark suit, Brennus is polished elegance, a king, as he surveys us beneath him. His eyes stop on me, taking in every inch of my body. "Genevieve," he says my name like a prayer, "me queen… me living darkness."

CHAPTER 11

The Specter
Of Regret

"It never seems ta lessen," Brennus says to me, while stepping with regal grace down the staircase toward our position in the cellar bar below. "Dis stabbing thrill of desire dat bleeds trough me whenever I behold ye, *mo chroí.*" The icy path is expanding around him, covering the surfaces of the pub with frost. Knowing that this is only an image of Brennus—a magical spell projected to us through his vast power, I still feel almost paralyzing fear that he has found me again.

"Keep him talking, love," Reed says in my ear. "Try to draw him in. We need him to physically come here."

I feign composure as I reply to Brennus, "Come in and get your overdose then." I straighten my shoulders and prepare for war. "I'm surprised that you're not tired of the hangover."

Brennus' light green eyes rivet on me, like he's scouring me for any minute changes that might have occurred since I was last within his embrace. "Ye've a devious wee mind. I tought for sure dat we had ye trapped on yer isle in da blue sea," he remarks, coming ever nearer to me and ignoring everyone else.

"I'm sorry, it must have been so disappointing sifting through the carnage and not finding pieces of me," I reply, seeing my breath forming icy tendrils in the frigid air.

"'Tis whah I tought I wanted, too, Genevieve—ta see ye extinguished from all existence. 'Twas my only ambition, truth be told. However, when yer wee isle incinerated and I believed dat me fellas had annihilated ye, someting happened ta me," Brennus breathes, his image coming close to me. He leans very near, trying to inhale the scent of my hair, only to frown and look dissatisfied in the obvious fact that he cannot.

"You were sorry it wasn't you who pulled the trigger?" I ask, confused by the contradictory behavior he is displaying.

"I learned dat dere is a raging depth of pain dat I had yet ta experience," he explains, watching my reaction.

"You mean you had a moment of remorse?" I ask, quirking my eyebrow in disbelief. "What a vexing situation for you, Brenn: to be at the pinnacle of your triumph and to be daunted by the specter of regret."

"'Twas na remorse," he replies in a harsh tone. "'Twas loss on a scale I had never imagined possible. 'Twas an agony dat even da death of me own heart, or da heart of me brudder, could na equal."

"Well, you appear to have recovered fully from it," I reply, raising my chin. "Judging by the Werree you sent to me, you're leaning toward killing me again?" I ask, trying to sound calm, but hearing the accusation in my tone.

"Dey were na here by me orders!" Brennus hisses, looking outraged. "'Twas Lonan dat banjaxed me orders." Seeing the deep scowl on his face and the way that his lower lip is thinning menacingly, I can tell he means it. "'Tis his hatred for da other dat has him blind ta whah is truly important here."

"And what's that?" I ask, unable to stop myself.

Sighing heavily, Brennus asks in a tired tone, "Ye have ta ask me dat? Ye do na know dat ye are all dat madders ta me?"

"I'm sorry—my bad!" I retort with sarcasm, hitting my forehead in mock surprise. "I must've totally misread your intentions! I thought that you were trying to—what was it—extinguish me from all existence?" I ask. "But now that you tell me that I'm all that matters to you, I feel so much better."

"Ye are aware, Genevieve, dat sarcasm is da lowest form of humor?" Brennus replies, completely serious.

"You need some lithium for your mood swings, Brenn," I reply, shaking my head in disgust.

"Have ye na heard a word I've been tellin' ye?" he asks in frustration. "I'm trying ta explain dat I tought I killed ye and for several hours afterward, 'twas da most agonizing moments I've ever experienced."

"Oh," I murmur, surprise leaking into my tone. "So…you've decided to let me live?" I ask, knowing he wouldn't be coming here if that were the case.

"Well…dat's na entirely accurate. If by live ye mean dat I'll drain ye and share me blood wi' ye so dat ye become me undead queen, den ye get ta live. Ye will na even have ta beg me, 'twill be enough dat ye submit ta me."

Looking at Reed, he immediately says, "No."

"Ahh, I'm sorry, Brennus," I reply sheepishly. "My attorney has advised me against your offer. You see, we kinda have this other deal in motion that should do the trick."

Russell closes his eyes briefly, like I'm giving away a huge secret. Seeing Russell's reaction, Brennus' expression turns sour. "Deal? Whah deal, Genevieve?" he asks.

"Well, it's kinda in the planning stages right now, but I guess I can let you in on it," I say in a conspiratorial tone.

"Red, don't tell him nothin'," Russell retorts in agitation.

"It's okay, Russell. He can't stop us now," I reply, giving him a wink.

"Speak," Brennus barks abruptly, like a leader used to ruling.

"We did some recon," I say in a serious tone. "You've assembled a legion of the fallen army, not to mention Inikwi and my personal favorite, Werree—Lachlan would be so mad at you."

"I already explained dat da Werree are na here by me orders, but da Fallen and da Inikwi were necessary. Ye can na be allowed ta escape from here. I miss ye, *mo chroí*—more dan ye can imagine. I need ye ta be at me side now," he replies, calmly explaining his position.

"You've made it clear that we're not getting out of here alive," I explain, watching his reaction. "You're the king and you're coming here to crush us."

"'Tis difficult to remember dat ye are jus a wee lass still. When ye speak ta me like dat and set me blood on fire," Brennus murmurs, smiling in approval, "'tis making me wish dat I could really be here now, so dat I could inhale da scent of all dat intoxicating blood pounding trough yer veins."

I wrinkle my nose at him. "Yes, so disappointing for me, too," I agree, feeling a shiver of dread pass through me.

"Ye plan ta bargain wi' me? Do ye propose another contract in order ta spare deir lives?" he inquires, barely hiding his grin.

"No," I sigh sadly. "I know that you're not going to spare their lives, no matter what I offer you, Brennus," I reply, gazing back at him and seeing his smile broaden.

"Dat is interesting, Genevieve. I tought dat ye would attempt ta grovel for deir lives," he grins, raising his brow like he's intrigued.

"Ahh...*tristitiae*, that means sorrow, right?" I ask, seeing him nod his head. "You always said that it's my weakness."

"I did," he affirms, his eyes slowly narrowing.

"And yours is me," I say without a doubt.

"Whah are ye saying?" he asks, suddenly not looking so confident.

"Like I said, I haven't worked out all the details, but essentially, you're wasting your time coming here, because I'll be gone," I reply. "Anya, that's the angel over there, has been dying to kill me since she met me," I explain, pointing to Anya who's standing next to Russell.

"Why?" Brennus asks in a stiff tone, circling Anya and hearing her growl a warning at his magical image.

"It's complicated," I mutter, waving my hand absently. "Russell is kinda her *aspire* and I've been keeping him from her—blah, blah, blah. Suffice it to say, she hates my guts."

Brennus' lips contort in a sneer. "Kill her," he orders me, looking fierce.

"Can't," I say, shrugging my shoulders. "If I kill her, then I'll have to rely on either Russell or Reed to kill me and that's a lot to ask of them. No, Anya is my best choice. Or, I could walk out right now and hope that a Fallen kills me in the heat of the moment, but you might have promised them something or they could double-cross you and take me to Sheol and I really don't feel like taking that chance."

Brennus begins to swear softly in Faerie—at least, I think he's swearing. He takes a deep breath and switches back to English, "Listen ta me, Genevieve. Ye can walk out dis doorway right now and surrender ta Lonan. He'll keep ye safe until I arrive. I'll agree ta let yer friends live." He watches me sit down on the sofa and dig my hand into the bag of pretzels, pulling out a handful.

"You know, pretzels as a last meal is not so bad. I'm really craving Twinkies, but this is okay. At least I get water this time," I say, popping a pretzel in my mouth and watching his reaction.

"Whah about da other and da *aingeal?*" Brennus asks, trying to find the angle that will get me to submit to him.

"Well, once Anya kills me, my soul might ascend to Paradise. If I get there, I'll try to convince the hierarchy to call Reed, Russell, and Anya back to Paradise, too, before you're able to hurt them," I answer with goose bumps rising as I think of the countless barriers to such a plan.

"Dat is a wrong move, Genevieve. Dey'll never agree ta dat," Brennus responds immediately, like he has intimate knowledge of how Paradise operates.

"Then it's plan B for them. Reed can kill Russell…he might even enjoy that a little," I say as I look at Reed and then Russell. "If he does that, then Anya will be willing to kill him, too," I reply, feeling my throat get tight at the thought of losing either Reed or Russell.

The grim expression on Brennus' face tells me just what he thinks of my new plan. Anger flares in his voice when he approaches Russell, saying, "I order ye ta protect Genevieve 'til I arrive."

With a growing frown, Russell says, "You know, it's funny…there's somethin' in me now that actually wants to obey you."

"Ye've been bitten, Russell," Brennus replies in a menacing tone. "My venom is in ye now, because it all stems from me. I'm yer king and ye'll follow me orders."

"Is that it? I was wonderin' why you almost seem appealin' to me now," Russell says off-handedly. "But, naw, you're not my king. I don't subscribe to the whole evil dictator vibe you got goin' on."

"Ye won't subscribe ta anyting ever again if ye go along wi' Genevieve's plan," Brennus counters. "She's planning ta kill ye."

"Normally, I'm not one to drink the grape kool-aid, Brennus, knowin' it's poisoned," Russell replies calmly. "I'm more of a 'see how many bad guys I can take with me' type. So I may still be here when you arrive, but I'm gonna make sure that Red is gone 'cuz her soul is the most important thing to me. I'm not gonna let you send it to Sheol."

Seeing that he's not getting what he wants from Russell, Brennus turns to Reed, eyeing him in an assessing way. "Ye're awfully calm about dis," he remarks.

"Yes," Reed agrees.

"Dis does na bother ye—dat she plans on dying here—cut down in a seedy, underground hovel?" Brennus asks with disgust in his voice, gesturing around him.

"What matter the place?" Reed replies in a grim tone. "The world ends for us both when she's gone."

"'Tis ironic dat ye are da only other one ta understand dat," Brennus replies in a soft tone.

"Isn't it?" Reed agrees.

"We two have a vested interest in seeing her stay alive. Can we na find a solution ta dis?" Brennus asks, his face looks somehow paler than normal.

"I have an interest in her remaining alive. You have an interest in her becoming undead," Reed counters.

"Too, true," Brennus responds, exhaling a sigh. "'Tis jus dat I can na control her while she's alive—na dat I object ta her being alive because I enjoy every sensual breath dat she takes."

"Yes, there is that, and the fact that she won't be the same after you suck out her soul," Reed replies, his eyes narrowing minutely.

"'Tis disconcerting," Brennus agrees.

"You love her purity of spirit," Reed states, watching Brennus.

"Dere is na one ting dat I do na love about her," Brennus says thoughtfully.

"Except for her love for Russell and me," Reed replies, his deep green eyes scanning me lovingly.

"Except for dat," Brennus scowls in agreement. "So, we're aligned in our tinking."

"You've forced her into a corner and now she only sees one way out," Reed says. "It was the same in the caves in Houghton—she'll evade you the only way she can."

"So ye're saying dat me only option is ta let her escape now, if I want ta have a chance of ever having her again," Brennus asks Reed with an ironic twist of his lips.

"Either that, or you have to arrive here and stop her before she dies...tick, tock, tick, tock...Or...you could eliminate the threat outside," Reed advises with a cunning smile on his perfect lips. "That means turning on the Inikwi, the Fallen, and the Werree in order to save her."

"'Tis frowned upon ta turn on one's allies," Brennus states blandly.

"Tell all of your friends 'goodbye,'" Reed smiles, knowing that the Gancanagh will be hunted by the Fallen again if they betray them now.

"How much time do I have ta clear a path for yer escape?" Brennus asks, looking tormented.

"How much time do you need?" Reed counters, looking at the clock on the wall.

"Several hours," he replies.

"How about two?" Reed asks.

"Four," Brennus returns.

"Done," Reed replies.

Brennus reaches out and tries to stroke my cheek, but his hand slips right through me. "Do na go somewhere I can na ever find ye, Genevieve," he says, his eyes softening.

"Don't make me," I murmur.

Leaning near my ear, Brennus whispers, "I did na understand how love can haunt...ye keep teaching me new tings." Pulling back, his light green eyes infiltrate mine.

"I wish I could teach you to let me go before you get burned," I whisper back.

"I'm already burning," he says, before falling away in a dark, shadowy swirl of smoke.

My breath exhales in a rush. "He's going to make the Fallen leave!" I hiss. I turn in agitation to Reed.

A small smile forms on Reed's lips. "No, he won't. He was just buying time to work out another plan. He's too far gone to let you go now, but you rattled him with your suicide pact." Reed walks to my side to cup my cheek. "He'll counter quickly. We need to be prepared for an onslaught. I think he'll try to come in *en masse.*"

"You do?" I ask, feeling my stomach swirl with conflicting emotions.

Before Reed can reply, a howling wind streams in through the opening from the street, bringing with it swirling, drifting snow. "Hooo, it is gettin' nasty out there," Russell shivers. "I bet the fallen aren't used to this kind of cold."

"It's cover," Reed murmurs, nearing the entrance of the pub.

"Huh?" Russell asks, following Reed.

"We can't wage this kind of war in the open, and yet, we have no choice," Reed explains, taking a position by the staircase.

"We...you mean angels?" Russell asks, taking a position on the adjacent wall, looking up the staircase.

"Yes, I mean angels. The Fallen are being overt. The weather has turned to cover the fact that they're here. It will drive the humans from the streets, create whiteout conditions so that we have a chance of keeping this from them," he replies, glancing at Russell.

"Who's controllin' the weather?" Russell asks Reed. Not smiling, Reed uses his index finger to point up.

"Will it tip off our enemies to the fact that something is about to happen?" I ask, joining them and scanning the top of the stairs.

"Yes," Reed replies. "When Brennus can't change it, he'll understand and then he'll be even more desperate to get in here and extract you."

A screeching noise from a truck's squeaky brakes sounds from the street above, causing Reed's hand to wrap around my upper arm and push me back behind him. Scraping and mumbling voices issue as truck doors slam shut. I tense, knowing that something is coming and a bead of sweat slides down the side of my face despite the cold. And then, like someone turning on a hose in a slaughterhouse, blood begins cascading down the staircase like a scarlet fountain.

"Is that blood?" Russell asks grimly.

"Yes," Reed answers, his nose wrinkling in disgust.

"Why?" I ask, feeling my knees growing weak.

"Scare tactic?" Russell asks hopefully.

"Brennus is too practical for that," Reed replies, sounding calm.

"Marking his territory?" Russell tries again.

"Bait," Reed offers.

"Bait...bait for what?" Russell asks.

The truck doors open and slam again before the whine of an engine revving away quickly makes every hair on my arms stand on end.

"That is the question," Reed replies, evaluating everything in the room. He speaks to Anya in Angel and she collects her bow and quiver from the sofa, strapping them on her body.

THUMP.

"What the hell was that?" Russell asks with his eyes wide as streams of dust fall from the beams of the ceiling. We all take several collective steps back from the entrance, while looking up at the ceiling.

Reed says, "I don't—"

THUMP.

The ceiling bows and cracks split the stone in web-like patterns, while pieces of mortar fall to the floor, breaking like plaster. Feeling my heart lodge somewhere in my throat, my hand shoots out to Reed's arm, pulling him back with me. Russell, staring at the ceiling, says, "That's not good—"

THUMP.

The harrowing sound makes us all jump and Anya is beside Russell in an instant, holding on to him like I'm holding on to Reed. A wrenching sound like the roof being torn away emits from above, causing tables and chairs to rattle and the glasses on the bar shelves to tumble and shatter. Pulling Reed with me, I crouch down on one knee, holding my arm over my head as my wings try to umbrella the rest of me.

"Damn, that's freaky," Russell says under his breath, staring at the stone ceiling from his crouched position near the floor.

The pounding crash of falling debris hitting the floor above our heads, makes my hands tremble. Glancing at me, Reed grasps my hand, holding it in his before bringing my cold fingers to his lips and kissing them. "I'm here, love," he breathes, reassuring me.

I grit my teeth and duck my head reflexively as a THUMP comes from above us, like something really heavy just fell on the ceiling. Reed lets go of my hand, jetting to the bar and coming back with an armload of expensive liquor.

"Thanks," Russell says, uncapping a bottle of brown liquor and taking a huge gulp of it.

"Don't drink it, Russell," Reed says tersely. "Tear up some pieces of that table cloth and stick one in the bottle like a wick."

"That's alcohol abuse," Russell mutters, before complying with Reed's order. "You know I can conjure fire, right?" he asks Reed with a quirk of his brow.

"Yes, but some of us have to do it the old-fashioned way," Reed replies, looking annoyed as he grabs the bottle back from Russell to store it with the ones he has already made.

"Reed, I got your back," Russell says with zero humor in his tone.

"I know," Reed replies. "And I have yours."

"Well, shoot, we should be just fine then," Russell says seriously, holding Anya to his side.

"Here." I hand Russell some strips of tablecloth. "Wrap Anya's skin wherever you can, so the Gancanagh cannot make her their slave. Using a cloth napkin, I wrap it around Reed's face, tying it behind his head so that he looks like a train robber.

When I finish, I stare into his perfect eyes, feeling fear that I'll never see them again. I pull the cloth down, pressing my lips to his in a passionate kiss.

The stone ceiling caves in then; beams and rubble fall down everywhere, collapsing tables and shattering mirrors. Choking rock dust and a foul odor permeates the air, causing us all to cough and hack. In the darkness I hear something moving toward us from the staircase. Low, throaty snickering-laughter, like the sound a hyena would make, pushes through the dust clouds surrounding us.

Paralyzed by the sound, I search for what could've made it. The hair on my neck rises as several sets of eyes shine reflective as dark shapes descend the staircase. The click of claws scratching against the stone steps causes my jaw to clench.

Another terrorizing THUMP comes from above us. Whatever's up there wants its shot at us, too.

The shiny sets of eyes near the stairs snicker again. "What are they?" I ask Reed.

"Risers," Reed says, looking around and grasping a broken chair leg.

A shiver cuts through Russell. "Why're they laughin'?" Russell asks next to me.

"They aren't. They're arguing over who is the most dominate. The pitch of the voice determines who is the Alpha," Reed states.

"Why's that important?" Russell asks in a low tone.

"Because in Sheol, like every place else, the alpha gets to eat first," Reed replies.

A riser staggers forward to the bottom step, and as I look it over, I exhale a breath. Its head is canine with leather-like flesh pulled tightly over bone. It has ears, but they're paper-thin and ragged, like something bigger has gnawed them off. Roughly the size of a normal dog, the Riser resembles a greyhound, skinny to the point of being emaciated.

"We can't let them feed on the blood or they'll grow," Reed says in a low tone. He pulls a lighter from his pocket, igniting the homemade wick in one of the bottles. He heaves it towards the stairs. The bottle shatters and ignites the pool of blood, showering fire. I watch the smoke rise and with it, the shadows on the staircase become more prominent as five more sets of eyes gaze back at me. They're already lapping at the pools of blood on the steps.

"Ahh, hell! They're feedin'!" Russell points out agitatedly.

The high-pitched giggles from before begin to come in a lower frequency. As one Riser lifts its head from the blood, it begins to change; it jerks and pops as it rises up on its hind legs and it's spine straightens. The canine-like muzzle it used to possess flattens to become less dog-like, more human, no...more demon.

Russell conjures an elf dart in his hand, throwing it at a Riser. He hits the target square in the chest. The flames cover the demon, but it doesn't move; it doesn't even flinch. Instead, it giggles again, thereby calling its brethren to it.

"When they're risen like this, Russell, they're almost impervious to magic," Reed says with a frown.

"How am I supposed to kill it?" Russell asks in frustration.

"You kill them with brute strength. Pierce the heart or cut off the head," Reed advises.

"With what?" Russell scoffs. "I don't have any weapons."

"Improvise, Russell, anything can be a weapon. Stay behind me," Reed says, not looking at Russell but keeping his eyes locked on the demons that are beginning to creep further into the room.

A sweet, musical voice comes from the top of the stairs, "Don't touch the little female Seraph," she calls to the Riser below. In the darkness, I can just make out the delicate features of a lovely angel in the snowy doorway. Her hair is pulled back in a long, immaculate ponytail. I can't decipher its color because everything is shades of gray. If I were to guess, I would say she could be Seraphim; it's something in the shape of her wings, they're almost regal. The fur-fringed collar stirs against her cheek in the stormy air.

A low growl resonates from Reed as he follows my gaze up to the Fallen watching us.

"Your pets know what to do, Larken," the powerful angel next to Larken states as he crosses his arms over his chest and observes us from his stadium position above. A frown forms as his eyebrows draw together. "She does look very fragile, though...too fragile...I should go down and—"

"Hail"" Larken barks his name as she reaches out and pulls him back to her side. "She's stronger than she appears. Let Valerius subdue her first...we promised him..."

Anything else that Larken says is drowned out by the clownish-laughter coming from the Risers. They've grown into massive, powerful beasts in a matter of moments, with claws that are meant for shredding and jaws that drip saliva in anticipation of a meal. They spread out and seem to be pushing us back nearer to the hole in the ceiling at the center of the room.

Reed tenses; his muscles flex in his arms. "Please stay behind me, Evie," Reed says in a low tone, glancing at me to see my reaction.

"I promise," I nod.

Reed's wings spread wide, and for a moment, all I can see are his dark feathers as they serrate at the edges. With a leg from a chair grasped firmly in his hand, Reed leaps up and is across the room in half a second. He drives the stake downward, plunging it into a monster's neck thereby severing the nape like a matador kills a bull. The Riser in front topples to the ground. Reed breaks its paw off and uses the claws to slash the Riser on his left. Saliva spews from the creature's mouth, burning everything it touches like acid. Hackles elevate on the Riser nearest Reed; it grabs him in its powerful arms, squeezing Reed as its jaws latch onto Reed's wing.

My heart lurches into my throat. I pick up a broken bottle from the floor as Reed drives his head back into the face of the Riser, forcing the monster to unclench its teeth and free his wing. The demon continues trying to crush Reed, its laughter becoming high-pitched as Reed struggles to get free. I run at the Riser, using a chair as a springboard to propel me to them. Driving the bottle in my hand forward, I embed it in the Riser's temple, continuing on to sever its skullcap.

Immediately, Reed is released from the cage of arms as the Riser falls to the floor. Reed shoves me back as another Riser rushes forward, pouncing on him. I sprawl on the floor. As I sit up, I draw energy to me and channel it all at the Riser, letting it pulse out of my outstretched hand. The Riser absorbs the power surge from me; it only seems to grow larger as it tears at Reed.

I glance around for help, but Russell and Anya are under attack, attempting to fend off two Risers who are circling them. Russell is keeping Anya near his side, always pivoting and slashing at the Risers to keep himself between the Riser and Anya.

Looking for another weapon to use, I step back and scan the floor. Reed pulls himself from beneath the Riser, thrusting it back and then diving forward to tackle it to the ground. In my next breath, I feel swirling heat and smell the scent that has every fiber of my being on point to run. Looking up at the hole in the ceiling, one enormous, deep brown eyeball stares down at me. I shudder, unable to move.

The eyeball pulls back from the hole. "Russell," I want to scream his name, but it won't come out louder than a whisper as dread seeps through me.

Russell must've heard me, but he just grunts a response as this momentary distraction allows the Riser's claws to cut into his forearm.

"I need you," I beg, backing away from the hole on shaky legs.

"WHAT?" Russell hisses, straining to avoid the swipe at his head.

"MAGIC!" I find my voice, beginning to pull the energy in the room to me, but there isn't much because something is pulling it away from me—probably the scores of Gancanagh hanging around outside—or maybe the Ifrit himself—now that he has spotted me. Trying hard to concentrate, I close my eyes and grit my teeth. "WE NEED MAGIC!"

"IT DOESN'T WORK ON THEM! IT JUST MAKES THEM BIGGER!" Russell pants.

"IFRIT!" I yell, opening my eyes and seeing Russell stumble back, falling to the floor with the Riser on top of him. Anya pounces on its leathery back, thrusting a gold tipped arrow through it like a dagger.

The Ifrit squeezes himself through the hole in the ceiling. He's just like a human in every way but for the fact that he's currently a shrinking giant as he continues to reduce in size. "Valerius," I whisper, looking back toward the stairs and seeing Larken and Hail still watching us with avid fascination.

"You've heard of me," Valerius' cruel smile shows some of his perfectly straight teeth. "Did my brother, Valentine, mention me perhaps?" He's billboard-size now, looking like he could've just stepped off an ad in Time Square. I've seen their ability to shapeshift before, but it still makes me shiver in fear.

Ducking his head, Valerius reaches out and swipes me off my feet, crushing me in his fist like a paper doll. Reed, flying to my side, tries to pry the fingers of the Ifrit open to dislodge me from his grasp. Using his other hand, Valerius plucks Reed off his thumb, flinging him away so that Reed crashes into the wall by the bar.

Beginning to grow again, Valerius and I immediately clear the basement, breaking the plane of the first floor that is completely torn apart. The crushing pressure from the Ifrit's fist eases, probably because his hand is expanding rapidly. As he opens his fist, I rest against his palm and see that we're level with the snow-covered rooftops. Fallen angels cover the sloping roofs, watching and waiting for events to unfold. Gancanagh have blocked off the entrances to this street with military vehicles. There are no cars or humans about that I can see, maybe because there is at least three feet of snow covering everything.

The swirl of scorching breath burns the snow from the sky as Valerius snarls, "YOU ARE THE HALF-BREED WHO BARGAINED FOR VALENTINE'S DEATH."

My wing lifts up to shield my skin from the burning fire that passes from his lips. I smell the scent of my singed feathers as they smolder. "HE TORTURED MY FRIENDS!" I retort, lowering my wing a few inches to see his reaction.

"HE WAS A PRINCE!" Valerius replies in outrage. My wing again takes the brunt of the heat.

"HE WAS AN EVIL A-HOLE!" I shout, trying with no success to match his abrasive tone.

Somewhere in the distance, the high-pitched trumpeting of horns sound. In the next instant, like crows on a wire, the Fallen that have been crouching on the pitched rooftops take flight. Their wings flap in panic, scattering them in confusion. When the horns sound again it's like a signal for attention; the Fallen all hover in stasis, looking around at the skies above them with grim expressions.

Peeking from beneath my wing, I look above me at Valerius' face as he silently scans the skies above his head, too.

Thunk—the sound comes from an arrow piercing the chest of a fallen angel flying near us. Bristling, red feathers of the arrow's shaft protrude from him like a declaration of war. Then, *thunk, thunk, thunk, thunk, thunk,* several more arrows pepper his chest, causing blood to spew from his mouth while he freefalls through the air toward the ground.

Pulling my wing back from my face, I straighten just enough to feel the full impact of strong arms going around me, plucking me from the palm of the giant Ifrit with a bone-crunching jolt.

"UGHH," my breath comes out in a rush as all the wind is knocked out of my lungs.

"Sorry, love," Reed says, gritting his teeth and dodging through the arms of fallen angels who have zeroed in on us as their targets.

Missing us by centimeters, the streaming black hair of a beautiful fallen angel touches my skin. His strong hands reach out to try to pluck me from Reed's arms, but his hands fall away as another angel pounces onto his back. This blond-haired divine angel slips a dagger beneath the fallen one's throat and slits it with a grim expression while blood spatters back onto his chest from the velocity of flight.

"Who was that?" I breathe, watching the blond angel fling himself off the dead angel and onto the back of another fallen angel.

"One of Tau's army," Reed says, diving lower to avoid the broadsword that just about cut us both in half. Chaos has erupted in the air as both fallen and divine angels are flying around, engaging in a fierce battle.

Glancing behind us, I watch as Valerius shapeshifts again, growing wings from his arms that resemble a pterodactyl's while he has reduced in size to roughly fifteen feet in length.

"HE'S BEHIND US!" I shout a warning to Reed, but Valerius dives at us, striking Reed in the back with his fists and forcing us to spiral toward the ground below. Managing to gain control from the spin, Reed spreads his wings wide, gliding between buildings in a zigzag pattern as we near the snow-covered street below.

Valerius swipes at Reed's legs, causing him to lose balance. We plow into the ground, tumbling and skidding on the snow and ice. Landing softly beside me, the Ifrit hauls me to my feet by the scruff of my sweater, pulling me up to his eye level.

Reed picks up a parked car and swings it into Valerius' back. The roof of the car caves in around the Ifrit, but the monster barely notices the impact. Shrugging off the car, the Ifrit turns and breathes a stream of scorching breath at Reed, burning his chest and searing his left forearm as he brings it up to shield his face. Reed doesn't make a sound, even when I know he's in agony. Instead, he rushes the Ifrit, skewering it with a steal rod from the smashed car.

Valerius merely looks annoyed but little else. The monster ignores Reed, instead turning back to me. "Did you enjoy Valentines death?" he hisses, while holding me up a little higher with his arm extended in front of him. Reaching back with his other hand, he plucks Reed from his back, dangling Reed by his neck next to me.

"Is this your *aspire?*" he asks me of Reed, his eyebrows drawing together in a sneer. Desperately trying to pull energy to me, I feel it burn. "Answer me!" Valerius demands between gritted teeth, while shaking me roughly.

"YES!" I shout at him. "He's my *aspire!*"

Scowling at me, he growls, "Then he will be payment for Valentine."

Releasing pent-up energy, I whisper, "Ice like fire, cold and true, Freeze him quickly, through and through…"

Cracking ice streams up Valerius' forearm, stiffening him and covering him, so that in seconds, he resembles a fifteen-foot ice sculpture. Reed smashes his fists into Valerius' hand, cracking the ifrit's limb off. He drops to the ground, landing on his feet. Using his fist, Reed shatters Valerius' snowy hand that still has me suspended in air, breaking it off. When he catches me in his arms, he holds me to him in a death grip.

"You can kill Ifrits, Evie," Reed whispers in my ear, sounding like he's in awe. "That was a test. The Fallen wanted to see if you could kill it."

"You don't think the Ifrit was sent by Brennus?" I reply, feeling like I might go into shock at any second. Pulling back from me gently, Reed lets me go.

"I think Brennus is losing control. The Fallen want you, too, and he's not here to stop them. Larken and Hail, the two Fallen back at the bar, were attempting to capture you before Brennus arrives. They may also be preventing him from getting here," Reed says as he looks around, surveying the area.

He trudges through the snow to the smashed car and plucks a steel bar from it. Reed uses the bar like a bat, swinging it at the icy statue of Valerius and shattering him into a thousand pieces of ice.

"Brennus does want ye, Genevieve, and we're right: da only ting ye can trust about *aingeals* is dat dey'll turn on ye whenever it suits dem." Lonan says from near the street lamp twenty yards away. "Brennus is obsessed wi' ye. He was willing ta take dis risk ta get ye away from yer *aingeal*—ta kill him and erase him from yer heart." Turning to Reed, Lonan says, "He wants ye dead," his gaze shifts back to me, "and he wants his queen. We're ready ta see whah all da fuss is about…give us a taste of ye and we'll let ye be one of us again."

Stepping in front of me, Reed blocks me with his body from Lonan, Cavan, and Alastar. *Click, click, click,* Lonan and the fellas engage their fangs.

"Don't be a crackhead, Lonan," I plead with him as they spread out in front of us.

Reed reaches for a wrought-iron streetlamp and tears it out of the ground. Giant flashes of light and the sizzle and pop of electricity emits from the base of the lamp as the light extinguishes. He swings it effortlessly in front of us, grinning deviously at Lonan. Lonan grins back, pulling a whistle from his pocket and bringing it to his lips, he blows it loudly. Goose bumps form on my arms as Reed straightens and lowers his streetlamp. In moments, fallen Power angels and Archangels begin landing on parked cars and under shop eaves all around us.

My racing heart beats faster than the thoughts in my head as we're becoming outnumbered by more than a hundred-to-one in the space of ten seconds. Feeling my world spinning out of control, I go down on one knee, watching as a bright-white clone of myself pushes its way out of my body. Seeing it fly from me, I'm shocked by the direction it takes…it goes straight up.

Reed and I back up slowly, sheltered by the dark, closed shop front behind us. Lonan raises his hand, melting all of the snow between us. A brazen fallen Power angel with dark, falcon-like wings approaches us first. Pulling energy to me, I whisper hushed words while directing my spell at him.

As my magic hits him, he shrinks in his clothing; his shoes flop off him and his sweater becomes like a dress as he reduces in size to no taller than a garden gnome. He looks at me in panic before Reed swings the streetlamp at him, connecting with his abdomen and swatting him out of the park.

Growls of disbelief come from the Fallen who witness my magic work on an angel. I turn on them, throwing energy and whispering the "inside out" spell I'd made up myself. I hit several of them with it, causing the fallen angels to drop to their knees as they begin heaving their insides out through their mouths.

But, seconds after that, a fallen Archangel turns his automatic weapon on Reed and me, spraying the air with bullets. Blocking the projectiles from me, Reed takes several in the chest, stumbling back and falling to the ground in agony. He could've shapeshifted to avoid the bullets, but he didn't because I would've been hit. He took them for me. Panic steals my breath, seeing Reed struggle to rise to his knee.

As I look up, the Archangel aims his gun at me; his eyes squint in satisfaction when two bullets rip through my right side just below my ribs. The impact propels me backward and I expel most of the energy I was holding. With the little I now have, I manage to raise my hand and hurriedly erect a magical wall between my enemies and us, which stops the bullets like flies on a windscreen.

Gasping and holding my side, I reel backward, struggling to keep on my feet in front of Reed. Warm blood seeps between my fingers, bringing heat to their numbness.

Several Fallen advance on us immediately, but they find that they can only get within a few feet of me before they run into the wall I have created with my spell. A few fallen angels pace around us, looking for a weakness in my defenses. I growl at them, hoping to deter them.

Then, my skin prickles with quivering energy as Lonan tries to pull energy away from me in an attempt to dissolve my sanctuary. Quickly, my eyes go to his while I pant and fight for every ounce of energy to keep them all at bay.

Reed stumbles and falls beside me and then rises to his feet. His blood oozes out of his chest from the myriad of bullets he has taken for me. Seeing him struggle to stay on his feet, something within me feels like it's tearing—frayed by the sight of Reed in pain. I straighten up slowly, while this thread of pain inside of me grows more and more taut. Then, when this pain reaches an excruciating level, the thread snaps; it feels as if my heart is being torn from my chest. Without thinking, I find that I no longer need to strain for energy, it comes to me willingly. I don't whisper rhyming words, because I don't need them, they're just words, meaningless in this visceral state. Instead, I exude pure, raw, human rage.

A bright beam of light, intense enough to bleach the sky white, rolls out from my hands, creating a white-hot path straight through the Fallen and Gancanagh. It incinerates some of them so completely that all that is left behind are shadows of their corpses on the ground. Seeing ashy flakes of charred Angels billow like clouds and mix with the newly fallen snow, I sway on my feet. Before I realize what is happening, I'm the ground.

Cold drifts of snow collect near my cheek as Reed pulls my battered body toward him. Cradling my head on his lap, he strokes my hair as he leans against the door of a Polish shop. The flutter of more wings surrounds our position. I can't lift my head to see the angels. Reed growls a warning to someone approaching us, but all I see are his black boots and the bottom portion of his crimson wings.

A deep, masculine voice says, "Evie sent her messenger to me… she is my daughter."

CHAPTER 12

Dreamy Drew

My warm breath floats in swirls like smoke around me, mingling with the icy air. Drip...drip...blood falls from my fingertips to spatter the snow covering the frigid sidewalk by my feet. The Crestwood clock tower calls out a warning to me in the darkness: BONG...BONG...BONG...it intones, but it sounds more like: RUN...RUN...RUN...

Quiet voices, speaking in musical, lilting tones, interrupt the vicious death knell tolling in my dream. Waking with a lurch from the nightmare, I clutch my side, while trying to get on my feet to defend myself. A strong hand pushes me back down, forcing a growl out of me. Grasping the restraining hand, I try hard to focus my blurry vision on the faces above me.

"Get off," my lips curl in a snarl, while I push the hand away again. Unfamiliar faces of angels with searching eyes hover over me. Arching my back, I look around at the room behind me. It's a vaulting, ancient brick room decorated with medieval armor and tunics with black crosses—some sort of medieval tower.

The hand on me slowly lifts, allowing me to slip off a table and get to my feet. Stumbling back and coming up against a cold wall, I scan the rounded, medieval windows lining it. My eyes shift back to the five Powers in front of me and they narrow at the angel holding a scalpel. Killing scenarios pulse through my mind and now I just have to figure out which way I want to fight.

One of the angels speaks to me again in his musical language.

My head snaps in his direction and as my wings spread wide. I whisper, "This isn't a sing-a-long...I'm about to kill you..." Picking up a wooden chair, I smash it against the wall, before grasping splintered wood in each hand. As I adopt a defensive posture, they read it, looking at each other with uncomfortable expressions.

"Where am I? Where's Reed?" I demand, raising my hand like I'll stake the first one that moves, which I will. I inch toward the door on the far wall and see them watch with perplexed expressions.

"You are in the *Brama Mostowa*. You must lay back," one of the Powers answers, speaking in a soft tone, while gesturing toward the table again.

"Are we in Crestwood?" I ask. I have to make sure, even though the architecture still looks like Poland.

The angel frowns. "No. Torun," he states.

My eyes slip out of focus again. Reaching a hand up to rub my eyes, I notice that my palm is burned, like I touched it to fire. Disoriented, I try to remember how I got here and the nightmare I just had. The quiet voices of the angels speak to each other again in their language, causing me to stiffen.

"Whatever you have in mind...don't," I warn them, seeing they have a plan.

"You have broken ribs and you have been shot," the Power with the scalpel says, gesturing at me with the blade. "You will tear open what I have labored to mend."

Reaching down, my fingers brush over the gauzy bandages that cover my breasts and torso. Realizing I'm only wearing bandages and underwear, I growl, "I hate waking up half-naked."

This elicits a smile from one of them. Throwing one of my stakes at him, he catches it easily, but his eyebrows knit together. "Where's Reed?" I repeat in a stern tone, still brandishing the other stake.

"Fighting," the one with the scalpel replies, before setting it on the table. He flicks his wrist toward the wall behind me. Inching toward the windows again, I peer out. We're near the river, in one of the tower gates that line the city. I can just make out the medieval streets of Torun because of the snow.

My fingers curl on the window frame while snow-covered angels take off and land on the ancient fortification above. Flashes of light burst over the city, but they're obscured by the blizzard. Smelling the distant magic on the wind, my pulse beats painfully in my chest. Pushing away from the wall, I streak toward the door.

Wrenching it open, I plow into the angel on the other side. Phaedrus' arms wrap around me, clutching me to him. Feeling the downy feathers that cover the mantel of his owlish wings, my eyes open wide.

"Phaedrus! What are you..." I trail off when he pulls back from me and holds up some clothes. "I LOVE YOU!" I exclaim.

"I know," he says, his black eyes staring into mine and I remember that he can hear my thoughts. "It's good to see you," he adds in a quiet tone. He holds up his hand to the angels behind me. "I will speak to her."

Reading his face, I can tell that he's remembering the last time we were together. It was on the road outside the church where the Ifrit, Valentine, held Russell and Brownie captive. Phaedrus had to leave me there as I went into the church alone. The guilt of that moment is still there, in his expression. He's a Virtue angel, he performs miracles, but that mission was for me alone and it's still haunting him.

Putting my arms gingerly around him, I whisper in his ear, "You always appear when I need you." I let go of him and start to shrug into the clothes he has given me. "Were you sent here for me?" I ask, wondering if I'm his miracle mission again.

"Yes...of a sort," Phaedrus says. "I came with Tau."

"Tau? He's here?" I mumble, feeling a lump immediately lodge in my throat.

"He brought you in from the street, but then he went back out to fight. Reed went with him," he explains.

I panic, "But, Reed was shot—"

"It takes more than bullets to render a Power unfit to fight," Phaedrus says in a soothing tone.

"Russell and Anya?" I ask with fear building in me.

"Reed went out to search for them," he explains.

"Do you know where they are?" I ask urgently.

"No, but you do," he counters, taking my hand. I cringe in pain because it's still blistered with burns.

"Evie!" Phaedrus says, seeing my hands. "What—"

"I...think I burned them when I killed Lonan," I reply grimly. *I killed Lonan—turned him to dust—don't think about that now*, I warn myself.

With his hand on my shoulder, Phaedrus turns me down the hallway, leading me to another room. It's somebody's office with a desk and a few chairs. Phaedrus goes to a beautifully ornate rug spread out on the ancient floor and sits. Following him, I sit cross-legged, facing him stiffly because my side is aching.

"We need a controlled clone," Phaedrus advises me. "One that will follow Russell's energy to him and then be able to ask him his position so that you can send a different clone to Reed and direct him there."

"You taught Russell to do this...when I was with the Gancanagh?" I ask, trying to breathe steadily so that I can fight the adrenaline that just flashed into my system. I need to remain calm.

"I helped," Phaedrus replies in his modest way.

"Okay…so a clone," I murmur, taking another cleansing breath. "I should have practiced these more."

"Survival was more important," Phaedrus replies, "and you're weak right now so you'll need to concentrate."

Attempting to reach a meditative state, the first clone that juts from me is gone in an instant. Brushing my hair back from my face, I try again.

Another clone appears from me, bathed for a moment in a golden glow. Sweat breaks out on my forehead as I attempt to control her. I fly her through the wall of the tower gate and into the cold, softly illuminated city streets beyond. Her wings spread out as she soars, moving faster than I could in my body because there are restrictions on me: gravity, mass, force, to name a few.

As I gaze around through her eyes, it's like a lesson in quantum physics. Everything is energy and everyone and everything has its own signature and way to manipulate it, but it's all basically connected. In those terms, it's not too surprising that my clone knows exactly where Russell is on this vast tree of one-consciousness.

One-consciousness aside, my presence is agitating the Fallen. My clone is being noticed, and I've picked up a couple of trailers violently pursuing me. Slowing for a moment, I hover in one spot, letting them catch me. I don't want to lead them to Russell.

Not having the same need to flap my wings as they do, I seem to be disturbing the fallen Archangel with the streaming dark hair as a frown twists his lovely face. The Power with him swings his sword at me, hacking through the air that my image occupies.

"Give up," I say to the fallen Power, watching him continue to thrust his sword at me with the same result.

But, it is the fallen Archangel that speaks to me, "How do I surrender?" he asks.

The earnestness of his question makes my eyes snap to his face.

"Please…" he trails off, his expression tortured.

"I don't know," I reply, feeling tears prickling my eyes in response to the sadness I see in him.

"I want to go home," he admits with the kind of weariness that I know well.

"Me, too," I breathe.

When the fallen Power angel swings his sword at me again, this fallen Archangel with the sad eyes defends me. He uses his sword to hack the other's head clean off his body. A spray of blood slips through me as the dead angel's body freefalls away toward the ground in what seems like slow motion.

Howling wind and snow blow the Archangel's hair back as I stare into his eyes. I see something I've never seen in one of them before: regret. "Tell me how I'm to submit," he begs me, his face awash with pain as he searches my image for answers.

"I'm sorry, but if there is a way...I don't know it," I answer, feeling powerless to help him.

"What if I joined your army?" he asks, his brown eyes imploring mine.

"My army?" I ask. "I don't have an army."

"This is your army," he says, spreading his arms wide and indicating the chaos and carnage going on all around us.

"No," I deny it, shaking my head. "They don't follow me."

"They're here for you—both sides," he counters. "We will follow you. The Halfling—many of us will follow you."

"I prefer half-breed," I reply without thinking.

"What matters a name?" he asks tiredly. "You have power that none of us possesses. You can lead this army—all of us, not just Divine."

"But, we fight each other," I point out.

"I would follow you," he replies without a hint of subterfuge.

"Follow me where?" I ask.

"Home," he replies.

"I don't understand..." I trail off, seeing something in his eyes. Something like hope. "You want my help to get back to Paradise?" I ask.

"You would consider it?" he asks, his eyes widening.

I nod numbly, seeing a brief smile appear in the corners of his lips right before a divine Power angel pauses behind him and drives his sword through the back of this fallen angel and out the front of his chest. Blood spews from his mouth, but the smile doesn't leave his face.

"NO! DON'T!" I scream, startled as I reach out to the dying fallen angel, but my clone's hands slip right through him.

"Are you hurt?" the divine angel asks me as the fallen Archangel falls limply away from us toward the ground, dead and broken. All I can do is shake my clone's head, while turning her away. My eyesight within my clone fades as my concentration wavers.

A warm hand touches my skin as Phaedrus says, "Stay focused, Evie. You have to find Russell. He needs you."

I take a deep breath, keeping my own eyes closed as I try to calm my racing heart. In moments, I'm fully conscious again within my clone. I reach out and feel a pull toward the center of the city. Streaking as fast as I can towards that pull of energy, my clone enters a clock tower through the black clock face covered with a gold, twelve-pointed star.

I locate Russell and Anya on the interior stairway of the clock tower, fighting back to back as Fallen pour at them from all angles.

"I found them," I breathe to Phaedrus next to me.

"Good, where are they?" he asks.

"Clock tower—black face, golden star on it," I describe.

"The Town Hall," Phaedrus says quickly. "You need to create another clone and send it to Reed with this information."

"That's possible?" I ask. "Sssheeesh—" I hiss, seeing Anya receive a slash to her thigh.

I direct my clone to hop up on the railing of the staircase above Russell and Anya. Waving my clone's hands in the air to get the attention of the Fallen, I yell, "HEY! EVIL FREAKS!"

The instant the Fallen surrounding Anya see me, I dive off the edge of the railing and plummet through the open air surrounding the winding staircase. Mock falling toward the ground like a wounded bird, they all abandon Russell and Anya to pursue me.

"You're alive," Russell's clone says, falling next to mine an instant later.

"I'm at the *Brama Mostowa*—it's the medieval tower near the river," I reply, grinning at him in relief.

"Oh, the Bridge Gate," he translates for me, probably remembering it from 600 years ago. "Nice, huh?" he asks as he touches down on the Town Hall's marble-tiled floor by my side.

"Nice? Not so much. It's more like a medieval prison meets corporate office building, but it does have one perk: no Fallen," I reply.

"Sounds fine by me. Now we just need help gettin' there," he says with a frown. "It's thick with the smell of rotten Fallen outside and I've got Anya. I need to go back up to her." He points to where he'd left his body and Anya. "I think she's hurt."

The Fallen begin hacking at our clones with their weapons, but we ignore them.

"I'll tell Reed where you are—maybe he can help," I say quickly.

"Okay," Russell agrees as his clone dematerializes, causing the Fallen surrounding me to growl in frustration.

"Phaedrus, I need to stay in this clone so the Fallen don't go back up and try to get Russell—" I begin.

"Shatter," Phaedrus advises me softly, like a voice inside my head.

"What?" I ask in confusion.

"I want you to shatter as if you were a broken piece of glass. Send Reed a fragment of the clone you are in now," he explains. "It will be a soft whisper of you, but enough for him to feel—to hear, smell, follow—"

"A piece of me," I murmur, feeling stumped and wishing I were more like Russell—more of a doer than a thinker. "Shatter..." I breathe. Nothing happens. "Break..."

"Reed could be in trouble. You should get him here as fast as you can," Phaedrus' voice says in my head.

Instantly I feel brittle. Cracks begin crawling slowly up my arms as light from within me shines out through them. The Fallen who have been surrounding me step back, distancing themselves from what they don't understand. A piece of me, from where my heart resides, breaks out of my clone. Glowing golden, a soft orb floats briefly in front of the fallen angels before shooting through the side of the brown brick wall.

As the Fallen continue to circle me, I attempt to ignore their trash talking because some of the stuff they want to do to me and my soul is really terrifying. Feeling Phaedrus reach out and take my hand, I understand that he can hear what the Fallen are saying as he listens to the thoughts in my mind. And then, as if by magic, they all stop speaking while two of them lay prone in pieces on the floor. Reed, covered in carnage stands before me, staring into my clone's eyes as several divine angels cut down the rest of the Fallen angels surrounding us.

"What are you doing here, love?" Reed asks.

Pointing up, I say, "Russell and Anya are up there."

A smile pulls at the corners of his mouth while he calls out, "Russell?"

"Yeah! You got my back now?" Russell asks in a sour tone, looking over the railing from the tower above. "'Cuz one of them freaky demon things almost ate me after y'all left!"

"A Riser nearly ate you?" Reed asks with humor in his tone.

"Yeah, whatever—it's not funny!" he calls down, sounding irritated. "Next time, I want Zee for my wingman."

"That is because I am the ultimate assassin," Zephyr replies from behind Reed.

Russell flies down from the tower above with Anya in his arms. "Zee!" Russell says, grinning.

"Russell," Zephyr replies, and his tone is a little tight as he rests his hand on Russell's shoulder. "The last time I saw you, you were being eaten by Gancanagh."

"Apparently, I'm delicious," Russell says with a cheeky grin as Zephyr drops his hand. "Is Buns here, too?" he asks Zephyr.

"Nearby. She is not fighting," Zephyr answers with a frown, "at least, she better not be. She was told to stay in the tower gate."

"Did she go postal?" Russell grins at him, "You know, for pullin' her portal on the island and sendin' her to your safe house before the fight?"

"Define postal?" Zephyr counters, his brows pulling together further.

"Insanely angry," Russell says.

"Yes," Zephyr nods his head adamantly, pointing at him. "She has not called me 'sweetie' since."

"Oooo," Russell says, ducking his head and wrinkling his nose. "Doghouse."

"Yes," Zephyr agrees blandly. "We must discuss how I am to get out of it. But, who is this?" Zephyr asks, indicating Anya.

"Long story," Russell mutters, pulling Anya closer to him.

"My favorite kind," Zephyr replies, his assassin's eyes almost twinkling.

"I need to get her somewhere safe and warm, she's freezin'. You think you can help me out with that?" Russell asks, looking a little cold himself.

"We'll take you to the Bridge Gate," Zephyr replies. "Maybe she can give Buns a project—"

"Any sign of Brennus?" I interrupt them, holding my breath.

"He either never made it here, or he left soon after the battle began because we haven't seen him. Nor have we seen any of the Gancanagh since you took care of the ones in the street," Reed replies, gauging my reaction. I don't know how I feel about it, so maybe he can tell me later.

The huge, arching doors that open to the street swing in, emitting a legion of divine angels. Attired from head to foot in white armor, spattered in blood, the leader in the front stands out from the rest not only for his extremely long set of crimson wings, but also for his short, auburn hair that is the exact same color as mine. Knowing that this incredibly confident angel striding toward me is my father, I become mute as I stare at him.

Sparing only a glance around, he speaks to Reed, "I see you have located Russell and Anya," Tau says in a direct way, nodding towards Russell.

"Evie found them, we just secured the area," Reed replies, just as directly.

Tau pauses before turning his face to look at me for the first time. Recognition creeps over me as my jaw falls open. He has gray eyes, too, almost like mine, but mine are darker…and his face hasn't changed…it's still like an angel's, beautiful and perfect in every way…just like I remember it…

"Drew…Dreamy Drew is my father…" I whisper, before my clone dissolves into the air and I open my eyes to look at Phaedrus by my side.

"AHH," I breathe out, feeling really, really confused. Getting up from the floor, my hands in fists, I pace around the small, medieval office of the Bridge Gate.

Holding his head, Phaedrus says, "Can you slow down, I can't keep up with all those pictures in your mind."

"Then get out of my head," I retort in anger, putting my hand to my forehead.

"Tau was the high school Homecoming King?" Phaedrus asks, a small smile forming on his lips, like he can't help himself. He's probably reliving that cool, September night with me in my mind, watching the halftime celebration on the football field as Drew, I mean Tau, was crowned king while standing next to Stacy Hingus.

"He was everything. He was class president, captain of the cross-country team, and captain of the soccer team—debate. He sat right behind me in calculus. I TOLD MOLLY THAT HE LOOKED LIKE AN ADULT IN THE NINTH GRADE!" I yell, gesturing wildly while freaking out. "NOBODY LOOKS LIKE HIM AT FOURTEEN! THAT'S WHY EVERYONE CALLED HIM 'DREAMY DREW' BECAUSE HE WAS–IS–INCREDIBLY HOT."

"Technically, he's much older than an adult," Phaedrus replies in a rational tone.

"You think?" I retort sarcastically.

"So, you've known him for a while," Phaedrus says, prompting me.

"NO! Not really—since freshman year of high school. He was always mean to me," I reply in a small voice, completely pissed off when tears come to my eyes. I try to stuff them back down.

"He was mean to you?" Phaedrus asks, frowning.

"Yeah, I'd say 'hi' to him because he sat by me in a lot of my classes…every class and he'd just ignore me, like I was a total loser. And then…I'm pretty sure he spread some stupid rumors about me," I say in a scathing tone.

"Rumors?" Phaedrus asks.

"Not important," I reply, my face flushing.

"Cheesy?" he asks me, reading my thoughts. My head tilts back as I look at the ceiling in frustration.

"He told everyone I smell...like cheese, so for a while, kids called me 'cheesy' in the halls instead of Evie," I explain, feeling humiliated all over again.

"You don't smell like cheese—far from it," Phaedrus says, looking confused.

"THANK YOU!" I answer, while feeling a little vindicated. "I didn't then either, but once you get a label, forget it, you're done."

"Done?" he asks.

"It's like a stigma. Who wants to date 'cheesy?'" I question.

"But, it has to wear off?" he asks.

"Oh, there was more, trust me," I say, wringing my hands. "I have to get out of here."

"What? Why?" he asks, his eyes widening.

"Because all of my illusions are gone, Phaedrus," I reply, trying to explain the unexplainable. "He's this...and I'm just...and he hates me."

"Why would he hate you?" Phaedrus asks in a reasonable tone.

"I don't know, Phaedrus, but I'll take a stab at it," I retort. "Maybe, if you're Tau and you're used to being in God's inner circle and you enjoy killing rotten, stinky fallen angels and going on dangerous missions to Sheol to parley with evil a-holes, you could see hanging out with me in some small-town high school a little beneath you."

"But, you are his daughter," Phaedrus says with a reverence that makes me wish that *he* was my father for a moment.

"And what makes you sure he wanted to *be* my father?" I ask.

"You are here," Phaedrus replies.

"Yes, but do you really ever say 'no thanks' when God asks you to do something?" I counter.

"Hmm," Phaedrus responds, reluctant to see my point.

"Yeah," I say with a derisive laugh, knowing that I have one.

"You just defined his role, what he does, not who he is. You want to leave before you give him a chance to explain: to talk to you on a level that he was probably never allowed before now?" he inquires.

Putting both my hands over my face, I exhale in frustration, "Ughh. Okay, you have a point. But, to use Russell's words this is 'awkward as ass.'"

"Your forte," Phaedrus replies.

"My plate is a little full of awkward right now, Phaedrus," I reply.

"You can handle it," he says with reassurance, and I narrow my eyes at him.

"Is this your mission?" I ask, seeing him smile.

"Virtue angels get to do many things—" he begins.

Holding up my hand I say, "Got it. We'll need a miracle to understand each other."

"Perhaps," he smiles.

"Whatever," I frown back. "Do you hear that?" I ask, going to the window and looking out. Swarms of divine angels are landing all around the ancient walls of the tower. They look like they're celebrating victory as they boisterously greet each other.

Frowning, he moves to the window and looks out at the crowd. He smiles, saying, "The battle must be over."

"That means we won, right?" I ask him, looking to be reassured.

He nods. "That means we won this battle."

"Where will we be going now?" I ask.

"Good question. Maybe you can ask your dad," he replies innocently.

"Sure, and maybe he'll give me the keys to the car and a little money for the movies once we get there," I counter.

"There's the spirit," he replies.

"Should I thank him?" I ask in a soft tone. Seeing Phaedrus' brow rise in question, I add, "For saving me today."

"That would be nice. Gratitude is a good ice breaker," he replies as we both stare out the window at the angels reveling in victory.

"Now, I'll just have to try to find some," I say quietly.

"About the other thing…I do not think it is a topic you will want to lead with," Phaedrus says, not taking his black eyes from the scene outside the window.

"Hmm?" I ask, pretending ignorance.

"I was listening when the fallen one asked you to help him," he replies. "I felt your regret at his demise."

"You think Tau will be resistant to finding out if there can ever be absolution for the Fallen," I ask, my heart beating harder.

"He knows there is not," Phaedrus responds.

"Yes, well, there's never been an angel with a soul before either," I reply.

"Hmm," he murmurs. "Heresy from the heretic. You are brave, aren't you?" he asks in a teasing way.

Before I can answer him, there is a nasty reverb from the P.A. system in the phones. Then, "ATTENTION ALL SWEETIES! THIS IS BUNS SPEAKING! WE HAVE DANCING ON THE PARAPETS AND A RAGING PARTY NEAR THE RIVER. BRING YOUR PARKAS!

EVIE, GET YOUR ASS TO THE ROOF FOR AN INSANE REUNION! THAT IS ALL!"

"I love her," I murmur.

"Yes," Phaedrus agrees. "There is something reverent in her irreverence."

"Exactly," I say with a smile. "Shall we go see her?" I ask.

"After you," he says.

CHAPTER 13

Rebellion

I follow Phaedrus up the ancient staircase of the Bridge Gate to the roof. Every angel I pass steps aside for me. It makes me feel like I'm back with the Gancanagh where I'm the queen and they have to defer to me. Exiting an exterior door, I'm blasted by the cold, snowy air. I spot Buns and Brownie amid several Powers all hanging on the Reaper's every word. Buns is wearing a long, gray coat with a matching military-style hat—the kind with the ear flaps. Funky music that I've never heard before is playing from an ancient sound system someone dragged out here.

When Buns sees me, she calls out, "Sweetie!" Breaking away from the crowd, she throws her arms around me, hugging me tight.

"Nice bonnet," I say, smiling as Brownie hugs me, too.

"Don't let the Russians hear you call it that. It's an ushanka! I brought one for you from St. Petersburg," she says, grinning at me and putting the hat on my head. She drapes a matching, long coat around me, too.

"Russia? Is that where you went?" I ask, grateful for the warmth.

"Da, comrade. That was Zee's idea," she says, rolling her eyes. "He wanted us to try out the spas, but he's in BIG trouble with me, so I think he was relieved that this whole epic battle surfaced." She waves her hand like he lucked out or something.

"Timely," I agree. "So, nice party."

"It's retro, right?" she asks me, looking around at the medieval walls of the city. "Straight out of the Dark Ages. I love it!"

"It's straight out of something," I reply, smiling as she hands me a pierogi wrapped in paper.

"I wanted to do fireworks, but we're trying to keep it quiet, so we thought less is more—like you've been teaching us—minivans not Ferraris," she says.

"I think that any secret you had is out in Torun. After the night of fighting, I doubt if any of the humans will be in the dark about the existence of angels," I reply, before taking a bite of the pierogi she gave me.

"It's all taken care of," Buns says nonchalantly. "Everything within the city is probably back to normal by now."

"What?" I ask. "The whole town is a mess. Dead angels every-where, trashed buildings, bullet holes, mortar in the streets…blood… smashed cars…" I trail off, watching her shaking her head.

"They sent in the Cherubim," she says with an easy smile.

"I thought those angels keep track of sins," I counter, watching her smile grow bigger.

"Some do and some, well, some clean up the sinners. I'll bet the Virtues are helping, too," she adds. I glance at Phaedrus who nods his head.

"The tavern we were in was destroyed—" I start to say, but I stop as she shakes her head no. "Reed's house—" she continues to shake her head.

"They probably look the same now as they did the moment before you arrived here," she replies.

"How?" I wonder aloud.

"Divine design," she replies.

Frustrated by her explanation, I turn to Brownie. "How did you get here?" I ask.

"I hitched a ride with Preben," Brownie says, pointing her thumb at the tall, silver-haired Power I remember from Dominion's chateau. He once helped me when I was on trial there for my life.

"Preben!" I exclaim. His tall frame is covered by white, protective armor, but his light-brown wings are unadorned.

"Are you responsible for this?" he asks with mock sternness.

"Uh, that all depends," I reply.

"Does it? On what?" he asks with a look of intrigue.

"Have my rights changed at all?" I ask. I cross my arms, remem-bering that when I was at Dominion he had told me that the only right I had was to "pray for death."

"Considerably changed—we touch you and Tau will have our wings," he says.

"And your heads," Brownie adds, reaching out and patting his cheek lightly.

"Heads will roll!" Buns chimes in with glee. The Powers standing around her all seem amused rather than offended by her.

Seeing the way that Preben is looking at Brownie, like she's edible, I straighten up, glancing at Buns. Buns's eyebrow rises as she nods her head to my question.

"Brownie, how did you happen to find Preben?" I ask while Brownie's fingertips gently lift from Preben's cheek.

"Uh, hmm, well, he kinda found my safe house," she says, her face turning red.

"He did?" I ask, while she plays with the ends of her platinum-blond hair.

"She mentioned something to me once, when we were in China together—after the Gancanagh had taken you. She said she wanted to find you and then she wanted to rest for a while. She said she had a little place in Austria, in the Alps…" he trails off, when Brownie smiles.

"So, you looked for it?" I ask. "I'm surprised you didn't follow Reed here when he came through his portal after Brownie."

"I was distracted at that moment," Preben says, a small smile on his lips as Brownie's blush deepens. "I wasn't expecting him to be there. After Reed freed you from Brennus' lair in Ireland, we had lost contact with all of you," he replies ruefully, his light gray eyes falling on me.

"We went to the island," I mutter, knowing he was purposefully not told our location.

"Yes, I know," he replies. "You wanted to protect Russell from us—from Dominion."

"He has an *aspire* now, a Throne, so you can't have him," I respond quickly, making sure that Preben knows that Russell will never be their pawn.

"WHAT!" Both Brownie and Buns ask in unison.

Preben's brow rises in surprise as he says, "I did not see that coming."

"Get in line!" Buns and Brownie say together, their eyes wide.

"*Aspire* aside, it is no longer up to us—what happens to him or to you," he says.

"Is Dominion backing down?" I ask, relieved that we won't have to scuffle over Russell.

"We are outranked," he replies. "The Seraphim have arrived."

"Ah," I say, my face filling with heat. "There's a new sheriff in town."

"There is indeed," he says, his eyes lifting from me to the space behind me.

Feeling cold wind, goose bumps rise on my arms as all the angels stand up just a little straighter. Buns leans toward my ear, saying teasingly, "Sweetie, your dad is smokin' hot!"

"Shut up, Buns," I mutter, and her eyes dance with laughter at my comment.

"Who's that with him? Do you know them, sweetie?" she asks, forcing me to glance behind me at the Seraphim who just landed amid the Powers on the parapet. Tau, standing a few yards away, is staring at me. He hasn't changed since the battle; blood is crisscrossing his white, full-body armor.

My eyes glide over the dark-haired angel standing next to Tau. I'm surprised to find that I do recognize him. He also attended my high school. "That one is Tau's best friend, Cole Martin. They did everything together in school." My eyes shift from Cole to the other Seraphim next to Cole and I forget to breathe. My face flushes hot as I stare into Xavier Reece's eyes.

Xavier is tall and as built as Tau with golden-blond hair, but it's his eyes that are shocking; one iris is blue and the other is green. Mr. Freidmen, our high school biology teacher, told us in class that it's a genetic anomaly called heterochromia iridium that causes one iris to have a different amount of melanin in it, making it a different color. Kenny called Xavier a genetic sideshow freak and told us he once saw a dog with two different colored eyes, too…Kenny transferred to a private school after that.

"What's wrong, sweetie? Do you know that one, too," Buns whispers to me, watching my visceral reaction to Xavier.

I stiffen. "Uhh…Xavier Reece," I murmur.

Buns looks from me to Xavier and then back to me again. "Was he your boyfriend or something?" she asks.

"Or something," I manage to say.

"Ex-boyfriend?" she guesses again.

"That's more like it," I mutter.

"How ex are we talking?" she asks.

"The kind where you have to take everything that he ever gave you and bury it in the backyard so there will be nothing to remind you of how much you loved him," I murmur, feeling almost as bad as I did on the night when I had dug that hole.

"Cheesy Claremont, how you've grown," Cole Martin says as his wings retract behind him in a sedate, regal way. The snow still clings to his black hair that is a little longer than he wore it in high school.

Taking a deep breath, I turn around to face them. "Cold Misery, you're looking fresh. Is that brain matter in your hair?" I ask him, seeing his hazel eyes soften in the corners in humor. I lean casually against an ancient stone wall behind me, crossing my legs negligently. Buns's brows pull together as she looks at them in confusion.

"I always loved that nickname," Cole replies, a smile touching his seductive lips. "Did you come up with it?"

"Yes, but I can't take all the credit—you earned it all on your own," I reply, crossing my arms in front of me while trying to keep my features blank.

"We had to be tough on you," he says, coming to stand by my side. "We had to prepare you for the challenges you faced—thicken your skin. I bet it's easier to take being called 'half-breed' after surviving high school as 'cheesy.'"

"Was that your reasoning?" I ask Cole in a bored tone.

"We also had to keep the hormonal humans away," Xavier adds.

"Bravo then. Mission accomplished," I reply with no emotion.

"Not really," Xavier replies. "We had to get creative with a few of the males in school, right, Tau?" he asks rhetorically. Tau nods. Xavier continues, "Greg Landon wanted to do more than watch the movie... but he was more of a lover than a fighter."

"Why would you care who I dated? You were the one who decided that we weren't right for each other," I say to Xavier. "Wait...was that an act? Were you just pretending to like me?" My heart constricts with betrayal. "Were you just there to spy on me?" I ask Xavier, not letting my voice change or show irritation. I can't let them get to me.

"I was protecting you," he states.

"By lying to me," I counter.

"I wasn't allowed to tell you anything," he frowns.

"You're an angel," I accuse him as he comes to stand next to me.

"So are you," he replies with a small smile.

"No. I'm not," I say without emotion. "You should've told me."

"You've adapted well since we last saw you," Cole says, flanking my other side and taking in all of my attributes. "Look at her lack of emotion, Xavier," he adds, like he's proud of my demeanor. "Who taught you to act like a Seraph?"

"A fallen angel named Casimir," I reply, watching the smile instantly leave Cole's face. They probably knew Casimir. He was Seraphim like them and may have even been their friend before the Fall. "He tried to take me to Sheol when I was with the Gancanagh."

"When you were Brennus' queen," Tau states, his mouth turning down in disdain. "We have been apprised of that incident." Approaching me, Tau's features become more unreadable than mine. "Reed killed Casimir, is that correct?" he asks.

"Yes, my *aspire*," I say and Xavier growls at my words, causing my eyes to narrow at him.

"Why do you have an *aspire*?" he asks, sounding angry.

"Why do you care?" I counter, frowning at him like he's boring me.

"I care for many, many reasons," Xavier replies, leaning nearer to me and invading my personal space.

I pretend to ignore him, but my wings react anyway. My coat falls off me as my wings spread out, pushing him back. Speaking in Angel, Xavier reaches out to gently stroke my wing. I straighten, feeling confused.

Turning to Buns, her mouth is falling open a little. "What did he just say?" I ask.

"He thinks your wings are adorable," she says before a smile spreads over her face. Then, she whispers, "I think he *likes* you."

Meeting Xavier's mismatched eyes, I frown. "No, he doesn't and he never really did," I reply, inching closer to Buns. "Well, thanks for coming today…Tau. I appreciate the help—killing the Fallen—good job. I guess I'll see you all at the ten-year class reunion. Keep in touch."

Standing up straighter, I hitch my arm in Buns's and try to move past them. They instantly create a wall in front of me so that we can't get to the door that leads down the tower.

Phaedrus says something to Tau in Angel.

"What did Phaedrus say?" I ask Buns.

She's just as startled as I am, probably because she's not used to coming up against Seraphim. "Basically, he just told them to relax—not to push you. He told them that they're being too aggressive," she whispers.

Tau replies to Phaedrus and I look to Buns to translate.

"Sweetie, uh…he wants to know how to tell you that he's assuming the protection of you without appearing too aggressive."

My eyes narrow. "How do you say 'get stuffed' in Angel, Buns?" I counter, before seeing Phaedrus cringe.

"You don't," Tau warns in a soft tone, his wings spreading out, making him look huge and frankly, terrifying.

Letting go of Buns, my wings spread out, too, mimicking Tau's aggressive posture.

While Tau frowns at me, Xavier grins saying, "Evie, you can't do that. I've been waiting for you to grow up. I have so much to teach you."

"Not interested," I reply.

Xavier's grin is gone, replaced by a frown. "Get interested," he says in a stern tone.

"Why? I already have mentors and protectors," I reply.

Xavier's eyebrow rises cunningly over his blue eye. "And you didn't need us at all today?" he asks calmly.

"Thanks for the hand today, but where were you when everything was falling apart? Where was he when this all started?" I ask, flicking my hand towards Tau. "When I began evolving into a TOTAL FREAK? You were nowhere—you're a little late and you're unreliable," I say as Xavier's eyelids hood over his mismatched eyes.

"We were called back!" Xavier responds in a harsh tone. "None of us wanted to leave you—and you're not a freak!"

"Easy, Xavier," Tau says as I struggle to keep the cool mask in place, but it's slipping and I'm trying not to cry.

A breeze touches my face and then Reed is next to me, taking me in his arms and holding me close to him. "We won, love," he breathes softly in my ear. "Now take a deep breath and we'll handle this together." He kisses me, causing crazy things to happen in my stomach and my knees to feel weak.

Xavier growls behind us. Reed grins, his green eyes showing humor. "Another admirer, love?" he asks me in a sexy, teasing tone. "You're really going to have to start telling them about me."

"Why tell them when I can show them?" I ask. My arms snake behind his neck and I brush my lips lightly over his, while pressing my body to him.

Hearing another low growl from Xavier, I break off our kiss, glancing at him. His crimson wings are stretched wide, and Tau has his hand on Xavier's arm, holding him firmly.

Reed gently nudges me back from him, before spreading his charcoal-colored wings wide and growling back at Xavier. Reed looks fierce with his brows drawn together and his jaw clenching. They look like they're about to pounce on each other, causing fear to creep up my spine.

Phaedrus steps between us all, facing Tau. He speaks rapidly to the Seraphim, looking like he's reasoning with them.

Then, Tau speaks to Xavier; his voice, although musical, has an authoritative tone to it that even I can recognize. Xavier, still frowning, slowly retracts his wings while his jaw tenses even more.

Next, Tau speaks to Reed in the same tone. Reed's charcoal-colored wings retract slowly, too, and come to rest elegantly behind him.

To me, Tau says, "I'm going to give my orders to the Powers. We will leave within the hour." He turns and strides toward the door to the tower with Cole next to him. Xavier stares at me for a moment before he reluctantly follows Tau into the Bridge Gate.

"Take Tau's number off speed-dial, Reed," I mutter.

"Listen, love...Tau is used to being in command. He has your best interest at heart, I'm certain, and I think you should give him a chance," Reed says, taking my hand. "We should consider going with him."

"Where is he going?" I ask, squeezing his hand tight in mine.

"There's a ship in the Baltic Sea waiting for us," he explains, looking up at the sky.

"Are Cole and Xavier coming, too?" I ask, hoping for a negative answer. I have too much history with Xavier. He had had a starring role in every daydream I had in high school...and then he broke my heart.

"It's their boat," he replies, watching my eyes close briefly.

"How are we getting there?" I ask.

"We're going to fly," he says, not looking happy about it.

"You mean...with our wings?" I ask with a sinking feeling. Reed nods. Half in denial about what's happening, I ask, "Where's the boat going to take us?"

"We can discuss that when we get there," Reed replies, his voice silky before he caresses his lips against mine. Somehow I know he's stalling me on the location.

"That bad, huh?" I ask, feeling uneasy. "We can't leave without Russell. Is he here?" Fear is threading through me.

"He's right behind me. We had to stop and get medical attention," Zephyr answers next to Buns. She turns and hugs him to her, letting her hands rove over him to make sure he's not hurt. "I caught the last part. Xavier will be an interesting challenge," he says, looking at Reed significantly.

"I look forward to it," Reed replies easily.

My eyes fall on Russell, seeing how exhausted he is. "Are you okay, Russell?" I ask. He's holding Anya's hand and they both have been bandaged in a few places.

"Yeah, I could use some food—a bed—ESPN," he replies with weariness in his tone.

"The army is pulling out to a new position," Reed says, watching Russell's reaction. "We're flying—with wings."

"Y'all are evil," Russell states tiredly.

Zephyr seems to agree with Russell. "How long do we allow this to go on?" Zephyr asks Reed in a serious tone. "The Seraphim believe that they are in charge of Evie."

"We need answers and they have them," Reed replies, "and Tau is Evie's father, so we attempt to compromise—"

Zephyr cuts in, "They are Seraphim, no offense Evie, but Seraphim are not known for their ability to compromise."

"None taken. I'm only half Seraphim," I reply, shrugging.

"They have information that Evie needs. I'm willing to cooperate to see some of those questions answered. Are we all in agreement that we play along for now?" Reed asks all of us, like we all have equal say.

"I'm in, sweetie," Buns says, smiling at me. "I like boats."

"Me, too," Brownie chimes in immediately, letting her copper butterfly wings spread out of her back. Preben's eyes follow their delicate lines.

"You will need me, so I will come," Zephyr says with the hubris that accompanies a few billion years of life experience.

My eyes drift to Russell's and he says, "It goes without sayin' that I'm goin' wherever you are, Red." I nod, expecting nothing less from him.

Everyone's eyes in our group fall on Anya. Reed speaks to her in Angel and she looks from Russell to me. Straightening her shoulders, she nods her assent.

My eyes drift to Phaedrus and he smiles, saying, "Oh, I have to go...I've been sent to aid Tau."

"You're on his side?" I ask him, feeling irritated.

"Perhaps he's the one praying for a miracle," Phaedrus murmurs.

"Are you sure you've never been a parent, Phaedrus?" I ask. "Because you've got that guilt thing down."

"It's a gift," he replies.

Around us, angels are lifting off into the air, having been given their orders to move out. "Okay, but if Tau turns out to be a stalker, we're gonna have words," I warn Phaedrus in a grave tone, knowing I'm in for trouble...aggravating, messy trouble.

❧

After flying for hours through what feels like a snowpocalypse, we land among the multitude of angels on the deck of one of the coolest ships I've ever seen. Militaristic and sleek, it is like a floating city with military grade aircraft on the vast deck. The sun is just beginning to rise over the aft of the ship, as a Power angel on board leads me to a room.

Pausing at the threshold, I say, "Uh, this is a single room." A single, berth-style bed, a small closet, and a tiny shower are the only appointments in the small space.

"This is the room I was told to give you," the angel replies.

Narrowing my eyes at him, I ask, "Who instructed you to give me this room?"

"Xavier," the angel offers the name freely.

"He's on my last nerve," I mutter, before stumbling into my room, feeling as stiff as a Popsicle. Reed follows me, and it's annoying that he doesn't even seem fatigued.

"Xavier was teasing you about your flying so that you'd get angry and try harder," Reed says, watching me step into the bathroom and turn on the shower.

Walking to him, I put my finger to his lips, saying, "Shhh, let's not talk about Xavier...in fact, let's not talk..." Dragging Reed into the small shower with me, we don't talk for a long, long time.

Reed leads me from the shower to the single bed. Wrapped in a towel with my head pillowed on Reed's chest, we fall asleep in each other's arms on the bed—grateful just to be together.

෴

Genevieve... Genevieve... come ta me, mo chroí... it will be ye dat wears me crown... forever from harm... ye belong ta me...

"EVIE!" Reed shakes me hard, and my eyes open to the glare of bright sunlight. Standing outside on the deck of the ship in my towel, I'm dizzy and disoriented. Reed, in a towel too, lifts me off my feet and carries me past gawking Powers as the breeze lifts my hair like a windsock.

"Ye will be returned ta me," I whisper as the warmth of Reed's body penetrates the thin layer of icy frost covering me.

Someone drapes a blanket around my shoulders as we enter a dim hallway. Several Powers usher us into a posh room as one tells Reed that Tau wants to see us. My eyes rest on a set of glass doors that lead to a balcony overlooking the sea. Reed sits down on a leather chair, settling me on his lap. He strokes my hair as I slowly become aware that I'm numb from cold. Trembling in his arms, he whispers words in Angel in my ear.

Lifting my head off Reed's chest with my teeth chattering, I become lucid enough to realize I'm not in our bed. Glancing around, it's plain that we're no longer in steerage, but in one of the presidential suites of the ship. It's masculine in its appointments with dark, wood floors and shelves—more like a den than what I'd expect to see on a ship.

Seeing Tau watching me from an elegant chair across from the one we're in, I look away, resting my cheek back against Reed's bare chest again.

"Does she do that often?" Tau asks Reed in a soft tone.

"I've never known her to walk away in her sleep," Reed replies, sounding concerned.

I feel muddled—my mind is foggy and it's hard to focus. "Dddid I jjjust…wwwalk outside in mmmy ttttowel?" I ask Reed in a small voice, my teeth chattering.

Rubbing my arms, Reed says lightly, "Yes, but don't worry, I think the crew enjoyed it."

"Where were you going?" Tau asks me.

"I dddon't kkknow," I reply, embarrassment creeping over me.

"Would you like something warm—coffee? Tea?" Tau offers, his gray eyes scanning my face.

"Cccofffeee," I reply, gritting my teeth, while pulling the blanket tighter to me.

Handing me a cup of coffee, I wrap my cold fingers around it. Someone pounds on the door of the cabin then, making me stiffen.

"Enter," Tau barks, not taking his eyes off of me.

"Red!" Russell says, bursting through the door. "You okay?" he asks, looking worried when he sees me on Reed's lap.

I nod with my teeth still chattering.

"I came lookin' for you when I felt their energy. I can smell the magic…it's thick—your room is foggy with it," he says, sitting down in the chair next to us. "Ah shoot, he's playin' with you, isn't he?" Russell asks.

"Wwhenn have yyyou known mmmee to wwalkk around nnnakked on the ddeeckkk of a ssship?" I ask him.

"Now, that's been awhile," he grins teasingly. "At least a few centuries."

"Was it Brennus?" Reed asks, his arms tightening.

"Uh huh," I nod.

"Was it a spell?" Russell asks.

"It didn't ffffeel like his other sssspells," I admit, after sipping my coffee. "It was like he wwwas inside my head—and exerting energy ffffrom without."

"Thrall," Tau says, "and magic, too. You were bitten recently?" he asks me.

"Yes," I answer, glancing at Tau.

"And you were bitten before—months ago?" Tau asks.

"Yes," I respond.

"More venom makes their thrall stronger—maybe it's beginning to work on you. But they still had to use magic, too. You're covered in frost," Tau says. He gestures to my skin that is just now losing the twinge of blue. "What did Brennus tell you to do?" he asks.

"He tttold me to come to hhhim," I reply in a small voice.

"You know where he is?" Tau asks.

"No," I say hesitantly.

"No…but?" he prompts me.

"No, nothing," I reply, not looking in his eyes.

Tau says nothing; he just watches me drink my coffee. I glance at Russell. He's aware that I have the means of locating Brennus—we both do. I begin to get warmer and my teeth stop chattering.

"I look forward to meeting him," Tau says.

"Do you know where he is?" I ask as confusing emotions erupt in me, fear the most dominant among them.

"Not at the moment, but I don't need to because he will come to me," he replies, before sipping his coffee.

"Why would he do that?" I counter.

"Because I'm going to make it so that he has no other option," he replies easily.

"How?" I ask.

"I will begin by insulting him," Tau says. "When I make him appear ridiculous, he will have to retaliate or risk losing his stature among his peers."

"How will you insult him?" I ask, my brows pulling together.

"I intend to move into his home, assume his throne…with his queen," he replies.

My stomach clenches in fear as my mouth goes dry. "We're going back to Ireland?" I ask in a raspy tone.

"Yes," he replies easily, like we're discussing the homework assignment for English class.

"You should be careful. Brennus is very clever and…determined," I say, meeting his eyes again.

Tau pauses, his gray eyes showing amusement. "Are you afraid for me?" he asks, his head tilting to the side as he assesses my demeanor.

I shake my head slowly. "No, I'm afraid for me," I reply angrily. "I've lived with them and it was a struggle for survival from one day to the next and you want to take me back there."

"You don't trust that I can protect you," he states, his brows pulling together in a frown.

"I don't trust you. Period," I shoot back.

"Yes, I can see that," Tau agrees. "You don't need to trust me. You just need to obey me."

My eyebrows rise in surprise. "Obey you?" I ask incredulously. "I don't even know you."

"If you don't respect that I am your father, then respect my rank," he says in a calm tone, his face a mask of tranquility. "I am the authority here."

Glancing at Russell, he's frowning at Tau, too. "Are you hearing this, Russ?" I ask him.

"Yeah, I'm hearin' it," he replies. "I'm just tryin' to understand it. I mean, I'm down for the whole insultin' Brennus part—I just got a problem with draggin' you back to the creepy castle. You want your daughter to be bait?" he asks Tau with agitation in his tone.

"I want what you want: my daughter to be safe, and she will be safe with me," Tau replies.

"Brennus wants me on my knees—you can't protect me from that," I retort, angrier with him than I probably should be. He's not doing this, it's Brennus, but my emotions are a tangled mess right now.

"He will grovel on his knees to you," Tau counters.

"I don't want that," I reply.

"What do you want?" he asks.

"I want him to stop…just stop," I breathe.

"Then, I will make him stop," Tau says.

"What if you can't," I whisper.

"I can," he replies, his eyes softening a little in the corners.

"You think you know him, but you don't," I say grimly, feeling a desperation I can't even begin to describe. "He's seductive and sweet one minute and then he turns ruthless and horrifying the next. He changes, adapts. He makes alliances with the most awful monsters. He kills women and he only craves one thing: me. You can't stop him—no one can stop him," I say, shaking my head.

Tau rises from his seat. Drawing nearer to me, he crouches by my side, looking into my eyes that are a replica of his own. "You don't have the benefit of my experience to know that he is not all-powerful. He has many, many weaknesses—especially when it comes to his desire for you." Tentatively, Tau reaches out, tucking a piece of my hair behind my ear. "I will show you how to bring down your enemies…you just need to remember that that is exactly what Brennus is: your enemy."

Stiffening, I pull back from his hand. "You don't think that I know that he's my enemy?" I ask.

"I think that if you truly believed that, you would have killed him already," he replies.

My eyes narrow at Tau menacingly. "You think that I want him in my life?" I ask between my teeth.

"I think you are reluctant to kill him," Tau replies honestly. He stands up and moves away from me. "He can't be allowed to exist, Evie. He's a killer. He preys upon the weak. When you see him for what he truly is, you may then be able to do what you were meant to do."

"And what am I meant to do?" I ask him.

"Protect the weak," he replies. "Draw out evil and dispatch it, not pity it."

"Black and white, good and evil, sinner and saint?" I ask him derisively.

"Yes," he replies.

"Then why can't I think in those terms?" I ask.

"Maybe it's your soul that always wants to leave room for the possibility of redemption," he answers contemplatively.

"Or maybe I'm just not like you," I counter in a not-so-nice tone. "Did you know that Brennus saved my life from an Ifrit?" I inquire.

"Yes, Valentine," Tau responds quietly. His back is to me as he's staring out at the sea beyond the glass doors. "He did it for him, not for you…and you saved him from the Werree, and that also, was done for him, not for you—although, with your life tied to his, it did work in your favor as well. I was at Dominion recently; they apprised me of what happened while you were with the Gancanagh."

"So you know everything?" I ask him in a derogatory way, because he can't possibly know everything—he has no idea how I felt when all of that was happening.

"Everything?" he asks me, glancing over his shoulder at my face. "No one among us can know everything," he replies. "And you haven't spoken to me about it, so I cannot know your perspective."

"That's right…you don't know my perspective. You haven't had a chance to speak to me about it," I agree softly, "because you've been, where exactly?" I ask him, trying to keep anger from leaking into my voice with little success.

"Paradise," he answers.

Nodding my head, I say, "Right, Paradise…a little R & R from all that parenting you were doing," I reply with sarcasm. "You must have been exhausted."

Tau slowly turns around to face me. He has lost his blank mask of calm and the scowl on his face speaks volumes.

"Okay, love, I think you need to rest now," Reed cuts in, lifting me in his arms as he rises from the chair.

Russell rises, too, saying, "Here, I'll get the door for you, Reed."

"You had an excellent parent…James. He loved you very much," Tau says and my throat closes as tears instantly come to my eyes.

Wiggling out of Reed's arms I make him put me down. Facing Tau I say, "He was the BEST parent and he LOVED me more than anyone and ANGELS killed him for it!" I sob as tears run down my cheeks. "They tore him apart in the house that we lived in because NOBODY WAS THERE TO PROTECT HIM—NOT YOU, NOT ME—AND HE SUFFERED…and he died," I whisper the last part as it becomes almost impossible to breathe. My hands go to my eyes and I feel like my heart is breaking all over again.

"Evie…you couldn't have protected him—" Tau says with concern.

"I have to get out of here," I breathe, before turning and bailing out of his room.

Running as fast as I can, everything is just a blur. I wind down halls and stairwells in fractions of seconds. Finding myself in an engine room, I hide behind a huge, metal bulkhead and cry my eyes out.

Russell

CHAPTER 14

I'm On A Boat

Roundin' the corner to the engine room, I hear someone sniffle and then hiccup. A small smile crosses my lips, 'cuz I know that hiccup. I push past the metal door and listen as another hiccup comes from around the bulkhead.

"Go away, Russell," Evie says, when I sit down next to her on the floor.

"Now you're askin' me to walk away from a damsel in distress. That's a guilt I can't carry," I reply.

Pullin' off my shirt, I hand it to Red. She takes it with a grudgin' look on her face. Shruggin' into it, it covers the towel and falls almost to her knees.

"Thanks," she grumbles. "You don't have to stay."

"Yeah…well, maybe I want to hide out, too," I say with a shrug, thinkin' of Anya in the cabin next to mine.

"Why? Your creepy-old dad show up, too?" she asks, rubbin' a tear away from her eye.

"Naw, but what's really creepy is he looks younger than me," I admit in an easy tone. "I bet I could take him."

Red rolls her eyes at me, sayin' sarcastically, "Yeah, Russ, you fighting Tau wouldn't add another layer of strange to this or anything." But she smiles.

"How 'bout that other one—Cole?" I ask her.

"Cole Martin?" she asks me. When I nod, her tone turns suspicious, "Why? What did Cold Misery do now?"

"He was airplane talkin' Anya all the way here," I say, and I hear the edge in my own tone. When I see the confused look on Red's face, I explain. "He was way too close to her on the flight here and he was talkin' in a loud voice, like he had to talk over the engine, 'cept there were no engines. I didn't know what he was sayin' to her 'cuz he was speakin' in Angel."

"They were just talking?" Red asks.

"Well…yeah," I admit in a low tone. "But, it was the *way* he was talkin' to her…all buddy-buddy and smooth…like 'I'm an angel and I know how to speak Angel…'" I trail off from the derogatory imitation when Red starts gigglin'.

"What?" I ask her, smilin' too. "The way I figure it, you and me have gotta knock someone's head off soon—show them we're not the new kids 'round here."

"And we're not putting up with their shen?" she asks, and then hiccups again.

"That's right," I agree. "We gotta show them we can carry our own weight."

"So, what you're saying is I should suck it up and stop crying?" she asks, bitin' her bottom lip so it'll stop pushin' out in a pout.

"Oh Lord, look at you now," I say in a gentle tone, leanin' over and wipin' at her last tear. "All tragic and beautiful. You know we have to get a plan together."

"A plan?" she asks, lookin' alarmed.

"They're takin' us back to the snake nest. We know what that means," I say significantly.

"All our angels are vulnerable," Red replies, followin' my line of thought exactly. Her need for a plan is makin' her sit up straighter.

"I don't like it. The cold freaks know every inch of that place. We saw the surface when we were there, but—"

"The Gancanagh's magic goes deep," she finishes.

"To the bone, Red," I agree. "We need to stop thinkin' in terms of humans and angels and start thinkin' like faeries."

"But their magic doesn't affect angels," she says.

"Naw, but they got that place rigged. You showed them how portals worked and they, well, they liked that so much they probably portaled the livin' crap outta that place. I could smell magic there before, but now it's gotta be everywhere. Just 'cuz the angels can't get slapped 'round by magic, doesn't mean those sneaky lil' devils won't use it to get close to them—close enough to touch 'em."

"Like Declan and the fellas did at Dominion," she breathes, while lookin' wide-eyed at me.

"And if they can turn one of us, they have an instant killin' machine 'cuz everyone would be reluctant to take out one of our own." Red's face turns pale, so I quickly press on. "The first thing we do when we get there is go room by room and look for anythin' that's…wrong. Now that their stink isn't workin' on me, it should be easier to smell other stuff," I explain, hopin' that if she can focus on a plan to be proactive, it will divert her from the fact that we're leadin' her back to her prison.

"That could eat up a year of our lives," she mutters, knowin' how big Brennus' castle is and that they probably have traps all throughout.

"We gotta make it quick, 'cuz if we don't, it could be open season on our friends," I say. "Brennus is gettin' smarter—adaptin'. He nearly plucked you off this ship already."

"What about you, Russell?" Red questions, lookin' scared. "What happens when Brennus realizes that you were bitten several more times than me?"

"Then he's gonna throw confetti in the air and make me his party," I answer, seein' her eyes widen in fear.

"We've gotta protect you, Russ! You can't go with us!" Red spits out as she jumps to her feet.

"Hush now, Red. We're just talkin' here—you and me," I say in a soothin' way meant to calm her down. I get to my feet, too. "Where does one hide from magical creatures anyway?" I ask rhetorically, 'cuz we both know that those demons will always find us.

"He can't have you!" she says, pointin' her finger at me.

"You're damn right he can't have me," I agree. "I may be new to this magic thing, but I'm catchin' up quick." Openin' my palm, I whisper words to myself that create a small orb of light. Throwin' it against the wall, it shoots 'round us and ricochets, like a kid's rubber superball. When it bounces by my head, I make it pause it midair for a moment before it explodes into a shower of Twinkies.

Red picks up a Twinkie from the pile on the floor. "How did you do that?" she asks with a laugh.

"Well, it wasn't that hard. Twinkies are in season this time of year," I grin.

"I love you, Russ," Red says impulsively, walkin' into my arms and huggin' me tight with her face pressin' against my chest.

My arms go around her instantly, almost like habit as I stroke her soft hair. Somethin' inside my heart leaps, like it always does when she's near me, but…somethin' else is missin'. I'm not itchin' to tear her clothin' off and make love to her on the floor of the engine room and that's what's strange 'bout it. I plant a soft kiss on top of her head, and then wild crickets begin bouncin' 'round in my belly, the way they do when Anya is…

A low growl comes from the doorway of the engine room. My wings shoot out of my back at the sound and I push Red behind me, adoptin' a defensive posture. I straighten again when I see Anya's black wings spread out in response to mine. She's livid, if her emerald, snappin' eyes are any indication. Reed is holdin' her upper arm, in case she decides that she's seen enough.

Reed speaks to Anya in Angel and she turns her head to glare at him. Then she unleashes a torrent of words on him and me that have me blushin' even though I have no idea of what she's sayin'. But the way she's shakin' her finger at me is sorta tellin'.

Turnin', I see Red's face. She's gone completely pale as she's starin' at Reed. He's got a look I haven't seen since Crestwood: suppressed rage.

"Whoa, what just happened here?" I ask Reed. "You know this is just us talkin', right?" I ask, gesturin' between Red and me.

"Is that what it was?" Reed responds quietly. "It's getting more and more difficult to tell."

Anger creeps into my voice too, when I say, "You think this is seduction...right now? Here on the open water with Gancanagh tryin' to drag her off the ship and her father showin' up to claim her?" I ask, feelin' like my integrity is bein' questioned.

"I hugged him...it was me," Evie says from behind me. She moves to stand beside me, wringin' her hands in front of her and makin' us look guilty.

Reed's face turns blank and then he asks, "How could you resist when he brought the Twinkies?" Reed lets go of Anya's arm and walks out of the engine room. Red pushes past me as she tries to catch up to Reed, leavin' me to deal with Anya alone.

Shufflin' my foot, I feel like a criminal that's truly innocent of the charges this time. "Why are you here, Anya?" I ask, knowin' that she doesn't understand me. I rub my forehead where it's startin' to ache. "This world is only gonna break your heart."

"You break heart. You throw all away," she responds immediately, her hands on her hips as she glares at me.

"You understand me?" I murmur, my mouth droppin' open.

"Buns and Brownie—help Anya," she retorts. "Teach words and..." she pulls a pocket dictionary from the back pocket of her tight, shape-huggin' low rise jeans, "and Webster."

"Yeah? Well that's good. That means you're smart, right? So you'll understand this then. I don't know you," I say as anger over the situation I'm findin' myself in erupts.

"You not try to know Anya," she responds in a tense tone.

"That's right. I don't want to know you," I agree, not wantin' to have this conversation now, but since she's forcin' the issue, I'm thinkin' that maybe this is as good a time as any. I need her to leave before we get to Ireland. She's not supposed to be a part of this and if I remove the reason for her bein' here, maybe she'll go somewhere safe.

"So, that is complication?" she asks in a soft tone. Her sleek, ebony wings retract to a restin' position behind her.

"Naw, not a complication. It's a wall between us," I reply, hopin' she'll get what I'm sayin'.

"Then…I remove wall," she says, takin' a step nearer to me.

Holdin' up my hand, I say, "I like the wall."

She pauses, and tilts her head at me, like she's processin' what I just said. "That is two complication," she replies with a blank expression, holdin' up two fingers.

"Here's number three: I want you to leave," I state in a firm tone, watchin' for her expression to change. She just stares at me like she doesn't understand what I just said. "I don't love you and I never will. So, you might as well just get a new tattoo or whatever it is y'all do in a situation like this." I point to her chest and see her fingers skim over the spot where the crimson wings are branded into her skin beneath her clothin'.

"This is blindness," she says in a quiet, restless tone. "You not see what we are," she adds, indicatin' her and me with her gesture.

"Don't tell me that you're one of those psychotic girls that can't hear when it's over?" I ask in my harshest tone, feelin' my stomach twist at the expression on her face. Pain and confusion break through her blank façade.

"What is 'psychotic?'" she interrupts me…she flips open her dictionary, searchin' for the word. "Spell for me."

"Crazy…coo-coo, loco, insane, demented," I reply, bein' as crass as I possibly can, but she still looks puzzled. "Non compos mentis—"

She gasps, like I slapped her and then her eyelids narrow to slits over her green eyes. "Anya Throne…THRONE," she growls, slappin' her chest with her fist. She begins readin' me the riot act with her Angelic words, like she's tellin' me where I can go if I have a mind to. Finally, after a few minutes she switches back to English. "You leave me and say, 'I be back for you.' That make you liar, not me non compos mantis—cra-zee."

She's breathin' hard now, lookin' wild and fierce…exotic and unbelievably beautiful. Her black hair is flowin' down her back in waves and her face is flushin' pink with emotion.

Stay the course, man, I think, givin' myself a quick pep talk in my mind, while bein' distracted by her incredible allure.

"I don't need a broken-hearted savior," I say, pointin' my finger at her.

Her spine straightens instantly, as her mouth thins in a grim line. "Yes, I have eyes—I see what you want now." She takes a step back from me and the feelin' of crickets jumpin' 'round in my stomach is makin' me want to move nearer to her again.

"Good," I nod, but I feel sick. My face is a mirror of her grim expression. "So, you'll be goin' soon," I state with a sinkin' feelin' of regret.

"I decide what I do," she replies.

Unthinkingly, my hand shoots out to her upper arm, holdin' her when she would have walked away. "You're gettin' off this boat."

"This angel no longer belongs to you," Anya replies in a soft tone. "You shun—you throw away...you get no..." she flounders for a second, searchin' for words. "You get no thinking in what Anya do."

"You're wrong. I get thinkin' about what you do, 'cuz as long as you're here, you're my responsibility. You should leave here and go home," I counter as my hand tightens on her arm.

"You think you know so much?" she asks me in a derisive way. "You baby compared with Anya. I take care of me."

"I know I'm not gonna let up on you until you leave," I reply in a menacin' tone as my face draws closer to hers.

"Your words are wrong," she says, puzzled. "I am not understanding you. You say you don't want me. I say I take care of me...you want me away...why care if here, or not here? I will not bother you anymore."

"It bothers me to see you here," I clarify.

Pullin' her arm out of my grasp, Anya crosses her arms over her chest defensively before askin', "Why? I say to you I leave Russell be to run after Evie," her mouth twists like she's tastin' somethin' bad. "I have no home to go to," she admits in a soft tone. "I know no one here...I misunderstanding very much. Reapers offer to help Anya... Brownie is kind."

"'Cuz I don't want you here, so you can't stay. Brownie is my friend, not yours," I retort. I have to squeeze my hands in fists to keep from takin' her in my arms when I see the tragic look that comes to her eyes before she can hide it.

"You would deny Anya any help?" she asks, her face registerin' shock.

"You said you could take care of yourself. Prove it," I say, but the bitterness in my tone is from havin' to say the words, not 'cuz I mean them. On the contrary, I feel almost desperate to comfort her, but then I wouldn't be protectin' her. I have to keep her away from Brennus.

"I not know you...not my *aspire*...on a different day, you would help Anya...you love me...you would make me feel safe in my own skin, not like this—ugly...a stranger," Anya says like she's chokin'.

"I'll talk to Zee. He has places you can stay. He knows tons of angels. You'll be all right," I say in a gruff tone.

"NO!" Anya says, her brows pullin' together. "That will feel like corrosion, slowly eating through me. Stop speaking. You only hurt. Try hard to destroy. I will find my way without you."

"That sounds fine," I retort acidly, but my chest feels tight; it aches.

She nods her head once. Then, she asks, "Do you want to see Phaedrus now then?"

"Huh?" I ask, not understandin' what she's talkin' 'bout.

"You say Anya not yours. You tell Phaedrus, he remove your mark from me," she replies, lookin' pale and tired all of a sudden.

"I gotta do what now?" I ask, feelin' somethin' twist in my chest, like my heart's dyin'.

"You say Anya not *aspire*—you must release me," she says in a tight voice.

"Is that really—do I have to do that now?" I ask, and for some reason, I feel totally enraged with her for even mentionin' that to me.

"Yes—it's what you must do to have your Evie again. You say the words and make it the end of our acquaintance," she replies.

"Well, I'm kinda busy plannin' an attack on the Gancanagh right now," I reply, runnin' my hand through my hair in agitation.

Lookin' confused and crushed, Anya just shakes her head at me. "When time comes to you, then?"

"Yeah, when I have time," I respond in a gruff tone. "You're gonna be all right." I can't help myself from sayin' it again when she begins walkin' towards the door.

She pauses, but doesn't turn around. She leaves then, which is good 'cuz I can't say anythin' more to her now, anyway. Instead, I crush the handle to the steel door near the bulkhead in frustration. I sit down on the floor and hang my head, wonderin' if I even know who I am anymore.

I don't know how long I sit in this small space, but when I get up from the floor, my legs feel stiff. Slowly, I walk back towards my cabin and when I near it, I feel Brownie and Buns join me on either side. They both link arms with me, like they're escortin' a prisoner to his execution. My eyebrows rise as I notice that they're dressed in bathin' suits and revealin' cover-ups, even though we're dodgin' icebergs outside. I can't really say anythin' to them 'bout it, since I just gave away the only shirt that I had to Red.

"A word?" Brownie asks me in a stern tone, while pullin' me into her cabin and shuttin' the door.

"'Trap' is a word. 'Detainee' is another one," I say when they both lean against the door with their arms crossed and their faces even crosser.

"We know you, Russell," Buns says like a sneer. "You're super chivalrous—"

"To a fault," Brownie chimes in like an accusation.

"And a sucker for a female in need," Buns says.

"HUGE sucker," Brownie adds, tappin' her kitten-heel clad foot.

"What's your angle here, cowboy? Where did you get the black hat?" Buns asks, her blue eyes narrowin'.

"Do wut?" I drawl.

"Cut the country bumpkin crap," Brownie warns me. "We know how crafty you are—"

"Crafty," Buns agrees with a nod.

"You're gonna have to explain to me what you're referrin' to," I say again, stallin' for time to try to figure out what to tell them.

"Sounds like Russell could use some time with the mermaids, Brownie," Buns says with an evil smile twistin' her lips.

"Or, the Undines," Brownie hisses.

"What do y'all want to know?" I ask them with a resigned sigh.

"Let's start with Evie and work our way up to Anya, shall we?" Buns asks. "I've never seen Reed and Evie argue—disagree, sure but argue, never."

"They're fightin'?" I say, surprised to find that I don't feel good 'bout that.

"They are," Brownie says in a shamin' way that makes my face burn.

"It's about you. What did you do?" Buns asks, wrinklin' her nose at me like I smell foul.

"We hugged...and I kissed her on the top of the head—comfortingly, not passionately," I blurt out. "Just like I would've done if either one of you were cryin' your eyes out."

Brownie and Buns both look at each other and lose a little of their swagger. "Oh," Buns says in a cowed tone.

"Can I go now?" I ask them, feelin' like I won a battle, but the war is still ahead of me if I don't retreat now.

"And Anya?" Brownie asks, causin' me to shut my eyes briefly. Smellin' blood, they rally and go in for the kill. "Spill it," she demands.

"She's gotta go, y'all," I state in an authoritative tone.

"What do you mean she has to go? She is your *aspire*," Brownie retorts. "I examined the binding emblem myself. They're your wings—"

"No question," Buns finishes for Brownie.

"So what?" I ask them in agitation. "I don't know her at all—at all at all!"

"So you get to know her," Brownie says, like I'm slow.

"Now? This has to happen now?" I ask them, while pullin' my hand through my hair in exasperation. "This can't wait until after we kill Brennus? After we get rid of all the evil freaks stalkin' us?"

"There's probably always going to be some kind of evil freaks stalking you," Brownie points out.

"You kinda taunt them into it by your very nature," Buns agrees.

"Not like Brennus. He'd like nothin' better than to get close to Anya. If he so much as touched her…" I trail off.

"She'd be his minion," Brownie finishes, causin' my eyes to shoot to her blue ones in anger.

"His *sclábhaí*," I mutter, usin' Brennus' word for slave.

"There's the white hat!" Buns says excitedly, nudgin' Brownie with her elbow.

"I KNEW IT!" Brownie agrees with glee. "So you told her to go away—that you don't want her—so she'll be out of danger!"

"It's very old-fashion of you, Russell," Buns says, her stern tone creepin' back in.

"Very Dark Ages meets—" and then she says something in Angel I can't understand.

"Yes, very—" and Buns hisses the word in Angel, too, as she nods her head.

"Fine, I'm—" and I try to say the word, fail miserably, and shrug when I see them both grin. "Can I go now?"

"Nope," Buns says with a frown.

"Not a chance," Brownie agrees.

"Why not?" I ask them with a sigh.

"You just made a big mess," Buns says.

"HUGE mess," Brownie adds.

"You don't shun a Throne," Buns warns.

"I mean, are you crazy?" Brownie asks with an incredulous grin.

"Naw…it's a good plan. I tell her to go away. I take away any chance of reconciliation, and she's safe," I explain, watchin' their frowns deepen.

"Horrible plan," Brownie states.

"The worst," Buns agrees.

"Why?" I ask them in a frustrated tone as my brows pull together.

"THRONE," they say in unison.

"So?" I mutter, and see them glance at each other again in exasperation. "You're all angels. How much different can she be from y'all?"

They both snort in unison.

"Karma is what they do, Russell," Buns says sympathetically.

"Everything to them is a circle," Brownie chimes in. "Reap what you sow kind of thing—and this is personal."

"Very personal," Buns agrees.

"You made it personal," Brownie continues.

"So, what're y'all sayin'?" I ask them warily.

"You ignore her," Buns says, "and you get paid back ten fold."

"Huh?" I ask.

"You say go away, she could go so far you'll never see her again," Brownie explains, and a pain I wasn't expectin' squeezes my chest.

"Or, she could get so close and never let you touch her again," Buns counters.

"Or, she could just get off this boat and leave before the Gancanagh get a chance to touch her," I counter right back.

"Ughh, I almost feel sorry for him," Buns says to Brownie.

"I know, right?" Brownie agrees. "You need our help."

"Desperately," Buns states, twistin' her blond hair like a bratty little sister.

"Ahhh, y'all are trippin'," I sigh, wavin' my hand at them. "I've been around. I know a thing or two and I don't want her here."

"O-kayyy," Buns says.

"Splendid," Brownie agrees.

"I love fireworks," Buns says, steppin' aside and openin' the door to the cabin for me.

"Big, noisy ones with lots of fire," Brownie adds.

"All the colors of the spectrum—you know, Brownie, this makes Anya sorta single, right?" Buns asks slyly.

"I do believe you are correct, Buns," Brownie agrees.

"When are you removing your mark from Anya, Russell?" Buns inquires.

"Can't we deal with all the formalities after we battle the Gancanagh?" I grumble.

"Why wait?" They ask.

"'Cuz I don't want to deal with it now," I retort angrily.

"There's something there," Brownie states intuitively.

"You feel something for her," Buns agrees.

"I don't know what I feel," I reply. "The thought of her stayin' makes me hurt and the thought of her goin' is…confusin'."

"The weight of love…" Brownie whispers, lookin' at me the way she did when we were trapped together in the basement of the evil church. She had told me then that she wanted to live 'cuz she had never been in love. "You should know for sure that you don't love her before you let her go, Russell. You can't just let Phaedrus remove the binding between you, not without truly knowing what you were to each other. And she deserves an honest explanation for why you would like her to leave now."

"Because you can't make her do anything—she's her own angel," Buns explains.

I scowl at them. "But, if I'm honest and she decides to stay then I've lost this chance of convincin' her to go."

"Stub-born," Buns replies.

"Psych-o," Brownie agrees in a sing-song voice.

"Y'all just keep your mouths shut 'bout any of this conversation. I don't want y'all blabbin' it to Anya," I say, lettin' my eyes narrow as I look at each of them sternly.

Buns gasps, "Russell! We are the very epitome of discretion."

"We're Reapers!" Brownie says, like that explains everythin'.

"Yeah, well…good," I say, pushin' past them and out into the hallway.

Buns sticks her head out of the cabin sayin', "We'll pray for you!"

"You're gonna need it," Brownie calls emphatically.

"We can still help you. Come to our beach party—it's tomorrow—on the port side basketball courts," Buns calls after me. I shake my head at them like they're the ones who need prayers.

CHAPTER 15

Don't Go

"Powers don't know what to make of Anya," Zephyr says as he comes to stand next to me by a basketball hoop. He must've caught me watchin' Anya standin' with Brownie and Buns by the refreshment table two courts away. This ship is equipped like a luxury liner but with the capabilities of a battleship. From what I've been told, it rarely docks at any port, but is serviced by a steady stream of companion ships organized and maintained by Powers.

"What do you mean?" I ask Zephyr, seein' that Buns has gotten to him and made him wear board shorts and flip flops to the beach party. I had nothin' else to wear but what Brownie gave me, so I'm wearin' them, too.

"She's a Throne. She outranks Powers, but she's gone rogue, so she's taboo now," Zephyr replies.

"So, they'll stay away from her?" I ask, feelin' better than I should 'bout that. My eyes slip over her long, dark hair, lingerin' on the seriously sexy, black bikini top and wrap skirt she's sportin' this evenin'. With her supple, black wings elegantly displayed, she's absolutely stunnin'.

"The Powers might stay away, but she seems to have intrigued the Seraphim," Zephyr says as we both watch Cole walk up to our girls and engage them in conversation. Everyone here speaks in Angel, a fact that irritates me to no end. I'm tryin' hard to learn it, but I feel like a cockroach tryin' to learn English.

"I hate that guy," I mutter under my breath, but Zephyr still hears it.

"He is annoying," Zephyr agrees, seein' Cole reach out and touch a flower on Buns's lei.

"Why's he hangin' 'round us?" I ask Zee, changin' my position so that I can better observe Cole. *He favors his right hand.*

"It's not us...it's them," Zephyr replies, noddin' his head toward the girls. "Our Reapers are fascinating, alluring—" he says.

"Sexy," I add.

"That, too," Zee agrees. "And Anya is intrepid and seductive..." he trails off when I growl at him involuntarily. Zephyr tries to suppress his grin when he adds, "I have already found the angel for me."

"I'm sorry. I didn't mean that—it just came out—" I begin.

"I know—it is instinct. She is definitely your *aspire.* You must speak with her, Russell. She put herself at risk to come here," Zephyr says.

"Don't you think I get that?" I ask him in frustration. "She's vulnerable here. She's not gonna get a second chance, Zee! If I die, my soul still has a shot at Paradise. All y'all just..." I trail off, unable to put into words what I'd feel if she or any of them were harmed.

"It is worth the risk to our lives," Zephyr replies calmly.

"Is it?" I shoot back.

"You have seen Brennus. You tell me if it is better to ignore his evil," Zephyr says.

"I'm not plannin' on ignorin' him," I respond in a low tone. "I just don't think we need all y'all to come with us to Ireland. Buns and Brownie should take Anya somewhere else."

"You want to tell them that?" Zephyr asks, while watchin' the girls chattin' it up.

"They might listen, if it was comin' from you," I say, lookin' for his help.

"And I might get called back to Paradise in the next few seconds..." he says, and then he pauses and looks up at the ceilin'. "Nope. That's not going to happen either."

"When did you learn sarcasm, Zee?" I ask sullenly.

"It was forced upon me when I began associating with half-humans," he replies smoothly.

"Well, it's unbecomin' of an angel of your stature," I retort sourly, while his grin widens.

"We fought them in Ireland before this," Zephyr points out, indicatin' when Evie was in Ireland with the Gancanagh and we stalked them, lookin' for a way to rescue her.

"I know, but this feels different to me. We're not in control," I say, tryin' to see if he's pickin' up what I'm layin' down. The Seraphim are callin' the shots now.

"Yes, that is a problem," Zephyr agrees in a low tone.

Lookin' across the courts, I see Cole lean in close to Anya and whisper somethin' in her ear. Another low growl rumbles from me as my eyes narrow to slits and killin' scenarios flicker through my brain.

Zephyr grasps my upper arms, sayin', "You are going to be living on raw emotion where Anya is concerned—like anyone would who is newly committed."

"Why are you so sure she's my *aspire?*" I retort in a snarl.

"One need only to look at you now to know," Zephyr says, his ice blue eyes borin' into mine. "If your goal is to make her go away, you will completely rule that out if you show her that you are jealous."

"I can take him," I state as my hands become fists.

"I have no doubt, after all, I trained you," Zephyr replies with a genuine grin.

"Naw, I think I'll go pick a fight," I reply, tryin' to pull away from Zephyr.

"That is not indifference, Russell," he says in a determined tone.

"Indifference has never been a weapon in my arsenal," I admit, takin' a deep breath and tryin' to calm down.

"I did not come up with this plan. I am merely attempting to help you execute it if this is what you believe you have to do," Zephyr replies, while soundin' like a true wingman.

"Yeah, okay " I growl, before lightly shruggin' off his hand from my arm. "Maybe I should go back to my cabin then," I add, while searchin' for the nearest exit. I'm just in time to see Evie arrive.

Dressed for the party in a white bikini top, Red smoothes her hands nervously over her matchin' wrap skirt. Loose, auburn hair flows down her back between her crimson wings and a white, exotic flower peeks seductively from behind her ear. As she searches the room, she worries the long strand of wooden beads 'round her neck.

"Evie's here," I tell Zephyr.

"Yes, and she has an escort," Zephyr replies. My eyes narrow as I look behind Red to see Xavier trailin' her. He's even bigger and broader without his body armor on and his powerful, crimson wings make mine look, well, small. Dressed for the party in board shorts and wooden necklace equipped with a shark tooth, I wonder briefly what he's up to.

Xavier leans in close to Red's cheek and whispers somethin' in her ear while gesturin' toward the dance floor. She wrinkles her nose at him and says "no," which makes a slow grin tug at the corners of Xavier's mouth.

Glancin' 'round again, Evie spots Buns and Brownie, but she ignores them and continues to search the room, until finally, her eyes rest on Zee and me. A moment after that, she is at my side with her hand on Zephyr's arm.

"Zee," she says, her voice full of worry, "you have to tell him that I'm fully capable of going with him—I'm a scary monster now, you know—you've seen me—"

"Where is Reed going?" Zephyr asks 'cuz like me, he knows by her demeanor that the only one she could be talkin' 'bout is Reed.

"He volunteered to go on ahead of the ship with the detail from Dominion to Brennus' estate. They're supposed to secure the position and ferret out any unforeseen complications there. It's dangerous—he can't smell magic like I can and they won't let me go too," Evie says in a rush of words that can only be accomplished by a female.

"Who won't let you go?" I ask.

"The idiot Seraphim, Preben and his stupid Dominion Powers... Reed," she replies sullenly, before clenchin' her teeth when Xavier chuckles behind her. "Would you mind telling Xavier that if he doesn't want to become an albatross, he should stop laughing," she mutters, which only makes him laugh harder.

"I'll go," I volunteer, ignorin' Xavier and focusin' on Red.

"Thanks, Russell, but I think Zee will be able to convince Reed to let me go...he's still a little raw about the Twinkie thing—" Red replies, before I interrupt her.

"Naw, I mean I'll go to Brennus' crib. I can smell the magic, maybe even better than you can, and he's not as focused on me as he is on you—" I explain.

"NO!" she interrupts me with her hands on her hips. "You have to stay here."

"Why?" I ask, my eyes narrowin'.

"Because you've been bitten too many times for it not to affect you. Brennus' thrall is no joke—he can control you—" she starts.

"No, he can't," I reply. "He tried to get me to kill Anya when we were in the pub, but I didn't do it, did I?" I ask her rhetorically.

"He wasn't there," she retorts. "That was a hologram of him. What happens when he's in the same room with you and he uses magic too?" she asks me.

"Then it will be a war of words and I've been workin' on some spells," I reply.

"You're being ridiculous. Zee, tell him that he's being ridiculous," Evie says, while turnin' back to Zee with a look of frustration.

"We'll locate body armor—get briefed on the mission," Zephyr says to me over the top of Evie's head.

"WHAT!" Red glares at Zephyr.

A grin breaks over Zephyr's face before he kisses Evie on the forehead. "I will go and protect them both for you. There is no need to worry."

"I'm going with you!" she insists, her small hands in fists.

"You will remain on this ship," Xavier says behind her in a stern voice that at once surprises me as it irritates me.

"Who is this guy again?" I ask Red in a derogatory way.

"I'm her shadow," Xavier cuts in, answerin' my question with a blank expression, not the least bit intimidated by me.

"She has a shadow, and it looks nothin' like you," I reply, standin' up to him.

"And you have an *aspire* that has been waiting for you for a long while. Perhaps it's time you cast your shadow beside hers," he replies, unruffled.

"Ah, naw! You didn't just go there," I grit out, before comin' eye to eye with Xavier.

"But, I did," he replies with an easy grace that is like a hallmark of the Seraphim. "You once told me that you could see forever in Anya's eyes, but trust me when I tell you that she'd be satisfied with you just knowing that they're green."

"What?" I respond, feelin' like he just hit me in the gut.

"Exactly. You know very little, so don't interfere with how we decide to protect Evie," he replies with the complete assurance that he has the upper hand.

"I may not know much, but I know I'm not the one that left her alone here to fend for herself, all the while not knowin' what she was or where she came from," I counter, takin' back some of the power he just took from me.

"It's such a shame, you know even less than that—you know nothing," he volleys back. "If you plan to go with the contingent from Dominion, you had best hurry. They're not like Anya, they will not wait for you."

While ponderin' ways to smash his face in, I feel small flakes of snow drift onto my face and arms, meltin' like gentle kisses against my skin. Xavier, on the other hand, is covered in big, fat clumps of slushy snow that Evie has created with the flick of her wrist.

Xavier's lips twitch while he turns toward Evie to see her cross her arms over her chest and glare at him.

"Evie!" Xavier grins at her. In an instant, he pulls her up off her feet in a bear-like hug while he shakes his blond hair, showerin' large dollops of meltin' snow onto her silky skin.

For a moment, I feel as if I'm watchin' two angelic lovers engagin' in a form of adolescent flirtation. Xavier rubs his cold, wet cheek against Evie's and she gasps as the combination of frigid water and masculine skin combine to cause an unwillin', feminine giggle to tumble from her.

"Xavier, stop!" she breathes. "Put me down!"

"You stop first," he retorts, lookin' up as the snow continues to fall upon them.

"Fine," she manages, flickin' her wrist again to make the snow stop fallin'.

To say that I'm freaked out by what I just saw would lessen the impact it has on me. Glancin' at Zee, I see that he's disturbed, too.

"How long have you known each other?" Zephyr asks in a calm voice.

"High school," Evie frowns, and swats at Xavier's hand when he doesn't release her right away once her feet are on the ground.

"And how long have you known Evie?" Zee asks while his eyes shift to Xavier's.

"A little longer than that," he replies, no longer smilin'.

"How much longer?" I ask.

"Longer," he shoots back with a blank expression.

"Russell," Zephyr says next to me, but his eyes don't leave Xavier's. "We should prepare to leave."

"Yeah...okay," I murmur, before glancin' at Evie. "It'll be okay, Red. I'll make sure they don't miss anthin' ugly or undead."

She reaches out to Zephyr and me, huggin' us like she'll never see us again. "Take me with you," she says, and the force with which she holds us translates her growin' desperation and fear.

"We will return to you," Zephyr says in a gentle voice.

"Of course we're comin' back. We're not punks," I say, glancin' at Xavier and seein' him scowl back at me. *Where's your empty expression now*, I think with a slow smile.

"If you let me go with you, I'll be able to show you where all their surveillance was set up—how they operate, what shifts consisted of—" She continues, employin' another angle to convince us of her position.

"Zephyr is a Prostat Power, Evie," Xavier says, usin' an Angelic word that I'd never heard before now. "Very few angels ever reach his level of excellence. The Gancanagh will never hear him coming if they're still there."

"I know he's a wicked assassin, Xavier. He's the one who trained me," Evie says, while lettin' us go.

"You've been trained?" he asks in a deadly calm tone.

"Yes," she replies.

"When?" he counters.

"When what?" she responds, turnin' to face him.

"When were you trained?" he asks. "Before or after your evolution?"

"Uh…that's a gray area for me," she replies evasively.

Lookin' over the top of her head, Xavier asks Zephyr, "When was she trained?"

"We began during the latter part of her evolution into angel," Zephyr replies calmly, and he doesn't flinch when Xavier's brows draw together and a low growl escapes from him. Red and I both adopt defensive postures in front of Zee, just in case Xavier decides to attack him. The entire room quiets at once, while everyone's focus falls on us.

"Interesting," Xavier murmurs, the picture of composure once again.

"She was an excellent student. She cut me right here once," Zephyr says proudly, holdin' up his wrist and pointin' to the spot.

"I would have liked to have witnessed that," he replies, his voice full of humor.

"Naw, you wouldn't've," I scoff at him, "'cuz she healed him right after that and we had to watch her flesh break open and her bleed all over herself before Reed cleaned her up." The look on Xavier's face turns grim while he glances at me. "Ah, you didn't know she'd do somethin' like that, did you—hurt herself to save her friends? But, that's what she does. She'd never abandon anyone. C'mon, Zee, we gotta catch a flight to faerie-tale-horror-town and make sure that no evil freaks are there when she arrives."

"What am I supposed to do?" Evie calls after us.

"Enjoy the party," I call back.

Zee and I walk out of the courts and down a few hallways before I ask, "What do you think?"

He glances at me before sayin', "She knows him."

"You picked up on that, too," I say, exhalin' a large breath.

"She doesn't know that she knows him," he adds. "But, that's nothing compared to how well he knows her. He has the look."

"The look?" I question.

"Buns can probably explain it better to you, but I will do my best. When a soul arrives in Paradise after a lifetime on earth, it will sometimes pine for the soul mate that was left behind," Zephyr says.

"He has that look?" I ask.

"No…he has the other look," Zephyr replies with a grim expression.

"The other look?" My eyebrow quirks.

"The look of that soul when it reunites with its soul mate," he replies solemnly.

"Naw, you're wrong!" I blurt out, before haltin' where I stand in the narrow hallway. "How is that possible when I'm her soul mate?" I point to my chest.

"I don't know, Russell," he says plainly. "He's an angel and he doesn't even have a soul. I am just telling you what I saw."

I walk next to Zee again, but this time at a slower pace. "Why haven't the Seraphim met with us—told us what's happenin', where they've been, what they've been doin'?" I ask. "It'd be nice to know the game plan, instead of havin' to react when the room starts blowin' up."

"We have to start doing our own intel before we become obsolete," Zephyr says. "That's what Reed's been doing. He's getting close to them—to Tau."

"I have a distinct disadvantage, Zee," I say, thinkin' 'bout what he said. "I can't speak Angel."

"You have an insider, Russell," Zee says quietly. When I look at him, he says, "Anya—"

"No way," I growl at him. "I'm not usin' her for nothin'."

"She knows possibly as much or more than them," he says. "She probably knows what happened between you and Evie, have you thought of that?"

"Of course I've thought of it! It's almost all I think 'bout, but my need to know isn't as strong as my need to get her outta here," I reply defensively.

Roundin' the corner to the corridor that leads to my room, I find Reed standin' outside my door. He's already attired in full, black combat armor. He nods to Zephyr and me as we approach him.

"I requisitioned armor for you both, in case you wanted to join us," Reed says, and gestures toward my room. I open the door and see the armor hangin' in my closet.

"Ah, you're gettin' the band back together. Look, Zee, we got new uniforms," I grin at Reed and see his reluctant smile.

"I wish I could offer you a better venue, but it's the same old dive as last time," Reed replies with a negligent shrug. I gesture for Reed and Zephyr to come in and then I close the door behind them.

"I'm down—it's gotta be hotter than that beach party we were just subjected to," I say off-handedly.

"Bad?" Reed asks.

"If by bad you mean good, then no. Powers are appallingly lame players, no offense," I flash him a grin for the slur I just shot his way.

"Paper gangstas?" Reed asks me with humor.

"Somethin' like that. Now, Prostat Powers on the other hand…" I leave my comment to hang in the air between us, acknowledgin' that he's elite.

"Have sick style," Zephyr chimes in, showin' that he's been hangin' out with Buns.

"Decidedly so," I agree. "So, how's this goin' down?" I ask Reed, pullin' out the black armor and seein' that it'll fit me.

"We're the opening act. We go in stealth, search for incendiaries, pockets of magic, latent spells intended for half-angels," he says, lookin' directly at me.

"Don't forget portals," I add.

"Those can be your special project, Russell," Reed smiles at me as he adds, "you have the nose for it."

"Whatever. You're just jealous of my new angelic nose—I got a lot of play with the old one…" I trail off when the crickets in my stomach begin jumpin' 'round and I hear the door next to my room open and close. It could only mean that Anya just got in.

Reed glances at his watch and says, "Meet us on the deck when you're ready, we have to leave soon."

"I'll be along in a second," I say as Reed and Zee walk out into the hallway.

Reed turns back and says, "Russell…about the thing—with you and Evie…I was out of line—I—"

"Reed, we're good," I reply. "I can't explain it, but I can honestly say that I'm not sweatin' it for once."

A crooked smile comes to his lips as he says, "Those crickets still bothering you?" he asks.

"You could say that," I reply.

"You'll let me know if you want to talk about them?" he asks.

"Yeah, I'll let you know," I say, before closin' the door.

Hurriedly, I change into the body armor. Openin' the door to my room, I step out into the hall just as Anya walks past me toward the end of the hallway. My wings unfurl *snap* when I see the skintight, black body armor coverin' her dangerous curves. She looks more like a dominatrix than a soldier with her black hair pulled back in a massive ponytail and her golden bow slung carelessly over her shoulder.

Before I can think 'bout what I'm doin', I've gotten directly in front of her, blockin' her way to the deck.

"Ah, naw!" I say with a dark scowl on my face. "Where do you think you're goin'?"

She doesn't answer me, but attempts to step around me. My hands go to her upper arms to hold her in place in front of me. Her eyes narrow to slits as she raises her angelic voice in frustration. Sweet music falls from her lips as she jabs at the air near my face with her finger.

"Yeah, yeah, yeah—I'm probably all of that and more," I agree in a stern tone, "but don't think for one second I'm lettin' you off this ship, so you can turn 'round right now and go back to your room."

"Leave ship! Stay on ship!" Anya rants in a derogatory way as she wildly gestures with her hands. "You non compos mentis, Russell. You cannot decide what you are wanting."

"Don't try to twist this," I respond with equal heat. "I want you to go somewhere else—not the exact same place I'm goin'."

"How am I to know that you volunteer for the mission, too? You do not share your intentions with me. I do not possess the magic to read your mind!" she replies.

"Yeah, well, I bet you can tell what I'm thinkin' right now," I retort angrily.

"I no longer care what you are thinking," she replies. "I volunteer for this mission and I am going." She attempts to step 'round me again, but I block her.

"Anya," I growl when she tries to duck by me the other way. "You're stayin' here until I get back," I order as I pick her up off her feet and heft her over my shoulder. Carryin' her back down the hall to my room, I dump her quickly on my bed.

"Russell!" she squeaks at me, too angry to even yell at me in Angel.

"We'll talk later 'bout this," I say, before backin' out of the room. Closin' the door, I whisper words to it, sealin' it shut tight for the next hour or so with a spell. Grinnin' when I hear Anya try to kick down the door and it holds tight, I turn and run back down the hall to the deck of the ship.

Military grade helicopters with advanced weaponry speckle the deck with their rotors warmin' up. Spottin' Zee already seated in one, I run to it, climbin' in next to him. "We're not gonna fly with our wings?" I ask.

Zee shrugs, "This will get us near the castle faster. It is also less taxing. We will bail out before we get there so they do not hear us coming. I thought you were going to miss it," Zee comments next to me, usin' a loud voice to be heard over the engines.

"I ran into a complication," I yell, but smile when I remember the feelin' of Anya's body against mine. The crickets are still buzzin' 'round wildly inside of me.

"I think your complication has followed you," Zephyr replies above the noise of the rotors. Anya emerges onto the deck of the ship and strolls over to our helicopter.

As she brushes past me to a seat, small pieces of wood and fiberglass fall off her armor, lettin' me know that she couldn't break through the door I had put a spell on, so she went through the wall.

Sittin' kitty-corner from me, she smoothes her hair back delicately like a cat, raisin' her eyebrow cunningly when I scowl at her. As I tear my eyes away from hers, I try hard to get control of the warrin' emotions her presence instills in me. I don't know if I want to shake her or kiss her...or both.

Through the open doorway, I see Reed standin' among the Seraphim on the deck of the ship. He nods his head when Tau places his hand on Reed's shoulder in a gesture of respect. When he drops his hand, Reed turns toward the main door. I glance over in that direction too and see Red standin' by the entryway with her arms crossed over her chest and her hair whippin' wildly 'round her in the wind. Reed walks to her and when he reaches her, he picks her up off her feet and kisses her like he'll never let her go.

I frown then, not 'cuz I'm jealous—I mean I am, but it has lost its intensity somehow...it's different. Glancin' at Anya, she's no longer lookin' at me, but out the other doorway at the sea. A few moments later, Reed climbs into the seat across from mine and the helicopter leaves the deck.

While Anya continues to stare at the sea, my eyes wander down the delicate slope of her neck. I wonder what she is thinkin' 'bout and what it would be like to kiss her like I dream of kissin' her whenever I close my eyes.

Evie

CHAPTER 16

Everlasting Love

Cold, fine drops of rain fall softly on my cheeks as I emerge from the darkness of the ship's interior to the gray, overcast sky of the main deck. Pulling my dark pea coat tighter to my body, the wind lifts red tendrils of my hair. I walk slowly to the railing overlooking the water.

Even though the initial reports from Reed and his team are good, I had felt suffocated listening to them in the comfort of the Seraphim's control room. Envisioning Reed, Russell, and Zephyr roaming the shadowy rooms of Brennus' castle has me unable to sit still or think clearly. I spared little thought for what the Seraphim would think before I had left their meeting abruptly. They're the ones that insisted that I stay with them; so right now upgrading their opinion of me isn't a priority.

I catch my first sight of the Irish coastline; its craggy landscape makes me shiver in dread. I find it difficult to imagine now how the Gancanagh had made this their home for so long without anyone realizing it. The cold, moss-covered edifices practically scream their presence. As I study the shadows between the falling-down stone, I imagine creeping shapes of undead Faeries grasping the rock, waiting for our ship to draw nearer to their position.

Tipping my face up, I let the rain wash over me. It bathes away the frigid sweat of fear that has broken on my brow.

"You don't know how fiercely beautiful you are, do you?" A quiet voice behind me asks, causing me to stiffen and fix my eyes on the rocks along the shoreline.

"Xavier," I say in a tight voice, "if there was ever a time to leave me alone, it would be now."

"I have left you alone—too long alone," he replies.

I glance at him over my shoulder and I see the strange expression on his face that resembles something disturbingly like regret. "Continue the trend, I don't mind," I reply.

Xavier grins, "When your insult is accompanied by your winsome smile, it takes all the edge out of the remark."

"I'll try to affect a scowl next time," I say.

He joins me at the railing. "You could try, but they're just as seductive—" he begins.

"What do you want?" I interrupt, stiffening in confusion.

"I saw you slip out of the strategy meeting. Why did you leave?" he asks.

"Strategy," I murmur the word like it's an illusive concept, "the art of planning."

"I remember your fondness for it. You used to have a strategy for everything—studying, entertaining, shopping…you used to lay out your clothing each night before school," Xavier says with another grin. "Cole and I would wager whether you'd actually wear the outfits that you chose or change them at the last second."

"You were spying on me in my bedroom? That sounds perverted," I reply, wrinkling my nose at him. My cheeks burn not only with that thought, but also at my stupidity for not knowing that they were there.

"I was guarding you," he corrects me. "So why did you leave the strategy meeting? It's not like you to let any detail escape your attention." His mouth curves in a cunning smile as he watches me frown.

"You go ahead and make your plans," I reply in a dismissive way, irritated that he thinks he knows me well.

"You sound as if you believe it is futile to do so," Xavier remarks.

Facing him, I see both his blue eye and his green eye. He is so big, like Russell, in fact, they have a similar look to them, but Xavier's hair is much lighter than Russell's tawny color—more golden…extremely handsome. I used to like his size, but right now it's annoying because it makes me feel small.

"It is futile," I reply. My knuckles tighten on the railing in front of me, causing them to turn whiter.

"There can always be a plan, if you know your enemy," Xavier says in a quiet voice.

"I know my enemy. That's why I'm not making plans," I reply.

"What does Brennus want from you? Do you know?" Xavier asks.

I flinch at the mention of Brennus' name. "He wants me to be his undead queen," I answer in a voice that quivers a little.

"Why?" he questions with his eyebrows pulling together in concentration.

"Why what?" I ask as drops of rain slide down my cheeks.

"What is it about you that he desires?" he asks in a probing tone. "Apart from the fact that you're a beautiful, tempting morsel..."

My face flushes with color again as his eyes rove over me and I want to hit him when he chuckles. Raising my chin, I reply, "I think it's important to him that I see the good in him that didn't die." The smile falls away from Xavier's lips to be replaced by a deepening frown. "Something good survived in him that Aodh, his maker, couldn't kill and that part of him craves love—yearns for it."

"You're wrong," Xavier disagrees in a tight voice. "Nothing good survived his transformation from Faerie to Gancanagh."

"How do you know?" I counter.

"Because he follows you even though it's wrong. If his love were pure, he'd let you go so that you could pursue what you desire. He wouldn't try to change you into one of them because he knows that it'd be the death of you," Xavier replies, his breathing increasing with restrained emotion.

"Brennus hasn't changed me yet and he's had plenty of opportunity," I point out. "He's not what he seems...and I think he's different around me."

"He's different? How is he different?" Xavier asks while his jaw tightens.

"He...he's nicer. I make him nicer," I admit.

"Nicer?" he asks like he doesn't know the word.

"He doesn't want to hurt anyone when he's with me. Maybe I do that to him. Maybe it's because he says I'm always giving him my energy. He says he craves it like an addiction. Maybe I make him nice," I explain.

"You defend him?" Xavier asks, his eyes narrowing. "He's reprehensible."

"He wanted to survive," I say between my teeth.

"At the expense of all else," Xavier says.

"He did it for his brother Finn. Finn was turned first and he believed that Finn wouldn't survive Aodh's cruelty without him," I argue, unable to stop myself.

"A noble reason for a tragic error in judgment, one that I'm sure he's looking to you to correct," Xavier states with a renewed patience.

"Meaning what exactly?" I ask, feeling something cold climb down my spine.

"If I were to cease to be...I could think of no better place than within the arms of an angel, especially if she loved me—" he says, but I interrupt him.

"I don't love Brennus," I whisper, perplexed by the stab of guilt that rushes through me.

"You have a great propensity for love. It's in your nature. You make others gravitate to you like sheep to a shepherdess...and you love them, even if they're wrong," Xavier says, while reaching out and wiping away the rain from my cheek with his warm, rough fingers. "But for Brennus, it will be only revenge now: his thoughts of you are ugly and twisted. He's been drinking dust after tasting your blood, and that craving for you is just as strong in him. He's had time to plot his horror—design his torture for you."

"Why are you telling me this?" I ask as I shy away from his touch.

"I don't want you to hesitate to kill him," he replies, staring into my eyes. "Don't let your human side and your need to be empathetic get in the way of destroying his vulgarity. Don't be fooled by the falseness of his love and deny the ones who really love you."

"What do you know about my friends? You don't know any of them," I retort.

"I was referring to your family who loves you: Tau, Cole and I," he corrects me as his face turns blank to hide his emotions.

Stunned, I stammer, "My family? Let's be real—I never really knew you—any of you and what I do know of you I don't like! You've been lying to me since I met you in high school!"

"You know me, Evie. I was your..." he trails off.

"My boyfriend?" I ask. "See, you can't even say it now, just like you couldn't say it when we were in school! You acted like we were sometimes, and then you'd act like I was just some girl you knew."

"You've never been just *some girl*. I couldn't tell you what I am because I wasn't allowed to say it then," he replies.

"And I'm supposed to believe you because you've been so honest with me?" I ask.

"I've always been honest with you, except for when I had to keep things from you in order to protect you."

"Like the fact that you're an angel?" I say accusingly.

"Yes, like that," he frowns.

"What else have you kept from me?" I wonder aloud.

"A lot," he admits with a guilty frown.

"Lucy Clark," I say, thinking of the very popular and very beautiful girl that Xavier dated after he broke up with me in the summer before our senior year.

"She was an attempt to make you angry instead of sad...because you were really sad—"

"I was sad because you broke my heart when you broke up with me so abruptly and you didn't even give me a good reason," I say, pointing my finger at him.

"I told you we were getting too close," he counters, like that's a good excuse.

"Being close is a good thing," I retort with a frown.

"Not when I can crush you. I almost did, so many times," he says in exasperation. "Tau told me I was losing perspective. He ordered me not to date you."

"And you listened to him!" I remark with scorn, not wanting to hear his excuses. I was the one who had to watch Xavier walking in the halls at school with Lucy hanging on him. We had been friends since the first day of freshman year and he acted like he didn't know me. I was nothing—no, I had been less than nothing.

"Tau *is* your father," he says in a stern tone. "You'll have to reconcile yourself to that fact."

"I realize that, but you're not. You're just some random angel who had the sheer misfortune of having to watch over the half-breed," I reply in a stilted tone.

"Don't call yourself that!" Xavier says in an angry tone that startles me. "You're the first of your kind—that alone makes you valiant!"

"What do you want from me?" I whisper the question again.

Xavier's jaw clenches as the spray of the water crashes loudly against the side of the ship far below. "I want you to know me as more than just a random angel that was assigned to protect you," he responds.

"Why? Are you saying that it wasn't random?" I ask in a raspy tone. "Why did you agree to this mission to protect me?"

Xavier hangs his head as he watches the water far below the railing. Rain drips from the sides of his face as he growls, "Would that I could've fought for you at Dominion—protected you there. I wouldn't have been content to destroy just Pagan for you. I would've annihilated the entire war council for trying you as a…" he trails off.

"As a freak," I finish, frowning.

Xavier tips his head back in frustration while a steady stream of Angelic words flows from his lips. It appears to me like he's speaking directly to Heaven. When he gazes back at me, he's calmer. "Never demean yourself like that in front of me again. You're not a freak. You're exceptional."

I must look surprised because Xavier's expression softens. "You don't know how perfect you are," he says in a meditative tone.

"I know that I don't smell like cheese," I reply. A reluctant smile comes to my lips before he begins laughing.

"That's a start," he says. His large hand covers mine on the railing. I withdraw mine and hide it within the pocket of my woolen coat.

Xavier's hand remains where mine had been as he states, "You're quarreling with your *aspire.*"

"We're fine," I say, brushing off his segue to pry into my personal life. My eyes shift to the swells of the sea.

Feeling the weight of Xavier's stare, I glance at him as he says, "You needed him...when you were alone...when we...when I..." he trails off again, sounding like he's struggling to find words.

"Yes, I need Reed," I agree. "He helped me when I couldn't help myself—when no one else would."

"He has earned your respect," Xavier says, his knuckles becoming whiter as they tense on the railing.

"He has earned my devotion," I correct him. My eyes widen when his fingers bend the metal of the railing with a crunching sound.

Xavier closes his eyes, like he's fighting some internal demons. He lets go of the railing. "I can see why he would merit your loyalty, but it was his duty to assist you. You're Seraphim, while he is a Power—" Xavier begins.

"You're wasting your time explaining angel rank to me because I find it a meaningless concept," I reply with narrowing eyes.

"When did you become so unreasonable?" he asks. "It's not meaningless when you consider that what he did for you was nothing less than his job," Xavier shoots back as if his point is important in the least, which it isn't to me.

"Protecting me was Reed's job?" I ask Xavier in a tone that implies he's insane.

He nods arrogantly. "Yes, every divine Power you encountered should've protected you."

"All of them?" I ask in a calm tone.

"Yes," he affirms.

"But, that's not what happened," I say with my eyebrow quirking.

"No," he agrees grimly.

"You're aware that angels mostly wanted to kill me?" I ask matter-of-factly.

"I am now," he counters with his eyebrows drawing together in a black look.

"How did you find out?" I ask out of morbid curiosity.

"Dominion gave us a report when we returned and began searching for you—" he starts to say.

"You had to search for me?" I interrupt to ask him derisively. "Why? Didn't you just say that you came from Paradise?"

"Yes," he affirms.

"Then shouldn't you have known where I was? What I've been doing? How things were going? Don't you guys do recon? Have a plan?" I ask, finding his answers to be suspect.

"Where you're concerned, it doesn't work like that—information regarding you is highly guarded. I'm not omnipotent and I've been deliberately kept uninformed about your work here—"

"Why?" I ask, interrupting him again.

"Because I wasn't allowed to be part of the equation again until now," he replies, attempting to sound civil, but anger leaks into his tone.

"Okay, let's say I believe you," I say skeptically, which makes him frown at me again.

"Are you questioning my integrity?" he asks in a stern tone.

I hold up my hand to ebb the irritation caused by my last comment. "Fine—you didn't know where I was or what I was doing. So, you went to Dominion for help?" I prompt him to continue.

He relaxes a little, but his jaw remains tense when he says, "Yes, we sought council with Dominion, and then…" he trails off, turning his back to the ocean, he leans against the bent railing to look at the ship behind me.

"And then what?" I ask.

"And then Tau and Cole had to stop me from tearing Gunnar apart," Xavier says in a dark tone as his arms cross over his chest.

My mouth falls open at the mention of Gunnar's name. Gunnar is the Power who was against me in my trial at Dominion—Pagan's special friend on the war council. "Why would you do that?" I ask, still not comprehending him at all.

"Because Gunnar made your binding ceremony with Reed a realistic course of action," he replies in a sullen tone.

"And you don't approve of my *aspire*?" I ask, not sure if I find him amusing or offensive.

"No," he retorts through gritted teeth.

"Why not?" I ask with growing anger, decidedly offended.

"You owe Reed nothing," Xavier replies in a bitter tone, "certainly far less than the forever that you promised him."

"You don't know what you're talking about, Reece," I retort, using his last name to sever some of the familiarity between us.

"Reece...Reed...isn't that a silly coincidence?" he asks, his mouth twisting in a grim smile that neither reaches his blue eye nor his green one.

"What are you talking about?" I ask while my mouth goes dry and dread creeps over me like a cold sweat.

"You don't remember what I'm talking about," he replies in an intense tone, while he points his finger at me. "And you bound your heart and soul to Reed without even knowing—" He doesn't finish, but clamps his teeth together tightly. Slowly, he drops the finger he'd been shaking at me.

Knowing that my face has gone from flushed to pale, I ask, "Without even knowing what, Xavier?" The need to hold my breath is almost irresistible as I wait for him to answer me.

He pushes away from the railing while saying, "I'll take care of it." He begins to stride away from me toward the entrance of the ship.

"You'll take care of what?" I ask his broad, retreating back.

"Everything," his response drifts back to me.

I allow him to take five more steps toward the interior of the ship before I cast my spell. Xavier stops abruptly, brought up short as he bumps into the invisible wall of energy I created in front of him.

"Evie!" he growls as he turns to look back at me. He rubs his nose like he would if he had just run into a closed door.

"I'm sorry, but your last comment sounded eerily like a threat to me. What did you mean when you said that you'd take care of everything, Xavier?" I ask calmly.

He just glares at me before he takes a few steps in my direction. I flick my wrist and his forward progress is halted as he collides with another invisible wall. "Reverse your spell," Xavier demands.

I take a step back in response to his anger. "Answer the question," I reply.

"No," he rejects stubbornly.

"What did you say?" I ask, before closing my eyes and whispering lyrical words to myself.

When I open them, I slowly move my hand laterally. Xavier's eyes widen as he stumbles sideways. He pushes back against the moving energy that continues to edge him toward the railing of the ship. As he resists my magic, I feel the sheer force of his strength as he literally pushes back. It causes some of the power to surge at me, stinging me inside. "Last chance, Xavier," I grunt, forcing him closer to the side of the ship.

When he shakes his head "no," I drive both my hands sideways in the air, pushing him to the railing.

Xavier holds on tight to it. "Evie," he growls my name, causing goose bumps to break out over my skin.

"Sorry, I can't hear your answer," I respond with *faux* calm, cupping my hand to my ear.

Xavier doesn't respond, but instead, he lets go of the railing before leaping up onto it. Poised above me, his wings spread wide as he flies straight up when he finds the weakness in my magic; my wall has no ceiling.

"Uh oh," I breathe. Searching the sky to locate where Xavier went, I quickly conclude that I've lost him. "Not good," I mutter clenching my teeth in fear.

Defensive strategies pulse through my mind. I react to the first viable solution that presents itself. Concentrating, I crouch down on one knee as a hundred of my clones explode from me; the perfect replicas stand on the deck like images in a house of mirrors, camouflaging me from the menace stalking me from the sky.

I wait a few moments before I decide that I'm better off inside the ship. As I inch forward toward the companionway, I send my clones to wander around ahead of me, but I pause when Xavier materializes on the deck twenty yards away.

Dripping wet from the rain and thoroughly pissed off, he wipes his mouth with the back of his hand while his huge, red wings move restlessly. I attempt to adopt a serene expression in order to blend in better with my clones, but my breathing is coming out in soft pants that I find hard to control.

Sniffing the air like a wolf, Xavier growls low, causing my heart to speed up and lodge somewhere in my throat. While his eyes scan all the clones on the deck to my left, I stand perfectly still and watch water drip from his chin onto his now bare chest. My knees weaken as his eyes drift to mine and then narrow when they lock on.

Xavier stretches his arms out wide from his sides as he walks negligently toward me. Each clone that he touches on his path to me swirls like fairy dust in the air, disappearing in winding billows of smoke, but he never even glances at them because his eyes never leave mine.

When he reaches me, I'm weak with fear. I don't even struggle when he grasps the lapels of my pea coat, pulling me the last few inches toward him.

"How did you know which one was me?" I ask him weakly.

"I know your heart," he replies. Pulling me up to him, he kisses me tenderly, his lips a plea against mine. Then, he whispers sadly against my mouth, "Remember me." His grip eases on my lapels and he reluctantly lets me go.

"Don't ever kiss me again," I say as I look in his eyes. "This isn't high school. I'm not in love with you anymore. I'm not the same girl—"

"I'm not talking about high school. Remember me," he says again as he looks into my eyes with his hands holding my shoulders.

Too stunned to react for a moment, I just stare up at him before a flood of color rushes to my cheeks. "Remember you? Don't tell me that you were my soul mate, too," I say in a strange, choked voice.

"No," he replies in an equally strained tone. "You only get one soul mate—human. I'm an angel."

"Oh," I murmur, exhaling deeply, "then...you're saying, what? That we knew each other...before...when we were..." Using my index finger, I point up toward the sky.

Sadness enters his eyes as he gazes at me. "I wasn't your soul mate in Paradise, Evie...I was your angel," Xavier replies.

"Xavier...that's not funny," I stutter.

"I assure you, Evie, there is nothing I find less amusing," he replies with a grim expression as his hand reaches up to cup my cheek.

"Xavier, you have no binding mark on you," I say, pointing to his chest.

"We said we'd wait until this was over—until we return together to Paradise," he answers.

"I can't hear this right now," I say while panic makes my heart beat out of control. Placing my hand on his chest, I try to push him away, but he doesn't move except to cover my hand with his own. I focus on it. *Strong*, I think.

"This isn't going away, Evie. I'm not leaving you again," he says, sounding resolved.

"You have to go away!" I reply in a plea, not looking at his face. "I have an *aspire!* You're too late."

His hand tightens over mine. "The binding with Reed was a commitment exacted under duress."

"No," I reply, shaking my head, "I wanted Reed."

"It was coercion," he counters.

"It was free will!" I say plainly. Xavier's jaw tightens as his frown deepens.

"You haven't had free will since I saw you last," he replies. "Everything after that has been survival—compulsion—force," Xavier says while his fingers curl around mine.

"Who else knows about this?" I ask, feeling the heat of his fingers warming mine.

"About us?" he asks, and I blanch and nod. "Tau, Cole, Phaedrus—" he says, and he smiles when my eyes shoot to his in surprise.

"Phaedrus knows? How long has he known?" I ask.

"I spoke to him at Dominion. I needed answers and…his council," Xavier admits.

"And he advised you to tell me that we were friends before we came here…forget high school, I mean, before high school… umm…before I was born?" I ask as I worry my lower lip in concentration.

"We were more than friends in high school, and yes, we were much more than friends before Earth, but…no, he didn't advise me to tell you," he replies. Holding my fingers in his, he brings them to his lips and kisses them.

"Don't," I say, pulling my hand from his. "What did Phaedrus say?" I ask, needing to hear Phaedrus' opinion. Phaedrus is a Virtue, not to mention the angel who performed the binding rites between Reed and me.

"He has his philosophy…and I have mine," Xavier states cryptically.

"What's his philosophy?" I counter.

"You are as tenacious as ever," he smiles.

"Xavier," I growl at him while he tucks a wisp of my hair behind my ear.

"Time," he responds. "He thought that you might need time to know me again—"

"THAT WAS GOOD ADVICE!" I scold him.

"No," he objects, "you've been running wild on your own without me. You've had to keep moving just to stay alive. I need you to know that I'm here for you…and why. I need you to know me again—that it was your plan for me to be here with you."

"Why should I believe you or trust you ever again? If what you're telling me is true, then that means you left me here alone," I accuse as my voice turns raw with emotion, for which I can't account.

"I hope that you never learn the exacting toll of being ripped apart like that," he replies quietly. Pain registers in his eyes as his hands close around mine. "To ache from the knowledge that I may never hold you again—to count the moments, like grains of sand, while we were parted only to escape the sky and find that you still only know me as a boy from school…" He trails off. His eyes search mine for any glimmer of recognition from me.

"Xavier, I don't remember anything but this life," I say, my eyes imploring his. "I remember high school and you throwing wads of paper at me in the bleachers at assemblies." I point at him, "And Drivers Ed! You remember—the time you and Cole sat in the back seat of the Drivers Ed car and pretended like every turn I made would be our last?"

"You were being too cautious," Xavier says tenderly. He reaches his hand up to stroke my damp hair. "If you had taken those turns any slower, we'd still be there."

"Whatever," I retort, irritated that he's still able to tease me, even in the midst of this conversation. "My point is that what I remember of you is not flattering."

"Junior Prom was nice," he says softly.

"Yes and you told me a few weeks later that you didn't think we were right for each other," I point out, surprised to realize that I still feel the sting of that rejection, even after all that has happened since then.

"We were becoming too close," he replies with a frown. "You were too fragile…I was losing control." His eyes soften. "What if I told you that being with you gives the night its purpose?" he asks. "I have memorized the curve of your body when you've lain in my arms. I've listened to your delicate breath, while I've pillowed your head on my chest. And one day soon, I'll be the one who steals your strength with just a kiss," he says, while placing my hand back on his chest so that I feel the primal beat of his heart under my fingertips.

"I don't remember you ever holding me like that," I murmur, shaking my head and trying to pull my hand from him.

"You didn't know I was there," he says softly. "It was my job to protect you and part of that was protecting you from the knowledge of what we are."

"I don't know you at all. It was all lies," I repeat, nearing despair.

"You know me. Soon, you'll remember us," he murmurs.

"And if I don't?" I ask, seeing pain enter his eyes again.

"You will," he replies, like a promise.

"You can't tell Reed," I state abruptly, while my mind tumbles over itself for ways to exact a promise of silence from him.

"Why not? He has to be told about us," he replies, and my fingers on his chest curl into a tight fist.

"Why does he have to know? It's all in the past—high school. It's the kind of thing that would make him…" I trail off as I bite my lower lip.

"He has to be told, Evie," Xavier replies with his eyes narrowing into a frown. "It's not something that I plan to keep a secret."

"WHY!" I shout, while I pull my hand away from him again. Color floods my cheeks at the thought of Xavier telling Reed anything about what we may have been to each other in a time that I can hardly even imagine, let alone remember.

"It will answer questions that he must've been asking himself since he met you," he replies.

"What questions?" I retort, panic rising in me again.

"He must have wondered how he came between two soul mates," he says in a gentle voice. "It is an alliance that is virtually unbreakable."

"You're saying you did that?" I ask in a rush. "You came between Russell and me?"

"Not me...you," he says quietly. "It was what you asked for: a reward for your mission here on Earth."

"I'm sorry," I say in confusion. "I don't understand."

"You asked for a love of your own choosing, not one that had been created for you. Soul mates are corresponding halves of a whole created to fit together in perfect symmetry. You wanted a love of your own making—your own creation...the ultimate free will. You did it for me—for us," Xavier says in a reverent tone that only causes me to panic more.

"No, you're lying! I'd never do that to Russell," I say, shaking my head.

"Things were different between both of you," he says.

"Why? Why were they different?" I ask.

"They were different because you love me," he replies with a smile touching his lips.

"I love you? You're saying I chose this mission for you? I chose to be the first angel with a soul?" I ask.

He nods with a solemn expression. "And I came with you to protect you."

"But, then you left me here," I reply, feeling stiff and taut.

Xavier's expression turns almost desperate. "I was called back! I had no choice in the matter: no free will," he says grimly. "Every moment away from you has been a crushing weight with no relief."

"Xavier," I say, trying to shrug his hands off my arms, but he pulls me against his chest and hugs me.

Whispering against my hair, he says, "You know me. You must remember me, Evie. It is your singular sweetness—your fire that burns within me and I have to find a way to bring you back to me."

"Xavier, I can't come back to you," I whisper.

He tightens his embrace for an instant before his arms ease from around me as he lets go of me. "You have no choice, Evie," he says with a sad smile. "Our futures are weft in patterns that will not allow us to fall away from each other. The fabric of time will tell our story, with or without you willing it. You will know me again."

"And Reed?" I ask, fearing what he's telling me.

His mouth thins in a narrow line. "Maybe he can become like the sea and forget the shape of things that once were, but now are lost," he replies.

"His shape is burned into me," I respond with intensity, pointing at my chest. "I will never forget him."

"'Never' is a deceptive concept, Evie," Xavier replies with an air of calm. "I prefer to wager on always—the infinity ahead to kiss your lips, to touch your skin—to help you rediscover the love between us."

"There's nothing between us, not anymore!" I disagree sternly, crossing my arms over my chest.

"There is!" he counters with equal heat. "I made you a promise that I wouldn't allow you to forget me and I intend to keep that promise."

"This is insane," I mutter as I rub my brow with a shaky hand. "You're speaking of things I can't even begin to respond to."

"What else can I do?" he asks while he threads his hands pensively through his blond hair.

"You can promise me that you won't tell Reed anything about this," I counter.

"By 'this' you mean 'us?'" Xavier asks, his brows coming together in frustration.

"Fine—us," I state with equal frustration.

"No," he states emphatically.

"No?" I retort as my breathing increases.

"No, I won't promise you that," he replies. "He needs to know."

A voice from behind Xavier interrupts my thoughts. "Xavier...you told her?" Tau asks with his eyes fixed on me. He's dressed warmly in a seaman's coat with a knit cap covering his auburn hair. Beside him, Cole is similarly attired as he scans Xavier's dripping wet form in front of me.

"Yes," Xavier affirms with a single nod. He drops his hands to his sides when he sees Cole standing beside Tau on the cold deck.

My eyebrows draw together in a scowl. "We've just been chatting. Anything else you guys want to tell me?" I ask them all with sarcasm dripping from my voice. "You're not my mother, are you Cole?"

A wide grin forms on his mouth before he laughs. "No, Evie," he says, shaking his dark head. "I'm not your mother. But, we've been friends for a very long time."

Tau frowns, "I thought we agreed to wait until after we dealt with the Gancanagh." His gray eyes bore into Xavier's.

"She pressed the issue. She tried to throw me overboard," Xavier responds with a reluctant smile.

"Evie?" Cole asks, intrigued.

"This will bring on complications that we don't need, Xavier," Tau continues, ignoring his last comment.

"Complications that I will field," Xavier replies calmly.

"Phaedrus said—" Tau begins.

"I know what he said," Xavier cuts him off in frustration.

Tau gives Xavier a disapproving look before his eyes shift back to me. I raise my chin as I stare back at him, feeling acutely uncomfortable in his presence. "Can we talk?" Tau asks me gently.

"What would you like to discuss?" I question, turning on him with thinly veiled hostility in my tone. "My *aspire*—my forgotten lover—my soul mate—or, I know! Let's talk about my undead stalker! Those are all topics I want to discuss with my long-lost father!"

"We don't have to discuss anything that makes you uncomfortable. I'd like to just try being in the same room with you…uh, maybe share a meal with you. We don't have to even talk if you don't wish to…" he trails off.

"You want to have dinner with me?" I ask. A confusing rush of guilt and fear mixed with an appalling sense of hope attacks me. Quickly, I try to swallow past the lump in my throat that the hope has elicited.

"Yes," he replies, and I get the sense that he is studying me.

"Alone? Just the two of us?" I ask, before glancing at Xavier and seeing his jaw tense in irritation.

"Yes," Tau replies again, his eyebrow lifting in quite the same way that mine does.

"When?" I ask.

"Tonight?" Tau counters.

"But, aren't we supposed to arrive at the castle by this afternoon?" I inquire.

"We should arrive within the hour," Tau replies.

"We'll be there that soon?" I ask. The air suddenly feels suffocating and heavy. Adrenaline ripples through my bloodstream, like water through narrowing channels, making me feel lightheaded.

I must look wobbly because Tau pulls me into his arms and holds me lightly against his chest. "Close your eyes." I struggle to take a deeper breath. "Picture yourself wandering beneath the moon's golden reflection," he says in a gentle voice as my cheek rests against his shoulder, "the heady scent of languid flowers in their first blush, carried on a balmy breeze; the elemental feeling of cool, evening sand beneath your feet; and the secret knowledge that you are one with it all."

A tear slips from my eye to roll down my cheek while I inhale his scent and find it to be so familiar to me—the scent of my home—of my childhood. Slowly, my hands come up to lightly touch his back. "You smell like the night to me," I whisper as my arms involuntarily tighten around him.

"Evening was when I could get the closest to you," he replies in a soothing voice. "When you were a baby, I could hold you through the dark hours...just you and me."

"You could?" I ask.

"You were so gentle and sweet...I was afraid to touch you at first. You were so human then...fragile and tiny."

"You were afraid of me?" I ask, not picking my head up from his shoulder. "Don't you meet with the Fallen in Sheol?"

"Yes," he replies, "but none of them has ever stolen my heart nor left me without words to ponder its loss." I close my eyes tighter so that I won't cry. "Will you have dinner with me tonight?" he asks me again as my arms loosen on him.

"Okay," I agree in a voice that is barely audible.

"Thank you," he replies with a smile in his tone.

Letting go of him, I keep my eyes averted from Tau as I walk toward the companionway of the ship. "Evie," Xavier calls to me. "We need to talk as well."

I pause for a moment before I glance at Xavier. "You're eternal, right?" I ask him in a rhetorical way. "I'm betting that you can wait."

Russell

CHAPTER 17

Ireland

Long, slantin' shadows fall like fence posts over the deep-red, embroidered tapestries linin' the wall in the hallway. This corridor, with its tall, narrow windows leads to the Archive Room. Knowin' where everythin' is in the Gancanagh estate doesn't make it less creepy; in fact, it might be more so 'cuz I'm used to seein' it well maintained and full of activity. Now, shattered glass and broken furniture litter the rooms like a frat house at the end of the term.

Anya rubs her nose again, tryin' hard to ease the burn of the sweet, cloyin' odor of the Gancanagh. If I wasn't so completely infuriated with her, I'd feel bad for her, but as things stand, it just makes me smile.

"You should've smelled it before they were evicted," I mutter to her. "Naw, come to think of it, you should've been in the caves with them. Now that was rank."

Anya ignores my comment and moves her hand back to a ready position on her bow. She stalks ahead of me a few paces, gettin' closer to Reed, Sorin, and Elan at the front of our unit, which is exactly where I want her to be: protected in the center.

I glance behind us several times as we make our way down the hall to ensure nothin' is comin' at us from behind. In this position, I have a clear view of Anya, and I plan on keepin' it until we know what we're dealin' with here.

Reed speaks into his wireless headset, which sends his voice echoin' to the earphone, "Approaching the Archive Room."

Preben's voice responds in our ears, "North Tower's clear—anything interesting in the Archive?"

"We'll let you know when we get in," Reed replies.

Preben says somethin' in Angel, which makes Zephyr smile.

"What'd he say, Zee?" I ask, 'cuz I hate bein' left out.

Zee shrugs negligibly. "He called dibs on any Faerie armor," he replies with a twinkle in his eyes. "Faeries are known for their intricate metalwork, especially armor and weapons."

"Does he know they sing?" I ask, rememberin' Red's memories of the weapons in the Archive Room singin' for her when I used my clone to talk to her in her captivity.

"Yes—that is essentially why Preben wants one," Zephyr answers, speakin' of the tall, silver-haired leader of the Dominion Powers.

Reed left the assignment of the other Dominion teams to Preben after choosin' ours. Sorin, Elan, and Tycho are the only Powers Reed let accompany us, 'cuz I think that he worked with them in China and they earned his trust.

I look ahead then to the enormous, wooden doors encompassin' the far wall. They're not merely ostentatious 'cuz they almost reach the ceilin', they're also adorned with intricately carved dragonheads clawin' outward, like vicious sentinels frozen in the instant before they could surge forth from their mahogany prison.

Sniffin' the air, I say in a low tone, "Hold up, Reed."

The angels ahead of me halt, becomin' still as I creep forward toward the doors.

"What is it?" Reed asks.

I sniff the air again. "I don't know…magic, I think, but the smell is different…ashen and smoky, like a campfire," I explain, tryin' to find the source of the energy. "Y'all got marshmallows?" I ask, over my shoulder with a slow smile.

Glancin' behind me, the angels all stare back at me, puzzled.

"Never mind," I mumble, wishin' Red was here.

Reachin' out to the doors cautiously, all the hairs on my arms rise in response. Light shines swiftly from the carved Faerie writin' on the archin' eaves above the doors, while frightenin' crackin' and creakin' come from the wood. Hastily, I step back from the edifice.

A curlin', dark roil of smoke tumbles and rises from the large nostrils of the fire-breathin' beast etched within the doors. The dragonheads' expressions change from tragic to fierce while they animate and move with struggling jerks to free themselves from the timbered plane.

"Naw, don't get up on our account," I murmur in a sanguine tone I'm not feelin'.

The heads pivot toward me as one scaly cranium lurches violently in my direction, its serpentine neck comin' within inches of my face. A thunderin' voice punctures the air as it speaks. The voice is somethin' between the sound of a biker gang startin' up their engines and a launch at Cape Canaveral. The vibration from it causes what is left on nearby tables to shatter before they hit the ground. Couple that with the smell of brimstone and burnin' flesh that rolls out of its mouths in smoky plumes and it's enough to make me feel a second of regret for havin' come on this mission.

When the rumblin' voice from the dragonhead subsides, I ask, "Anyone catch that?" while backin' up further from the snarlin' beast tearin' away from the door inch by inch.

Wood splinters in tremblin' cracks as the two-headed dragon strains to get out of it. Spatterin' flames leap into the air like the inferno from fire-breathers at a carnival sideshow, while the heat from them rushes oven-hot around me.

"Y'all can feel that, right?" I ask Reed and Zephyr at my sides.

"No, faerie magic is useless against us. Is it warm?" Zephyr inquires with a grin.

"Yeah, it sorta is, actually," I nod with an ironic twist of my lip. "What'd it say?" I ask, sweatin'. "Do y'all know?"

The ground rumbles as one huge claw scrapes the floor in front of the door. Sharp, mahogany talons tear the ancient rug in long, jagged knife-lines, while the stone floor cracks beneath its weight.

"Please tell me that someone knows Faerie," I say hopefully.

"I know it," Reed replies, soundin' like he's concentratin'.

"You gonna let me in on what it said or not?" I ask, before cringin' when the beast throws back its heads and roars triumphantly as its second set of talons dislodge from the wood, poundin' on the floor with a startlin' BUMP.

Reed, ever the professional, says calmly, "It asked this question: 'When confronted by the knowledge that all is lost, save the disgrace of death, what is your weapon of choice?'"

"It wants to know what weapon I'd pick if I know I'm gonna die?" I ask, frownin' at his face.

"Yes," he states.

"Do you think it's a trick question?" I shoot back. "I mean, if we're wrong, what do you think will happen?" I ask, attemptin' to sound casual.

"I think the beast will continue to grow until we solve the enigma or it kills you," Reed replies without much expression. "Do you know any anti-dragon charms?"

I give him an are-you-serious look. "Naw, I think I'm gonna have to wing it," I reply sarcastically.

"A shield might be helpful," Reed suggests as both dragonheads inhale deep, powerful breaths. "Heat-resistant," he adds with both his eyebrows risin'.

"Noted," I reply with an air of confidence I don't really feel.

The dark, knotty eyes of the dragon shift dully while it spews a torrent of flames from its mouths. I just have time to whisper words that cause an invisible wall of energy to form in front of me. Kneelin' behind it, heat wraps 'round the wall and singes the edge of my wing along my left flank.

When I open my eyes, Anya is standin' directly in front of me, tryin' unsuccessfully to block the magical fire. Reachin' behind her back, she pulls a golden arrow from her quiver, quickly ratchetin' it on her bow. Releasin' the shaft, the bow makes a low, musical twang as the arrow flies straight through the head of a dragon, like mist, and embeds in the door.

In frustration, she turns on Reed with a torrent of Angelic words.

"I *am* thinking, Anya," Reed replies, unruffled. "Russell will just have to play with it until we decipher the enigma."

Zee frowns. "There are more weapons than words to describe them," Zephyr says in a low tone to Reed.

As a suggestion, I offer, "Could it be magic?"

In response to my answer, the enraged dragon roars, breathin' brimstone at me again. Feelin' like I'm meltin', I hunch down behind the shield I had created. When I glance up again, the dragon appears to have grown, its heads nearin' the vaulted ceilin'.

"No, not magic," Reed replies, standin' within the inferno, like it is a mirage, as the flames abate.

With a feminine growl, Anya grasps Zephyr's broadsword from his idle hand and rushes the dragon, choppin' at its heads. She is only successful at cuttin' the air as the sword passes through it like an apparition.

"Why can't y'all touch it?" I ask with my jaw clenched. But then, the dragon tears free from the door with a rain of shatterin' wood. Sweat glides down the side of my face; I swipe at it irritably.

The monstrous, wooden reptile lunges, snarlin' at us, but the angels all hold their ground in its presence. Anya's ebony wings stretch in front of me like the night sky in her attempt to stop the creature from reachin' me. Ripples of energy, like waves in a pool, distort its polished scales when it passes through her like a dream.

"Its faerie magic doesn't truly exist for us," Reed answers my question, while the dragon rams its head at me, knockin' me back, as a whoosh of air expels from my lungs. "But, it seems to work well on half-humans. We have to solve its riddle by naming the weapon to open the door."

"A battle-axe?" Sorin asks the dragon.

Enraged by his answer, the dragon's wooden wings unfold. Destroyin' a tapestry, the fabric tears loudly on its serrated edge. Shriekin' and growin' in size, it takes up a wider girth of corridor.

I cringe inwardly and call out, "It's gettin' bigger," while dodgin' the crushin' blows from the dragon's tail as it labors by me.

The angels form a huddle in front of the door. "Let's not guess— for Russell's sake," Reed orders the Powers with a modicum of pity.

"Yeah, don't guess!" I agree grimly, as I back up. My hands are slick with sweat. "What was the question again?" I ask Zee with a look of supplication.

Zephyr responds with an air of patience, "When confronted by the knowledge that all is lost, save the disgrace of death, what is your weapon of choice?'"

Reed's head snaps up as a smile spreads from his eyes to his lips. He utters somethin' that has to be Faerie. Then, he murmurs, "Immortality."

I crouch down low so I can lurch away from the next burst of fire before it fries me, but instead, the energy in the room instantly shifts. Then, not unlike a vacuum suckin' up a dust particle, the dragon is swept up off its feet; its scales liftin' like shingles in a windstorm.

I'm pulled off my feet, too, bein' sucked toward the Archive Room doors in a rush of wind. Anya flies from the ground then, to get directly in my path in order to keep me from becomin' part of the enchanted door by clutchin' me to her.

As the wind eases, her hypnotic-green eyes stare up into mine while we both use our wings to remain aloft. My hand slips from her back to her face, cuppin' her cheek, as my thumb caresses her luminous skin. Her eyes close and I don't know if I can survive not kissin' her where her sooty lashes contrast against her pale complexion.

Leanin' down, my lips near hers, but just as they would've connected, she eases back from me. Openin' her eyes, she looks away, causin' my hand to slip from her cheek.

"Immortality," she says in a thin, haunted tone. "It is a weapon with a double-edge."

Turnin' away from me, she flies back down to the ground, before followin' Sorin, Elan, and Tycho into the Archive Room. Reed and Zephyr wait for me by the carved door that is now just that: a door.

"Injured?" Reed asks in an assassin' way.

I shrug, noncommittal. "Just my pride," I reply before punchin' one of the inanimate dragonheads on the door, splinterin' it to pieces.

"Good thing you are not in short supply," Zephyr grins.

"I'll say," I agree, flexin' my fingers and watchin' Anya gaze 'round the nearly empty room. "Looks like they took almost everythin'."

"All but one suit of armor and a battle-axe," Zephyr comments.

An exquisite suit of silver armor, edged in gold, stands alone in the center of the room. The tunic-style plackart of the armor is deeply etched with intricate scrolls, and on the breastplate, a set of golden wings is centered. I don't need to look behind the plackart to know that the back of it has two, long plackets, slits in the armor, created to accommodate the wings of the wearer.

Matching, silver chainmail cuisse protect the wearer's thighs from harm as the greaves, in this case silver metal boots resemblin' the framin' of a lead glass window, protect the calves and feet.

One silver gauntlet of the armor holds a seriously deadly-lookin' battle-axe. The serrated edge of the silver axe-head resembles the arch of a wing, while the long shaft of the axe is notched for grippin'.

"That's Evie's," I state with a growin' frown. "Brennus gave it to her 'cuz she went right to it when he brought her here. It belonged to him. He made it himself." My gaze shifts to Reed's. "Damn, it's like he knew we were comin here."

"I told him that I would come when the contract was broken," Reed replies.

"Do we let Red see this thing?" I ask, indicatin' the armor.

Reed walks slowly to the armor and pauses in front of it. A reflection of Reed's face shines on it, etched with complex scrollin' marks. He reaches his hand out, restin' it gently against the cold metal of the breastplate where his face had been. His hand tenses and he crushes the golden wings affixed there. When he pulls his hand away, the metal moves too, poppin' back out and smoothin' until it is like new again.

"She would look beautiful in this armor. Did you know that it will mold to her shape if it desires her?" Reed asks me, not lookin' away from it.

"Is that right?" I ask, tryin' to imagine somethin' like that.

"Yes. But then, it would always remind me of Brennus," he adds, frownin'.

I frown at the armor now, too, sayin', "We could use it for target practice when we work on our spells."

"It's for her. She'll decide what she wants to do with it," Reed says in a low tone. He squeezes the device on his ear, activatin' his microphone. "Archive Room clear."

Preben's voice sounds in our ears, "Weapons?" he asks.

"Gone—just a present here for Evie," he replies. "We're moving on to the South Tower—the Harem."

"We're nearing the East Tower," Preben reports.

"Most of the dead freaks were housed in that part of the castle," I chime in.

"It should smell lovely then," Preben replies. It's obvious to me that some of Brownie's sarcasm is rubbin' off on him to claim another victim.

"Yeah, good luck with that," I reply with a reluctant smile.

Leavin' the Archive Room, we move down the corridor connectin' the West Tower to the South Tower. This hallway is even more disturbin' than the last one, 'cuz pools of dried blood lie in testament to what can only be tantamount to a slaughter. Overturned tables and broken vases make it look more like a barroom after a brawl than the palace I remember.

Passin' by bloody handprints smeared across a wall, I hold mine up to it. Mine's much larger. It must be from a woman.

"They've redecorated," I say in a low tone.

Glancin' at Anya, she looks stone white against her midnight wings. "Stay with me," I order her with a stern look.

"Why?" she shoots back with her shoulders straightenin'.

"'Cuz cannibals *are* what they eat," I reply matter-of-factly. Her eyes narrow at me, but she doesn't disagree.

More eerie wooden doors hang at the entrance to the South Tower, otherwise known as the Harem, but these doors are capriciously left un-enchanted.

"Movement," Reed warns.

I strain my ears, tryin' to hear somethin', but the silence only grows louder the more I try. "Remind me never to be your neighbor," I whisper to Reed. "Should we knock?" I ask, liftin' my chin toward the doors ahead of us.

"No," Reed replies. "They already know we're here." Reed pushes one of the doors back slowly. A strong reek of Gancanagh mixed with blood seeps out from it. My flesh crawls when Reed says softly, "They're attempting to surround us."

I search the intervenin' spaces between the end of the corridors and us. Our position in front of the doors leaves us vulnerable not only to what's in the Harem, but also to the south corridor and the east corridor that both connect in front of it in an L-shape.

A fragile, feminine voice pleads softly, "Help me…please," as a young woman staggers over the debris-ridden stone floor toward us from the adjacent east corridor.

Goose bumps run the length of me when I notice her neck above the sexy collar of her white blouse. Bloody trails from puncture wounds no longer cry like tears from her.

Glancin' at Reed, he says in a low tone to me, "Be ready." His eyes focus not on the girl in the hallway, but on the tower doors juxtaposed to us.

"I need help," the girl whispers again, and somethin' in my chest tightens. My eyes fly to Anya as I imagine her with the same bloody tear streaks on her neck.

"There are more behind her at the end of the corridor," Zephyr informs me in so low a tone, that I don't think anyone but me hears him.

The dark wings on Anya's back recoil in reaction to the pitiful plea from the apparently fragile victim, pinnin' them back as if in dread. She steps forward when the girl falters again, intent, it would seem, on helpin' her.

"Anya!" I growl in a sinister voice that doesn't sound like my own.

It works 'cuz she stops several paces away from the girl. But when Anya looks back at me over her shoulder, she misses the intimate smile that flickers over the injured girl's lips, revealin' her nefarious nature. A fraction of a second after that, the newly formed Gancanagh leaps forward, runnin' at Anya with the supernatural speed of a born predator.

Anya must've seen the horror on my face, 'cuz she turns back and tries to raise her bow, but her fingers fumble on the string and the arrow slips from it. A *click* resonates in the hallway while the fangs of this fresh-turned Gancanagh engage in her mouth. The flash of white from their syringe-sharpness triggers me. I disregard the onslaught of other undead females comin' at us from inside the tower doors at my side.

In this moment, I finally understand the problem viscerally: this illness is terminal. One touch will render all of my pathetically conceived plans to protect Anya obsolete. She'll respond only to them and she'll never be mine again—not once, not ever.

With a risin' tide of feminine Gancanagh crestin' the threshold of the Harem tower, I ignore both their ambush and the fact that gettin' to Anya is likely a doomed effort. The beautiful bloodsucker is almost on top of her. I sprint past Zee, who blocks a slue of reekin' killers from gang-swarmin' me. He uses his broad sword in a sweepin' motion, carvin' a sprawlin' tideline of blood as heads flail from bodies.

Reed is almost invisible the way he moves through the Gancanagh; he's a shadowy silhouette leavin' a trail of dead corpses littered on the floor. I brush past Sorin, Tycho, and Elan, all locked in battle with the nearest enemy.

Red, polished nails reach out toward Anya's face as a girlish leer lives within dead eyes. The irony of this moment is that my illness is just as terminal as the one that destroyed the soul of this stark-white killer. I know that if she touches Anya, I'll be as good as dead inside, too. I understand now that Anya is what she says she is: she is my *aspire*.

As I acknowledge that fact, I surrender to the darkness that grows 'round me in my need to be fast enough—to be the wall that stops the toxic fingertips from reachin' the delicate skin of my angel. Cold-black emptiness surrounds me at once as I become blind and deaf in less time than a heartbeat. In an empty, torturous ache of utter nothingness, I'm pulled through darkness to materialize in front of Anya.

The cold hand of the undead touches my neck. Shock registers in her lackluster eyes when she realizes I'm the recipient of the soft caress meant for Anya's cheek.

"That's *my* angel," I growl while my red wings block her from Anya.

She spares one glance to where I had been a second ago, several yards away, and like me, she doesn't really know how I got here. Placin' my hand on her icy forehead, a glow of light issues from it, liftin' her off her feet and throwin' her backward. She lands in the middle of the corridor, now completely dead.

Screams come from the other Gancanagh amassin' in the east corridor, but they're more like shrieks of horror at what I've done to their friend than war cries. These are not hard-edged faeries who met their undeaths fightin' for their lives. They were human women, many of which are teenagers, who succumbed first to the seductive intoxication of the Gancanagh skin, most likely becomin' a meal for one or more of the fellas, and then turned into vicious killers and were left, much like a rodent problem, for the new tenants.

A ripplin' murmur of feminine voices permeates the air, while I reach back and pull Anya protectively into my arms. My wings curve 'round her instinctually as phrases like "The Red Menace" and "The Other" are spoken in dread-filled whispers. The Gancanagh nearest us in the east corridor attempt to retreat by turnin' and pushin' each other as if we've dispensed tear-gas on a crowd of protesters.

But, somewhere at the back of them, comes a barkin' command for attack.

"OY! Da other is nuting," a clipped, masculine voice says. "Ye're powerful now—immortal and he is merely lunch." It's apparent by their continual shovin' to get away from me that they aren't buyin' Declan's lie.

"Ah, no, you gotta be kiddin' me," I breathe, seein' Declan and Faolan standin' behind the females, urgin' them on. "You're hidin' behind girls now?" I call to them. "I thought I smelled the stink of cowardice."

"'Tis na cowardice," Declan calls back, soundin' offended. "'Tis strategy. We're teaching dem domination trough war...and we're teachin' ye dat when ye kill us we'll jus make more."

"You're hidin' behind their skirts," I taunt them. "And y'all know that they're not powerful."

"Ahh, but dey've a powerful effect on ye, do dey na? 'Twould hurt ye ta kill dem, especially since dey were once so very human," Declan explains with a calculated grin.

"Whah would hurt him more is takin' his *aspire* from him," Faolan says in a conversational tone to Declan. "Ye know, since being wi' our queen, I've had a real craving for *aingeal*, and her dark wings are terribly sexy."

Faolan's fangs shoot forward in his mouth with a decisive *click* as he smiles coyly towards Anya. Anya growls at him as her eyes narrow to slits. With the sound of fightin' still goin' on behind us, I know that I need to keep them at bay for now.

"Fay," Declan asks, "would ye say dat 'tis a mite greedy ta try ta keep two *aingeals?*"

"'Tis, Deck. 'Tis really very greedy, da other," he agrees, shakin' his head at me, while several undead females plow past him in the other direction. "Whah do ye say ye give us Genevieve and ye can keep da other one?" he asks, lookin' at Anya.

I stiffen.

"Would dat make her da other's other?" Declan asks Faolan with a grin.

"'Twould," Faolan agrees with a nod.

"Anyway," Declan smiles at me, "we're already very partial ta our queen—no offense—ye're really quite lovely and under different circumstances, I'd luv ta taste ye," he adds, shruggin' at Anya.

"Look here," Faolan smiles, "we'll trow in da house for ye—sorta a weddin' present."

"'Tis more yer style now, anyway—whah wi' all da destruction, 'tis much more like da trailer park dat ye're used ta," Declan says smugly, and then his face takes on a grim visage. "Now, where is our queen?" he asks me between his gritted teeth.

"You look dead-serious, Declan," I say, smilin'. "Red said y'all have a tendency to turn moody all of a sudden—it could be from all those female hormones all y'all been drinkin'. It makes you edgy."

Without even tryin', Declan creates a fireball and throws it at me. I tense, pullin' energy to me and lettin' it pulse out of my hand. My magic stops the fireball midway between him and me.

"Your elf dart looks like it has lost its way," I say, allowin' the fire to shimmer in stasis for a few seconds before I shatter it in flaming shards of fire and spew it back at them.

The fire misses them as Declan deflects it. It hits several of the fleein' Gancanagh females, catchin' their clothin' and hair on fire, but although they scream in terror, it's apparent when the flames die out almost instantly that their toxic skin is unharmed by it.

"She taught ye magic?" Declan accuses, like Red betrayed him personally.

"You're surprised?" I ask him. "She's my soul mate."

"And our queen," Faolan counters grimly.

"And my *aspire*," Reed replies.

Reed, standin' next to me, looks like he walked through a meat grinder. Pieces of flesh and blood cling to his dark armor, but I can't see his face 'cuz it's covered by a black, assassin's hood.

"Da *aingeal*," Declan calls. "How is it dat ye haven't killed da other yet?"

"He grows on one," Reed replies smoothly.

"Like a callus?" Declan asks with a sneer.

"Something like that," Reed replies as he starts stridin' in an invisible stream of speed at Declan.

With his sword drawn, Reed hefts it to strike the Gancanagh in the hallway, choppin' through everyone in his path to Red's former bodyguards. Declan, seein' him comin', pulls out a small, jeweled compact from his pocket.

"Ye'll give her our regards, won't ye?" he asks, before flippin' open the lid of the compact.

Instantly, Declan and Faolan distort, shiftin' into the mirror, like someone flushed them down a toilet. The mirror drops to the floor where their feet had been, and stands wide open.

Reed comes to a halt in front of it, before throwin' his powerful sword in an uncharacteristic display of anger. Zee flies past me, followin' Reed, and I watch in disbelief as Reed explodes into a swarm of angry, buzzin' honeybees.

The swarm hovers over the mirror, circlin' it in preparation of followin' the dead guys to their lair. Zephyr, reachin' the mirror, picks it up and snaps it closed before the bees have a chance to enter it.

"You are going to let them taunt you into following them?" Zephyr angrily asks the swarm hoverin' in the air.

The bees morph into the shape of Reed's outline, before implodin' into his angelic form again. Grimly, Reed pulls the assassin's hood back from his face, revealin' his clenched jaw while he glares at Zephyr and the mirror in his hand. Zee sees him look at the mirror, so he crushes the metal under his fingers without blinkin' an eye.

"ZEE!" Reed explodes with frustration in every line of his demeanor. "That was a direct line to Brennus!" he shouts, pointin' his finger at the now useless metal pebble in Zee's palm.

"And now, it's a paperweight," he replies. "Since when do we do anything on their terms?" he asks Reed rationally.

Reed tenses. "I could've killed him—killed them all on my terms!" he shouts at Zee. I haven't seen Reed this out of control since Brennus took Evie.

"NO!" Zephyr yells back, pointin' right back at Reed. "You don't know what was waiting for you at the other end of this portal."

"The perfect opportunity," Reed replies heatedly.

"Or your perfect demise," Zephyr counters coolly.

"What am I supposed to do now?" Reed asks Zee roughly. "He's a coward that won't face me."

"For now, rejoice in this deliverance from evil," Zephyr replies in a calm tone. "Sorin, Tycho, Elan—let us find the rest of the newly turned Gancanagh and dispose of them. Evie will be upset if she sees them." To Reed he says, "Stay with Russell and help him protect Anya."

As Zee walks away to hunt Gancanagh, Reed reaches down and picks up his sword. Then, he leans it against the wall and reluctantly pulls the blood-smeared, black armor off of him.

"You okay?" I ask Anya, whom I've pressed tight to my side.

She nods her head solemnly, not sayin' a word. I lean down and kiss her temple lightly, wantin' to do more but not knowin' how she'll react to me kissin' her lips.

"It is fortunate for me that they were not as interested in me as they were in Evie," Anya says in a soft, shaky voice.

"Huh?" I mutter, rattled by the very scent of her skin. It makes my heart pound harder in my chest as my hand runs lightly over the contours of her soft wings. The crickets in my stomach are reactin' wildly to holdin' her. I want to crush her to me now, as I think of what could've happened to her only minutes ago.

Her hand shakes as she puts it to her forehead. "It would have solved two of your problems with one, small solution," she replies, pullin' away from my side. "Lucky for me, they were not interested in a trade." She exhales like she has been holdin' her breath in dread.

Lookin' at her pale face, there is fear in her eyes as she tries hard to avoid mine. My eyes narrow when what she just said registers.

"You think—you believe I'd give you to them if they agreed to the trade? Your life for Evie's?" I ask her, afraid that I'm right—that that is what she believes.

She stumbles away from me on shaky legs, goin' to where she had dropped her golden bow. Pickin' it up, her fingers are stiff and she has trouble adjustin' an arrow on it.

"Are you gonna answer me?" I ask her angrily, now completely offended by what she implied.

She stiffens even more. "I did not know," she replies with the numb voice of someone who just experienced trauma. "I do not know to what lengths you will go to be rid of me. I am merely the other's other."

"AHHH, C'MON!" I say with exasperation while my stomach twists into knots. "You can't listen to them—you can't really believe that I'd give you to those monsters, Anya!"

Her bow trembles in her hand as she stammers in a haunted voice, "I...I was next to you...listening. I hear what they say to you... that you greedy to want two angels. I close my eyes and I hold my breath because they do not know that you do not want me—that I am nothing to you," she breathes, and a small tear falls from the corner of her eye. Her hand comes swiftly up to dash it away before she continues. "And this fear—fear like I do not know before is making me sick—ache." She holds her fist against her heart before finally lookin' at my face. "Not fear that they will kill me, but fear that you will betray me and I will welcome their death."

"I would never do that," I say grimly. "You must know that I'd never do that to you."

More tears fall from her green eyes as she looks 'round at the bloody walls, appearin' more afraid than I've ever seen her look. "I want...I need..." she swallows hard against the obvious lump in her throat.

"Anya," I say her name softly, 'cuz she looks so lost and I did that to her. I made her afraid of me...and maybe afraid of her love for me.

Somethin' squeezes tight in my chest. But, when I step closer to her to pull her into my arms, she backs away from me. With her teeth clenched, she raises her bow, pointin' it at me while she continues to back away from me.

"Anya," Reed says her name gently. "I know it's very tempting to kill Russell, but please don't. I need him to sniff out the portals that the Gancanagh have stashed all over this estate."

Dressed now in just a t-shirt and black, athletic pants, Reed approaches Anya slowly. Holdin' his hand out to her, she weakly lowers her bow, like she can't hold it up any longer.

"She has battle-fatigue, Russell," Reed says to me in a low tone. "She's in shock—this has to be the first time she's ever been witness to this kind of slaughter."

I glance 'round at the floor, seein' body parts everywhere. The last battle we were in was bad, but this is just plain gory.

My eyes narrow, not only 'cuz of what he just said, but 'cuz Anya just walked into Reed's open arms, lettin' him comfort her against his chest. A low, mean growl rumbles in my throat, makin' a smile immediately appear on Reed's lips. His hand slips to Anya's back, holdin' her against him.

"There is nothing like a Throne to bring just the right amount of karma," he says, when she leans her pale cheek against his shoulder. "I've watched you comfort Evie just like this and felt the same way— like I could tear your heart out through your back."

"I was thinkin' of just crushin' yours and leavin' it where I'd found it," I reply in a salty tone.

His grin widens. "Yes...karma," Reed says in a knowin' voice.

He speaks softly in Angel to Anya, but she doesn't respond. She looks numb. Liftin' her up into his arms, he tries not to smile again when another growl comes from me. Reed walks the few feet to me. Shiftin' Anya into my arms, her head rests against my chest and I try not to squeeze her too tight.

Reed says, "There were some comfortable-looking sofas in the library we passed in the North Tower. Let's go find one for Anya."

"Do you think she'll be okay?" I ask worriedly. I've seen soldiers with stares like hers before…in many, many, lifetimes, but I've never seen it happen to an angel.

"Yes. We'll locate some clean blankets and we'll keep her warm," Reed assures me.

Reed collects his armor before walkin' next to Anya and me in the corridor.

"Damn, Reed, do you know what this means?" I ask as we walk.

Lookin' puzzled he asks, "No, what?"

"It means you're not the stiff, emotionless, soul mate-stealin', a-hole I thought you were," I reply with irritation in my voice.

Reed's brows come together as he thinks about what I've just said. "And you are not the—" and he says somethin' in Angel I don't know, "that I thought you were."

A reluctant smile touches my lips. "Well, shhhheeeeeeeit, right?" I ask, as we turn down another long corridor together.

"Yes, exactly," he agrees, noddin'.

Evie

CHAPTER 18

Welcome Home

The cloudy night sky lends little light to the surrounding grounds of Brennus' estate, but my angel vision is such that I can see everything very well—too well. Spent shell casings litter the ground like acorns from an ancient oak tree, while uprooted pines and torn sod remain like fallen soldiers in the aftermath of a horrible war.

Under my own power, I fly past the cliffs from the ship moored off the Irish coastline. I can still see the fading telltale tire tracks across the lawn, a testament to my desperate escape from this prison. The starry sky had broken open for Reed and me when we had driven over the edge of the rock face and entered the portal leading to London. Now, the same sky that had been a co-conspirator in my quest to be with Reed seems to be coldly disapproving of my presence. The wind, lashing my hair into my face, seems angry with me for returning after it had given its last, best effort to save my life.

Touching down, my feet crunch the gravel on the circular drive in front of the massive gray, stone façade of Brennus' fortress. Interior lights shine through panes of glass, while the froth of white curtains waft in the open air from the shattered ones. I concentrate on putting one foot in front of the other. It's a simple plan that should require very little effort. Should.

Approaching the imposing stone gargoyles at the illuminated front entrance, I falter for a moment, losing my single-mindedness when the damp chill from one falls upon me. Flanked by Tau on one side of me and Xavier on the other, Xavier wastes no time in smashing his fist into the iniquitous snarl of the gargoyle. Pieces of stone shower the ground at my feet.

"Not a fan of the arts?" I ask him with a wry smile, trying to cover my hesitation.

Xavier flashes me a perfect smile, saying, "No, just not a fan of evil."

Glancing through the doors of the front entrance, Powers are moving everywhere I look. Recognizing none of them, I hesitate again. All I want to do is find Reed, Russell, and Zee and make sure they're okay, but I don't know how these unfamiliar angels will react to my presence, so I start plotting an alternate route.

"Is there a problem?" Tau asks in a gentle voice.

"Do you know them?" I ask him. My gray eyes meet his and my hand gestures in the general direction of the war-like angels inside as they move around the fortress, like a swarm in the nerve-center of a hive.

"The Powers?" Tau asks for clarification, his auburn eyebrow arching in question.

When I nod, he scans the crowd. Some are removing broken furniture, while others are repairing the glass ceiling that had been shattered by Casmir's army of fallen angels when they had attacked Brennus to get to me. But some, upon sighting us, are already staring with blank expressions.

Tau says patiently, "I recognize several, but I'm not acquainted with the majority."

"Do they know I'm coming?" I ask. My nails dig into my palms because I can't discern if they're "friendlies" as they move around at preternatural speeds.

"Yes, why?" he questions, puzzled. I happen to glance from his face to that of Xavier's and when he reads my body language, he frowns.

I shrug, saying as calmly as I can, "Because the ones that don't know about me usually freak when they see me." Xavier's eyes run the length of me, which makes me lift my chin. I shift agitatedly as I think of other less populated entrances than this one.

"Things aren't like they used to be," Tau responds while his fingers lightly take mine.

"Then, why do I feel like a criminal about to walk into a law enforcement convention?" I counter. I refrain from mentioning that just going inside is like walking into one of the cellar rooms of Brennus' cave in Houghton, but I don't want to discuss that with them.

"We're here to protect you now," Tau says in a serious tone.

"As I recall, you wouldn't even tell me the homework assignment for Calc when I missed class," I counter with an edge in my tone. "And, if you haven't noticed, there are only two of you and there are over a hundred of them, maybe more—not great odds if things turn ugly."

"You're a divine Seraph," Xavier answers for Tau. "You outrank them. And, skipping class to go sledding with cafeteria trays is not behavior we reward."

"How did you know about that?" I ask suspiciously, but then I hold up my hand to stop him from answering. "Never mind. Being Seraphim is a matter of degree to them. I'm also flagrantly human." Feeling uncomfortable, I pull my hand from Tau's.

Xavier's frown softens. "You are a refinement of both and I will kill anyone who doesn't agree," he replies.

Rolling my eyes at him, I ask, "Can you please be serious?"

"I am serious," Xavier says soberly. "Show me those who object and I will end them."

Startled by his demeanor, I reply, "Let's not act crazy—most angels are just used to the same old thing—status quo. We shouldn't hurt them if it can be avoided."

"Do you think that I'm misguided? You really don't remember anything about Paradise, do you?" Xavier asks pointedly. When I shake my head and look down, he says, "I intend to establish supremacy here—our supremacy."

"Why does it have to be like that? They probably already think I'm a nightmare," I sigh.

Xavier ignores my sigh, saying, "Powers are strong—warriors. Everything is about power. I'll make sure they know yours extends with mine."

Moving with purpose, he strides into the middle of the medieval foyer that I have always regarded as the "lobby" of the castle. Standing near a twisted, wrought-iron pillar beneath a clear view of the turrets, Xavier begins to speak in Angel to the Powers surrounding him.

Entering the hall with Tau, the heat of the stone fireplace at my side warms me as I observe Xavier in the center of the room. His enormous wings spread out around him in a magnificent, crimson exhibition of strength. A ripple of nervous energy envelopes me seeing them thus displayed.

"What's he saying?" I ask Tau while he looks on with an approving smile.

"He has just announced your arrival," Tau replies.

"Oh…is that all?" I ask skeptically, "Because it sounded to me like he said a lot more than 'we're home.'"

"He also declared today as 'Ruination Day' for all who oppose you," Tau adds, his lips twitching while his gray eyes turn to mine.

"Ruination Day? Who talks like that?" I ask as my narrowing eyes go to Xavier again. "What does that even mean?"

"It means that anyone who objects to your presence is invited to fight him in order to demonstrate his dissention," Tau replies with an undeniable degree of satisfaction. "They respect strength, so he'll show them strength."

My eyes drift back to Xavier who is staring down every other angel in the room like a ruthless dictator at a book burning, while the light from the fireplace dances over the planes of his skin. Every line of his body denotes the fact that he is ready to pounce on someone at the least provocation. My skin prickles, assessing the several tiers of angels within the room.

How long could he last against them? I wonder as dread fills me at the mental image of it.

"They also respect being treated as equals," I reply matter-of-factly.

I walk over and I stand beside Xavier. "Um, can I just say something?" I ask in an exasperated voice. Every eye in the hall is already on me, so I continue. "Hi, I'm Evie," I introduce myself uncomfortably, looking around. "There's a slight change in plans—there'll be no ruination today," I glare at Xavier, "instead, I'd like to thank you all for coming to help us. Maybe once you've all been around me for a while, you'll see that I'm not creepy and then we can all be...uh, friends?"

A ripple of musical voices sound around us as the angels study me like they'd like to melt me down to see what I'm made of, but thankfully, Tau steps in to address them. He speaks in Angel so I have no way of following him, but it sounds like he's giving them orders. The unmistakable look of respect is on every one of their faces as they listen to him.

Xavier's eyes dance as he leans near my ear and says, "Was that your best attempt to win them over?"

I frown at him. "No, I was just trying to give them a reason not to attack you," I whisper back. "But now I'm not sure why I bothered."

Xavier's cheek brushes against mine as he leans closer. "So you came to save me?" he asks with a hint of humor in his seductive tone. "You have so much courage. I had forgotten some of what it's like to be near you—your vicious appeal—the savage longing you create. I find that I have to learn how to breathe again."

"Right," I reply sarcastically, while wetting my lips that have gone dry. "I hate to ruin your illusions of me, but I was only trying to protect me."

"No, if that were the case, you would've found a means of escape, but you didn't. You entered the arena and stood right beside me," he replies, and seeing his point, I bite my lip.

"It was just a normal response to a perceived threat," I contradict him.

"It's a normal response for an angel protecting her mate," Xavier counters, like a skilled tactician.

"No, any normal female would try to talk her way out of trouble," I say with a brittle smile.

Xavier's fingers come up to play with a strand of my hair as he says, "There is nothing remotely ordinary about you—accept it. I'll show you what you are."

"And, what am I?" I ask with a raise of my eyebrow while I pull my hair back from his large hand.

"Mine," he replies softly with conviction. The light from the chandelier overhead makes his hair golden and his wings a deep, blood-red color. "I will tear open the sky to make you see it."

Wildly careening butterflies take flight in my stomach, causing my eyes to shift from the intense, mismatched ones to the doors that lead to the West Tower. Despite my agitation, a smile curves my lips as I breathe, "Reed," with relief so strong it makes my legs weak.

As Reed walks toward me, I admire the seductive way he moves while my eyes wander from his green ones to his bare chest. His dark-gray wings, tucked casually behind him, unfold when mine flutter in some kind of primal signal to him. I can't help touching him when he reaches me, letting my arms wrap around the back of his neck while my red wings spread out. Rising up on tiptoes, my cheek brushes his. I whisper near his ear, "You're okay?" half in question and half in relief.

Feeling his arms wrap around me, he presses me to him and responds, "Yes, you?" The incredible scent of him assails me, causing my fingers to reach up and entwine lightly in his hair.

Before I can answer him, Xavier gives a low snarl next to us. Reed instantly stiffens, but otherwise he doesn't outwardly react, except to plant a long, sensual kiss on my lips. Ending our kiss, he leans his forehead against mine, while saying, "I missed you," with a sublime smile.

"You wouldn't have had to miss me if you'd let me come with you," I reply, my hand slipping to his shoulder, while I straighten.

"Flawless reasoning," he replies with a small smile.

"Did you find anything...bad?" I ask while trying not to hold my breath.

"Yes, I did," he says with a look of supplication. "Ostentatious decor is everywhere."

I give him a furtive look, knowing he is purposefully not answering my question. Reed's hand slips from my back to my side, positioning me next to him so that he can face Tau and Xavier. Addressing Tau, Reed says, "The residence and grounds are still being secured. Zephyr and Russell are continuing to locate latent spells and portals, but there are layers of them—what we anticipated. It may be some time before we can safely allow Evie access to the entire estate."

"She will be well protected," Xavier says in a cold voice. "I will not leave her side."

"You are not needed in that regard," Reed counters in an equal tone. His fingers lightly touch the mark of my wings on his chest. "I will see to her."

Tau's gray eyes are on me when he says, "Xavier is Evie's guardian. He is well acquainted with the role."

Reed, still outwardly calm, squeezes me tighter to him. Feeling him tense, my heart accelerates while my face flushes, like I've just been caught in something tawdry. "Her guardian? But, he's a Seraph," Reed replies with a tilt of his head, clearly unhappy with the news.

"Yes, I am," Xavier agrees in answer to the implied question. "I have been hers since her inception."

"Clearly, it's time that you were reassigned to another soul," Reed replies with his green eyes narrowing. "This one now has an *aspire*."

"There is no other soul for me, nor angel for that matter," Xavier says without emotion. "And if you believe that you deserve her, I'm here to let you know just how misguided you have become."

"I look forward to your challenge then," Reed replies with a genuine smile of pleasure.

"I will not keep you waiting long," Xavier returns with the same kind of smile.

Alarmed by the satisfied looks on both their faces, I ask them, "What are you talking about? What challenge?"

"I will explain it to you later, love," Reed says gently, while petting my cheek with the back of his fingers.

Tau doesn't share their smiles as he says, "Evie has agreed to dine with me this evening. I'll meet with Preben and make the arrangements." Then, his eyes soften when they find mine again. "Would you like to rest before we dine?" he asks me.

"No, I'm good. I'd like to be alone with my *aspire*," I reply in a firm tone, still feeling awkward with him.

"Then, I'll meet you later tonight," he says with a small smile.

"Okay," I reply, shyly. I try not to stiffen when he leans forward and places a kiss on my brow. "You're taking him with you, right?" I ask Tau, shifting my gaze to Xavier.

Tau says something to Xavier, which makes Xavier's smile turn into a grim line.

Shaking his head slowly, Xavier says in a determined voice, "I'm staying with her."

Reed sounds calm as he says, "I'll be with her. She will have my protection."

"Brennus was able to get to her under your protection," Xavier counters Reed with elegant disdain.

"Everything was able to get to her when you withdrew yours," Reed responds.

As Xavier loses his calm look of disdain and steps aggressively forward in anger, Reed slips me behind him. Tau moves faster than Xavier, holding him back from Reed with both hands on his chest. Reed's dark wings match the menacing width of Xavier's crimson ones at full extension.

Still holding Xavier, Tau says over his shoulder, "Take Evie to see her friends, she has been worried about them."

Frozen where I am, I stare at Xavier. Breathing heavily, like he's trying to gain control of himself, his eyes slip to mine. He speaks to me in Angel: it sounds painful and unmusical, falling from his lips to hang in the air between us.

Reed has to tug gently on my hand to get me to move away toward the corridor leading toward the West Tower. I walk midway down the hallway next to Reed before I know it.

Glancing at Reed's severe expression, I ask, "What did Xavier say?"

Reed instantly changes direction and ushers me into an adjacent alcove, pinning me to the stone wall with the cage of his arms flanking me. "Who is he to you, Evie?" Reed asks me, while searching my eyes for answers.

A guilty panic hits me then, and I try to explain, "I knew Xavier in high school—we were friends. Well, maybe we were a little more than friends at times, but then he'd get weird and moody and act like he didn't like me...I don't know. Xavier said...he said we knew each other before I was sent here—that we were a lot more than friends, but I don't remember him, I swear! I don't remember Paradise at all—"

Reed pulls me in his arms, kissing me passionately. "I'm sorry—of course you don't know," Reed says against my lips. His hand presses to my heart as it beats hard in fear.

"What did he say to me?" I ask again.

Reed doesn't answer right away, and then he murmurs, "He said, 'What has been, will be again.'" Seeing my confusion, Reed adds, "It's our mantra—it means that one day, the war of Heaven will end and we will be united once again under God in Paradise."

"Oh," I exhale, lowering my eyes from Reed's in relief that Xavier hadn't been saying something about me.

"But," Reed says softly, causing my eyes to lift to his again, "I don't think that's what he meant when he said it. I think he was speaking of you and him: what has been, will be again."

I lift my arms to him, hugging him and saying, "You know that I love you. It's you and me—it will always be you and me."

"I thought he must be dead," Reed says in a low tone, "your guardian angel. When you showed up at Crestwood and you were alone…and I began to know you—I was certain that you would have had one. The only conclusion that I could come to was that he had been killed."

"He said he was called back to Heaven. He said he couldn't refuse them," I murmur, not fully understanding what that means.

"You were present when a soul ascended, Evie, you know the pull of it, and should he have tried to resist, he would've been taken by force," Reed replies grimly.

"Then…Heaven could take you back—make you leave me?" I ask with a chill of dread filling me at the thought of them taking Reed from me.

"They could take you from me, and then make you forget that you were ever loved by me…or wanted me," Reed replies sadly. "It would seem that they've already done that to Xavier."

"They can't do that to us! I'll rebel—I'll fight for you," I say in a harsh voice before Reed covers my lips with his, kissing me almost senseless.

"Don't say that, Evie," he whispers against my mouth. "You are beloved in their eyes—whatever they conceal from you has a purpose. You must trust in that purpose."

"If they took you from me, it would be like they concealed my heart from me," I say in a hushed voice.

Reed's eyes soften then, as he says, "And you have just proved to me how beloved I am in your eyes and in the eyes of Paradise. I have lived for centuries and never hoped to hear my own emotion echoed so passionately by the lips of one so fair."

Feeling somehow better after hearing that, I rest my cheek against his shoulder. "Xavier said he has been with me since my inception," I say in a shallow voice. "Does that mean that I was always intended for this—that this, all my lifetimes with Russell—everything has been leading to this…it's all still one single on-going mission?"

"Are you asking me if I believe that you were created for just this purpose?" Reed asks.

"Uh huh," I reply.

"I think that you have been given the freedom to choose your own destiny, and that's what makes you so supremely unpredictable—lethal. You have the perfect poker face because you hardly know what you'll do until you do it," Reed says with a gentle squeeze. "You follow your infallible instincts that are ruled by your heart."

"I don't know how infallible my instincts are—I agreed to have dinner with Tau tonight," I say quietly.

"That was very accommodating of you," Reed says with an encouraging smile.

"Do you think so?" I ask with *faux* cheeriness. "Because I was just thinking that it will be a perfect opportunity to rise up and take back some of the control the Seraphim have wrestled away from me."

"Really?" he asks sounding amused.

"Uh huh," I nod. "I want them to know that we are a unit—unified. We make the decisions that affect our lives, not them."

"How do you perceive that going?" he asks.

"Hmm, not well," I reply with a quirk of my eyebrow.

"As long as you have no illusions going into it," Reed smiles. "There is almost no rank higher than Tau's and you're his daughter. He has only just found you again, and he never meant to leave you."

"So, you're saying he'll try to hold onto every ounce of control with both fists?" I ask warily.

"By any means necessary," Reed warns me.

"Great," I sigh. "I'll see if anyone has antacids for this meal."

"Why don't you go and try to get to know him instead?" Reed asks while he puts his arm around my waist and leads me back into the corridor.

"You mean try to form a relationship with him?" I wrinkle my nose. We turn down several hallways and I realize that he's taking me toward the North Tower.

"Yes," Reed says.

"I don't trust him," I reply softly.

"Maybe, if you allow him to, he can earn it," Reed says, stopping in front of the closed doors to the library. "There's something else you can do, too, Evie."

"There is?" I ask curiously.

"Anya could use someone she can trust," he says gently. "She's just seen some things that were less than optimal for a newly arrived angel."

"Oh, what happened?" I ask.

A reluctant look crosses his face, "We had to end some new Gancanagh. They were females from the harem. It was somewhat gruesome." For him to say it was gruesome means that it was off the charts disgusting.

"Oh," I reply as my face loses some of its color. "Is she okay?"

"She could use a friend," he admits, opening the doors to the library.

Looking around the room, many of the Power angels who had been with us in China mill around on the brown-leather couches and chairs. Most of the French doors that line this room and over-look the stone terrace are intact, only a few have been boarded up. The exposed beams of the ceiling makes the room appear like the structure of a ship—very much like the ceiling in the kirk. At the far end of the room, a cheerful fire snaps in the grand fireplace. I almost don't see Anya on one of the chairs facing the fire. She looks so small and unmoving.

Brennus had ordered me to avoid this room because the elite fellas used it as a kind of gentlemen's club. Just being in here makes me feel disobedient. Suddenly, the realization that I'm stranded once again in my elegant prison begins to creep over me, causing goose bumps to rise on my skin. My throat tightens as the oppressive walls creep closer around me. My hand goes to my neck as it searches for the moon pen-dant that used to hang there, but it's gone, incinerated on the island along with several of the fellas that used to call this home.

"Are you okay?" Reed asks worriedly.

"I'm fine," I murmur with a small smile. "I'll go sit with Anya for a while."

On shaky legs, I move towards Anya's chair. She doesn't look up when I near her, but continues to gaze hazily at the fire. I don't bother pulling the other chair nearer to hers. Instead, I sit down on the floor in front of her chair and lean my back next to her legs to watch the fire with her. When she doesn't object to my presence, I reach up and take her hand in mine, resting my cheek against her knee. It occurs to me that maybe she is the only other being that can possibly know how I feel.

I'm not sure how long we sit there like that, holding hands, but I look up when Russell lifts Anya into his arms and then sits back down in her seat with her on his lap.

"Stop lookin' at the fire with that doll-eye stare, Red. You're startin' to freak me out," Russell says as he strokes Anya's long, dark hair.

"I do not have a doll-eye stare," I reply, blinking my eyes that have gone dry.

"Yeah, right! My sister Scarlett's American Girl dolls have more of an expression than either of y'all," he replies. "And they were adopted."

I smile, forgetting where I am for a second. "I was thinking," I say, straightening up and stretching my legs that are numb.

"Good, 'cuz I've been thinkin', too, and I'm thinkin' you're not allowed anywhere near that room with the knight's armor in front of it without me," he says agitatedly.

"The kirk—uh, the Knight's Bar?" I ask, paying closer attention to him. He looks really tired—older.

"That's the one," Russell says, running his hand through his tawny hair. "I just had to walk by it and all my hair stood straight up on my arms like somethin' walked 'cross my grave," he explains.

"You are not dead, yet," Anya says softly, looking him over to make sure her assessment is correct.

"It's an expression," he explains gently. "I just meant that it was toxic with bad energy. Zee went in while I waited out in the hallway, but he couldn't find anythin'. I think I'm gonna need your help if we go in there. There's somethin' not right 'bout it."

"Let's not go in there, then," I reply with my eyes widening in concern. "There are plenty of other rooms around here for us to play in."

"Deal," Russell agrees so quickly, it makes me nervous. "I'll stay out if you do."

"I really wouldn't mind never seeing the inside of that room again, anyway," I reply, remembering being shot in that room by Casmir before I nearly destroyed it with a spell. In that room, Brennus was forced to free me from the magical contract that bound us together.

"We thought you'd feel that way, so we're cleanin' up the East and South Towers. You weren't allowed in them when you were here, so they should be less painful—less memories for you to deal with," Russell says.

"Thanks, Russ," I murmur, choked up by his thoughtfulness.

"It was Reed's idea," Russell replies. "And then frick and frack took the ball and ran with it. You're gonna be in the Harem Tower whether you like it or not 'cuz the Reapers freaked when they saw it. I mean they freaked in a good way," he adds for Anya's benefit.

"So, 'freaked' can be good and bad?" Anya asks softly, with her head still listlessly resting against Russell's shoulder.

"Yeah, I know it's confusin', but you're so quick, you'll have it in no time," he says, using his sweetest, most charming tone.

"What is frick and frack?" Anya asks, seeming to be snapping out of the fog that she has been in.

"Ah, that'd be Buns and Brownie," he smiles, brushing her hair behind her ear tenderly.

"When did they get here?" I ask.

"Not long before you, but they came in like a couple of generals. They've been givin' orders to the Powers—makin' them move furniture 'round, which is kinda funny 'cuz you know they're strong enough to do it themselves," he smirks. "I just think they enjoy tellin' them what to do."

"How's that going over?" I ask.

"Shoot, they've got those angels followin' them 'round like they're presents that need openin'," Russell winks. "Did you expect less?"

"No," I reply. "That sounds about right."

"Naw, those two've got the world on a string," Russell smiles. "They've been down in the kitchen, too, plannin' some kind of pizza party or other. It sounded good to me—I'm half-starvin'. I just came up here to get Anya. You want to eat with us?" he asks.

"I can't," I say with a sigh of regret. "I'm supposed to have dinner with Tau, but could you please take Reed and make sure he eats something?" I look across the room to see Reed sitting with some other Power. My eyes meet his and I get the impression that he has been watching me for a while—maybe even the whole time.

Russell follows my gaze to Reed, and says, "He's worried 'bout us bein' here. Maybe you can talk to your dad 'bout it and find out the game plan."

"Sure, maybe I'll bring it up after I ask him to tell me how he met my mom," I scoff with a sarcastic twist of my lips.

"Your mother is his *aspire*," Anya murmurs, causing both our eyes to lock on Anya's face. Seeing my strained expression, Anya adds, "I met her only once, but she was very good...urr, kind?"

Russell nods. His eyes are as round as mine when I look at him.

"Now that's freaky—and I'm not even gonna guess if it's good freaky or bad freaky," Russell breathes before looking at Anya. "You met her mom?" he prompts.

Anya shrugs "For a small time."

"Briefly?" I ask.

"Briefly," Anya accepts the correction. "She had just transitioned back from Earth. She's an old soul, very sage-urr, wise?" she asks us.

"Yeah, that's the right word," Russell says with a "holy shit" expression that I'm totally sharing.

"What was her name?" I ask Anya. I want clarity; I want proof of her knowledge.

"I get so confused. You are meaning 'is,' correct? She is, not was. She exists—not as past tense," she replies, shaking her head. "I do not know her Earth name, but she is known as—" and then Anya says a word in Angel that crudely sounds like "Vivian," but she draws it out so that it's lyrical—more beautiful than I can express with human syllables.

My heart lurches in my chest as what Anya relates shakes me to the core. I have always thought of everything to do with Paradise as an abstract—it exists, but as a distant concept or destination. It was like envisioning a far-off place, like Mars or a moon of Saturn. One could certainly go there if one met the requirements to exist on that plane. But, because I had never known my mother, could never envision her beyond the pictures I'd seen of her, she never really existed for me. She was not, and never could be, real…until now.

"What…what did you two talk about—when you met?" I ask Anya while other questions tumble around in my mind.

"She leave you behind—she cannot protect you like she wanted to…and she leave her *aspire*, too—very…hard?" she asks.

"Yes…hard," I reply in a shallow voice.

"How do you say: to give up something valued to you—something without compare in worth to do what is right?" she asks.

"Sacrifice," I say softly.

"Very hard sacrifice for her," Anya murmurs, "and for him, too." She lifts her chin in the direction of the doors where Tau has just entered. "She said she died in his arms."

Rising from my seat on the floor, I see Reed greet Tau while I run my hands over my jeans to straighten them. Russell gets up too, holding Anya at his side as Tau and Reed walk casually over to greet us. After Tau nods in acknowledgement of Russell, he speaks a few words to Anya in Angel. She smiles, and nods, looking a little awestruck at being in his presence.

Turning to me, Tau asks, "Are you ready?"

"Uh, yeah," I say shyly, feeling color flood my cheeks as my eyes nervously shift to Reed's. "I'll come find you when we're finished."

"I'll be waiting," he says with a smile. He steps forward and hugs me, while whispering in my ear, "Relax."

"Trying," I whisper back before letting him go.

"Shall we?" Tau asks, and when I nod, he leads me to the doors of the library.

CHAPTER 19

Dinner

"Where are we going?" I ask Tau, following next to him as he turns toward the East corridor. Things are beginning to become unfamiliar to me because I was never allowed in this part of the estate when Brennus was in charge.

Tau slows as we come upon black-lacquered doors, each designed with ornate scrollwork etched into the veneer. Massive, gold door knockers in the shape of fangs hang grotesquely in the center of each door.

"Should we knock?" I ask, raising my brow.

"That won't be necessary," Tau smiles as he pushes the doors open.

Gesturing for me to enter, I walk in front of Tau across the black, polished hardwood floor. A beautiful, round table, set for the two of us, is in the center of the room beneath a black chandelier. Gilded, Celtic infinity knots embellish the cathedral ceiling. Soft pools of light fall upon the crisp, white tablecloth, while elegant bone china, edged in black and gold, compliment the centerpiece of dark red roses.

Tau pulls out one of the large, red-velvet covered chairs for me to sit in. My fingertips brush over the golden nail heads that secure the fabric as I sit and glance around the room. A sophisticated, black wine rack encompasses the entire wall behind the stylish bar.

"Are you hungry, Evie?" Tau asks me after he takes his seat across the table.

"Yes," I manage to say with a nod, while picking up my napkin and placing it in my lap.

"I am as well," Tau smiles and looks over my shoulder at the angel that just entered the room from the door behind the bar. "Ah, Aldo."

As Aldo comes abreast of the table, I stiffen when a buzz, the rapid flutter of his paper-like dragonfly wings, vibrates with the intensity of a mechanized saw. The eerie sound causes adrenaline to intoxicate my muscles, while my wings tear out of my back with a snap.

Freddie! I think as a sick dread invades my mind.

Without thought, I grasp my dinner knife, spinning out of my chair at a dizzying speed to press the sharp point to Aldo's throat from behind him. His wings buzz again, making me almost insane with a need to tear them from him.

"On your knees," I order between my teeth near the Reaper's ear. He complies immediately by kneeling in supplication. "What do you want?" I ask him, pressing the knife deeper to his neck, but I haven't cut him yet.

"I've come to meet you and to discern what I can prepare for you…" he trails off.

My gaze shifts to Tau's as my breathing continues at a steady pace. I'm in control here, not the Reaper. I can rip his head from his body if I need to with just a flick of my knife.

Tau's eyes narrow as if reading my mind. "Evie, put down the knife," he murmurs in a calm tone. Then, he speaks in Angel to Aldo.

"Who is he?" I ask Tau suspiciously, not complying with his order.

"He's a Reaper," Tau says with a blank expression. "He's one of the best chefs I've ever had the pleasure of meeting, but now, I doubt if he'll serve us anything but burnt toast. Put the knife away before Aldo gets the impression that we don't like him."

My eyes run over his iridescent wings that are not the blue-green color of Freddie's, but an intricate blending of purple and fuchsia. Immediately, the blood drains from my face. Dropping the knife, it falls to the floor with a loud clatter.

I step away from Aldo. "I'm…sorry. Your wings—they reminded me of someone…" I utter in a distant voice, horrified by what I just did to him.

Tau rises from his chair, coming to me and pulling me against the soft fabric of his pressed shirt. Hiding my face against his chest, I listen while he speaks to Aldo in Angel. Aldo rises from his knees and walks quietly to the door behind the bar, leaving us alone.

Tau strokes the feathers of my wings lightly. "You have impressive speed," he says with a squeeze, before pulling me away from him so that he can see my face.

I avoid his eyes when I mutter, "Thanks," allowing him to guide me back to my seat. Locating my napkin, he hands it back to me.

When he takes his seat across from me again, he pours from an elegant carafe, filling my glass goblet. When I sip it, it tastes like grape juice.

"I would love something a little stronger," I say, nodding to my glass.

"Unfortunately, this wine rack lacks its namesake. It's filled with blood—human and…other," he says with a frown. I study the wine rack that encompasses the entire wall. The selection of bottles is enormous.

Sitting back in his chair, he watches me while I sip my juice. "You surprised me just now," he admits.

"Really? You didn't expect me to attack the chef?" I ask with sarcasm, before setting my goblet on the table and feeling embarrassed.

"Well then, welcome to my world: where the unexpected becomes the norm."

"Why did you attack him?" he asks. "I perceived no threat."

"You wouldn't, right?" I ask rhetorically. "He's just a Reaper to you. But, if you were ever human, you'd know that Reapers are strong—brutally strong."

His eyes narrow. "You will have to explain to me what you mean. Does this have something to do with the Reaper that made a deal with the Gancanagh in exchange for your soul?" he asks.

"His name was Freddie—Alfred Standish," I reply, and something like recognition shines in his eyes. "I met him at Crestwood and I thought…I thought he was a human, like me," I explain, while raising my gray eyes to his.

"But, you're not just human, are you?" he asks, seeing my point.

"No, and he knew that, too," I reply.

"So he stalked you," he prompts me to continue.

"Stalked me…besides Russell, he was my best friend. I told him everything," I say, hearing Aldo approaching us again. He places a basket of rolls directly in front of Tau and his stiff wings seem somehow stiffer as he refuses to look at me.

"Allow me to order for you, Evie," Tau states, and I nod.

When Tau finishes, Aldo turns to go back into the kitchen. I stop him before he walks past me by putting my hand on his arm.

"Aldo," I say softly, meeting his lovely brown eyes. "Please accept my apology for attacking you. I was frightened by your wings and I reacted in a way that I truly regret."

Aldo's eyes go from my hand on his sleeve to my face. The soft lighting from above gives his dark-brown hair a golden glow as a smile inches to the corners of his lips.

"You think my wings are frightening?" he asks with a smile.

"Very scary," I admit with a serious nod, unable to discern any other similarities in him to Freddie. He's much taller than Freddie had been. Freddie had been shorter than me with blue eyes and blond hair.

Aldo puffs up then, like I have just given him a compliment. "I can put them away if it will help," he says.

"No, you don't have to...I'll just have to be braver," I reply with a ghost of a smile.

"Who among us could be braver?" Aldo asks, and my eyes widen in surprise. Seeing it, his smile deepens. "I will make you something special." I let my hand drop from his before he walks to the door behind the bar again.

"I should've killed him," Tau says softly, causing my eyes to grow bigger as they turn to him. For a second, I think he's talking about Aldo. Tau must have sensed my confusion, because he adds, "Alfred. Xavier wanted to, but I thought we should wait to see what they were plotting."

"What?" is all I can say as my mouth goes dry.

"He was around before you went to Crestwood. You went to his house prior to school—for a brunch?" he asks me, looking grim.

I nod dumbly.

"Xavier would've torn him apart—he argued vehemently for it, but I allowed you to go, to see what he was after," Tau says. "I didn't know then that I would be leaving you unprotected from him."

"You knew that Freddie—Alfred, was going to follow me to Crestwood and you did nothing?" I ask for clarity.

A frown darkens his perfect brow. "I thought that we'd be able to take care of him there after he led us to his associates. I wanted to know all the players...what exactly the fallen Seraphim planned for you," Tau explains.

"When was the last time you saw me? When did you get called back?" I ask.

"Your first day at Crestwood. We had been planning to go with you. Cole had secured our housing so that we could wait until the moment that you began to evolve," he pauses.

"Why wait? Why couldn't you just tell me what I needed to know?" I ask him, upset that he hadn't told me anything when he had a chance—so many, many chances.

"Evie, you were happy being human. That world made sense to you," he says sadly. "There was so much that you were facing—I wanted you to be a child for as long as possible, because the minute you knew, all of that would end."

I try to calm the raw emotions inside of me while holding tight to my glass and waiting for him to continue.

"You were really nervous the morning you left for school, remember?" he asks me with a wry smile. "You kept checking to make sure that Jim had enough groceries for the week—posting notes everywhere to remind him to pick up his dry-cleaning…"

I look at him, seeing his eyes soften, and then I nod my head, hoping he will continue. The same nervousness that I felt on the morning before leaving for school settles over me once again.

"I watched you climb into your car—so hopeful, and yet, sad at the same time," he says.

"You were there," I whisper with the realization that what he has been telling me is true. He was there—they all were.

"It happened almost the instant you pulled out of your driveway," he explains, and he sounds almost bitter.

"What did?" I ask.

"Cole began to ascend. He resisted the pull, but his struggles were in vain. He knew it. The pull is as strong for us as it is when a soul ascends…he began to fade becoming a shadow of his form…"

I can't help saying numbly, "I witnessed a soul ascending when I was hiding from Pagan."

"Yes, Pagan," he says her name like he just ate something sour. "Then you know the intensity of it—the encompassing need to comply with the host of angels that call out to you…" he trails off when I nod my head.

"So, you and Xavier ascended with Cole?" I question.

Tau shakes his head, saying, "No, we resisted—"

"You did?" I interrupt him, stunned by his admission of noncompliance with Heaven.

Tau nods as his jaw tenses. "We followed you to Crestwood. The sky above us resonated with the call of voices for our return, but when we didn't comply, they decided to take us by force. Xavier began to fade when he made it to your room at Crestwood, but he felt sure you saw him, because you called out to him, asking who was there—" he says, sounding haunted.

"Oh my God!" I breathe, remembering returning to my room alone for the first time and thinking I saw a shadow pass over my wall as I entered. "That shadow was—"

"Xavier," Tau replies. "He was faster—he made it there before me. I was fading, too. When I arrived, I could only watch you from your fire escape—you cut your finger." I can only nod at him in response. "I wanted to tell you then about us—about everything... but that wasn't to be...I ascended," he says softly. "I—we were confused—angry," he replies in a salty tone. "We felt betrayed."

My eyes grow wide. "Wasn't that the plan?" I ask.

"It was never my plan...or Xavier's—he was inconsolable," he replies, lacking even a hint of levity.

"But, you were in Paradise, right?" I ask in confusion.

"You think that it matters?" he asks with equal confusion.

"Doesn't it? It's Paradise...you know, Heaven," I reply.

He pauses for a moment, and then he asks, "You know nothing of Paradise but human speculation and second-hand accounts. Am I correct?"

"That's right," I reply.

"I want you to do something for me. I want you to close your eyes," he says, and waits for me to do as he asks.

Closing my eyes, I listen to the beautiful resonance of his voice, when he says; "I want you to picture Jim in your mind." I squeeze my eyes tighter at the mention of my uncle's name. "Picture leaving him behind, knowing very well just how vulnerable he is to any fallen angel that happens upon him—knowing that he will both attract them and consume them with envy." My heart tightens painfully in my chest.

Tau continues, "You know how fragile Jim is—that you could easily snap him in half now without any effort. Then, consider my vast knowledge of killing. If you were to imagine every scenario and possible torture that you've witnessed and apply it to him, it could not possibly compare to what I can imagine," he murmurs.

Tears slip from my closed eyes.

"Now, imagine the most gruesome place that you can. Imagine Sheol where to smell rotting flesh would be a relief and imagine them taking him there. Jim, so beloved to you, now nearly unrecognizable as ever having been divine because he has either perished at their hands or been turned into something so ugly you hardly dare to look upon him and mark the violation he has suffered to become so vile."

My eyes open slowly when Tau's hand reaches across the table to take mine. "Do you think that Heaven could console me, knowing that I left my daughter behind?" he asks.

Shaking my head, I can hardly look at him. "Did you see Jim?" I ask, but it comes out like a croak.

"Xavier and I tracked him down," Tau replies with a nod.

"What did they do to him?" I ask, trying hard to hold back tears of despair and anger. "I have imagined every possible scenario. Did they torture him?"

"He couldn't remember anything about his death—no torture or pain. He is content," he says gently, and I can't help weeping in grief and a modicum of relief. "He gave me something to give to you when I saw you…and the moment was right," Tau says in a gentle tone, letting go of my hand.

"What?" I ask him breathlessly.

Rising from his chair, he walks to mine. Leaning down, he places a tender kiss on my wet cheek. When my eyes connect with his, he says, "He said to say, 'Being your human father was the greatest honor of all of his lifetimes.'"

"How could he say that?" I ask Tau as he crouches near my seat. Using his napkin, he wipes the tears from my cheeks. "I didn't protect him."

"You couldn't protect him. It's not your fault—it's mine," he replies.

"Why is it your fault?" I ask, sniffling. "You got shanghaied to Paradise."

Tau straightens and returns to his seat. "All of this wouldn't have happened if Alfred had been taken out in the beginning. We wouldn't be sitting in the defunct castle of the Gancanagh if I had."

A grim line twists his lips as he watches me sadly. I try to pull myself together as I pick up the breadbasket, taking a roll and placing it on my plate before extending it to him. "You know what Russell would say to us right now?" I ask, waiting for him to take the bread from me.

"I haven't any idea," my father replies, accepting the basket from me.

Breaking open my roll, I explain, "He'd say we're stupid."

Setting a roll on the small plate, he asks, "Would he?"

"Yes," I nod, nibbling my roll. It takes me a while before I can swallow past the lump in my throat. But then, using Russell's accent, I say, "He'd say, 'You're stupid and arrogant if you think that you're capable of doin' any of this without the help of Heaven. This was meant—I can feel it and you can either cry 'bout it or you can man up.'"

"He would say that?" Tau asks, following my lead and taking a bite of his roll.

"Uh huh," I reply.

"Should we kill him?" Tau asks, and smiles when I laugh.

Taking a sip of my juice, my throat eases a little. "Not just yet. I like having him around." I chew my roll for a while, thinking, and then I ask, "So, you didn't know us before—Russ and me?"

"No," Tau replies. "I met you the human way—when you were born."

"Really!" I ask, my eyes widening.

"Really," he smiles. "It was determined that you would feel more like my daughter if we never met in Paradise. I believe the hope was that I would bond with you if I felt that you were created as my child."

"Did it work?" I ask him.

"Am I here?" he counters.

"Oh," I smile as a light feeling within me makes my cheeks blush warmly.

"Cole knew you, and of course Xavier knew everything there was to know about you. He used to tell us stories of your past lifetimes—your adventures, escapades. Hearing some of them, there can be no doubt why you were chosen for this."

The fact that Xavier has always been with me begins to sink in. "Can I ask you something?" I inquire.

"Yes," he grins, highlighting the fact that I've been asking him lots of things.

I blush before I ask, "If a guardian angel has always been with a particular soul, does that mean that he would know more about that soul than even her soul mate?"

"Possibly, he would be witness to much more than the soul mate," he replies. "Then there is the fact that they could remain together in Paradise until the soul reunited with its mate."

"Is that common?" I ask.

"It's not," he responds slowly. His reply seems to imply something that I don't want to pursue at the moment.

"What about Russell's guardian angel? Where is he?" I ask.

"Russell has had many, a different one for different lifetimes on Earth. It's uncommon to have only one guardian angel over such a lifespan," he replies.

"How uncommon?" I ask, not being able to stop myself.

"I've never heard of another pair like you and Xavier. Nor is it common for a Seraph to guard a soul," Tau states. I cringe inwardly at this little nugget of information.

"Why wasn't Russell given another guardian angel for this life?" I ask, irritated that he didn't have any protection from Heaven while growing up.

"Not every soul has a guardian. Mostly, they're reserved for souls doing specific work," Tau says.

"They are?" I ask, uncomfortable, since I apparently have always had a guardian angel who now thinks he owns me.

"Virtues aid most souls when necessary. It was thought that a guardian angel for Russell would draw attention to him—attention that we didn't want. He was much safer born with the masses, camouflaged within the human race. He was born first, you'll recall. That was done on purpose," Tau says. "He was human, he would not attract attention."

"Not like a half-angel would," I say.

"Not like a half-angel would," Tau agrees.

"Yes, but when he went to school to meet me, why not give him some protection then?" I ask.

"I believe you know the answer to that," he replies.

Dinner arrives and I smile politely and nod at Aldo who explains to me what he has prepared for me. I don't hear what he says, but instead I'm thinking about Tau's last comment. Russell hadn't been given protection because he wasn't supposed to stay here on Earth. I had changed the plan, but maybe the plan had already changed. Tau had to leave and that was not his plan. Freddie was able to get to me, again, not Tau's plan. Maybe Heaven has its own agenda and it seems to be a secret known only to them.

I manage to smile and thank Aldo before he leaves the room again. We eat in silence for a little while until Tau asks, "What was it like?" When my eyebrow lifts, he adds, "Finding out that you were an angel—evolving?"

"I...wow," I stammer, not knowing what to say, "that's a...hard question to answer."

"I'm sorry. I shouldn't have asked you," he says with a frown. "How is your meal?"

"No, it's okay. Um...close your eyes," I murmur, and wait patiently for him to do it. "Maybe...maybe it's a little like being alone on a moving train for the first time. The excitement and wonder at the new experience slowly gives way to the creeping feeling that something isn't quite right. You check your ticket again and see that you may have made a mistake—it's not the train you intended to be on. At first, you try to deny it. You watch the scenery slipping past and try to find a familiar landmark, and for a while, you take solace in denial."

"But soon, the terrifyingly unfamiliarity of the terrain outside the window causes you to panic. Crushing fear that you can't ignore makes you rush around, looking for a way off it. But, it's moving so fast that you know there is no getting off until it stops somewhere. So, you creep back to your seat and try not to attract attention to yourself, because the strangers on the train have taken on a weird, plastic appearance. Any camaraderie that you may have shared with them before is gone since you're no longer one of them: you're a trespasser meant to be on a different train."

"The knowledge begins to weigh on you as you slide farther and farther from where you wanted to go. You try to reign in your fear and convince yourself that maybe this new destination will be better than the one you had planned for yourself."

"Then, somewhere along the way you discover that all your baggage is wrong, too, and you find that you're ill-equipped to survive the trip you're on," I whisper as my voice falters. My eyes brighten with tears again. "That's a tough one…" I pause when Tau's eyes open and connect with mine.

I take a deep breath, choking back my tears and say, "But then… then you notice that the stranger sitting next to you isn't like any of the other passengers…that even though you sat in his seat, he's going to try to help you sort out the tangle you're in. And, because this stranger is so perfect, you begin to relax a little and forget that you're on the wrong train at all."

"Reed is the stranger in this scenario," Tau says, not at all like a question.

"Yes," I reply.

"What about Xavier?" he asks.

"What about him?" I reply with a sinking feeling.

"He's not going away," Tau replies. "He loves you."

"I hardly know him," I say uncomfortably. "He's not really the person I knew in high school, is he?"

"What happens when your soul awakens and that changes? What happens when you do remember him?" he asks me.

"I don't know—maybe it will never happen," I reply.

"I forget just how young you are, Evie," he frowns. "There will be an alignment of your heart, your soul, and your mind, and then… you may feel differently."

"You think so?" I ask as irritation enters my tone. "Because Russell has been trying to get me to remember all of our past lives, but I can't. I do, however, feel the connection that I have with him. My soul recognizes his. Why don't I feel anything remotely like that for Xavier?"

"I don't know why the passionate substance of your soul doesn't recognize him," Tau says with a renewed calm. "But, because of your mission, the very stars have had to hide their fire from you. Does it not, then, stand to reason that it's just well hidden?" he asks.

"Do we ever really know entirely what is in our own hearts?" I ask. "I'm sitting here, surrounded by Brennus' empire—bottles of blood lining the walls like trophies and I still have a hard time believing that this is truly all he is—a killer."

"Don't perceive with just your heart, Evie," Tau says. "You haven't seen him clearly since he took you from that northern library…feel him—his taste, his scent…he feels your love but gives none."

"Brennus wants me to survive," I sigh in frustration.

"For his own pleasure only—not for you to exist without him," Tau counters. "And he will hold on to you until you sever that thread."

"And Xavier? Will he hold on, too?" I ask. "Because I have an *aspire*."

"He doesn't see it as a legitimate binding—none of us do," Tau says softly.

"Why?" I ask him, completely offended.

"Do not misunderstand me," he explains in a serious tone. "I am grateful to Reed for protecting you and it speaks of his feelings for you that he was willing to bind his life to yours. But, the threat of death was present in the decision…and the offer. I am worried that there will come a time when the grace of the offer will not be enough to satisfy either of you."

"You think it was unfair of me to have accepted Reed's offer?" I ask, feeling shame stain my cheeks at having my fears echoed so eloquently.

"I'm afraid that the beauty of your love can enslave the unsuspecting…and a love like that is…dismaying," he says carefully.

"Reed's not my slave," I say defensively. "Our relationship is a partnership."

"His life has utterly changed—it is chained to yours," he replies. "That he has shown such strength in pain is a testament to his love for you, but was it just the cold, winter wind that swept you into his arms?" he asks me.

"You doubt my love for him?" I ask him incredulously. "You think I committed to him to garner his help?"

"You fled from him—straight into Brennus' arms," he replies.

"I was trying to protect him!" I retort. "You don't know what it was like. I had finally figured out that even the Divine wanted me dead. I had only just barely escaped Pagan who hunted me within an inch of my life. They would've killed him had they found us together."

"If you loved him, why go to Dominion and beg them to kill you?" he asks me.

"I didn't beg them to kill me. I presented it as an option and I did it to save him! I had given up hope that they would spare my life, but I thought that maybe they would spare Reed and Zee if I went to them and turned myself in," I explain.

"And you didn't know then that your death would've killed everything inside of him?" he asks me with narrowing eyes.

A sad smile twists my lips when I reply, "You know, you're the one who made sure that I was raised like a human, and then you're surprised when I think like one. I hadn't invested much thought into how he'd survive eternity without me; I just hoped that he would."

"I was surprised to hear that you disregarded all the sacrifices he made for you to keep you alive," Tau replies.

"That's the perspective of an angel," I respond. "Maybe you can understand this: I will fight for him with all that I am. I won't let him go—I can't."

Tau's brow darkens again as he stares at me and I can tell he's worried about something because my brow does the same thing.

"What?" I ask.

"I was just thinking that you may not get a choice in that," he replies. "Xavier will challenge Reed—"

"Challenge him? Challenge him for what?" I ask.

"For you," Tau replies.

"No, he won't," I say, setting my fork down because I can no longer eat. "I can't let that happen."

"How will you stop it?" he asks. "It's between them."

"We'll leave," I reply succinctly.

"Without us?" Tau asks, setting his fork down as well and leaning back in his chair.

"It's been a little slice of heaven being with you," I say with a little sarcasm, "but I can protect myself now—and what's mine," I reply, placing my napkin on the table.

"You propose to leave? Just like that?" he asks, and I'm getting the feeling that he thinks I'm very naïve.

"I was proposing to leave after we deal with Brennus," I correct him. "I'm aware that there's a mission here. When it's over, there won't be any reason to stay together."

"Can't you think of at least one other reason?" he asks me, sounding irritated.

Looking up at the ceiling for a second, I shrug when our eyes meet again, "Well, there's the fact that you're my dad, but I'm nineteen now—time for me to leave the nest anyway."

"And the fact that I'm your superior has no weight with you?" he inquires.

"Wait a minute, you mean like rank?" I ask and roll my eyes.

"That is exactly what I mean," he responds coolly.

"I don't respond to rank," I reply.

"What do you respond to?" he asks me. "Is it force?"

My eyebrows come together slowly in a frown. "What are you saying?" I ask him.

Tau leans forward and places his hands flat on the table. It takes an extreme effort not to lean away from his aggressive posture and break eye contact with him.

He studies me for a moment before he says, "I'm saying that if you plan on leaving without my permission, you had best hit the ground running and never stop because I will find you and then you will answer to me."

"You would make me hide from you?" I ask.

"You would make me hunt for you?" he counters.

"You do realize that I'm no longer the little girl that you left behind?" I murmur softly, almost menacingly.

I lean closer to him, mimicking his posture while pulling energy to me. I allow it to leak from my fingertips and spread slowly over the table, covering everything on his side with a crystallizing frost. He doesn't even glance at his frozen water glass or look away from my face when his wings storm out of his back, destroying the chair behind him as he stands.

"Should you try magic on me, you had best kill me, because if you don't, I will make you pay for it," Tau says with equal menace in his tone.

"I don't want to kill you—I just want autonomy," I reply, standing too and feeling myself pale. He's way better at this than me. I feel like a child trying to negotiate a later bedtime.

"There is no autonomy. You don't exist for your own amusement," he says.

"I don't exist for your amusement either," I counter.

Pointing at me from across the table, he says, "You're an angel—that makes you subject to our laws and right now, I find nothing amusing about you."

I cross my arms. "Does this mean I've outgrown the adorable stage?" I ask with a hint of derision. "You forget that I'm also human."

"How can I forget that when you're so much like your mother?" he asks me, and his wings lower perceptibly.

"My mother..." I trail off, feeling the grim line of my mouth relax a little.

"Would have been better at this," he replies, gesturing to the table and indicating dinner.

"She couldn't have been worse," I say under my breath, but bite my lip when I see him frown. "You did smash your chair," I point out, gesturing behind him to the lumber on the floor.

"You are difficult to fathom, Evie," he says with a frustrated sigh. "There are so many facets to you and all of them are dichotomies. "You're naïve yet wise, independent with a dependence, guilelessly sophisticated, obstinately compliant..."

"I get it: I'm flawed," I say, holding up my hand to stop him as my spine straightens.

"You're perfectly flawed—that is what is so endearing about you," he explains softly. "You're very much like your mother."

"And you're insultingly flattering, so it would seem I'm more like you," I reply, while rubbing my aching forehead.

"Maybe so...we're both very strong-willed," he replies.

"So, what now?" I ask, before adding, "And don't say dessert because I'm not hungry."

"Are you asking me what my plans are for you?" he asks, and I nod. "I plan to train you."

"I know how to fight," I counter.

"You know some techniques, but true strategy?" he shakes his head. "I also plan to teach you about your position here as well as in Paradise. You need help with language acquisition, protocol, negotiation, angelic cognition..."

"What's angelic cognition?" I ask.

"The ability to perceive what your angelic opponent is thinking—how he thinks—behaves," he explains.

"All these things I can learn from Reed," I reply.

"You can learn how a Power will react and perceive from Reed, but what of the Seraphim and especially the fallen Seraphim? He can't teach you that," Tau replies.

"You would be surprised at what he knows. He could teach you a lot about half-humans," I reply.

"I'm counting on it, since I seem to be at a disadvantage" he replies. "I'd value his council."

"I'm willing to learn all of the things you've outlined while we're here, but I want something in return," I say, and watch his head tilt just a little to the side, the way Reed's does when I've captured his full attention.

"What are your terms?" he asks.

"I want to know about her—my mother," I say, wanting to hold my breath, but forcing myself to breathe evenly.

"What do you want to know?" he asks.

"Everything," I reply.

"I would like to tell you about her," he agrees softly.

"Good," I reply with a nod. "We can start tomorrow." I turn and begin walking across the floor to the doors.

"Evie, you said, 'while we're here.' What did you mean by that?" Tau asks behind me.

I stop, closing my eyes and mouthing, "fffffffaaaa." I open my eyes and slowly turn back to face my father. "I meant that when we get Brennus, the terms of our agreement will be fulfilled," I say.

"That is what I thought you meant," he replies, looking unaffected. "May I add a small caveat here?" he asks me rhetorically. "The conditions that you are attempting to stipulate are not within your realm of control. You will be here until I determine otherwise, at which time we, you and I, will be elsewhere. Together. Failure to comply with that stipulation will lead to severe penalties. Is that clear?" he asks me.

"Mmm," I mutter, turning once again toward the doors.

In a fraction of a second, he is standing in front of me with his fingers lightly lifting my chin so that our eyes meet, "I asked if that was clear," he says.

"It's crystal," I reply with a sinking feeling.

"Good," he smiles. "Then I will walk back with you to find your friends."

CHAPTER 20

Don't Look Back

Tau and I leave dinner behind in the Black Café as we walk together toward the library. Neither one of us speaks on our way, since dinner has apparently not lived up to either one of our expectations. When we arrive at our destination, I know instantly that Reed is not here because there are no butterflies in my stomach. Disappointed, I slump into a wing-backed chair and listen with half an ear as Tau speaks to one of the Powers.

"Your friends have left word for you to join them in the South Tower. I believe it was the Harem when you were here last," Tau says to me.

"I know where it is," I say with relief, while getting up from the chair. "I'll find them."

"No," Tau says with authority. "You'll stay with me until I can deliver you to them."

"I'm not defenseless," I mutter.

"You cannot walk around here alone," Tau states calmly.

"Fine," I say with as much dignity as I can.

"Cole and Xavier are in the West Tower," Tau says. "I need to speak with them."

Indicating with a sweep of his hand that he's ready to go, I follow him out into the hall as we walk toward the tower of rooms that Brennus had created just for me. I have no interest in seeing them again. The things that I cherish the most, like the pictures of my childhood, are gone now, having been stolen back by my friends. Peeking at Tau, I wonder what he'll think of the archive—the homage to my past.

Will he recognize anything? I wonder.

On our way, we're stopped by several groups of angels all vying for a chance to speak with Tau. Some seem to have business with him, but others just act like they're meeting a roackstar for the first time. I try to be polite, but after a while I start to feel like a kid in the backseat of a station wagon while her parent runs tedious errands.

Finally, we break away from Tau's adoring fans and turn onto the corridor leading past the Knight's Bar. I almost stumble to a halt. Opulent decay, like that of the weathered seawalls in Venice, is present around the foundation in this corridor, caused by the saltwater that had flooded out of the Knights Bar after my escape. The flotsam from the contents of the room had washed here to be stranded below the fearsome, slithering beasts woven within the tapestries when the water abated.

As we pick our way around the debris, a dark, eerie energy permeates the air. It grows stronger with every step nearer to the double doors that are guarded by two heavy, medieval suits of armor.

"Uhh," I groan, instinctively shying away from the precipice of the doors. Low energy, like cold, glacial water winding downstream, flows over my skin on its way under the doors and between the cracks in the wood to deposit, like silt, into the basin of the room.

Tau's wings shield me from the entrance to the room. "Is there something here?" Tau asks me with concern.

"You could say that," I reply, and I almost have a heart attack when Tau moves forward to push both the doors open. "NO, DON'T!" I yell, grasping him by the upper arm and pulling him back from the room's threshold.

"It's okay, Evie," Tau says in a gentle voice while he turns to me and strokes my hair back from my forehead. Looking into my eyes, he asks, "Do you sense magic?"

I nod, holding on to his arm tighter as he turns to get a better view through the open doors. "Don't—"

"The Gancanagh's magic won't hurt me. It's an amusing illusion to me, Evie," Tau says in a soothing tone. "Parlor tricks for angels..." he trails off, while easing my hand off of his forearm. "I'll investigate the room for you, if you will agree to wait here."

"Maybe we should wait—I promised Russell I'd stay away until he came with me," I state.

Glancing hesitantly inside the room, it's as if I'm gazing through a delicate, hazy-blue, silk scarf. The effect causes a soft blurring and rounding of shapes so that everything takes on a very seductive and tranquil appeal. If I were to reach out, I feel that I could then tug away the hem of the scarf to reveal the true contents of the room, but without removing it, the veil creates the aura of what the room had been like before I completely swamped it with water from the ocean.

"Tell me what you see," Tau says as he takes a step through the doorway.

"I see...I see the Knight's Bar—how it was originally with the rosette windows intact—throwing colored light on the wooden bar—"

"It's evening," Tau remarks. "You do know that?"

"Not in there it isn't," I reply. "In there, it's sunny."

"What else do you see?" he asks.

"Suits of armor lining the wall, delicate chandeliers over elegant wooden tables, rows of exotic bottles of liquor behind the bar..."

"Enticing?" he asks.

"It would be, if it weren't for the..." I pause.

"The?" Tau prompts, walking further into the room out of arms reach.

My voice sounds a little higher than normal when I say, "I'm aware that you're known for raising the level of bravery into the stratosphere, but you're making me nervous." I take a step closer to the precipice, doing a little hand-wringing. "If you come back this way, I'll tell you."

"Are you worried for me?" Tau asks, sounding amused.

"Why is that funny?" I furl my brow, while gesturing to him with a frown to come back.

"I don't know, it just is," he smiles, coming closer to me, but stopping just inside the room. "You were saying it would be enticing if..." he prompts.

"If it didn't also feel like this room was made for only one type of species: Gancanagh," I explain.

"Ahh, depauperate," he says, his eyes lifting towards the rosette windows.

"Uhh...yeah, that...let me put it to you another way. Everything I see inside it beckons me in—I'm almost dazzled by the elegant details—its ethereal glow. But, it instinctually freaks me out, too."

"I see," he says thoughtfully.

"You do?" I counter.

"Yes," he nods, "you are attracted to the magical mimicry and repulsed by it."

"It's more than that," I admit. "This room is drawing low level energy to it like dead meat attracts flies."

"Low energy?" he asks.

My forehead wrinkles as I try to think. "Umm, that's hard to explain. Low energy feels cold and it acts cold. It's slower and it feels more solid—like ice. Higher energy burns and is quick like water slipping over the falls."

"The room is filled with low energy?" Tau asks.

"Yeah, but the problem with the magic in this room is that it's not holding still to disguise its contours from me—it's almost fluid… watery. It's acting like high energy."

"Maybe Brennus doesn't know how sensitive you are becoming to his magic," Tau says. "He may have thought the room would charm you enough so that you would walk in here…and once in here, it could trap you or harm you."

"Maybe…or maybe it's the opposite, a deception to serve as a disguise. You're a stealth-hunter, so you don't usually require camouflage. But, what if…what if he planned for me to notice its confusing energy?" I ask with a raise of my eyebrow. "What if he doesn't want me in this room?" I near the threshold.

Tau stands in my way, "Confound the adversary into entering," he says softly, not letting me walk around him into the room. "It is nothing like you described, Evie. It's dark—the only light in it is shed from the stars through the shattered windows."

A shiver passes over my skin, while the empty shape in my heart seems to grow bigger. "What if his plan is to be counterintuitive?"

I want that to be true. Suddenly, I feel a bittersweet urge to go in, to see if it's different from the nightmares I've had about it since my escape. I inch closer as the hazy fabric of magic dances and waves. The effect is hypnotic, making me feel languid.

"What?" I ask the murmur of secretive voices coming from the room. "Yes, I hear you…why have you been waiting so long?"

"Evie," Tau says, standing directly in front of me and blocking my way with his tall frame. Slowly, I crane my neck to see his face. "No one's there. To whom are you speaking?"

"The one true lover…he has a hundred kisses for me," I say softly as my breath comes from me in cold swirls.

Instantly, Tau closes the doors and then takes my elbow and makes me walk with him to one of the suits of armor. Pulling the lance from its grasp, he lets go of me and walks back to the doors, thrusting the lance through the handles and essentially barring them.

With the doors closed, I find it easier to think. "Wow, that was a trip," I say under my breath.

Pointing his finger at me with a frown, Tau says adamantly, "You're not allowed in there."

"Yeah…okay," I agree in confusion, feeling muddled.

"You're not allowed in this corridor either," he orders, "and I want no less than two bodyguards with you at all times."

"Bodyguards?" I groan, finding it hard to think. "I hate bodyguards."

"You'll adjust," he says, glancing at the doors grimly. "Their magic is rampant in this house and you're susceptible to it."

Scanning his face, I see he's bothered by my vulnerability. "Don't worry, they're susceptible to mine, too."

"Don't worry, she says," Tau replies exasperatedly, looking toward the ceiling like he's talking to Heaven. Frowning at me, he continues, "You were just speaking to the magic in that room."

"Weird, huh? It's even stranger when you hear it speak back," I reply with a grim smile.

"What did it say?" he asks, looking like he is gearing up for an interrogation.

My cheeks burn while I straighten and shrug, "It asked me to look upon the room with lover's eyes...to see the aesthetics as a reflection of what will become mine if I just take the steps to seize it...something like that."

"You're aware that it's merely a beautiful theatre?" he asks tensely.

"It's more like a peep-show," I reply. "The Gancanagh aren't sentimental—they're sensual and mercurial."

"This estate is strong—contradictory. You cannot become complacent here," he cautions me.

I want to roll my eyes. Having lived here with the killers gives me some insight as to what I can expect. "I'm aware it's not the setting that the postcard makes it out to be. And, may I add, that the lance you used to bar the door isn't going to keep anyone from getting out of there," I point out.

"It's not a lance, it's a type of polearm called a bardiche, not to be confused with a halberd—that resembles an axe-head. I had meant the bardiche more as a warning to angels not to enter," he states.

"Oh, well, it's very subtle—you're message," I say for clarity, before pulling energy to me and then releasing it in the direction of the hollow armor enshrined in their alcoves beside the doors.

The loud screech of metal rubbing against metal sounds as the armor animates; the knees of the dull iron bend outward. Then, heavy boots clamor against the floor when the ancient warriors both jump down from their stone niches. Straightening up, they march forward, much like the guards of Buckingham Palace, to block the doors and serve as a deterrent to anyone planning to investigate this room.

I glance at Tau to gauge his reaction to what I've just done and see his eyebrow arch. "What, too much?" I ask innocently, as both my eyebrows rise, too. He shrugs, while leading me away from the doors with his arm linked to mine. "You didn't think that was stellar?" I ask in an attempt at playfulness. "I made them march—"

"I know, I saw them," he says with as close to an eye-roll as I've ever seen from him, but I also see the suppressed smile in the corners of his lips. "Your soldiers seemed a little innocuous," he states, and then he grins when he sees my eyes narrow.

"But, it's hard for you to judge as a casual observer, right?" I ask, knowing he's teasing me. "No, no, don't answer that," I advise, seeing the gleam in his eye.

As we walk farther down the West Corridor, I find it harder and harder to breathe, let alone trade insults with Tau. Memories of Eion dragging Lachlan from the attacking Werree destroy any pleasant feelings that my sanctuary used to evoke. Passing through the doors carved with angel wings, I pause when Tau stops just inside. His expression, usually so sedate, now appears rattled, like he hadn't expected this.

The furniture from the house that I grew up in with Uncle Jim is still here, largely untouched. Buns and Brownie had helped Zee, Reed, and Russell pilfer the room of many of my pictures and sentimental items from my childhood. They had also taken the portrait that Mr. MacKinnon had painted of me, too. But some things still remain: things that Tau clearly recognizes. My focus is not on the distant past. It's centered on the mantle. The crystal box is still here, gracing the space just above the grate.

"This was my favorite chair," Tau says weakly, going to a chair near the fireplace and touching it lightly with his fingertips. "I can still smell home on it—it's soft."

"Uh huh," I say absently, passing near him to the mantle. "It's from a time when things were never hard."

Reaching the fireplace, I lift the cold, smooth lid of the box and I'm not surprised to see that the letter-opener that had been inside it is now missing. It was my weapon; the one I had used to fend off Brennus when he had kidnapped me at the library. It's the one relic that means something to him. He had given me his; he would take mine.

"Tau," Cole says from one of the levels above. I close the lid of the box and follow Tau beneath the balconies to the three upper levels. Looking up toward the rounded ceiling, I see Cole leaning casually against the balcony two stories above us. Cole calls out, "I found home movies of Evie, you have to take a look."

Tau glances at me in silent question and I shrug. Smiling, he flies into the air and becomes almost a blur as he passes by the second floor library tier to the third floor media room. I follow a bit slower because I haven't got nearly as much power in my wings as he does.

"Oh, hey," Cole says when he sees me, tipping his chin up at me like he would when we sat next to each other in class. His black hair falls over his brow before he sweeps it away from his hazel eyes.

"Hey," I acknowledge him with a chin nod, too.

The theatre screen, mounted on the wall, shows images of seven-year-old girls in pink jerseys and pink knee socks over shin guards. They are passing a black and white soccer ball to each other as they wind down a viridescent field lined with white chalk.

"Evie's about to go in," Cole narrates with his eyes affixed to the screen and the remote in his hand.

Tau, standing next to me, stills. Then, the far away crowd noises are blotted out by my Uncle Jim's voice, cheering, "Let's go, Evie!" while the picture bounces and struggles to focus.

Tightness squeezes my throat at the sound. I want to wrap myself in the resonance of his voice in one second and hide from it in the next. Through tear-clouded eyes, I glance at Tau, who smiles broadly, while still watching as the seven-year-old me runs after the ball and kicks it, causing red pigtails to bounce and sway.

Tau inches forward, slowly sitting on the brown leather couch in fascination. "The Pink Pixies," he murmurs my team's name. Goose bumps rise on my forearms.

"She's about to score," Cole informs Tau with anticipation, while sitting next to him.

They both are riveted to the screen as the little girl that I used to be sprints by the yellow-jersey defender to boot the ball at the goal.

"YAH!" they both cheer, standing and applauding as if it just happened a second ago and not twelve years in the past.

The camera zooms in to watch me run back toward the center of the field. In the background, parents crowd the sidelines. Cole raises the remote, making the film play in slow motion.

"There's Xavier," he says with a grin, pointing to the screen.

Xavier, unmistakable and unchanged, stands grinning on the sideline, clapping loudly and then whistling like a besotted parent. He had only been feet from me. I cover my gaping mouth with my hand, while Tau and Cole continue to watch the game. I turn, unable to deal with the reality slapping me in the face. Finding the stairs, I climb them to the floor above—my room.

Stumbling from the stairwell, I stop when a gruff, deep voice growls, "I told you I wanted to be alone."

Xavier, stretched out on my teenage bed with his feet dangling over the edge, has his forearm slung over his eyes. His beautiful lips are twisted in a frown.

"I'm sorry…" I stutter. "I didn't know you were in here—"

"Evie," Xavier exhales my name, while sliding his arm back from his face to look at me. Music spills out from headphones as he pulls them from his ears. He turns it off.

"I didn't mean to bother you. I'll leave you alone," I begin.

"No," Xavier says while gracefully rising from the bed. His blond hair, rumpled from lying against the pillow, gives him a sexy, sultry air as his t-shirt straightens and falls back over the bare skin of his torso. "Stay," he says in a silky voice.

I lean against the wall just inside the door, unsure of what to do. "They're playing home-movies downstairs," I say nervously, hitching my thumb over my shoulder.

"I know," he says, while his hyper-masculine body draws nearer to me. "Cole was unrelenting with them. That's why I retreated up here."

"Me, too," I admit with a nervous smile as I look up at his face.

His shoulders round toward me as he says in a secretive tone, "Someone stole your troll."

"They did?" I ask, mirroring his tone and glancing at the shelf near my Nirvana poster.

He nods gravely, while saying, "The one with the purple hair. It was always on the second shelf in your room. You can still see the outline of its feet in the dust."

"It was probably Eion," I say as my eyes shift back to his. "He found it ironic because he said that trolls look nothing like it."

"That is why I liked it," Xavier remarks with an alluring smirk. "I'll hunt him down and kill him for you."

I look away from him as I admit, "He's already dead. Russell killed him."

"That will just make finding your troll more interesting," he replies, undaunted.

"It doesn't matter," I say absently, while catching his scent and having it stir strange emotions in me.

"It does matter," Xavier contradicts me.

"Why, it's just a stupid toy?" I ask.

"It was *your* stupid toy," he replies slowly, "and I won't allow any-one to take another thing from you without severe repercussions."

For a moment, I find the hubris of that statement very appealing. Something in my body language must be telling him that because his eyes become heavy-lidded.

"I saw you—just now," I blurt out, "on the film downstairs. It was you—I was only seven and you were there…"

"Did I just become real to you?" he asks me seriously, while his hand reaches out to cup my cheek. His shoulders cave in toward me as concern touches his features.

Biting my lip, I nod, "Really real—you look…you look exactly the same." My heartbeat pounds against the walls of my chest.

"You do know that we don't age?" he asks me with his eyebrows coming together, while his thumb caresses my skin.

"Yeah, but seeing you there was like, I don't know, like seeing a ghost," I breathe, and then I think to add, " and, yes, I've seen one of those before, too."

"I believe they prefer to be called souls," he corrects me with humor in his tone.

"Whatever," I reply because it's such a small point right now.

Xavier's gaze lingers on my face and his smile grows wider. Seeing it, uninvited feelings of attraction edge to the surface, causing a blush to creep to my cheeks.

"Yes, I *am* becoming real to you," Xavier says to himself while his finger traces the line of my jaw.

Brushing his hand away, I suddenly ask, "Why…why'd you come back? You were free of all this—of me. You had a chance to be happy and you ruined it."

Xavier lifts his hand to thread his fingers through my hair at the back of my head. Pulling me toward him, he lowers his lips to mine, kissing me with unrestrained desire. After a momentary pause for shock, I push against his chest to get him to stop kissing me. I feel the reluctance in him as he lifts his lips from mine. Still, his face remains inches from me when he says, "I came back for you…I love you."

"No, Xavier, don't say that," I say, closing my eyes.

"Say my name again," he demands, softly. "I will live in the sound of it."

My eyes fly open again. "You can't kiss me," I say instead with a shaky voice. "You can never kiss me again."

Xavier's lips twist in a lazy smile. "I will kiss you again and you will kiss me in return," he replies, like a promise.

"I have an *aspire*," I retort, upset by his blasé attitude.

Losing some of his smile, he replies, "You don't even know what that means. The only reason you're with him is because you had lost my aegis. I'm back now—you don't need him."

"You don't know what I need," I retort accusingly, as anger, coming from deep inside of me, bursts to the surface. "You deserted me!" I say between my teeth, feeling a betrayal so deep, that I hardly know where it originated.

Xavier's face turns grim before he engulfs me in his arms, picking me up off my feet and holding me to him. "I tried my hardest to stay," he says in a ragged voice before his lips brush tenderly over my hair.

As my cheek rests against his shoulder, I whisper, "Now, you have to try your hardest to let me go."

He stiffens, holding me tighter. "I have no intention of letting you go, not now, not ever, so you'll have to eventually forgive me."

I have to hush my urge to cry. "I'll forgive you if you promise not to challenge Reed."

"Your terms are unacceptable," he replies in a gruff tone. "I'll have to live without your forgiveness because I'm unwilling to live without you. I need your smile, your kisses, your love—"

"You sound just like Brennus: I, me, mine..." I say slowly. "You barely know me anymore."

"I'm nothing like him," Xavier says, nuzzling my neck. "He's dead...I'm very much alive."

"You're both overly affectionate," I add, trying to pull away from him.

Putting me back on my feet, he reaches down and tips my chin up so that I'll look at him. His blond hair falls over his brow when he looks down at me. "I've been gone for two long years, yes, but...we've sailed through thousands of years together—far beyond lifetimes. I used to know all of your secrets. I will again," he says earnestly.

"Then know this secret, Xavier: I love Reed. I will protect him with my life," I say plainly. "If you challenge him, you challenge me."

Xavier's eyes narrow to slits as he says through clenched teeth, "AHHH, Evie! Don't say that! Let him go!"

"I can't," I reply, shaking my head. "I couldn't turn back the tide of feelings that I have for him, even if I wanted to."

"He was never meant to be a part of this," Xavier says, stabbing his finger at me in anger.

"I'm not about to apologize to you for pulling him in," I say, watching Xavier's posture become rigid. "I wouldn't even be here right now if it weren't for him."

"I won't lose you," he warns softly.

"I don't know how you can prevent it," I reply, looking down at my feet so I don't have to see the pain in his eyes.

"There are a thousand ways to get you back. I just need one," he says, lifting my chin again so that I'll look at him.

Seeing the fire of determination in his eyes, I take a step back from him. "What are you going to do?" I ask suspiciously.

His face goes blank, revealing little. "For the answer to that, you'll have to learn my secrets." His eyes give no reverence to my concerns. "There was a time when I knew your every action before you made it. If you want to stay ahead of me, you'll have to learn mine."

I turn my back on him and walk to the balcony. My eyes rise to the broken skylights in the ceiling. Sighing heavily, I say, "I won't let you ruin what I have with Reed."

"And, I won't let you ruin what we had," he counters while his arms grip the balcony on either side of me. The heat from his body radiates to me to be subsumed by mine. Xavier leans near my ear to whisper, "You have filled the void that I left in you with false love… I've returned to reclaim my territory within your heart."

"False love! Are you serious?" I ask, responding to his provocative words. I have to turn toward him to see his face.

"Yes," he replies.

My eyebrows lower in a scowl as I say, "I don't even know what to say to you. Oh, wait. Yes I do. You're delusional."

I put my hand on his chest to push him back from me. He covers my hand with his, bringing it to his lips. When he kisses it, some sort of déjà vu leaks into my consciousness. Goose bumps, beginning at my wrist and traveling down the length of me, mingle with the intense, mental image of Xavier kissing me passionately beneath a tree in a place I've never been, at least, not recently. I blink as the hazy memory falls away, leaving me staring up at Xavier. My eyes scan his face as I think …*it was definitely him—his mismatched eyes smiling at me…*

"Evie," Xavier says in a gentle voice as he turns my hand over in his and kisses my open palm.

In the next second, panic makes the color drain from my face. *I know him,* I think. *I REALLY know him.*

Xavier stills as he studies me. Then, his eyes widen perceptively as his head tilts to one side. "Evie, what is it?" he asks.

"Huh?" I manage to say. I try to pull my hand back from him. "It's nothing." I look away evasively.

"Not nothing," he replies thoughtfully, holding my hand tighter.

"Let go, Xavier," I order in a salty tone, trying to hide my panic, but my heart feels like it's going to pound out of my chest.

"Not until you tell me what just happened," he replies. "You… were staring at me with the sweetest expression for a second there… just as if…" He freezes. I attempt to pull my hand back again, while I bite my lower lip. "You remember something!" he says with a mixture of accusation and elation.

"No," I say weakly, then add, "I don't know…"

"What? What do you remember?" he asks.

"Let go of me," I insist. "I can't think."

Those are the magic words that gain my release. Xavier, looking upon me with an expectant air, sparks a tumult of vague images in my mind: Xavier holding my hand, Xavier laughing, Xavier walking by my side, Xavier kissing me… Suddenly, the air is becoming too thin to breathe. Instead of answering him, I turn toward the open platform of the balcony and I bolt. Leaping into the air, my wings spread out as I dive towards the floor far below.

"Evie!" Xavier calls out behind me, but I ignore him.

When my feet touch the ground I don't hesitate, but I run full-out for the door. Hearing Xavier behind me, I use a spell to quickly close the doors to the tower as I run past them, locking him inside. I pause just beyond them to glance down the adjoining corridors and find them empty. My heart pounds harder in my chest and I jump when Xavier reaches the doors and beats against them. The doors strain against the jamb and even with magic, they won't hold long. I pivot on my heels and I sprint with supernatural speed in the direction of the South Tower.

Cccrackkk, the wood splinters as Xavier makes it into the corridor as I round the corner. Behind me his angry voice echoes off the stone walls, "EVIE, STOP!"

I run faster, feeling hunted. Ducking into a room halfway down the corridor leading to the South Tower, I realize it's the room I used for combat training with my Gancanagh bodyguards. Molly and I had dubbed it the "War Room," even though at one time it had clearly been a music room.

High ceilings with intricately cut molding, interspersed with exquisite, stone roundels, surround the room with a stately grace. Soft mats, an addition to the room when I began training here, still cover the dark wooden floors. But, beyond them, there is little else in the room to hide behind except for a large piano in the corner.

I creep back from the doors, breathing heavily and hoping that Xavier will pass right by this darkened room. Coming to rest against the back wall, I wait, trying to slow my breathing. But, when the doors are pushed inward and Xavier's large frame fills it, there is no controlling it.

Hide, I think, and instantly, my clothing tears from me; they fall in tatters to the floor as my skin flattens and takes on the tones and contours of the wall behind me. Rigidity engulfs me as I press into the stone of the wall.

"Evie," Xavier's voice echoes in the cavernous room.

I can't answer him, even if I wanted to; my skin, cold and gray, camouflages me from his sight. Xavier sniffs the air like a wolf. My heart beats faster.

Following his nose, Xavier scans the room, his eyes passing over me without seeing me. "I know you're in here," he says, turning in circles. "I can smell your scent…" he glances toward me again. Closing his eyes, he takes a step in my direction…then another. "I would know you anywhere by scent alone…so light, sweet…" he comes nearer, "you're beginning to remember me, aren't you?"

I try to move, but I only manage to tear away a small seam where my arm meets the wall because I'm mortared in place. "Don't be afraid of me," he says, like a caress. "I only want for you to know me again."

Nearing me, he opens his eyes again and spots my shredded clothing on the floor in front of me. His eyes rise from them as if following the contours of my shape against the wall. Leaning down he picks up my clothes before saying softly, "That is a brilliant façade, Evie, and if I hadn't been the one who suggested this sort of trait be added to your arsenal, I may have been fooled by it."

His hand reaches out and traces my shape up, following my silhouette. His fingers are soft against my hardened, rough exterior. He whispers something to me in Angel before he adds, "Amazing." His fingers trace my face, and finding my lips, he caresses them with his thumb. "I want to be your love again, but for now, I'll have to be content with being your mentor. You'll be safe with me, I promise."

He leans near, touching his full lips to my stony ones, kissing me with a gentleness that makes me want to cry. In the next instant, I change shape again, shedding my rock-like prison to burst forth into a swarm of swirling, bright-red butterflies. Shimmering around Xavier in a storming color of crimson, I ratchet upward in a twisting stream away from him.

"No, Evie, don't go…" Xavier says in a voice full of pain, "I won't become just a part of your past…"

Ignoring Xavier's order, I fly in a mass of fluttering, velvety wings toward the broken glass doors that lead outside. As I escape through a shattered windowpane, I pass swiftly into the cold, night sky.

The air is crisp with the icy aroma of the sea. Spiraling around the outer edifice of the South Tower, I'm swept and tossed by the salty wind. Drawn to a corner garden room by a different scent, one that is like nectar to me, I fly above a sleeping, walled garden and stone path to a set of lead-glass windows. I use magic to unlatch its wrought-iron clasp. The wooden-framed glass opens enough to fly through.

Reed, reclined on a massive, four-poster bed, reading an old, leather-bound book, sits up when the first of my butterflies land on his chest. One-by-one, I cover him in scarlet-winged creatures. Gently, Reed lays his book aside. Then, when the last of me flitters to rest upon him, my shape implodes to become my true form. Lying on his chest, I shiver from the cold before his arms snake possessively around me.

I kiss him with a panic-filled passion that only the fear of loss can elicit. "Never let me go," I breathe against his mouth.

"Never," Reed promises me without question.

CHAPTER 21

Dancing In Rings

Lying on top of Reed in the luxurious, four-poster bed, he flips me over with carnal strength, pinning me beneath him. Green eyes, so perfect to mine, are covered in a fall of dark hair over his brow. Reaching up, I gently push it to the side, feeling the icy chill in my heart warm at the sight of him.

"Your entrance was poetic, love," Reed says softly, as he smiles down at me. "I could just make out your delicate lines within the soft wave of scarlet, and not a minute too soon. I was trying my hardest not to search for you." Then he frowns, "Why are you unaccompanied?"

"Dinner didn't go as I planned," I respond with a frown.

"You're shivering," he says while wrapping a thick blanket around me. "What happened?"

"What if I told you that we have to leave as soon as this is over, what would you say?" I ask with my eyes searching his.

Reed's eyebrows draw together in concern, "You want to leave without the Seraphim?"

I nod solemnly.

He exhales, concern clouding his beautiful green eyes. "I'd say that I trust your judgment, but I'd wonder what brought you to that conclusion."

"Can it be done?" I ask.

"Yes," he says as the concern on his face grows. "That's not the hard part, Evie. The hard part is remaining one step ahead of them. They're very resourceful."

"But, we can do it, right?" I ask with desperation in my tone.

"If it became necessary, we could," he agrees grimly.

Throwing my arms around his neck, I hug him to me. "Good," I whisper-breathe. "Let's have a contingency plan. Keep it between us, just our group—Zee, Russell, Buns, Brownie, and Anya."

"What about Preben?" Reed asks, and then he shrugs at my raised eyebrow, saying, "He and Brownie have a thing."

I bite my thumbnail. "I don't know...let's work out the details with Zee and Russell, and then we can approach Preben later, okay?" I ask anxiously.

Reed's frown deepens. "Evie, what happened at dinner?" he asks.

I shrug as I try to downplay what must look like a complete freak out in Reed's eyes. "I got the distinct impression that their plans for me may not include my friends," I answer.

Reed relaxes a little. "We knew that they would have their own ideas about other angels. It's rare for Reapers to be involved in fighting. They don't know Buns and Brownie, yet. They'll see the benefit of having them around as companionship for you," Reed replies reassuringly.

"No, you don't understand...I mean *all* of my friends..." I trail off as anger makes a blush come to my cheeks. Understanding filters into Reed's expression. "They outrank us, don't they?" I ask.

"They do," he agrees.

Quickly, I tell him what happened at dinner tonight. "If you wanted to tear us apart, what would you do?" I ask Reed feebly.

"I'd send us on separate missions," he responds without hesitating.

"Could we say no?" I ask.

"No, but Tau will see reason," Reed says, straightening. "He hasn't had an opportunity to observe us together. You're his daughter. He's concerned about the circumstances of our binding."

"Why should we have to explain ourselves to anyone?" I ask. "It's not his decision. It's ours and we already made it."

A sexy smile twists Reed's lips despite the seriousness of our discussion. "Yes, we did, didn't we?" he agrees.

Leaning forward, he slips the blanket from my bare shoulder. His lips trace where the blanket had been, causing me to lose my breath.

"We need a plan," I whisper as I lay back against the soft mattress. Reed follows me.

"We'll have an egress if diplomacy doesn't succeed," he says, trailing kisses over my sensitive skin. "Let's just hope that we won't need it."

"Why?" I ask.

"Because there will be a price to pay if they catch up to us," he replies in a low tone.

"I love you," I whisper softly in his ear, wrapping my arms around him again. "You're worth any price to me."

"And you are priceless," he states.

"You'll fight to stay with me?" I ask, feeling his lips slip lower. I bite my bottom lip as my eyes close.

"There is nothing more important to me than you," he says with his lips hovering just above my skin. Then he kisses me again and I gasp softly.

A loud rap on the wooden door of our room makes me jump before Russell's voice comes through it.

"Reed, you in there?" Russell asks with a strained tone.

A growl comes from Reed before he rises from our bed. He waits while I wrap the blanket around me before he opens the door.

Russell continues rapidly, "They lost Evie. Xavier is having a complete hissy fit lookin' for her…" he trails off when Reed reluctantly opens the door wider and he sees me sit up on the bed. "AHH, RED!" he exclaims with a mixture of relief and irritation. "What the hell?"

"Long story. You can tell them I'm okay," I say.

"Naw, you can tell him," Russell says, shaking his head in disgust. "I've already got one angel pissed off at me at the moment and that's all I can handle."

"Anya?" I ask.

"Who else?" he responds sullenly. "All's I wanted her to do was share my bedroom, 'cuz there's no way I'm lettin' her stay here in a room all by herself and she started cussin' me out in Angel—and before you ask me how I know she was cussin', let me just say that all y'all have cussed me out enough for me to know," Russell says while glaring at Reed.

"Russell," I cut off his rant, "where is Xavier now?"

"Oh, you mean where'd he go *after* he tossed my room around lookin' for you?" he asks with a sarcastic twist of his lip.

I pale before I nod.

"Zee told him that Reed was in the North Tower and hinted that you probably went there, too. Then, he sent me here to get Reed," Russell replies with a cheeky grin.

"Remind me to thank Zee," I remark to Reed.

Reed nods in agreement and says, "I'll go and tell Tau that you're here. Russell, can you stay with Evie until I return?"

Russell glances at my worried face and relents. "Sure, Zee's watchin' Anya for me. She probably prefers him to me right now. I'll babysit 'til you get back."

Walking to the beautiful, mahogany chest, Reed sifts through it and pulls out a long, deep-red nightgown. Coming to my side, he hands it to me. Eyeing it like it's a cold, dead creature, I arch my eyebrow at him.

"Would you prefer a corset?" he asks me with a smile.

"No," I sigh. "This is fine." I lift it above my head and let the silky fabric slip over my body under the blanket.

"Please stay here until I return," he requests.

"Okay," I answer. But, when he turns to go I bound out of the bed saying, "Wait!"

Turning back towards me, he catches me in his arms when I throw mine around him. Reed's kiss makes me forget about Russell until Russell clears his throat behind us.

"I'm still here," Russell says sourly.

Reed, eyeing the nightgown hugging every curve I possess on its way to the floor says, "I'll be right back."

"Hurry," I reply, and in a second, he's gone.

Closing the door, I slip back to the bed, pulling a blanket off it and wrapping it around me like a shawl.

"Your room's nice," Russell remarks, looking around it.

It is nice. It has a rustic-cottage feel to it. The large bed is somewhat imposing, but the only other furniture in the room is the simple chest and a couple of soft chairs near the stone fireplace. In the corner of the room, near the fire, a door leads out to a walled garden I had seen before I came in. I walk to the door, opening the top portion of it that swings in leaving the bottom in place. Cold sea air lifts my hair.

"I thought it would be different in this tower—the Harem," I say over my shoulder.

Russell walks to the fire and picks up the poker, stoking it before laying another log on.

"It's not all like this...most of it looks like a brothel, except for this room. This room was..." he trails off.

"Brennus'," I finish for him, knowing that this is his style—simple elegance. Everything else is for show: to display wealth and power. But, this is more to his taste: quiet beauty.

"Yeah," he says. "Are you gonna tell me what's goin' on?" Russell asks.

Taking my last look at the wintry garden outside, I close the door and turn to face Russell. "This is all my fault," I say while wringing my hands.

"Don't sweat it, Red. Xavier is a..." he trails off, seeing me shaking my head.

"No, I mean, this mess—why we're here," I choke.

"Ah, yeah, no shit, Red," he says with his crooked smile. "I already figured out it wasn't me. I like stuff simple—you're the one that's always gotta prove the world isn't flat."

"No, Russell...I'm sorry," I say with remorse, "I think it was all me—what went wrong between us."

Russell stills. "Why, what did you find out?" he asks, losing his smile.

"Xavier said...some stuff about being my guardian angel for centuries..." I swallow hard, before continuing, "and, he said that I sort of asked to do this so that I could have the ultimate free will."

"The ultimate free will, Red, what's that?" he questions in a quiet tone.

"Uhh, I feel sick," I murmur, stumbling to a chair and sitting in it.

"What's the ultimate free will?" Russell asks again, taking the seat next to mine.

"It's the ability to choose...I asked to choose my own love—one that wasn't created for me," I admit as insane guilt hits me in waves. "Soul mates are created for one another—not really much free will there."

"Why would you do something like that?" he asks, sounding confused.

"I don't know," I say, shaking my head and staring into his brown eyes. "Xavier said I did it for him, that we were in love..."

"NAH! NO WAY!" Russell says angrily. "You wouldn't come here just 'cuz of him. You would've come, but not for him. I know you," Russell says, pointing at his chest. "You'd accept this and make the best of it, but you wouldn't have done it at my expense."

"What if I'm that selfish, Russell," I ask him sadly.

"You're not," he says adamantly. "We need to talk to Anya. She'll know."

"Do you think she'll tell us?" I ask.

"Yeah, I think she will. She's not a player. She'll either tell us or she won't, but she won't distort the information in her favor."

"Why do you say that?" I ask.

"'Cuz they have an agenda, Red," Russell says. "Xavier obviously wants you and your dad wants control. Our team threatens both those things."

I blink, seeing his point. "How do you know that?" I ask.

"'Cuz I've lived thousands of times and I've been a parent in almost every one of them. We've had daughters, you and me...many,

many daughters. You'd be surprised 'bout what you'll say to get your daughter to do what you want—to protect her."

I think about what he just said for a moment before a small smile twists my lips. "Those angels are out-gunned with that kind of arsenal, Russell," I say.

"They should start takin' notes," Russell replies with a cocky lift of his eyebrow. "Now, if you're done eatin' that shame sandwich, you can tell me what else they said."

I tell him about dinner with Tau and then my confrontation with Xavier. He shakes his head grimly. "They want to break us up?" he asks.

"I don't know. They're really only interested in me...everyone else is ancillary to them," I admit. "Tau wants to school me on being a Seraphim—rank, position, blah, blah, blah."

"And, you're not down with that?" Russell asks with approval.

"Naw," I say, using his drawl. "They're all just angels to me. Equals."

"Agreed," he says with a nod.

We both fall silent then, staring at the flames in the grate that slowly begin to make me feel tipsy with their hypnotic dance. The soughs of sea air against the windowpanes create a strange music that wafts around me in a blanket of comfort.

"I remember this," Russell says with a heavy-lidded smile as he gazes at me from his chair.

"Hmm?" I ask sleepily.

"I forgot how much I like this...just this," he says, reaching out and taking my hand gently in his. He gives it a light squeeze before he lets me go again.

"What do you mean?" I ask with a limp smile.

"Just sittin' with my best friend, watchin' the fire slowly die..." he explains, trailing off to relive some distant memory of us.

"I like it, too," I admit with my eyes transfixed on the embers.

"It usually only happens later, when our passion for each other's replaced with ole bones," Russell says and smiles wearily.

I smile back dreamily, "Either I'm losing my touch or Anya has eclipsed me because we're not aging."

"She's done somethin'," Russell says. "I'm all snake-venom and recoil when I'm around her—ready to strike out at anyone who gets too close to her."

"Yeah?" I ask as my eyebrow lifts in intrigue.

"Yeah," he admits. "Then, when we're alone together...it's like it was with you 'cept," he glances at me.

"Don't leave me hanging. Except what?" I prompt him.

"'Cept I got those butterfly things you got for Reed," he replies, watching me for my reaction.

"Ohhh," I say with a little smirk. "Those. What are they like for you?"

"Ahh, you really want to hear this?" he asks, looking slightly embarrassed for having brought it up.

"Uh huh," I nod without hesitation.

He exhales a deep breath before saying, "Shoot, it's like... it's like I'm prowlin' 'round her, so full of wolf-fire and raw emotion that I want to throw back my head and howl at the top of my lungs, but it won't stop the avalanche of attraction from fallin' down on me. The more I'm with her, the more perfectly alive I feel and greedier I am for her attention."

I nod my head. "Yep, that sounds about right," I agree. "What are you going to do about it?"

"I don't know," Russell replies, frowning. "I think I messed up huge already. I treated her like a second-rate hand-me-down. She hates me."

"It's impossible to hate you, Russell," I reply honestly.

"Impossible for you...she's doin' a pretty good job at it," he replies with a sigh.

"You'll think of something," I say, believing every word.

"My track record's not very good lately," he says, eyeing me.

"Ahh, but you have the advantage, because I'll bet that she has the same butterflies for you that you have for her," I reply with a wry smile. "They seem to come in pairs."

"You think?" he asks.

I nod, adding quietly, "She'll have to come with us."

"We're leavin' then?" he asks me just as softly.

"I'm not letting them break us up," I reply sourly.

"When?" he asks, already onboard with whatever plan we make.

A warm feeling enters my chest at his answer. "We'll have to work that out," I answer.

"I hope it's soon," he sighs tiredly, "bein' here is exhaustin'."

I yawn. "Yeah," I agree.

I close my eyes against the blurring firelight, deciding that I'll make an attempt to rise and stumble to bed in a second, after I rest for a moment.

The soft sound of a latch releasing from its idle makes my eyes open. That sound is replaced by a low, enchanting strain of music whose instrument completely eludes me...maybe it's a steel guitar? Glancing towards the garden door, the purplish, bruising shadows are being pushed back by a sliver of golden light, peering through the crack.

A warm, sultry breeze, with the reminiscent scent of sun-baked sand, creeps around me. I glance to Russell's chair next to mine; it's empty. Confused, I sit forward and search the room, but it's empty, too.

"Russell?" my soft voice intones, hoping to hear his reply, but nothing comes.

Slowly, I rise from the chair and walk in front of the fire to the garden door. Inching it open, I peek outside. The rhythm of the far-away music softens, making me strain to hear it as my eyes adjust to the dazzling glow of sunlight. Squinting against the glare, the moss-covered, stone path leading away from the door is the only part of the garden that is illuminated; the rest is dark and shadowy night.

Prepared to bar the door, I hear Russell's distinctive laughter coming from behind the small copse of trees where the garden path leads. I hesitate, but the humorous timbre of Russell's laugh floats to me again, along with woodland sounds of winsome fauna.

I open the door and step through, my bare feet peeking out beneath the silken froth of the ruby-colored nightgown while its train trails behind me. With each step I take beyond the door, flora grows up along the path, chasing away the hopscotch of dead leaves and replacing them with explosions of vibrant greenery. My legs begin to tremble beneath me with apprehension.

"Russell, where are you?" I whisper cautiously into the receding night.

All around me, the lushness of the garden keeps growing as dewy vines sprawl-climb the slate-gray walls. My wings splay out in anticipation of flight while their edges serrate to knife-like points. A shiver of fear erupts through me when a wiry rabbit scampers from behind a white-petal tree blossoming before my eyes; the fragrant shower of ivory speckles the rabbit's brown, downy hair.

Balmy air, filled with exotic, intoxicating scents, gently touches my skin, bringing with it the lulling melody. Resisting it's calming effect, I whisper-yell, "RUSSELL MARX!" into the darkness just beyond the path.

"Yeah, yeah...I hear you, Red," Russell answers me in a distracted tone. "I'm over here."

I blow out a huge sigh of relief and straighten up out of my defensive posture. "What are you doing out here?" I ask with irritation dripping from my tone. "Is this your magic?"

I walk forward on the path and round the trees of the small arbor. Then, I stumble to a halt as my stomach turns to ice. Russell is standing amid Faolan and Declan beneath a lovely, pink-flowering tree. The fellas flank him as Faolan shows Russell a wind conjuring spell—twisting a dust devil in an intricate dance around the garden floor. The wind harasses a shower of soft petals to fall upon their hair and shoulders.

Declan and Faolan appear outwardly friendly, laughing together when Russell magically takes over the whirling dust cloud and makes it turn in the opposite direction. My legs and arms are heavy with paralyzing fear as I discard several attack scenarios in my mind because they all have the potential of resulting in Russell's death. Declan, comprehending my predatory watchfulness, puts his arm around Russell in a show of camaraderie, or a threat to me, depending on the interpretation. Thwarted, I have to suppress the instinctive urge to growl at him.

Reading my enemies, they seem to have changed their appearance. Faolan, tall and slender, has lost his pale veneer, and now looks almost ruddy. Declan, too, has a normal-looking skin tone. As Declan turns with Russell to follow the path of the chaotic windstorm, my mouth drops open, spying silvery wings slicing outward from his back in tall, arching lines. Declan's ears also look faerie-like, with elongated points where they had once been rounded.

"Red," Russell calls to me, "did you see that?" he asks, looking dazed as the wind dissipates into nothingness. He gestures for me to join them with a lean of his head, but then it lolls forward, indicating to me that he is under some kind of charm or spell.

The music continues to float in the garden like a merry-go-round of sound, being here, and then there, moving in stereo. My eyes shift to the far wall covered in ivy and bittersweet vines, looking for the source of it. I find Finn, leaning casually against the ivy, playing some sort of long stringed guitar that I cannot name. The guitar hangs low in front of him, more like a steely weapon than an instrument. His head bends forward while he plucks at it, concentrating solely on the mesmerizing notes of the music. My eyes shift to his white, pointed wings beyond his shoulders.

There are layers to his music, twisting melodies within melodies, and something else…something beyond sound. It is sensual and tactile—heat that burns from an Arabian sun, casting a heady fragrance of Bedouin fires and cooking pots from just the other side of a sandy plane. The effect is potent, filling me with the sense of invulnerability…like being intoxicated. My mind struggles to remember that this is all fake—a faerie-tale. The fellas can conjure cunning illusions and cast lulling spells that make everything dream-like and surreal.

Beside Finn, Brennus slants idly against the wall, watching me with his light-green eyes. The golden laurel crown upon his head contrasts starkly with his black hair. White wings reach above his crown in thin points that resemble the jagged shape and texture of silken leaves and continues downward to just below his calves. Sun-kissed skin has replaced the paleness that I have grown accustomed to seeing in him. In short, he's breathtakingly beautiful and never more faerie-like.

Pulling casually at the pointed cuff of his elegant, white tunic, Brennus smoothes the wrinkles from his silken sleeve…and then, he waits.

"Russell," I purr in my sweetest tone, keeping my eyes on Brennus. "Why don't you go and show Anya your new wind trick?"

A slow smile spreads over Brennus' lips as Faolan says, "Wait, Russell, I've another spell ta show ye—dis one heals da pains 'o wounded pride," he says with a congenial lilt.

"They're goin' back to their own land now, Red," Russell interrupts Faolan, missing his obvious threat. "They figured out a cure for their condition, so now they can go home."

"Really, Russ? There's a cure for arrogance?" I ask him with the sinking realization that I'm alone in this fight, since Russell isn't all-there. He's been completely fooled by their elaborate façade—lie upon lie dancing in rings around one another.

Russell laughs drunkenly at that, slapping Declan playfully on the chest, not seeing his frown. "She's funny," he chuckles.

"She is," Declan agrees with a grudging smile.

"Russell," I try again, glancing at him, and then back to Brennus, "I don't think they can go home…and I'm pretty sure they're still Gancanagh."

Russell frowns before shaking his head, "Naw, see!" he says, pointing to Faolan's mouth, "no fangs!"

Anger surges through me along with terrifying fear. "WAKE UP, RUSSELL!" I shout at him. "Their fangs retract—you know that!"

"Huh?" Russell mutters, peering at Faolan in confusion. "You got more teeth hidin' in there?"

Straining with all my might, I try to pull energy to me to conjure a spell that will help Russell out of his cloud, but the air is thick as if the music is scattering the energy, suppressing it and keeping it from me. There must be a trick to it, because the fellas and Russell can still use magic.

Panting in frustration and effort, I glare at Finn. "Finn, can you play something else?" I call to him over the seductive notes.

"Whah would ye like ta hear?" Finn calls back with a small smile.

"I don't know...how about *Stairway To Heaven?*" I ask, trying to get him to stop weaving magic within his sinister inflections.

"I do na tink I know dat one, Genevieve," Finn replies softly, "ye'll have ta teach it ta me."

"He does na take requests," Brennus says, straightening and pushing effortlessly away from the wall. "But, I do."

I frown at Brennus. "Oh?" I ask as my eyebrow rises. "Do you know the song called 'Go-the hell-away-and-don't-ever-come-back?'"

Brennus smiles and says, "I do na know da melody, but da lyrics are familiar."

He prowls towards me with his eyes focused in on mine. Feeling the framework of his newest cage, I twitch with the urge to fly away. "If you plan on staying, maybe I could hum a few bars for you," I reply as a bluff, trying to keep him talking and not attacking. It's my only chance to save Russell. "It worked with Casimir."

Brennus, appearing unimpressed says, "Make yer Siren's call, *grá mo chroí*, but I'll na listen ta yer song. 'Tis time ye heard moin."

"So I'm once again the 'love of your heart?'" I ask with a fleeting smile, translating *grá mo chroí*.

"Dat has never changed," he replies, nearing me without any sign of caution or apprehension. "Ye'll always be me heart."

I try again to pull energy to me, managing only to get a little. I attempt to construct an invisible wall around me to protect myself from Brennus, but when he encounters it, he simply raises his hand and it dissipates.

I look at him in question and hear him say fiercely, "Dere is some magic I never taught ye."

Terrible, nightmarish fear makes my legs feel dead beneath me. Brennus' hand reaches out for me and the coldness of his touch belies the warm tones of his flesh. Taking me in his arms, I see the fury of a jealous lover in his green stare. I would scream, but it is far too late. Brennus raises his hand and brings it down hard on my cheek, slapping me with the force of payback.

Russell roars in rage, lunging away from Declan and Faolan towards us. Holding me around the waist, Brennus raises his other hand, pulsing energy at Russell. Lifting off his feet, Russell is tossed backward into the trunk of the flowering tree, scattering pink petals like the erratic fall of confetti. He crashes beneath it, but gets to his feet, only to be set upon by Declan and Faolan; their fangs engage *click, click.*

Pushing Declan back with a roundhouse kick to the face, Russell leaves Declan's jaw hanging at an odd angle. He then grasps the trunk of the tree, cracking and tearing it from the ground in a shower of twisted roots and spewing dirt.

Russell chokes up on the trunk with a come-and-get-some sneer to Faolan. Swinging the tree, a whiplash of pale pink petals thrashes the air amid plumes of lion-colored pollen that has a sticky-sweet scent. The lichen-covered branches of the tree connect with Faolan, crushing and splintering the wood. It drives Faolan into the shadowy part of the garden not illuminated by the sultry light of Finn's fabricated Eden.

Declan rushes Russell, plowing into him with the force of a freight train and causing him to drop the splintered timber. Dripping spattering trails of saliva from his broken jaw, Declan's arms encircle Russell's waist. The air is knocked out of Russell's lungs. He tumbles to the ground and lands beyond the trees out of my line of sight.

And Finn plays on.

I turn in Brennus' arms, trying desperately to pry them from my waist so that I can help Russell. Brennus uses his savage strength to pull me to him. With my back pressing against his chest, his cool lips trace a line of kisses along the column of my throat.

My wings push against his chest, but he only tightens his grip on my waist painfully. His magic swirls out, pushing back the carnival of fighting fellas, wild-sprawling garden, and fuming music to just shadows and impressions in the night.

"*Mo chroí*, I've ached ta hold ye in me arms," he roughly intones against my shivering skin. "Ye've torn me heart out."

I stop futilely struggling, hearing his accusation. Tilting my head back, I rest it against the soft, white fabric covering Brennus' chest. Panting from exertion, I wish that the thumping of my heart sledgehammering against the walls of my chest were the pounding of my feet against the ground, running from here.

With my throat tightening, I whisper bitterly to Brennus, "I'm so ashamed of what I've become," knowing that he'll understand better than anyone what I mean. Brennus' body stills behind mine, his cool lips hover inches from my skin. "I never wanted to hurt you…they said… they said I asked for this…that I agreed to become this jealousy-inducing thing and now I find that I'm exactly like you…an enticing monster."

Brennus' breath touches my neck gently. "Dat, right dere, is why I can na live wi'out ye. Ye confide such tings in me dat makes da darkest rage abate," he breathes. "Ye are a monster, Genevieve, 'tis whah I love da most: da dangerous, seductive killer in ye. Ye've da sweetness of a wee lass and da strength of a celestial being. But, shame is for da weak, *síorghrá*," he coos, calling me eternal love, "and I've a cure for it."

His fangs engage, *click*, before piercing the soft skin of my neck and finding an arterial pulse. I scream this time as the brutal pain slicing my veins brings me to the unrelenting reality that I'm now, truly, in a fight for my life. The loss of blood soon makes my eyes become blacker while I gasp in gulps of air. My fingernails claw his cheeks before becoming fists, knocking his hardened jaw, until a growing complacent-fluttering of my fingertips traces dizzy circles on his flesh, feeling it warming with the infusion of my blood.

The once frantic beat of my heart begins to slow; its pulse lessening, threatening never to move again; not for the beauty of love, nor for the anticipation of a lover, or for the alignment of another's heart. The darkness grows, killing all hope with pain. A warm tear slips from my cheek to fall gently on his. When my knees buckle, Brennus disengages his fangs from my neck, turning my pliant body in his arms. The hard lines of his beautiful face soften as it swims in my vision, a result of my blood weakening his power, making him drunkenly satiated.

Held like a doll to him, I search for Russell beyond the magical veil that has thinned and now wavers between impression and clarity. The fight between Russell and the fellas continues; in one instant they struggle ahead of us, and then fall behind, like Shriners in a desperate parade.

Brennus turns my face so that my eyes rest on his light green ones. His impassioned tone dimly registers in my mind, "Ye'll bend ta me desires dis time. Confess yer love for me and I'll bestow me affections on ye along wi' me blood—everyting will be yers again and we'll conquer dem all."

The hubris of his statement causes a slow smile to spread over my bluish lips as my blood seeps in trails down my neck. Reaching my shaking fingers up to touch his cheek, my response comes out in a croaking whisper, "You've already won. I'm dying…you have your revenge."

Fear makes his eyes widen and when my eyes close he shakes me so I'll open them again. The beat of my heart struggles from one to the next, stumbling as each contraction is slower than the last.

Brennus' eyebrows draw together in a dark scowl as he snarls at me, "'Tis na winning!" He shakes me again when my eyes lose focus on him. "Losing ye means mourning for eternity…"

I pat his cheek lightly, while whispering, "Then…you lose," before my hand slips from him.

Leaning his face nearer to mine, a slow smile creeps to the corners of his lips as he asks, "Genevieve, when have ye known me ta lose anyting?"

Cold, dark fear constricts my dying heart. "What?" I breathe.

"Kiss me goodbye, *mo chroí*," he says with a smile before his lips cover mine.

Nudging my lips apart with teasing kisses, Brennus then bites down hard on his lower lip. His blood, like the fall of tears, wets my lips and mouth.

Undeath, like an excruciating poison, winds through my lethargic limbs. My muscles grow hard and taut, causing painful spasms as they become rigid and rickety.

"No," I whisper accusingly into his exultant face when he pulls back to observe my transformation into an undead monster.

"Yes," Brennus whispers in reply, lovingly stroking my hair. "Ye're truly moin now."

Cradled in Brennus' arms, I writhe in the coldness of suffering and absolute sorrow.

Russell's voice sounds next to me as he speaks through his teeth, "Put her down, before I tear his head off."

My head lists toward Russell's voice and I see him, standing behind Finn with his hands grasping the metal instrument that Finn had been playing. He pulls it tighter to Finn's neck with a grim, determined look when Brennus glances in his direction. Russell only needs to jerk the sharp edge of the instrument back to sever Finn's head from his body.

"Ye're too late," Brennus replies softly.

Breathing hard, Russell scowls at him, yelling, "PUT. HER. DOWN!"

Gently, like I'm made of glass, Brennus lays me down on the cold, hard ground. Everywhere around us, the beautiful garden is retreating; the lush greenery is crawling back, crumbling into wintery darkness. Cold, twisting wind replaces the sultry heat of Finn's magic.

Finn and Brennus, too, begin to change; their brilliant, white wings melt away in a plume of smoke, while their skin pales to a deathly tone. The white, magical faerie garb is replaced with sleek, black suits, perfectly tailored and no less refined.

"Now, move back!" Russell orders, scowling fiercely at Brennus.

When Brennus steps back from me, Russell shuffles Finn forward to my side. Glancing down at me quickly, and then back up at Brennus, Russell says, "Get up, Red. Let's go."

"She can na move," Brennus informs him with a smug smile. "She's dying...or, undying, whichever ye prefer."

Declan limps his way to Brennus' side, the mask of magic gone, so that he appears as he always has: cold and ruthless—a Gancanagh killer.

"What?" Russell asks in a higher tone. His eyes coming back to me, while the blood drains from his face.

I try to tell Russell to run, but my jaws feel wired shut while I'm being burned by the coldest of ice from the inside out. My veins are turning black beneath the stark white skin of my hands and forearms as Brennus' poisonous blood creeps through them.

"Naw, naw, naw..." Russell's panicky voice sounds as if it comes from him involuntarily, as a bad, off-key tune. "She'd never drink your blood—"

"But, she has. 'Twas on me lips, ye see, when I kissed her goodbye," comes Brennus' smooth reply. "She'll remain on dis side of eternity wi' me now."

"HOW COULD YOU DO THAT TO HER?" Russell shouts like the hiss of snake-spit. "You damned her soul forever! It was supposed to be a choice!"

"'Twas a choice. 'Twas me choice," Brennus says, watching Russell pull the silvery instrument tighter against Finn's neck.

"Brenn," Finn says, his face sad as he looks at me, "'tis na da way 'tis done."

"'Tis done!" Brennus hisses back.

I groan in agony as I try to hold on to the edge of pain so I won't fall down the dark hole growing inside of me. An instant later, I'm cradled in Russell's arms with his face buried in my hair. He rocks me, groaning in pain along with me as his blood-red wings spread around us, in an attempt to shield us from the fellas. "Ahh, Red, no... I'm sorry..." Russell whispers hoarsely to me, pulling me so close that our cheeks meet. He's so warm that I want to pull his heat to me to wrap around me like a blanket.

Feeling his soft tears dampen my skin, Russell's voice cracks as he groans in my ear, "What do I do? How do I stop this?"

No plumes of cold air escape from my lips, for my breath is turning colder than the air outside, as I struggle to say, "Killll... meee."

When the words are out, Russell's hand tightens into a fist within my hair. He groans again, like he'll be sick. "I can't," he says in a tortured tone with his teeth gnashing together.

"Please..." I whisper, no louder than an autumn leaf tumbling over the wintery grass.

Finn bends nearer to us on the ground, saying sympathetically to Russell, "Ye can na save her now. We'll take care of her—she'll be our own dear one. Ye should leave now, so she does na make ye her first kill."

Russell's brow wrinkles as he snarls back, "You've no idea what I can do!"

"Ye can na stop it," Brennus says, coming menacingly closer and baring his fangs. "And, I tink ye'd make a fine first kill."

Faolan, mangled and beaten, drops on the ground right in front of Brennus' feet. He let's out a groan as his body rests next to us. Brennus hisses, looking up at the sky before Reed kicks him hard in the face, thereby forcing him off his feet and away from me.

Charcoal-colored wings, of which I know every line and contour, spread out between Brennus and us, blocking the Gancanagh from coming between Russell and me. Then, Reed hurls himself at Declan, instantly breaking his leg to match his lower jaw, while narrowly avoiding Declan's fist as it swings past his bare, unprotected cheek.

The sound of harrowing panic threads through Reed's tone as he orders Russell, "WHATEVER YOU'RE PLANNING TO DO, RUSSELL, DO IT!"

Russell's eyes turn wild, widening while he breathes in a massive breath. Exhaling with flaring nostrils, he puts his large hand on my chest. His fingers begin to glow, heating up like molten metal, penetrating my chest to melt the crystallized ice growing inside of me.

I scream, suffering again as the flow of blood within my veins changes current, running in the opposite direction. Russell falls next to me, sending us like a cascade of debris to the frozen ground. Lying side-by-side, Russell's hand remains on my chest, locked together like Siamese twins as he pulls the poisoned blood from my body to flow into his.

Finn, disturbed by what is happening between Russell and me, tries to pry Russell's hand from my heart. Russell reaches out his other hand to rest it on Faolon's chest beside him, and it, too, begins to glow. A stricken expression crosses Finn's face before he abruptly lets go of Russell's hand on me and tries to pry the other one off of

Faolan. When he can't move it, he looks around, seeing the fight between Reed and Brennus. He gets up then and moves to help his brother.

Faolan's face pales to a gray-white color while his veins become engorged, swelling up like black, twisting leeches under his smooth skin. His hair, normally as black as pitch, whitens with the age of centuries. Two deep wounds break open on Faolan's neck, the exact size and shape of Brennus' fangs. The wounds ooze with what looks more like thick, dirty motor-oil than blood. A brief second more and his leech-like veins burst, causing black blood to ooze up through Faolan's pores and from his eyes and ears. He stops struggling as his eyes become darker than the sky above us.

Soothing warmth, healing the raw-rotten flesh inside of me, leaves me trembling and weak. Russell's hand slips from me as it loses its light. I flail, trying to grip Russell's chest and pull him to me.

When he coughs and sputters for air, I begin to cry, crawling next to him on my hands and knees.

Hovering above his chest, I peer down on his face, seeing him look up at me in a daze. "Russell," I gasp, "are you okay?"

"Naw," he says, shaking his head slowly. "I feel burned from the inside out."

"Can you move?" I demand, trying to get him to sit up.

"You're alive," he says, looking stunned. Then his head moves to the side and he notices Faolan's all-dead body lying next to him. "It worked," he mutters.

"What worked?" I croak, searching the garden and then the sky for Reed and Brennus.

"I was gonna take it—your sickness, but when Faolan groaned beside me, I thought, 'You take it, you cold dead freak,' so I let your sickness travel through me to him," Russell explains with a gravelly voice, rubbing his hands together like they ache. "It must have fried him—they're so cold."

"So, it passed through you to him, like an electrical current?" I ask.

"Yeah, I guess," he replies absently.

Bright, white light flickers in the air near me as Declan's hands smooth over his broken leg. Immediately, his leg aligns, losing the compound fracture that Reed had just inflicted on him. Twisting his hand up, Declan applies it to his hanging jaw, pushing it back into place with a loud *crack* and welding it there with his magical light.

Then, Declan's menacing gaze turns to Russell and me, lying on the ground. A sinister growl comes from me while my eyes narrow, like a lioness protecting her young, when Declan's steely eyes stare past me to Russell.

"Ye killed Faolan!" Declan growls at Russell as he steps forward in furious anger.

Waving his hand toward the slate-gray stones of the wall, Declan makes them disassemble and fly toward us in a tidal wave of rock and mortar.

With Finn's magic gone, I'm able to pull energy to me, and then hurl it at the impending stones. The first slabs are pulverized into great puffs of dust, but a few break through, spinning just wide of us.

"Russell, we have to move!" I order him, not looking back but keeping my focus on the raging, hulking Gancanagh ahead of me.

"Why, I'm bigger than him?" Russell asks weakly, standing limply by my side. He leans slightly forward, favoring his left side.

"I'll hold him off. Go get help," I whisper to Russell.

"You go get help, I'll hold him off," Russell replies, wincing in pain.

"Don't be stubborn," I say between my teeth.

"You're stubborn," he shoots back.

Brennus and Reed materialize just beyond Declan. Twisting and turning, they fight fiercely with knives at supernatural speed. I can hardly mark their progression as my erratic pulse quickens seeing Reed avoid Brennus' brutal swings using the weapon I recognize well…it's a letter-opener…my weapon. Finn is also with him, using his own knife to try to kill Reed, but Reed's sole focus seems to be just on Brennus.

Brennus cricket-leaps around the garden, defying gravity with inertia and bursts of magic. Reed is Brennus' shadow, only a millisecond behind him, until he anticipates Brennus' next move. With a brutal slash, Reed manages to tear a jagged, bloody line of flesh out of Brennus' back. Another slice soon follows as Brennus begins to lose more blood.

I'm so consumed by their fight that I forget about Declan in front of me, but he hasn't forgotten me. Russell is laboring hard beside me to fend off the magic whirling out of Declan. In a powerful burst of glittering air, Declan hurls wind at us. The twirling streams enter our noses, collecting the oxygen within our lungs and snatching it out of us through our mouths. In tandem, Russell and I both drop to our knees, fighting for breath.

Declan reaches me, his hand encircling my neck as he lifts me off my feet. Wild-eyed from lack of oxygen, I stare into his scowling face.

"Faolan loved ye! Why could ye na jus obey us?" he asks me in a shaming tone, even though he probably knows I can't answer him. "Ye will be one o' us and ye'll spend da rest o' yer life making it up ta him...and ye can na...ye fool, ye can na make it up ta him!"

Scratching uselessly at Declan's hand, I choke and redden, doing a painful dance as my legs swing around. Declan's sneer deepens as he applies more pressure to my neck. Rage and anger darken Declan's eyes before mine shift away from his to the beautiful green ones just behind him.

The dull glint of a knife's blade penetrates through the back of Declan's neck to emerge in front of my eyes. With a vicious tug, Reed cuts through the tendons and sinew there. Declan's grip immediately slackens and I drop to the ground while his head ratchets forward, only halfway attached, making Declan all-the-way dead.

"Evie," Reed says, his eyes wide with concern. He reaches out to take me in his arms.

"Reed," I gasp with relief, but before he can touch me, Brennus appears behind him.

My eyes flare wide, panic causing my swollen throat to constrict in agony, while a soft sound of anguish tumbles from my lips. Reed must know by my expression, because he turns away from me to plunge his knife into Brennus' looming shoulder. Brennus winces, but he's still able to reach out and touch his cold, toxic fingertips to Reed's hand as it grips the knife handle embedded in him.

Horror twists my heart as the muscles in Reed's back relax. His wings slowly lower in complacency. Reed stands docilely in front of Brennus, staring at him as if he is his love, not me.

Placing his hand on Reed's strong chest, Brennus gives him a gentle push, easily turning Reed's passive body as he nudges past him to me. Pulling the knife from his shoulder with only a small wince, Brennus says to Reed, "Stay dere," and my angel obeys.

I hear something grating, something like screams, except they have little sound, no real pitch. It takes me a few moments to realize that I am making those noises. My damaged larynx won't allow my crushed spirit to vent its desolation and despair. Just soft whimpers emerge from my trembling body, while all of the ramifications of what just occurred tear my heart in two.

The sorrow in Brennus' eyes matches my own, when he reaches out and cups my damp cheek. A shudder of hatred, so deep and brutal, racks my body as I gaze at Brennus. He just delivered to Reed what is tantamount to a death sentence. Reed will die by

Brennus' hand or by another angel's, because the poison administered by Brennus' touch is lethal, almost as bad as tasting his blood...

Brennus' finger traces the path of my tears. "Would ye cry like dat for me, *mo chroí*, if he'd killed me instead?" he asks in agony.

Tears continue to fall from my eyes, but my mind screams, *WAS LETHAL...WAS...UNTIL RUSSELL SAVED ME...*

I hood my gaze. "I'll do anything you want—everything," I beg in a raspy voice that oscillates and breaks. My eyes drift to Reed who has the satisfied smile of one under the hazy thrall of the Gancanagh.

I will fight for you, my eyes promise Reed's before they shift back to Brennus'.

I turn my lips to kiss the palm of Brennus' hand in submission. His eyes soften and he seems somewhat comforted by what I just did. He traces my lips with his thumb. "I've never known anyone ta survive me blood," he utters meditatively, while gently stroking my cheek. "Ye're a marvel, Genevieve."

"I'll be your marvel, Brennus. Let Reed go with Russell. Then, I'm all yours," I say with what I hope is a seductive smile.

Brennus stiffens. "More conditions?" he asks with a calculated rise of his dark eyebrow.

"You love to bargain, Brennus. You live for it," I reply, trying to slow the beat of my heart that I'm sure he can hear. "Take me with you—leave him." I cast my gaze on Reed. "I see now that he's weak. You beat him—let the angels kill him."

"Naw, you ain't goin' nowhere with him," Russell growls, grasping my upper arm and yanking me out of Brennus' hands.

Brennus' demeanor turns deadly. He begins pulling energy to him immediately; I feel it traveling through me. "Ye killed Faolan," Brennus snarls at Russell. "Do na tink for one moment dat I'll let ye live."

"Naw, you killed him. It was your blood that I pushed into him, not mine," Russell spits back, while the energy in the air shifts to Russell, too. A clone shoots forth from Russell, fleeing in the direction of the castle. Brennus watches it streak away, and he knows what it means. Other angels will come now.

"He's na very bright, is he, *mo chroí?* Is dat why ye threw him aside for da *aingeal?*" he asks as his brows draw together. "Ye do realize, da other, dat I'm now in control of a lethal Power angel? He'll kill for me at my slightest whim."

"He'd expect me to kill him," Russell retorts, pushing me away from him.

I collapse on the ground and when I try to get up, I bump into an invisible wall that Russell creates to keep me from going with Brennus. I beat on the transparent barrier, my heart pounding in my chest because I have to go; it's the only way to save Reed.

"Here is yer chance ta kill him den," Brennus says with a scowl, before he turns to Reed and says softly, "*Aingeal,* kill da other…"

Reed's wings pin back as he runs full-out at Russell, but the wall of energy surrounding both Russell and me knocks him back. Growling low, Reed prowls forward and cases the energy, testing it for weakness by brutally throwing his shoulder against it. The fierce and cunning scowl on his face is scarier than his snarl because Reed has never looked at us like that before—like he'll eviscerate us if he can just reach us.

Shouts and commotion come from just beyond the path, up near the door to my garden room. The beautiful voices of angels calling into the night elicit desperation in me. I begin to struggle against Russell's magic, throwing myself against it to find a weakness, too.

"Russell, they're coming! You have to let me go! I have to go with Brennus," I plead, feeling Russell pushing more energy into his spell to keep me back.

"I can't let you do it," Russell says grimly.

Brennus winds his arm back and throws fire at Russell's wall, only to have it deflect in a shower of sparks.

Russell sneers, "I told you a long time ago that you should've been worried 'bout what I was becomin', but now it's too late. Your men are dead and you're next."

"Dat is na quite right, is it?" Brennus asks. "Yer weakness jus led yer friend ta a slaughter. She jus might kill ye before I do," he says, nodding his head at me. "Her *aingeal* is as good as dead, all because of ye."

"Russell! PLEASE! LET ME GO!" I beg hysterically, with my eyes on Reed who watches Russell like he's prey.

"I CAN'T!" Russell shouts back at me in a tone somewhere between rage and despair.

Brennus, seeing the need for retreat when the angel voices grow closer, pulls a compact from inside his disheveled suit coat. Flipping the portal open, he turns to Reed and orders, "Enter da portal and wait for me."

Reed immediately shape-shifts by exploding into a swarm of honeybees. He disappears into the portal in a moment.

"NO!" I scream as my mind pulses with the most horrendous torture scenarios that await Reed at the other end of that portal.

Brennus hesitates when I beat against the invisible cage surrounding me. "WAIT! BRENNUS, WAIT!" I scream desperately. "I will come to you. I promise, I will."

A slow smile forms on Brennus' lips. "Ye will?" he asks.

"I will! Don't turn Reed—promise me!" I beg him.

Brennus' eyebrow arches in question, "Why na?" he asks.

My fingertips slide down the barrier between us as I croak, "Because...because I want him for my *sclábhaí*," I lie. "He'll make a good slave."

Brennus' smile deepens. "He would, indeed," Brennus grins indulgently.

"Brenn, we must go now," Finn says, indicating the commotion building behind us. When he sees Brennus nod, he disappears inside the portal.

"Ye know where I'll be," Brennus says with a small smile.

"I do," I agree, knowing just where to go—the Knight's Bar.

"Hurry...I do na plan ta keep him for ye long," he advises.

"I'll come, I promise..." I say, splaying my hands against the barrier between us.

"Until den," he nods, before jumping into the portal and disappearing from the night.

CHAPTER 22

Spies And Allies

The portal that Brennus uses to make his escape falls to the frozen ground and lays there as an enticing invitation for me to follow them. Russell frees himself from the energy shielding him and walks to it. As he picks it up, I plead, "Don't—" but he smashes it tight in his fist, before waving his hand at me to release me from my invisible prison.

I'm driven to my knees under a weight of sorrow so heavy that I can't remain standing. Tears come in racking gasps while I cover my face with my hands to try to contain them. *I have to—to plan...I have to...I have to...Reed!* My heart gives a painful lurch. *He took Reed from me!* I silently scream as my mind struggles to surmount the torturous emotions overtaking me.

"Red," Russell's soft voice penetrates my frantic brain while angels with fierce weapons and even fiercer expressions assemble in a circle around us, scanning the terrain for threats.

I hold up a trembling hand to him to stop him from reaching out and taking me in his arms. I don't want Russell to comfort me. There is no comfort. *I need Zee—he's brilliant, resourceful—he'll help me save Reed,* I plot frantically, while rising to my feet.

I grab onto the first Power angel I encounter, clutching the front of his armor, I ask him in a frayed voice, "Zephyr King? I need to find him!"

His hands go to my upper arms to steady me because I sway when my world begins to spin. Without thought, a glowing clone emerges from me, causing the Power's eyes to widen in amazement. The image of me shoots through the crowd of angels, eliciting murmurs and musical commentary. Disorientated and confused, I back away from the watchful Powers and turn to stumble along on the garden path. Russell is at my side, attempting to help me by putting his arm around me.

"No!" I say bitterly, as I try to shrug his arm off, but he holds on to me.

"I had to stop you," Russell's voice pleads, struggling with me to make me look at him. "'Cuz I know what it feels like after they take you and I couldn't live through that again."

I turn on him, shoving my finger in his face. "NOT YOUR DECISION!" I growl in a croaking voice because Declan has left deep bruises on my throat. *Declan! Declan's dead,* my mind is screaming.

Russell, looking beaten up too, straightens, pointing his finger back at me. "I'm makin' it my decision! Reed would've wanted me to stop you. You're in no condition to take Brennus on now!" Russell counters in an angry voice. "And don't tell me you could've healed Reed before Brennus tried to eat you again, 'cuz I'm not buyin' it."

"Don't talk about Reed in the past tense!" I snarl before the painful twist of my heart reminds me that I'm wasting precious time. Time is finite now; there's almost no time left for Reed. Brushing Russell aside, I run towards the estate to search for Zee.

"EVIE!" Russell shouts, following me.

Xavier descends from the sky with a flourish of his powerful wings and lands directly in front of me with a scowl to match my own. I try to maneuver around him, but he's equally fast, catching me up in his arms. "We need to talk," he begins, before he really looks at me. When he does, his eyes grow darker. He grips my chin, turning it so he can examine my blackening neck.

"Put me down," I order in a raspy whisper. "I can't talk now!"

"I'm surprised you can speak at all," comes Xavier's retort. "Who did this to you?"

"Gancanagh," I say, pointing to Declan's still body for expediency. "You should go have a look—"

"You were attacked?" he asks for confirmation.

"Yes," I say, wiggling to get out of his grasp.

Zephyr's voice reaches me then. "Evie," he murmurs in a desolate tone.

"ZEE!" I breathe as my face distorts in anguish when my eyes meet his ice-blue ones. I reach out to him, putting my arms around his neck. I try to pull myself out of Xavier's grasp while giant, racking sobs shake my body.

As I cling tight to Zephyr, Xavier finally relents by handing me into the Power's arms. I try hard to speak, to tell him exactly what happened and what he needs to know to help Reed, but all that is coming out of me are indiscernible words interrupted by heaving sobs.

"Shh..." Zephyr says gently, stroking my hair. "I received your messenger, Evie. I know Brennus attacked you...I know Reed...was lost—"

"No," I shake my head, "not lost—"

Xavier turns on Zephyr with menace. "Brennus attacked Evie?" he snarls.

"Yeah, try to keep up," Russell retorts, fielding the question for Zee.

Xavier's expression turns dark as he leans aggressively towards Russell. "Tell me what happened before I shred you!"

"XAVIER," Tau barks a warning as he joins us with Cole at his side. Tau's eyes meet mine while his expression goes completely blank. I turn away from him, burying my face in Zephyr's neck. "Evie," Tau says my name with merciful softness, "you're hurt. Zephyr, bring her inside."

"I'm not hurt," I manage to say, "it's Reed—" I have to pause to hold back the urge to violently retch as my stomach twists like I had been bayoneted in the abdomen. I squeeze my eyes shut.

"Inside," Tau repeats grimly to Zephyr, not waiting for me to finish.

Chilling wind flows over my already numb limbs as Zephyr transports me in his arms. He follows Tau through the maze of corridors at dizzying speeds. Looking over Zephyr's shoulder, my eyes rest on Russell's who follows close behind us. The burn of betrayal constricts my throat, making me glance away from Russell to Xavier edging closer to me.

The ghostly hint of an expensive fragrance lingers in the air when Zephyr carries me through a sitting room to Brennus' office. The perfume had been a gift from Brennus, bought for me when I occupied the suite of rooms connected to this office. Pushing past the office door, I can see that the room is largely untouched by the battle that had damaged most of the estate. Brennus' enormous mahogany desk is still here, graced by silk-covered chairs.

Zephyr passes the small table where I once ate my breakfast every morning, taking me directly to an elegant sofa beneath the large, arching windows with their view of the sea. Placing me upon the cushions, he immediately starts assessing my injuries. Tau stands beside him, speaking to him in Angel and following every detail of the examination.

"No time for this!" I rasp laconically to Zephyr. "Reed needs us."

"What happened?" Tau asks.

I try to speak, to tell him everything that happened, but I can't; my lips twist in an anguished expression. Quickly, Russell comes to my rescue, recounting the night's events in gut-wrenching detail. When he's done, they all seem to be in shock.

"She was forced to drink Gancanagh blood and then you healed her?" Tau asks Russell.

"Yeah," Russell replies with a grimace, adding, "but it was my fault she was out there in the first place—"

"How could she have ingested Brennus' blood, Russell?" Tau asks quietly. "She's alive and she still retains her soul."

"I don't know," Russell answers honestly. "I was hopin' one of y'all could tell me how it works."

Ignoring them, I whisper in Zephyr's ear, "We can save him—I need to get close—touch him—take away his thrall—"

Tau interrupts me, "How do you know that you can heal the thrall of the Gancanagh in an angel like Reed?"

"Russell healed me—toxic skin is a weaker poison than their blood," I whisper in a raspy voice, "and I'm immune to it."

"Yes, but how do you know it will work for Reed?" he asks again. "You and Russell share a similar physiology...not so with Reed."

I still at his words, seeing that it questions the logic of my plan. "It will work," I state firmly.

Pessimism is in his tone when he replies, "It's a great risk."

My heart sinks another degree. "It won't be you taking the risk," I reply in a sinister, gravelly voice.

"Nor will it be you," Tau replies calmly. "Your plan is flawed. It could very well end with Reed killing you when it fails...or worse, Brennus turning you into his undead queen."

"Reed would never hurt me," I retort.

"He's not Reed anymore," Tau says grimly.

My throat constricts like he's put a noose around my neck. "What're you saying?" I ask as renewed panic heaps upon my already overwhelming sense of fear and dread to make me feel sicker inside.

"The best we can do is hunt for Reed, attempt to capture him, and then, perhaps, you may try to heal him if he were properly restrained..." Tau says as he begins to outline a totally ridiculous plan.

"You'll never get close to him!" I rasp. "He's being controlled by Brennus—the only chance we have is if I go to Brennus, meet him—"

Xavier's deep growl interrupts me. "No!" Xavier argues, shaking his head at me. He's by Brennus' desk and in his hand is the small statue that Reed had carved of me.

"No?" I ask, like I don't understand the word, but my heart stumbles on it.

Xavier sets the statue back down on the desk. "You must know that everything you're saying is completely irrational," Xavier says.

"Irrational?" I ask him rhetorically. "No, it's completely feasible!" I insist as cold sweat breaks out on my brow.

"You can't do it," Xavier says in a soothing tone, while his fingers linger on the figurine. "We'll take care of this for you."

"How?" I ask, feeling sick.

"I will kill him for you. He will not suffer," Xavier replies with compassion in his mismatched eyes.

"What?" I ask in shock.

"Reed has to die before he harms others," Xavier answers cautiously, gauging my reaction.

"Will you kill me next, then?" I ask in swelling fury, "because the angel that kills Reed before I can heal him will have to kill me, too. I'll never stop hunting him. It'll be my only mission."

Tau speaks to Xavier in Angel, effectively cutting me out of their conversation. Wanting a translator, I lift my eyes to Zee's. The soulful sadness in them makes me have to bite my lip against bursting out in tears again. I feel torn at the seams.

I ask Zephyr almost inaudibly, "What're they saying?"

"Shh...not here," he replies conspiratorially. Then to Tau, he raises his tone, saying, "Evie needs rest. I will take her to her room."

Tau's gray stare turns to me again with an unreadable expression. He says calmly, "I will take care of her." Then, Tau speaks to Zephyr in Angel.

Zephyr stiffens. Something's way more wrong than it was even a minute ago. My hand reaches out to Zephyr's, taking his, I ask, "What, Zee?"

"They are going to force me out, Evie," Zephyr replies in a cold tone.

"Force you out?" comes my numb question.

"The choice is not mine to make. I am outranked," Zephyr says with his eyebrows drawing together in a deep frown. "They have only to say that my mission here is concluded and I must leave."

My hand tightens in his as I shake my head. "But...I'm Seraphim, too. No one truly knows where I rank, right?" I ask, looking for a loophole in their laws.

"In what scenario would a daughter outrank her father?" Tau asks in a gentle tone.

"Why are you doing this?" I demand hollowly.

Reaching out, he touches my cheek, saying, "My desire is to help you."

Hostilely brushing his hand from my cheek, I retort, "How is sending my friend away possibly going to help me?"

"Without your friends, you will have to rely on me for help, council...guidance," Tau replies with cold logic. "If they're allowed to remain, you'll never let me in."

"WHOA!" Russell cuts in angrily. "You're not serious, 'cuz no one's breakin' us up!"

"I am very serious, Russell," Tau replies, unruffled.

"This is about control, isn't it?" I ask with narrowing eyes. "It's about getting me to do as I'm told."

"That would be the goal for now until you learn to trust me," Tau replies.

Gazing around at the contingent of Power angels guarding the windows and doors leading to the balcony and the sitting room, I calculate the odds of my fragile situation. It's bleak; they all answer to Tau. Then, my eyes shift to Xavier who watches me grimly, in full agreement with my father.

My eyes shift back to Tau. "I've never asked you for anything. I'm asking you now: please, please, help me get Reed back!" I beg him. "I'll trust you—I'll do anything you want me to do, I promise!"

"Every effort will be made to locate Reed," Tau replies.

"Good," I breathe in a sick kind of relief. "Whose team am I on?"

"You won't participate in the recovery," Tau says.

"But...you need me to heal him," I say slowly, my voice hitching.

"If we take him alive, you'll be informed," Tau says softly.

"*If* you take him alive?" I ask.

"Yes," he affirms with paternal tolerance.

"I'm gonna be sick," I groan. "Please don't do this. You have to help me," I plead.

"I am," Tau says with resolve. "I will not allow your idiosyncrasies and misguided loyalty to lead you to sacrifice yourself or your soul."

"My misguided loyalty?" I ask in a shallow voice. "Wouldn't you do anything—everything to save your *aspire* if you could?"

Tau frowns grimly, looking away from me.

"Evie," Xavier says in a tone meant to caution me. When I glance at him he shakes his head in warning.

"What, Xavier?" I ask him in an anguished tone, "am I supposed to just let Reed die like he let my mother die? Is that what we do in my family?" I ask in growing rage. "I can't do that! Reed doesn't get another chance. He won't go to Paradise if I let him die." I put my trembling hand to my chest where the pain is excruciating.

"He is a Power. He is prepared to make this kind of sacrifice," Xavier says while he edges closer to me. He stands just a little bit between Tau and me, looking tense.

Tau loses any hint of calm he had once possessed, as his frown grows deeper. In a stern voice, he answers me, "You will be protected in ways your mother was not."

"I don't want your protection!" I retort through my tears.

"You cannot be allowed to put yourself in the hands of your enemy. Going to Brennus in supplication is in direct violation to Angelic law," Tau's tone is askance, as he explains his point to me. "Your plan is flawed."

Refusing to see his point, I counter, "Is it coincidence then that I don't know your laws or your language? I'm learning that nothing is coincidence, so that leads me to conclude that I don't know them because they don't apply to me. I'm a more effective killer when I'm not hemmed in by protocol—and isn't that what you all want out of me, for me to be a killer?" I ask him with my eyebrows pulling together in anger. "Let me do what I was created to do. Let me kill Brennus."

Tau's eyes narrow, "You're deliberately being intransigent," he says accusingly.

"No! You're the one who's unwilling to see my point!" I deny his accusation, throwing it back at him.

"You cannot see clearly through your emotions. Until you can, I will be making all of the decisions that affect your life," he states with an attempt at calm and order.

"No," I say, stepping towards the door to the sitting room. Cole immediately blocks it as he crosses his arms over his chest. I hesitate, seeing his resolve. Slowly, I murmur, "You can't keep me here,"

"You will cooperate," Tau replies like a parent.

"No, I won't," I counter, giving him my severest look.

"Evie," Tau sighs my name in exasperation.

"How can you stop me?" I ask him. "You can't hold me here—I can shapeshift into butterflies and fly up the chimney if I want to."

"Phaedrus," Tau says softly.

"Phaedrus?" I ask with a sense of deepening dread.

"Will tell us what you're planning," he responds, indicating that he knows that Phaedrus is able to read most of my thoughts as I have them. He can hear them just as if I were speaking to him.

"Phaedrus would never do that," I reply with certainty.

"Phaedrus respects rank. He will follow orders," Tau says with the same kind of certainty that makes me blush. "Now, I will give you a moment to say goodbye to Zephyr and Russell."

"NAW!" Russell shouts in anger, while his wings spread out behind him and his hands ball into fists. "You're not breakin' us up!"

"You'll see her again when this mission is complete, but for now, you'll leave here for your own protection. Brennus has shown that he can control you at will. That makes you a dangerous liability, Russell," Tau says in a reasonable tone.

"I'm not leavin' her," Russell retorts, pointing at me.

"You have the potential to hurt her, Russell. You demonstrated that this evening, therefore, you'll leave here within the hour with Zephyr and the Reapers," he responds with his mask of calm firmly back in place.

"You're makin' a mistake!" Russell argues as he prowls back and forth. "Y'all need me to stop him and get Reed back. I can cure Reed, too."

"My decision is made. We will contact you when the Gancanagh have been eliminated," Tau replies emotionlessly.

With all the confusion and rage of a wild tiger being caged for the first time, Russell probably would've lunged at Tau, but Zephyr reads his body language and stops him by putting his hands on Russell's chest.

"Russell," Zephyr says, looking in his eyes. "We must go."

Russell, with his face reddening in anger, tries to shrug Zephyr off him. Zephyr grips him tighter, making Russell look at him. "Listen to me," Zee says adamantly, "we have our orders. There is nothing we can do now."

Russell must see something in Zephyr's eyes, because he stops struggling and stares at him.

"This is wrong, Zee, and you know it!" Russell argues, while looking around at the Powers closing in on him. He growls at them, making them hesitate.

"It is less than ideal," Zephyr agrees in a grim tone, adding, "but I can think of several ways we can occupy our time waiting to see Evie again."

"Zee! You can't go!" I plead with renewed panic. I need his help. He's like a big brother to me.

"You will see me again, Evie," Zephyr promises, letting go of Russell as I break into sobs.

"I need you. Reed needs you!" I cry, clinging to Zephyr while he hugs me. "You can't just walk away from us."

He squeezes me hard, "Hide the cracks in your armor, Evie," Zephyr says softly in my ear. "Show them no emotion and look for us where you found Buns." He presses something cold into my hand, which I immediately conceal in my sleeve.

In the next moment, I'm snatched out of Zephyr's arms and engulfed in Russell's. I cling to him in quiet desperation, trying hard to stop crying.

"I'm not goin' far," Russell whispers in my ear and my throat constricts to the point that I can barely speak.

My breath hitches again as I squeeze him tighter. "I know," I reply.

When Russell lets me go, he points at the Seraphim in the room saying, "Anythin' happens to her, and I'm comin' for all y'all."

Xavier's wings seem to grow even bigger than before. "Say goodbye," Xavier growls at Russell.

Russell's eyes narrow as he says, "I'll see you soon, Red."

I just nod to him, unable to speak. Finding it hard to breathe as Russell and Zephyr leave the room, I look around wildly for a means of escape.

"Phaedrus?" Tau speaks in a louder tone with his eyes on me.

Phaedrus enters the office from the sitting room. His black eyes focus on me while a grim expression twists his lips as he reads my thoughts. I resist the urge to run to him and press my wet cheek against his downy, caramel-colored wings.

"I need to know what Evie is planning," Tau says with his eyes never leaving mine.

I stiffen, and my eyes remain locked with Phaedrus' while I wait to see what he'll do.

Phaedrus takes a deep breath before he replies, "She was trying to devise a means of escape and locate Reed as I entered. Then... she saw me and had the urge to hug me for comfort—she likes my wings," he explains quickly.

"How would she attempt to escape?" Tau presses him with a frown.

"She contemplated shapeshifting into butterflies..." he trails off as I hurl insults at him in my mind, "rat" being foremost among them.

Phaedrus' frown deepens as he responds to my mental tirade. "I'm not a rat!" he insists with a blush creeping to his cheeks. "I have a duty—"

Tau interrupts him, saying in a stern tone, "Evie, should you consider shapeshifting, please know that I have but to capture one of your butterflies and contain it. You would then be unable to shift back until I released it, making you my prisoner."

"I'm already that," I retort in fury while my hands ball into fists.

"What is she thinking now?" Tau asks Phaedrus.

I try to stop thinking, so that I can conceal all of my thoughts, but I'm so filled with raw emotions that things keep swirling and tumbling around in my mind.

"She…" Phaedrus hesitates.

"Yes," Tau presses him.

"It has nothing to do with escape," Phaedrus replies, trying to hedge.

"What is she thinking?" he asks again sternly.

My eyes plead with Phaedrus, whose wings begin to sag when his shoulders round forward. In a low tone, he says, "She's seeing her dreams…"

"Dreams?" Tau asks him, confused.

"Pictures of you and her that she wanted to someday make real— they were so alive and vibrant, she wanted someday to call you dad— to find mercy in your arms, but now…" he trails off.

"Now?" Tau's tone is grim.

"They're fading, being replaced by scenarios that will exclude you from ever knowing her or her mind," Phaedrus reluctantly admits.

"You will find mercy in my arms, Evie," Tau says to me in a gentle voice.

I shake my head, feeling crushed by all that has happened. "If you wanted to know what I was thinking, you should've asked me. I could've shown you," I say hostilely.

Nearing me, his hand twitches, like he's resisting the urge to touch me. "I'd like you to show me what you're thinking," Tau says while his eyes stare into mine.

With my eyes narrowing, I gaze dangerously at him, knowing that he doesn't know what he's asking for, so I reply, "I'm not a mess for you to clean up, Tau."

His eyes bore into mine. "Then, make me understand you," Tau orders.

Sick with desperation, I say between my teeth, "This isn't about you and me. It's about Reed."

"I want us to see eye-to-eye," Tau says solemnly. "I want you to see that I'm unwilling to risk your life for his."

"He *is* my life!" I respond feverishly, fighting against Tau's indifference.

Xavier interrupts us, "He is a malignant obsession."

I feel myself pale. "If you believe that, Xavier, then you'll never know who I am," I reply without an ounce of insincerity. "You all have an opportunity to help me now, should you pass it up, there will not be another one."

"We will save you from the consequences of your actions, Genevieve," Tau states. "I don't relish the thought of entering Sheol to search for your languished soul! Forget your daydreams of Hell because anything that you can imagine will not measure up to the horror of the reality."

"I can suffer for my own sins. I never asked you to save me," I reply, unwavering.

"You'll never have to—you're my daughter," he retorts. "I'll do what I can for Reed and you'll stay out of it, if I have to gag and bind you myself."

My fingers clench tighter as the ache in my chest grows to an almost unbearable level. "Yeah, good luck with that," I say with dark sarcasm, adopting a defensive posture and backing away from him toward the balcony door.

Normally I'm in command of the energy surrounding me, but now I have to strain to collect it. My chaotic emotions are hindering me, refusing to hold onto it. As the energy leaks haphazardly from me, the walls around us freeze with the crackling-creak of an iceberg. Sparkling-cold crystals of ice prowl up them.

"She will use her magic to immobilize us," Phaedrus advises Tau with his coal-black eyes focusing solely on me. "She plans to go to Brennus alone—in the Knights Bar—"

Swinging an anguished spell at him, Phaedrus leaps out of its path with the agility of a bird. The chair behind him shrinks to doll-house-size when the spell makes contact with it.

Xavier materializes in front of me, blowing into the palm of his open, gloved hand. A pixilated swirl of dust colors the air around me like shiny, silver foil as it engulfs me in a super-fine cloud. Black spots swarm in my eyes as my legs weaken and buckle beneath me. Xavier catches me in his arms; his mismatched eyes swim above me while I try to clutch the soft fabric of his shirt. In a panic, several of my clones tear from my skin, glowing and rushing in different directions.

One sorrowful clone enters Xavier, disappearing into the contours of his broad chest. His eyes widen in agony, while all of my crazed emotions from the past few hours assault him. The fiery glow of another of my clones swamps Tau before disappearing within him. His face blanches as he bends forward with a feverish grimace. Cole and Phaedrus have similar reactions to the clones that hit them and dissolve away.

Xavier shifts his arm beneath my knees, lifting me up while whatever he blew at me makes me as docile as a favored pet. He coos in my ear, "I'm sorry, but you're safe now."

My numb cheek rests against his chest as I slur, "Never...forgive..." but I can't continue.

As I stare hazily at my father, Tau addresses the room in Angel, presumably giving orders and instructions to those assembled. My focus slips again while the chemicals continue to press down on me. When my eyes readjust, Tau is by my side. Reaching out to me, he strokes my hair gently. "This is for your benefit, Evie," Tau murmurs in an appeasing way.

"Liar," the word falls from my lips in a whisper, causing Tau's eyes to darken before mine shut against him.

ༀ

My eyes open slowly to the dim light of dusk. Shadows stretch and pull over the elegant side table next to the carved poster bed in Brennus' room. Sluggishly, I try to move my aching muscles, but I can't stretch my arms because they're twisted together by a downy, supple cord behind me. So too, my wings are locked in one position by a rope wound around them near my back, refusing to allow them to bend or move much. I groan. The pounding ache in my head forces it wearily forward onto the soft pillow sham.

Straightening my bent knees an inch, the silken rope tied around my ankles tightens. Linked to the ropes at my wrists, the cord locks me in a hog-tied position on top of the coverlet. A gag cuts into the corners of my mouth, stifling my gasping breaths of panic.

I still, willing myself not to be sick when frigid memories of Reed's dull, drugged expression comes to mind, causing a surge of adrenaline to jerk me fully awake. Then I realize what the shadows mean; they indicate that several hours must've passed and the sun is again setting on the horizon. I struggle to tear the ropes binding me, feeling sure that they'll be shredded at any moment and I'll be freed, but they hold firm, biting into my flesh.

Breathing hard, I stop struggling for a second, trying to think.

Shapeshift, I think. I concentrate, trying to imagine myself distorting into the swirling mass of wings.

My wings make a lurch to retract and I begin to feel the shift from mammal to Lepidoptera, but then searing pain stabs me near the base of my wings where they connect to my back. It feels like someone tried to sheer them from my body with an axe. The rope wrapped there is cutting into my wings with vicious intent and I'm sure that I will lose them if I try to shapeshift again. With a pathetic whimper, I cry weakly before struggling some more. Managing to flip onto my back, I look up at the ceiling and freeze instantly as the gag in my mouth silences the scream that erupts from me.

Levitating above me, Brennus clings to the ceiling just like a spider stalking his prey. His handsome face studies me as his mouth slowly forms a sensual smile. I stare back at him while broken thoughts of Reed make my heartbeat triple, threatening to smother me in darkness again. *Reed needs me—appease him*, I think, while I inhale raggedly through my nose, trying to calm my erratic breathing so I won't faint.

Brennus' fingertips let go of the ceiling, but he doesn't fall; he slowly descends to hover only a few inches above me. Cold, prickly air reaches out to me, caressing my skin, while I gaze into the fire in his light green eyes.

"Da way ye struggle...'tis a torment ta me," he says as he comes closer with a quiet laugh. He reaches out to tuck my tumbled hair back from my forehead before he sinks further to lie beside me on the bed facing me. He leans his cheek against his hand with his elbow against the mattress. The bed sags a little under his weight while he bends down, kissing a tear that falls near my bound lips.

A sultry smile twitches his mouth when I shiver. He asks, "Did I na tell ye dat ye could na trust da *aingeals?*"

I nod feebly, while more bitter tears cloud my eyes. He wipes them away for me with his thumbs. He is so gentle, it makes me want to cry harder, but I resist the need to do so.

"When ye did na come ta me right away, I tought ye had betrayed me again," Brennus says in a whisper, like he's telling me a secret. His fingertips are softer than a shadow when he trails them down my shoulder.

Something within me responds to it and I ache for him to touch me. *More venom...I want him more—he's under my skin—inside...*Wintery coldness creeps through my veins as dread and desire mix to make my legs feel heavy, but I use them to try to force the ropes from me again.

"Och, do na struggle, *mo chroí,* dat *aingeal* rope only gets stronger if ye do," Brennus says with a soft intake of breath. His head tilts a little as he adds, "Or...do struggle. I can na decide. Ye've made yerself bleed."

Brennus touches my wrists, coming away with a smear of blood on his fingertips that he touches to his tongue. Closing his eyes, he savors the taste of me. When he opens them again, he traces his finger lightly over the silken threads of the cord binding me. Gently, he nudges me over, examining my tethered hands closely.

Shifting me back, he says with an edge in his tone, "'Tis na a knot dat I know. Finn is da one who can unravel even da most complex hitch."

In the gathering darkness of the room, I try to ask him what he's talking about with my eyes. He notices, bringing his hands to my neck, he unties the silken scarf in my mouth. The corners of my lips throb painfully. I move them gingerly, grimacing as the bottom one cracks and splits. Feeling like I have a desert in my mouth, I croak, "Untie me, Brennus."

He brushes my hair back, exposing my neck. My arterial pulse beats harder as he touches his cool lips to my throat. "Did ye na hear whah I told ye?" he asks, his teeth scratch my skin lightly. I inhale as a shiver trails through me. "I do na know dis knot."

"Then break the rope," I suggest in a breathy voice as I look toward the door. I could scream for help, but then Reed is dead. If an angel walks through that door, I will never see Reed alive again. I need to keep Brennus safe now. He has Reed.

Brennus toys with the ruby-colored silk strap of the nightgown I'm wearing. The thin fabric falls over the round curve of my shoulder. He uses his finger to follow the strap down and trace the edge of the silk that rests over my heart. "I can na break da rope. 'Tis *aingeal* hair—" he pauses when I bite my lower lip to stifle the soft gasp that threatens to spill from me. Seeing my reaction to his caress makes his eyelids close a little with desire. "'Da rope is called dat because 'tis made from a special tree in Paradise. I can na break it wi' magic and since I do na know dis knot, one wrong turn would render it undecipherable—ye'd be tethered to it 'til da one who tied it sets ye free."

"You're kidding, right?" I breathe in shallowly, as my cheek rests against the pillow again.

"I am na," comes Brennus' reply. "Do dey na tell ye anyting?" he asks with a frown. His hand reaches behind my back. I feel him tug gently on the rope; it tightens it, causing my shoulders to pull back. The jewel silk nightgown slips lower, exposing more of my skin as it makes my breasts strain dangerously against the fabric. It also pushes me forward so that I'm pressed against Brennus' chest. "We'll need to get some of dis rope, *mo chroí*, for da future."

"Brennus! Just pick me up and take me with you then," I whisper. "Someone can figure it out later."

A wicked smile reaches his eyes as he shakes his head slowly, "Ye want me help ta escape da *aingeals*?" he asks.

"Is that too dangerous a precedent to set for you?" I counter with my eyebrow arching, knowing that brashness is like an aphrodisiac to him.

"Are ye finally willing ta let it all go, *mo chroí*?" he asks, while his stone-white finger traces my swollen lips, soothing them like ice.

"What?" I ask shallowly. "My life?"

"Yer life," he nods in agreement.

I look away from his eyes. "Since I've met you, Brennus, my life has not been mine," I say with more honesty than I like to admit to myself. "Time with you is visceral…white-knuckle moments that make me know that I'm alive. I think I have become addicted to the rush of fear and desire you create…the uncertainty that I was once forced to endure has now become a need, like those pills that people keep in their medicine cabinets."

"Ye're a hallion," Brennus breathes with a grin. "Anyting less den ye is tedious ta me now—'tis nap-inducing."

"You never sleep," I point out.

"See whah I mean, den?" he inquires with a raised eyebrow. "Ye're too ideal for yer own good."

"And you're too vicious for yours," I reply with no qualms about what I say because he gives another low laugh. He tugs on the rope binding my hands again just enough so that I let out a low exhale of pain as my breasts press firmly against his chest. Feeling his body against mine is confusing, bringing pleasure with pain.

Brennus sees my confusion and his smile grows a little. "Ye're beginning ta discern between da essential and da nonessential moments of life, *mo chroí*," Brennus replies. "Ye're na meant for a tepid existence, so maybe 'tis time ta leave da sandbox."

"I would, but you said you can't untie the knot," I reply sarcastically. He tugs harder on the rope and I grimace. He nuzzles my skin above the fabric of my nightgown until I want to cry out.

"Ye're resourceful," Brennus murmurs against my skin, before his eyes lift to meet mine, "and ye are, after all, a prototype weapon with a wicked aftertaste...I've every confidence dat ye'll find a way ta free yerself," Brennus intones, stroking the contour of my cheek with the back of his fingers.

He lets go of the rope behind my back; it slackens a little, creating space between our bodies again. "What?" I ask him breathlessly, like I haven't heard him correctly. "You're not going to help me?"

"I am na," he agrees softly.

"Why not?" I whisper-yell at him, and then look anxiously at the door to see if anyone is coming.

"Because I know dat ye'll come ta me as soon as ye can—I have whah ye want most in da world: yer *aingeal*. He is ta ye whah Finn was ta me: da tie dat binds..." he trails off, watching as my face turns white.

"Is he still alive?" I ask Brennus.

Brennus shrugs noncommittal, saying, "Ta find dat out, ye'll have ta come ta me."

"What difference does it make if I come to you?" I ask in frustration.

"Da difference is that ye'll na be alone. I want ye ta bring someone wi' ye," Brennus says with his eyes fixed to mine.

"Who?" I croak, but I already know the answer.

"Da other," he replies as his jaw clenches. His fingertip moves over the silk as it trails down between my breasts to my abdomen, and then his hands shift to my hips to rest there.

"Russell," I choke.

Brennus' nostrils flare at his name as rage enters his eyes, but his voice is cold when he says, "He is da price, *mo chroí*, for yer disobedience...for Faolan and Declan."

"Russell didn't mean to kill Faolan. He was just trying to save me," I try to explain. I struggle against the ropes binding my wrists again in a desperate attempt to free myself. "I can't bring you Russell," I pant, "you have to ask me for something else."

Brennus' hands slip to my bottom as he pulls me to him again. I come to rest against his tall frame. As I struggle, his hands tighten on me, holding me to him. When I wear out and still to catch my breath, he says, "'Tis impossible ta change me mind. Ye'll bring him ta me or I'll kill yer *aingeal*."

"I can't give you that kind of revenge," I whisper, shaking my head weakly and wanting to sob my heart out against his chest, but I refuse to give in to it.

"'Tis na entirely revenge," Brennus replies as he pulls back from me enough so I can see his calculating-look. "Ye see we'll need him. He's strong and one day he'll be powerful. He can control magic dat affects *aingeals,* jus like ye."

"So?" I reply, feeling sick.

"Russell will be one o' us—he'll be me *sclábhaí.* I'll groom him," Brennus reasons. "We'll have many enemies. He'll be useful."

"I thought you wanted Russell dead!" I object because I'm unable to stop myself.

"I did," Brennus agrees, "but dis is a much better revenge. He loses his soul ta Sheol and he'll be me slave for eternity."

"Russell will never agree. He'll die first," I state.

"He'll agree," Brennus says without a hint of doubt. "He'll do anyting for ye. He already agreed ta die in yer place when I gave ye me blood."

Scrambling desperately for ways to alter his plan, I ask, "Wouldn't it be better if you turn me first and then we hunt Russell together?"

Praying that Brennus will agree, I think that I might have a chance to save Reed without involving Russell at all.

Brennus shakes his head. "He would na submit if ye were already turned or I'd take ye now and turn ye, regardless of yer binds. He has ta believe dat 'tis da only way ta save ye...and I want it ta come from ye."

"Why?" I whisper-shout as my eyes open wide.

"Because betrayal cuts deep," Brennus' lips form a sensual smile. "'Twill be like a death blow ta him for eternity."

"I was so blind," I murmur. "You're completely evil."

"I am," Brennus agrees as his hands tighten on my bottom again, and he pulls me to him so that there is no doubting his desire for me. "And ye're completely naïve. Did ye believe dat I'd na make ye suffer, as I've suffered? I know more about pain den ye can imagine and I intend ta teach ye everyting I know."

"Then teach me," I gasp from the pain I've already learned. "It's all my fault."

"'Tis," Brennus agrees. "'Tis all yer fault. But, I know from experience dat I can na stay angry wi' ye for long—'tis me weakness for ye. So, da other will be me *sclábhaí* and ye'll be me queen," Brennus pronounces with a determined look. "Den, let our enemies come and dey'll all fall."

"I won't kill for you," I whisper.

A rueful smile grows on Brennus' lips. His mouth finds mine and as he kisses me, I have no way to stop him. I can't bite him because he'll bleed. I can't push him away because my hands are tied. He's controlling all of the energy in the room; I can't gather enough to light a candle.

It becomes apparent as he tugs on my bottom lip that he is not going to stop until I respond to his kiss. Tentatively, I kiss him back, but passion quickly ignites between us. I feel him smile before he leans away from me. "Ye'll kill, but ye'll na be killin' for me. Ye'll be killin' ta survive. 'Tis da only way dat ye will. Ye're in the middle, do ye not see dat? Do ye na see where dis is headed? Da *aingeals* will tear ye apart in deir struggle to own ye."

My eyes narrow, "That's what you're doing!"

"'Tis," Brennus admits, "but I do it because I love ye. Dey do it because dey want ta crush ye." He lets go of me completely before he glances down at the exquisite watch on his wrist. He shakes his head. "Ye've almost no time left. Yer *aingeal* grows weaker by da moment. He may na last much longer."

"Then...he's alive," I breathe with a sick sort of relief.

"He is...deliciously so," Brennus replies and I blanche, knowing that Brennus has been feeding on Reed.

"What are your plans for Reed?" I ask with a painful contraction of my heart.

"I'll allow ye ta turn him...he'll be an excellent bodyguard for me queen...jus as long as he understands dat he can never, ever touch ye again. If he does, I'll make ye end him," Brennus promises me.

I close my eyes against him and turn my head away. "And, if I don't come to you?" I ask with a hitch in my voice.

"Den, I'll turn him meself and we'll hunt ye together," Brennus replies.

He leans forward, pressing his cold lips to mine, kissing me with a passion that he no longer has the power to restrain. When he raises his head from me, he smiles down into my eyes.

"You're getting lost in me again, Brennus," I say as a warning.

"I'll na be satisfied 'til I'm buried in ye," Brennus replies, rising from the bed. "Playtime wi' ye is over. Bring me da other or I'll make yer *aingeal* undead and he will hunt ye ta da ends of da earth for me."

Nearing the regulator clock resting on the antique table near the window, Brennus opens its glass face. Without preamble, he distorts in a swirling jumble of flesh, being sucked through the portal with the alacrity of a seasoned traveler.

Other figurines on the table tremble and flip up, being consumed as the rest of the items in the room begin to distort, too. But then, just as abruptly as it occurs, it ends, indicating that Brennus has made it through and closed the portal at the other side.

Immediately, I begin to cry again, but softly, heartbrokenly. *It's over*, I think. *I can't betray Russell, so I can't save Reed. Brennus will make Reed hunt me and then, I'll let him kill me.* I sniffle loudly, while I cry harder.

A small *creak*, coming from the hinge of the door connecting the bathroom to the suite sounds. Glancing to it, I recognize the dark-haired Throne leaning negligently against the doorframe. Anya's musical voice penetrates the gloom as she says briskly, "Russell was correct: Brennus is an evil a-hole. If you promise to help me kill him, I'll untie you."

CHAPTER 23

Old Is New

"Anya!" I breathe, seeing her toss her sleek, black ponytail behind her shoulder. Anya walks swiftly from the doorway of the bathroom to the elegant, four-poster bed. She carries in her hand a glass of water, which she sets on the beautiful, bedside table. Her emerald-colored eyes study me appraisingly before she sweeps my hair back from my face.

"Shh…" she says with her finger to her lips, glancing over her shoulder to the door behind her. She moves from me to the window near the clock. Quickly, she opens it, waving her hands to try to ventilate the room. "Paah," she wrinkles her nose at me and makes a cringing face. "He stinks!" Anya whispers accusingly, speaking of the sweet, sticky scent Brennus left behind in the room.

When she notices the regulator clock on the table near her, she sticks her elbow out sharply, knocking it over. The clock crashes to the floor, smashing its glass face and scattering the gears and cogs onto the expensive rug. The door to the sitting room crashes open and four Dominion Power angels prowl in with swords drawn. One goes directly to the bathroom, inspecting it quickly while the others fan out, opening closets and windows.

Anya speaks in Angel to the tall Power with the light-gray wings. Her face looks conciliatory as she gestures to the clock with a shrug. The Power looks suspiciously around, seeing me tied up and tousled on Brennus' huge bed. With a frown, he turns back to Anya, speaking to her in Angel. She shrugs again, speaking while approaching me to sit by my side. Picking up the glass of water from the bedside table, Anya holds it to my lips, helping me take a sip of it. When I've had half the glass, she pulls it back from me, replacing it on the table.

The same Dominion Power edges closer to me, lifting the discarded scarf from the bed. He hands it to Anya. Gently, she pushes it back in my mouth, tying it loosely at the back of my neck. When she's done, she smiles demurely to the Power who is inching closer to her, his eyes drinking in every curve of her in her black, body armor. He speaks again, this time with a flirty little smile. She smiles back, responding in kind to whatever it was that he said. The Power from the bathroom playfully slaps his partner on the chest, shoving him towards the door to the sitting room. They exchange some kind of banter in musical tones. With a fleeting glance at Anya, the last Power exits the room, closing the door behind him.

"Powers," Anya sighs, looking at the closed door. "They've been here too long."

Glancing back at me, she unties the gag in my mouth, removing it. Then she bends close to me, staring into my eyes. "If I trust in you, do you promise to help me kill Brennus?" she asks with a frown. Before I can answer her, she adds, "I want to know if you're willing to reach into his chest and rip his icy heart from it. Anything less than that and I'm leaving you here and I'll take care of him myself."

"I promise," I whisper hoarsely, staring back at her.

"Good," she says with a decisive nod. Quickly, she begins to untie the rope binding my wrists.

Lying on my side, I ask, "Where's Russell?"

"Gone," she replies absently, concentrating her attention on the intricate knot.

"Russell left without you?" I ask incredulously.

"Not exactly," she replies.

"I don't understand," I say. "Is he here or isn't he?"

"He's gone, but he didn't leave willingly," she replies in a low tone. "It took Xavier, Cole, and more than twenty angels to get him to leave, but in the end, it was Zee that pulled Russell with him into a portal."

"Why didn't you go with him, Anya," I ask her in a raspy voice. "He loves you."

Her hand stills for a moment. "I wasn't ready to leave yet."

"Aww," I groan, "he's probably freaking out that you're still here!" I whisper, exasperated.

"The bad freaking out or the good freaking out?" she asks with a flat voice.

"The bad freaking out! Very, very, bad freaking out," I say with a frown. "He's insane about you. He was pushing you away because he was afraid of losing you. He told me how he feels when he's around you."

Anya's hands still again. "How does he feel?" she murmurs.

"He...he has those butterfly things—and don't tell me you don't know what I'm talking about because I know you have them, too," I reply, frustrated now because Russell will never forgive me if I let something happen to Anya.

Anya continues untying the knot, whispering, "That is attraction—not love. You did not hear the things he said to me before he left."

My heart sinks. "What did he say?" I ask.

"He demanded that I go with him...he said that my 'bad-assery' is going to get me killed." She pauses for a second, and then asks, "What is 'bad-assery?'"

"Uhh," I think quickly, "it means to act like a bad-ass—act really brave and cocky."

"He called me cocky, too," Anya admits. "What does that mean?"

"It means arrogant," I mutter, adding, "but, that's a good thing around here—no one respects you unless you have an edge."

"Then what does moron mean?" she inquires.

I cringe, prefacing, "He calls me that sometimes—"

"Moron?" she asks again between her teeth, realizing it must be bad by my tone.

I whisper quickly, "Someone who can't make common sense decisions, but—"

"Ballsy?" she asks between her teeth.

"Now that's a compliment—someone who takes risks...is courageous..." I sigh.

"Wickeddamnsexy?" she asks in an intense whisper.

I smile despite everything. "Wicked-damn-sexy is, well, the most beautifully alluring being you can imagine."

She gives a soft snort of frustration, before whisper-shouting, "Not all of this is in Webster's—if he would just adhere to English I wouldn't want to kill him all the time!"

"You're English has improved," I point out.

"I'm very intelligent," she replies stiltedly, like she doubts I think so.

"I know," I agree. "You must be to get in here."

"That was easy," she shrugs off my compliment. "Xavier believes that I'm at odds with you over Russell. He trusts me to watch you like prey and keep you from them while he searches for Reed."

"You're not at odds with me over Russell?" I inquire.

"No," she answers. "We both want the same thing."

My eyebrow rises. "What's that?" I murmur.

"For Russell to be safe—and that moron, Brennus, is threatening that," she whispers, while focusing on the ropes. I feel them loosen as she twists them back and forth. Then she mutters, "Ugh, Xavier must be desperate to keep you safe. He bound this with his heart strings."

"What?" I ask, hoping she isn't speaking literally. "Please tell me that was a metaphor."

"Yes—a metaphor. Xavier...he is afraid of losing you—he is also insane for you," she breathes, using my words absently. "Insane for you without the soul to join yours or the deep attraction to awaken you...but with the devotion to endure this Godless place for you."

"I didn't ask him to come here!" I whisper-retort.

"Are you sure about that?" she inquires softly.

"Why would I want him here when he does stuff like this to me?" I ask rhetorically, lifting my wrists an inch to indicate that they're tied behind my back.

"Because your guardian angel is fierce and scary—intelligent and venerable...and uncontrollably virile," she responds easily.

"Don't forget overbearing and cruel. He drugged me and tied me up!" I rage softly.

"I did not say he was perfect," she replies calmly. "I just meant that he loves you. He has always loved you, ever since your soul was created," Anya whispers, pulling tight on the rope.

I wince, but not from the rope. "Did I...did I love him, too?" I ask in a whisper.

"Of course," she sighs in frustration as the rope tightens again. "The two of you had your own language—you spent more time together than if you were soul mates. I warned him about it."

"What?" I ask, holding my breath.

"I told him it was bad karma to try to come between soul mates. I suggested that he reassign to protect another soul—he wasn't a very good guardian angel for you," she whispers ruefully.

"He wasn't?" I murmur my question, trying to see her face.

Anya shakes her head, explaining in a low tone, "Well, he was outstanding if your mission was to face extreme danger and to be thrown into harrowing situations. You found your way into more revolutions, upheavals, and catastrophes than the average soul. He said that you could handle them, but I think he was just trying to get you back to him sooner and away from Russell."

"How did he react to your warning?" I wonder aloud.

"Xavier made it seem like you two had some kind of mission together—covert. It had always seemed like a mission from the start, but then, he grew so close to you...he wouldn't discuss it with me. It was easy to see that there was something—"

"What was easy to see? What was suspicious about the fact that he was assigned to me?" I interrupt her.

"He's a high-ranking Seraphim, performing the duties of a Virtue," she explains. "And, his only assignment was you—he guarded no other soul in all that time. There was no rotation between your lifetimes to ensure that he wouldn't bond intrinsically to you. It was unheard of—" The rope around my wrists slips off me, leaving just the ropes strung tight around my ankles and wings to tackle. "It is a good thing I know Xavier so well, or I'd never have gotten this off!" she whispers in triumph.

"How do you know him so well?" my curious whisper rings in my ears like the accusation of an ex-girlfriend as I use my hand to rub the circulation back into my aching wrist.

"We were born of the same fire," she replies in a gentle tone, while making me sit up, "and I saw him often. I crossed paths with him because of you and Russell. Karma tends to erupt around you."

I almost can't speak...almost. "Okay, I have so many questions." I stretch my aching legs and arch my back, trying to remove the knots in my muscles. "Let me start small and work my way up. Okay? What does it mean to be born of the same fire?"

"It's shocking what you don't remember," she mutters. "Maybe it is a little like sharing the same womb, although, I don't know if that's true," Anya responds, sounding puzzled.

"So, you and Xavier are like siblings?" I ask her.

"Again, I don't know what that's like," she replies.

"Do you want to kiss Xavier?" I ask.

"Pah!" she wrinkles her nose like Russell does. "I'd rather kiss the stinky, dead moron!"

"Siblings," I decide quietly.

"So, the karma thing? What do you mean by that?" I ask.

"You always bring out extremes in others, Evie," she states like it's a fact.

"I do?" I ask.

"You do," she affirms. "You are notorious in my circles."

"I am?" I ask.

"You are," she replies.

"Why?"

"I don't understand," she says. "What do you mean, why?"

"Why? Why am I notorious?" I ask.

She snorts, like something I said is offensive. "You question every-thing. You are never satisfied with how things are. When you attempt to change things, you cause others to react, sometimes negatively, sometimes positively, but they always react. Thrones trail in your wake, sometimes rewarding the behavior of others and sometimes meting out justice."

"How?" I ask.

"Karma—good fortune, misfortune. Whatever is required. We dispense reward and retribution...earned fate and recompense."

"Is that how you fell in love with Russell?" I ask. "He always tries to do what's right."

"There is no one like him," she says.

"I know," I agree.

"I followed him too long...I couldn't help myself," she says. "I attempted to change my assignment because of my feelings. I was ignored. It was as if they wanted me to fall in love with Russell. It must have been worse for Xavier. He has been with you so much longer."

"You've followed us...Russell and me? How come you couldn't speak our language?" I ask.

"I came on my own. I did not get imprinted for a mission. It is taking me longer to recall all that I have learned in the past," she says.

She tugs on the rope lashed to my wings. I bite my bottom lip so that I won't gasp in pain as the silken strands cut deeper into me around the base of my wings. Anya's quick intake of breath is soft, before she hisses, "Did you try to shapeshift while you were tied up?"

"It didn't work," I wince.

"Of course it didn't," she scolds. "I'm surprised it didn't tear your wings off!"

"Me, too," I grunt, trying to catch my breath.

"You can't shift when your wings can't retract. Hold still," she says in a very gentle way. "Didn't anyone teach you how to be an angel?"

"Well...we've kind of been in reactionary mode—playing defense. Everything's on a need-to-know basis," I whisper. "I just learned to shift. I'm sure someone would've thought to tell me eventually."

Anya groans. "I forget that you're just a baby," she says, sounding contrite.

"I'm not a baby," I retort, somewhat offended.

"Your soul is not, but the angel part of you is," she comments wist-fully. "Old is new, just like your mission here..."

My breath catches in my chest. "What do you know about my mission here?" I rasp, trying to keep my voice from raising several octaves.

"I know what you told me," she replies absently, concentrating on the knots again.

"Why would I confide in you?" I ask.

"Because we had a common interest," she whispers, her voice straining.

"A common interest?" I counter. "Russell?"

"Russell," she agrees.

"It must not be a very strong alliance. You tried to shoot me with your arrow in Torun," I point out.

"You tried to keep my *aspire*," she replies sullenly. "How does Russell say it…I was 'pissed off.' That is the karma I felt you deserved."

"Really?" I reply sarcastically. "Anyway, he's my soul mate," I say with equal sullenness.

"He will always be your soul mate, but he is my *aspire* now. You pushed him away and now, you cannot have him back," she whisper-retorts, pulling on my wing a little harder than I think is necessary.

I hiss softly in pain.

"Karma," Anya whispers.

"I pushed him away?" I ask skeptically. "Why would I do that?"

"Your mission here was confidential. But, I have a theory," she says.

"Which is?" I ask.

"I think you believed that you wouldn't be coming back," she mutters. "You didn't want him to suffer forever."

My mouth feels dry again. "Oh…"

"He told me that something felt cut after you agreed to this mission…that intensity between your souls…it was, not gone, but it was not the same. I cannot describe it because I have never felt it—it's the connection, the link…"

"The thread," I whisper hollowly, thinking of the thread that connects me to Reed—the one that we both hold onto so tightly.

"You understand," she murmurs. "Then, you became very involved with the planning for this mission. You and Russell fought. He didn't want you to go."

"Why?" I wonder.

Anya is silent for a moment, before she whispers, "Because you were making yourself a target for the angels in Sheol."

I close my eyes. "So it's true?" I ask. "I wanted to come back to Earth and become half-angel and half-human...a weapon against evil."

Anya stills behind me. "You think that is the only reason you came here?" she asks.

"Isn't it?" I counter with my shoulders rounding.

"I know you well enough to say that there had to be more than killing Fallen to make you volunteer for this," she says in a tight voice. She gently tugs the rope embedded in my back out of my flesh. My fingers grasp the coverlet on the bed, balling it in my fists so that I won't cry out. Anya exhales softly, "I did not mean that one."

It takes me a second to open my eyes and pant, "S'okay."

The rope wrapped around my wings slips gently from my crimson feathers. Anya moves in front of me again in order to begin untying my ankles. "Thank you," I whisper.

"For what?" she asks, while her ebony wings pin back.

"Xavier is going to shred you when he finds out what you did," I say.

"That is less scary than what Brennus has planned for Russell. You could've left him out there alone...in the garden," she says, while her fingers work quickly.

"No, I couldn't have," I counter.

"You paid the ultimate price for it," she whispers. "I can see why you love Reed. He is different from any Power I've ever known—special."

"I have to get him back!" I choke past the enormous lump in my throat, praying that she'll understand.

"That is my plan," she responds immediately, and my arms reach out and hug her, making it hard for her to move.

"You have a plan?" my arms loosen on her while my throat aches with unshed tears.

Swiftly, she reaches into my sleeve, pulling out the cool thing that Zephyr had handed to me earlier. "While you were meeting with Tau, I wasn't just practicing my English with Buns and Brownie," she says quickly, holding up a sorority pin belonging to either Buns or Brownie. It is intricate, made of gold with tiny pearls on the face of it. Upon closer inspection, I see that it opens with minute hinges and a clasp attached to it. Anya continues, "We were coming up with ways to kill the undead monsters and then to get you away from the Seraphim. The Reapers were afraid of just this scenario. They're outranked by just about everyone here and to use their words, 'they found you first.'"

I blink as she presses the pin into my hand. "Is this—"

"A portal," Anya answers.

"To where?" I ask.

"To—" she's cut off as the door crashes open and Xavier's huge frame fills the opening.

His eyes immediately narrow into a scowl when he sees me untied on the bed. Xavier's eyebrows slash together. "Anya," he growls menacingly, raising the fine hairs on my arms.

Without even blinking, I pull energy to me and then thrust it outward, creating an invisible barrier halfway between Xavier and us. He doesn't notice it, because when he rushes at us, he hits it hard, knocking him back onto the exquisite rug covering the floor.

Xavier is up in an instant, stalking the wall I created, searching for an imperfection in the energy between us. Behind him, Tau walks quietly into the room; his eyes are on me as his skin seems to pale a little.

"You've recovered your magic," Tau states, ignoring Xavier's stealthy pacing in front of him.

My mouth turns down in a frown as I hold my hand to the rope wound tightly around my ankles, freezing it so that it becomes brittle. Moving my ankles, the rope cracks and splits like glass, shattering away from me easily.

"Intense emotion hinders your magic," Tau says calmly, studying me clinically, like a bug behind glass.

"That, and the fact that I was reluctant to hurt you, two things that don't seem to be affecting me much now," I reply with as much calm as I can find.

"I have found your *aspire*, Evie," Tau says, and then glances from me to Xavier.

My barrier crumbles for an instant, distracted as I am by what Tau has said. Xavier capitalizes on my slip, coming to within inches of the bed before he hits the hastily erected barrier I throw toward him.

Xavier snarls at Anya, speaking to her in angry, Angelic tones.

Anya retorts with an equal snarl, "She tried to shift with the lariat on!"

Xavier pales as he looks at the discarded rope saturated in places with my blood. His eyes pivot to mine, while he says in a hushed tone, "You cannot shift when your wings are bound."

"Really?" I ask, intending for my tone to sound sarcastic, but it sounds more hurt than I would like.

Xavier's hands splay on the barrier between us. "Are they severed?" he asks in panic.

My wings move of their own accord, spreading out painfully, but fully functional. The pain in Xavier's eyes eases a little, but only a little.

"I know where Reed is, Evie," Tau says again, gaining my attention, but the wall holding Xavier back remains intact.

"I know where he is, too," I reply above the sound of my racing heart as it pounds in my ears. "He's with Brennus, waiting for me to come and free him, so don't try to lie to me and tell me that you found him. Brennus was here, he—"

"BRENNUS WAS HERE?" Xavier roars.

His eyelids narrow to slits over his distinctly different colored eyes before he picks up a table and smashes it against the barrier between us, trying to get to me. I feel the energy push back at me as the table shatters into splinters on the floor, but it does nothing to gain him entry.

My heartbeat doubles, "Will you calm down?" I ask with a condescending frown. "You're freaking me out!"

"The bad freaking out!" Anya adds beside me, nodding in agreement while her hands tremble.

Tau joins Xavier at the edge of the barrier: two huge, red-winged angels standing side-by-side with grim expressions. Tau brushes his auburn hair back from his gray eyes. I think I see a flash of guilt in them before he asks, "How did you fend him off?"

"You believe that he was here?" I counter.

"I believe you," he corrects me.

"I didn't fend him off. He wasn't here to turn me," I reply before taking a deep breath to calm my raging heart.

"Did he harm you?" he asks with his eyes closing just a little.

I shake my head. "Physically? No," I reply, "unless you consider his kiss—"

Xavier turns away, picking up a chair and smashing it with his bare hands. Splinters and shards of it fall to the floor, but the really scary part is when he opens his fists and dust fall from them. He stands with his back turned to me, panting in frustration. "He will never touch you again," Xavier says tensely.

"Don't make me any more promises that you can't keep," I counter with a bitter edge.

Tau's hand reaches out to Xavier's shoulder when he sees it round a fraction. His hand rests on it before his eyes turn back to mine. My father's voice is calm when he asks, "Brennus wants something from you. What is it?" My eyebrow arches at his quick mind. "It's obvious," Tau replies perceptively. "He wants something very badly if he's willing to stave off his hunger to have you now. What is it?"

"Revenge," I croak.

"Will you give it to him?" he asks.

"No," I reply, shaking my head while a tear slides over my cheek.

"So, you will protect Russell and let Reed go?" he inquires with an unreadable expression.

My eyes grow wide at his intuitiveness.

Tau explains softly, "Russell is the only thing he could want...it's the only thing that would make sense as a reason for him not to turn you the minute he found you here. Russell is growing in power. He'll be as powerful as you one day—powerful enough to come between you and Brennus. Does he want you to bring him Russell?"

I nod, feeling my throat closing up again.

"He will not let him live. He cannot—neither will he turn Russell into a Gancanagh. You do know that, don't you?" Tau asks me. "He has to stop Russell from evolving into a more powerful being than him and he has to do it now, before Russell becomes a real threat. If he takes you now without killing Russell, Russell will hunt for you. He will find you, like he found you before. Brennus cannot afford to turn Russell because there is no guarantee that Russell will stop evolving if he were to become undead. Who was Brennus' maker?"

"Aodh," I murmur.

"Aodh taught him that," Tau says. "Aodh taught him never to turn anyone more powerful. Brennus killed his own maker, didn't he?" Tau asks.

"Yes," I reply softly.

"You give Russell to Brennus and he will kill Russell. Let me help you," Tau says gently.

I bridle at his words. "No thanks, I got this one," I reply bitterly.

Tau's eyes instantly fill with worry. "I know that you don't trust me—"

"Trust you?" I ask with a salty edge in my tone. "I can hardly stand being near you. I want to shed you like dead skin."

My father's eyebrows pull together in concern. "You don't want me to leave you," he counters. "You feel that I betrayed you, but that isn't the case. I only wanted to protect you," he reasons in a gentle tone.

"Don't tell me how I feel," I rasp. I flick the clasp to the pin-portal open. It lays docilely in my palm. Shifting my eyes to Anya, I say, "Anya, you should go first. When you get to the other side, pull me through."

She nods, bursting almost instantly into small, speckled ladybugs. The normally lumbering bugs are anything but as they pull themselves agilely through the small opening in the pin.

Tau's voice is filled with agitation, "Evie, stay with us! Brennus will not honor any agreement that he made with you—"

"I know that," I cut him off. "He's a known enemy—just like you."

"I'm not your enemy!" Tau retorts harshly, his eyes becoming a dark and stormy gray.

"Now who's being naïve?" I ask him hotly, wanting to hurt him. "I'm so relieved to be getting away from you, and if Brennus does manage to turn me, watch your back because you'll make a good first kill!"

"EVIE!" Tau growls my name, losing all pretense of being cool, while pounding viciously against the barrier with his fists.

His desperation to stop me from leaving does something to my heart; it hurts like he's squeezing it in his fist. Xavier joins him, hurting himself as he drives his shoulder into the unforgiving obstacle in front of him. Energy flares back at me in bursts. It burns as they push the barrier between us. I struggle to hang on to the energy so my wall won't crumble again.

Tau's frustration rings in each word as he says, "You don't know what you're saying! You're more precious than any of us—"

"Precious?" I laugh without humor. "You only see me as a weapon."

"I see you as my daughter!" Tau states.

My heart twists again as my throat gets even tighter. "You're very good at strategy. I almost believed for a second that I mean something to you," I breathe in a shallow tone.

Xavier, beside Tau, says urgently, "Can't you see what you mean to us? You stretch the very limits of our control, Evie."

I feel hollow: as thin as air. "You had a chance to help me, but instead, you drugged me and tied me up. You have made it impossible for me to trust you," I say, my throat raw now. I stare into his eyes as his mouth twists in pain. "Go back to your cloud, Xavier. I don't want you here."

"The only way I'll go again is if you come with me," he promises me, resting his hand against the barrier.

The air shifts direction abruptly, stirring my hair. "Xavier, we're *so* over," I say in a soft voice.

"You're wrong," he says with a growl. "We've just started."

Reaching down, I lay the open pin on top of the silken coverlet next to me.

Both Xavier and Tau growl at me, tensing like racers before the starting gun. When I distort, I won't be able to hold them back from me. It will be a race to the other side of the portal. Whoever gets there first, wins. With my heart thumping sharply and my palms sweating, my mind chants silently: *On your mark, get set....*

Russell

CHAPTER 24

Your Heart Grows Cold

Rubbin' my sweaty palms on the coarse, blue denim coverin' my knees, my leg bounces up and down involuntarily. I stare at the X-shaped portal propped open against the far wall of the library. Sunlight, streamin' in the floor-to-ceilin', leaded-glass windows, falls like a spotlight on it. The reflected light from its tarnished metal highlights the dust motes dancin' 'round it.

As far as portals go, this one's the sneakiest that I've ever encountered. Housed in Brownie's cheap-lookin' sorority placard, the dull, chi-shaped, Greek letter made from chrome hides the contours of distorted space within it.

I lean forward in my seat on the soft, brown leather sofa facin' it. A low, menacin' growl from my right makes me still for a second and grip the arm of the sofa tight. "Do not make me throw you out of this room, Russell," Zephyr says from his seat adjacent to mine in Reed's library.

I still. "I'd like to see you try," my growl is sinister, but I don't move toward the portal. It only takes a moment more for my leg to start bouncin' agitatedly again.

Brownie's voice comes from the other end of the sofa. "She'll get Evie. Anya is cunning—"

"If anythin' happens to Anya," I retort, "I'm blamin' you, Brownie."

"ME!" Brownie says incredulously. "It was Anya's plan!"

"And, you gave her the portal to do it!" I say between my teeth. "You should've protected her."

"Sweetie, she's a Throne," Buns points out from her seat next to Zee's. "She outranks us."

I scowl at Buns. "Ahh, don't even go there, Buns! I know you can give two figs 'bout rank when it suits you."

"True," Buns replies unrepentantly. "I also happen to know a good plan when I hear it."

My brow creases dangerously. "How is it a good plan to leave her there unprotected?" I shoot back with my leg bouncin' twice as fast.

"She's with an army of Powers," Brownie says in a gentle tone.

"And what're they gonna do to her when they find out that she's tryin' to liberate Red?" I ask Brownie pointedly. "What's the penalty for treason in your world?" Brownie has the decency to pale. "Right! That's what I thought!" I sneer at her speechless expression, while boltin' to my feet.

Instantly Zephyr is in front of me, blockin' my direct line to the portal with his killer-blue stare. "Do not lose your head."

My wings pin back, just like the ears on a cat. "You better move 'cuz you're fixin' to lose yours."

Zee braces for my attack, adoptin' a defensive posture.

Buns moves quickly in front of Zephyr with an implorin' expression. "They won't hurt her…Xavier and Anya are close. She insisted that he'd never let them harm her—"

"You also said that Xavier and Red had a thing before comin' here. If that's true, then Xavier will protect Red by any means necessary," I reply, while tryin' to pick up on any weaknesses in Zephyr's stance.

"Sweetie," Buns says calmly, "you haven't eaten since we've gotten back to Crestwood. Let me fix you something."

"I'm not hungry," I say childishly, while my stomach rumbles in retort.

Buns puts her hands on her hips and taps her toe. "Oh no?" she asks like a bratty little sister. "Then you can help us clean up this place!"

She casts her hands 'round Reed's elegant library, indicatin' that it's covered in dust. From the look of the place, no one has been here to clean since Dominion hauled Reed and Zephyr away to their compound to question them about Evie—when Pagan thought Evie was a Nephilim. Even though most of the stuff in this room is untouched, the rest of the house was ransacked by the Gancanagh when they were lookin' for Evie's possessions for Brennus' collection.

I found all of the clothes that I left in my room upstairs thrown on the floor and strewn over my bed. But, even without the mess, just bein' back in Reed's Crestwood estate is surreal; maybe kind of like returnin' to a childhood home. I'd moved in here when I was just startin' to become an angel—after Freddie had tried to kill Red and me and reap her soul.

I was a baby when I lived here before, just beginnin' to evolve angelic traits and abilities. Zee had begun my trainin' in the dinin' room just down the hall. It feels like a lifetime ago. I've been 'round the world since then…chased by monsters I never dreamed existed.

"I'll help y'all later," I say, never takin' my eyes off Zee's, waitin' for him to get distracted for a millisecond.

Buns's frustrated tone rings out, "We can't start on the clean up because we've had to guard you from trying to get into that portal. I don't know why we're bothering, it won't open on the other end until they're ready to come through."

My eyes shift to hers, knowin' she's right. Slowly, I sit back down in my seat. I ask softly, "Y'all have other portals back to Brennus' estate, right?"

Brownie nods. "Of course—we stashed them right near…" she trails off when Zephyr shoots her a warnin' glance.

"Where?" I prompt her.

"We'll tell you later," she mutters, lookin' away from my piercin' stare.

My leg resumes its bouncin'.

Buns relaxes a little before sayin' pleadingly, "Sweetie, let me fix you something to eat."

"Whatever," I breathe sullenly.

"Good!" Buns says quickly, before skippin' out of the room like a deranged sprite.

"I'll help you!" Brownie calls after Buns, exitin' in quite the same way.

Zephyr goes back to his seat cautiously, eyein' me the entire time.

"You never should've—" I growl, but Zee interrupts me.

"Do not start with me again. I am at my limit, too," he growls back, squeezin' his fists like he wants to crush somethin'. "I have been working on another plan—one that includes just you and me," he says in a tight voice.

"What's the plan?" I ask, mirrorin' his tone, while leanin' toward his seat, givin' him my full attention.

"We go back—find Brennus," he says laconically.

"And then…" I trail off, waitin' for more from him.

"That's it," he says grimly.

"No exit strategy?" I ask quietly.

"We either leave, or we do not," he replies, his voice strained. "We take out as many as we can. If we get the head, Brennus, the body of the Gancanagh will divide and fall apart—easy for the others to conquer. We just make sure that neither of us leaves undead."

"And Reed?" I ask.

His eyes close briefly. "I may need you to help me kill him," Zephyr admits. "I may hesitate. I cannot be sure," his tense voice stops abruptly, while he fights with emotions he's completely uncomfortable 'bout havin'.

"I can heal him," I say, reachin' out and puttin' my hand on Zephyr's shoulder for a second before I let it drop.

"Reed is a killer, Russell," Zephyr states softly. "He can move faster than any angel I've ever seen. You have to get close to him—touch him. The second you enter the room with him could be the last one you have."

"Then, I'll make sure that I don't waste any time," I reply with exaggerated confidence.

Zee doesn't smile. "If it comes down to it, you will need to kill him for your own survival. He will hunt you with the precision of billions of years of experience. There will be nowhere on Earth for you to hide," he utters, and goose bumps rise on my forearms. "You have to think of Evie."

"I am thinkin' of her. She won't survive it, Zee," I reply with absolute certainty.

"She is stronger than you think," Zephyr replies. "Buns and Brownie will keep her alive until she can recover herself...if Reed and Brennus are both destroyed, she will pick up the pieces in time."

"You forgot to consider how your death would affect her," I say softly. "You're like a brother to her."

Zephyr's chin raises a notch as his fists ease. "You are right, she may never recover," he says arrogantly.

The reluctant smile on my face fades as I face the portal across the room. "I'm ready to go, just say when," I murmur, thinkin' 'bout all the weapons in Reed's private armory. Then, I think of Anya again. My face falls more.

Readin' my mind, Zephyr says, "The Seraphim will keep them safe until you and I end this."

"You think Anya failed?" I ask him with a tight voice.

"I think she should have been here already," he replies agitatedly.

My teeth grind together while my leg bounces uncontrollably. "I should've been nicer to her...I was awful when I left. She doesn't even know how I feel 'bout her. Maybe that's better...maybe she shouldn't know since I may not be comin' back..."

"You believe that she would not grieve for you if she was unaware that you love her?" Zephyr asks in a calm tone.

"Well...I don't know—" I begin, before I see him shake his head.

"You are stupid. Love doesn't work that way," Zephyr replies. "She loves you in spite of your feelings for her."

My frown deepens. "I'm stupid?" I inquire wide-eyed. "When did you become an expert on love, Zee?"

"Buns is a very good teacher," Zephyr replies with a half-smile.

I run my hand through my hair in agitation, 'cuz the thought of never seein' Anya or Red again is doin' evil things to me. My heartbeat races faster, while guilt pushes down on me.

The dust motes near the portal jump abruptly, floatin' into the air and spiralin' in a wild, tangled dance. My leg stops bouncin'. I shoot to my feet at the same time as Zephyr. Holdin' my breath, I exhale when a small, fat ladybug crawls from the portal. Zephyr holds me back while a swarm of them flitter out, flyin' into the air and castin' tiny shadows on the floor and walls.

It takes only seconds for the little bugs to merge together in a sexy silhouette, implodin' into the most beautiful creature I've ever seen. A moment after that, I have Anya in my arms, pressed tight to my chest while I breathe in the sultry scent of her thick, black ponytail. The crickets that I get when she's near are back full force, bouncin' 'round inside of me and makin' it seem like I can't get close enough to her.

Not thinkin', I trail kisses over the slender column of her neck, followin' the soft contours over her cheek to her soft, full lips.

"Russell—" Anya protests, but my mouth ends whatever it is that she was gonna say.

I kiss her with the intense desire that I've been holdin' back since I met her. The passion she evokes chews through me, raw and unabated. I stand with her wrapped in my arms, with the sunlight from the glass panes pourin' down on us, and my soul soars with a new lightness, like the wings of a moth released from a deadly web.

"Where is Evie?" Zephyr inquires next to us, causin' me to lift my lips from Anya's.

I stare at Anya, watchin' her takin' ragged breaths as she stares back at me hazily.

"What?" she asks, while a rush of blood stains her cheeks.

Zephyr asks again, "Evie?"

Anya's expression turns startled as she looks away from me to Zephyr. "Let me down, Russell!" she says in a panic, which causes my arms to tighten 'round her. "I have to pull Evie through the portal! She's holding off Xavier and Tau!"

Zephyr moves quickly to the portal on the floor. He lays it down on its back before spinnin' it with a wild twist of his hand. The portal whirls swiftly as it gains momentum on its own. It lifts up to hover a few inches from the ground.

As the portal continues to spin in perpetual motion, Zephyr stands right beside it, tensin' as a soft, crimson feather ejects from the portal. The plume dances wildly above it, before makin' a slow descent and comin' to rest on the floor near the wall. Zee glances at Anya in my arms.

"She's coming," Anya assures him, her fingers curlin' tight on my sleeve while she watches the portal for signs of Evie.

Almost on cue, Evie pitches out of the portal like a newborn filly bein' birthed from a mare—except without all the slimy, gross stuff. Her arms flay near the portal, tryin' to reach for it.

The portal stops movin' when her fingers grasp its edge. Without much dexterity, she tries to close it by smashin' the two sides of it together. 'Cuz of the way it's still drawin' matter through it, the halves of the portal resist each other, like two polarized magnets.

Turnin' her pale face up to ours, Red pleads, "Help!"

In an effort to close it, Red leans all her weight on it to push the two sides together. She almost closes it, but then her body lurches upward, like someone is pushin' it open again from the other side of the portal. She holds on and her body slams back on top of the portal when it falls back to the floor again.

"HOLY CRAP, ZEE! HELP ME!" comes Red's desperate plea as she holds on to the portal so it won't ratchet completely open.

Zephyr grasps the edge of the portal near her hands, wrenchin' it closed with a decisive SNAP.

"Who was that?" Zephyr asks in awe.

"Xavier. He was right behind me!" Red pants in exhaustion.

Zephyr takes the portal from Red, beginnin' to crush it when she gasps, "DON'T!"

"Why?" Zephyr hesitates.

A dark shadow enters Red's eyes. "Will it hurt them?" Red asks while her face twists in fear. "Will they be trapped in there?"

"No," he replies, "they can exit back the way they came."

Red blows out the breath she was holdin', "Okay, trash it," she wheezes.

Smilin' broadly, Zephyr doesn't hesitate again. He walks to the dust-covered desk near us, placin' what's left of the portal on it.

Doubled over, Red continues to pant, her eyes adjustin' to the bright light as she looks 'round the room bewilderedly.

My attention returns to Anya in my arms. She, too, has a bewildered look as her green eyes stare back at me. "Are you okay?" I manage to ask her, even though my throat feels tight. *God, I want to pull the tie in her hair away and watch her hair spill over her shoulders*, I think, breathin' harder in an attempt not to do that.

"Hmm?" she mutters, like she's in a trance.

Leanin' my face nearer to hers, I press my lips gently to her temple, just where her soft, black hair sweeps back from her porcelain skin. A light, sweet scent lingers in her hair, and in my mind the fragrance is what Paradise must smell like. "Are you hurt?" I murmur against her skin when I recover my voice.

Her skin blushes pink, warmin' beneath my lips, while she shakes her head, almost numbly, not speakin'. Pullin' her closer to me, I touch her silky wing. My fingers trail a gentle line down it, seein' how her glossy feathers shine almost blue in the sunlight. Her cheek rests against my shoulder while her arms move tentatively, almost timidly, to the back of my neck. My heart contracts painfully in my chest, 'cuz I realize that she is not holdin' me tight, like I'm holdin' her. Her embrace is much more cautious, much more unsure.

"I'm not all right," I whisper near her ear and I feel her stiffen. "I've been goin' out of my mind worryin' 'bout you."

"But...didn't Brownie and Buns tell you our plan?" she asks, soundin' confused.

"Yeah, they told me—" I begin.

"Then, there was no need to worry," she says blankly. "I merely had to execute it."

Adrenaline filters through my system as every possible scenario for what could've gone wrong tortures me again. My brow furrows, "You could've been killed by the Gancanagh or any one of those angels if they caught you!"

"That is why I didn't let them catch me," Anya says in a quiet tone.

Her brash statement does nothin' to calm my racin' heart, in fact, it's like salt in a cut. "You shouldn't've been the one executin' the plan," I reply, breathin' harder.

Her arms go slack 'round my neck while she stiffens more. "It had to be me. I'm the only one among us they trusted."

"Anya was brilliant, Russell," Red's voice quivers. I see her lookin' around Reed's library as she's realizin' that we're back in Crestwood. Any color she had in her face before is gone as she strains to say; "We have to keep her away from Tau and Xavier. They're angry that she helped me."

More adrenaline is released in me, makin' me want to smash somethin'. "What can they do to her, Zee?" I ask, turnin' to see his eyes hood a little.

"We can discuss that later, Russell," Zephyr says evasively.

My hand stills on Anya's wing. "You're not tellin' me—that means it's bad."

"They can remand me to Dominion and put me on trial for trea-son," Anya says in a dull voice with her cheek still restin' lightly on my shoulder.

"The HELL they can!" I roar. I pull her away from me, holdin' her at arm's length with her feet danglin' off the ground so I can look into her eyes. "There's no way I'm lettin' them near you! Do you understand me?"

"Put me down. I can take care of myself," Anya says in a calm tone.

"Naw, you can't!" I retort hotly.

"Yes. I. Can." Anya counters, enunciatin' every word.

I frown. "You're no bigger than Red—you can't do magic—no one's trained you to fight—you'd probably have a hard time even passin' as human!"

Her face is bright red when I'm done pointin' out all of her flaws. "Yes, all of that is probably true," she admits, "but unlike you, I have a plan that will work."

"You have a plan?" I ask as my eyebrows shoot up. "A plan to do what?"

"A plan to kill your evil, undead Faerie," she replies with a frown.

"Ha!" I fake laugh like she made a bad joke. "I'm not even gonna discuss the undead freaks with you! You're not goin' anywhere near them. But, I hope you have a plan to get outta trouble with the red-winged egomaniacs." I reply while my emotions boil over. "Those guys tend to be grudge-holders."

She waves her hand like she was swattin' my worry right out of the air. "Xavier will eventually forgive me—especially when the, uhh... undead freaks?" she asks and then goes on, "are, well, dead." I lower Anya to her feet, but I don't let go of her.

"ANYA! EVIE!" Buns and Brownie say in tandem as they burst into the library. The Reapers flitter to them, group huggin' them like teenage girls do when they run across each other at the mall.

"We have lunch ready in the kitchen," Buns says, strokin' Evie's wing. "You need to eat so we can discuss the plan."

"I'm fine," Red says immediately. "What's your plan?"

"Sorry," Buns replies, shakin' her head. "We can't discuss it unless you're chewing on something."

"Buns!" Evie begins to argue, but when she sees Buns's eyes narrow, she knows it'll be quicker if she does what Buns wants. In a flash, Red is out of the room and down the hall to the kitchen. She's back a second later with a wad of food stuffed in her mouth. "Mmm, griiilll cheesh," she mucks with pieces of grilled cheese sandwich spittin' out of her mouth. "Whaass da pllaan."

Anya seems a little disgusted when she says, "It's you and me on the inside, Evie. We go in together. You're going to pretend that I'm your prisoner—another 'tie that binds' that Brennus will believe will make Russell come to him—"

"WHAT!" I yell in irritation.

Red stops chewin' as we both stare at Anya, shocked.

Anya ignores me, continuin', "Brennus must have something planned for you and Russell—something that he thinks will render your magic benign—something like the melody he used in the garden. You've both become very powerful, and he can't be sure that he and his men can contain you, especially since Russell beat him by keeping Evie from him in the garden. He will most definitely execute his trap on Evie when we arrive, so she can't fight back. But, since Russell won't be coming in with us, he won't be hit with the...uhh, magic...eraser..."

Anya trails off as her leafy-green eyes dart to me. It takes me a second to realize that there are deep, rumblin' snarls comin' from me, almost like the sound that a jungle cat makes when it's wardin' off other predators from its kill. I stop growlin' abruptly, but I can't stop myself from askin', "You're plannin' on walkin' into the same room with Brennus?"

"All of his men will probably be there, too," Anya adds, like it's an overlooked detail, before she continues. "He'll be intrigued by this new twist in his revenge—possessing the *aspire* of his bitterest enemy will thrill him. It will at once placate him as it distracts him. That is the key to this plan, if we can distract him for long enough, Russell can sneak in and steal their energy, take away whatever magic they've been using to camouflage themselves within that evil, little church on their estate."

Evie manages to swallow her mouthful of food. "You know where they are?" she asks Anya, her eyes wide and waterin'.

"Of course," she says with a nod. "I can't be sure what kind of magic they're using to hide there but it's there," she says. Anya explains, "I sensed them there while I was exploring the church. It was like a shade had been drawn between two planes of reality— theirs and ours—but it was thin, like they occupied the same space that I did, just not in the same reality or dimension…does that make sense to you? Am I explaining it well?" she asks us.

I see Red nod before she says, "Yeah, it's like there's a hazy veil between us, and if you listen you can hear them through it—in their version of the Knight's Bar."

"Yes," she agrees slowly, while her eyes look dreamy, imaginin' the parallel world.

I can't keep my mouth shut any longer, or my cool. "So, let me recap the play, coach. I'm supposed to let you walk into Brennus' den of torture so that you can distract him for me to come and annihilate them with magic?" She wrinkles her nose at me, probably 'cuz I get more and more agitated when I highlight the STUPIDEST points of her plan.

"You will not be alone—" Anya starts, but I cut her off.

"Oh, right," I continue sarcastically, "you're comin', too, aren't you, Zee?"

Zephyr gives me a pensive look.

"Not just Zee," Anya says between her teeth.

"What? THE REAPERS!" I hiss, pointin' at Buns and Brownie angrily.

They both gasp, offended, while crossin' their arms huffily.

"NO!" Anya retorts, "I already coordinated a signal with Preben so he can lead his team in. All you need to do is take out the magic that keeps them hidden. Once you do that, the Powers will have fun tearing them open and whittling knife handles from their bones."

"And what happens when Brennus touches you before I can unweave all the ancient magic he's got layered around that place?" I glare at her, pointin' heatedly in the direction I think Ireland might lie in. "I don't even have the remotest clue 'bout that kind of magic. What happens if he runs his cold fingers over your cheek?" I ask, feelin' so edgy that I may have to smash somethin' with my fist soon.

"I'm not afraid of his thrall anymore. You can heal me," she replies with amazin' calm.

"IN THEORY!" I shout at her. "I can heal you *in theory!*"

"I prefer to have faith," she counters.

"THAT'S 'CUZ YOU'RE AN ANGEL!" I yell, completely losin' my head. "He's gonna try to snuff you out like a candle!"

Anya stills for a moment before deep-seated anger registers in her lethal stare. "I'm not a candle, Russell, I'm a fire—a raging, pissed off inferno! Brennus has threatened something that belongs to me so he's getting retribution—paid out tenfold, but I need your help to do it."

"Thrones," I hear Zephyr say under his breath, shakin' his head ruefully.

I run my hand through my hair in agitation, tryin' to calm down. Then, I direct my next question to Zephyr, "Okay, what's plan B?"

Before Zephyr can respond, Red says quietly, "I'll go in alone and offer Brennus something else."

Anger engulfs me again at the thought of Red goin' in there at all. "Naw!"

"What else would he want?" Zephyr asks her in a low tone.

"I could offer to heal him…" she says, palin' more, "to take away the stain of the Gancanagh."

"YES!" Anya says excitedly. "When we go in together, you could offer him that! It will take him by surprise! Then, Russell can steal his energy and the Powers can come in and…"

"You can't do that, Red! You can't take his sickness—you could lose your soul! You're NOT goin' in there!" I reiterate tersely, feelin' like she's deliberately ignorin' me.

"It's a good plan," Red says next to me. Her face is drawn with dark circles under her eyes.

With my frown deepenin', I retort, "It's only a good plan to you 'cuz it gives your *aspire* a chance, but it just might get mine killed!"

"It gives us all a chance," Red replies with a sorry-look. "Brennus will use Reed to hunt us. He's an assassin, Russell. We can't run from Reed if Brennus turns him into a Gancanagh. He knows us. He'll slaughter the Reapers without even thinking twice and when he catches you and me…" she trails off, lookin' green and sick. "He'll turn us into monsters."

"Maybe your dad could—" I begin.

"HE WON'T HELP!" Red screams at me, losin' it. "He'll search for Reed, but it'll be too late and then all he will do is protect me. Not you, not Zee, or Buns and Brownie. Just me. And as for Anya, she's practically an outlaw now."

"She's right," Anya agrees. "You all are expendable and I will be punished. Our only chance is to kill the Gancanagh before they kill us."

Brownie's voice is calm when she asks, "What do we do?"

Anya's eyebrow arches when she replies, "You get to distract the Seraphim."

"Sweetie, I have just the shoes for that," Buns says with an evil grin.

"I don't like your plan," I say softly, decidin' that changin' my tone might help get their attention.

"What don't you like about the plan?" Anya asks me with a sigh.

"With so much to hate, where should I begin?" I counter. "Could the fact that you're gonna get up close and personal with Brennus, a fact that would make most grown men cry, have anythin' to do with it?"

"He is—" Anya says, but I talk over her.

"What makes you think that he won't just crack you open like a bottle of Merlot the second you enter with Red?" I ask in a cold tone.

Anya shudders at the visual I present before sayin', "He won't. He wants revenge. He'll wait to do it when he has you for an audience."

"How do you know that?" I ask her.

"I'm a Throne. Vengeance is what I do. I understand it."

"What makes you think it will be any different if I'm there? Do you think that magic is a game of rock, paper, scissors?" I ask, shiftin' to my next point.

"No, but—" she sputters.

"Do you want to know a secret?" my question comes out louder than a whisper. "I don't even know what's gonna happen half the time when I unleash a spell. Sometimes I feel like my mind has been fractured and insanity is bleedin' into reality. Just talkin' 'bout magic makes me feel like I'm caught in some crappy online chat room with shut-ins who call themselves 'Wick-tastrophy' and 'Fro-dope.'"

Anya glances from me to Red. "I don't know—what is an online chat room?" she asks, lookin' like a little lost lamb.

Red says defensively, "Really, Russell?"

"Fine, Red," I say between my teeth, liftin' my finger to jab it at Anya. "Maybe *you* should explain the weakness of her plan. Tell her I don't know what's gonna happen when I try to do magic. Explain that you could be trapped in there, waitin' for help from me to save y'all from Brennus' greedy maw, only to find out that I let you down again—like I've been lettin' her down this entire time…and I don't even know why it's torturin' me 'cuz she's practically a stranger."

Anya's wings droop forward and her beautiful, sooty eyelashes come together briefly, like I'd hurt her with my comment. My heart squeezes in my chest again before she speaks with cold assurance,

"You won't be letting me down—either way—if it works or it doesn't... it won't matter."

The sadness in Anya's voice chills me enough to make me ask, "What do you mean it won't matter?"

Her jaw is set too tight, like she's tryin' too hard to show no emotion. "It won't matter because with or without you, Evie is going into that room...and so am I," she says, straightenin' her shoulders.

I see somethin' then, deep in Anya's eyes that causes my gut to ache like someone kicked me there. I don't know how I know what it is, maybe it's because I've had that look before, when I thought I had nothin' left to lose—when Red was dyin' in Brennus' caves.

"It matters to me," I reply in a gentle tone. "I care 'bout what happens to you."

Anya's eyes widen a little before they narrow again. "Guilt inspired by a stranger shouldn't pain you too long, Russell," she replies, usin' my words that take on the sharp edge of a knife twistin' in my chest. "I'm bound to Earth now—pinned-down here on my own. I don't regret coming; I wouldn't change it if I could, but this is not my home." She looks away from my eyes.

"So, you're sayin' that there's no point in stayin'?" I ask, knowin' that we're not talkin' 'bout her goin' somewhere else, but dyin' in Brennus arms with his cold lips destroyin' everthin' that's perfect in her.

"I'm saying that I believe the sacrifice is worth it," she says, avoidin' my eyes. "Revenge for what he's done."

A chill runs through me and I've never felt so cold in my life. "I need a second alone with Anya," I say to no one in particular because my eyes never leave her face.

Red's voice is urgent as she says, "But we need to plan—"

"I *said* I need to talk to my *aspire*. Alone," I say forcefully, my eyes leave Anya to look at the gray eyes I feel I've known forever.

Evie argues, "There's almost no time left—"

Buns puts her arm 'round Red's shoulders. "We'll start getting ready, Evie," Buns states firmly, while pullin' her away. "I have just the right weapons for you. Black silk, I think."

Buns and Brownie move with Evie toward the library door. After they file out, Zee gives me a "be cool" look. My chin raises just a notch in recognition of his silent advice. When the door closes behind Zee, I turn back to look at Anya, but her hand connects loudly with my cheek in a *slap* that turns my face away from her for a moment. My eyes narrow instantly, as it registers in my mind that she just hit me.

"What the hell?" I growl. My shirt rips from me as my wings fly out of my back and spread out wide 'round me.

"So NOW I'm your *aspire!*" she growls back with her eyes even narrower than mine.

She storms towards the door of the library to leave, but I'm faster than her, gettin' in front of her and blockin' her way. When I put my hands on her shoulders to stop her, she grabs my finger, wrenchin' it back. I grunt as I'm driven down on one knee in front of her. "And I'm *not* a *moron*. I can make decisions that affect my life," she says in a silky tone.

An instant later, I spring up, pickin' her up off her feet and heftin' her over my shoulder, movin' to press her against the nearest built-in bookcase. Books topple and fall from the shelves as Anya thrusts her hands to them, tryin' to gain some leverage against me.

"Stop," I growl. Then I look into her eyes. The churning butterflies in my gut make it imperative that I get even closer to her. My body shifts to hold her to the bookcase. Her hands fall to my shoulders to push me away, but she can't move me at all. I'm havin' trouble breathin' now because she may be the most beautiful creature I've ever seen. Her cheeks are flushed and her breath is comin' out of her in short gasps. Black lashes make her green eyes sparkle in comparison as her beautiful eyebrows scowl at me.

I lower my lips to hers, kissin' her like I'm askin' her the question, *Are you mine?*

She doesn't respond at first, ignorin' my question. My lips brush over hers as they silently ask again, *Are you mine?*

I feel the need to hold my breath, like I've been waitin' for this moment all my life.

Tentatively, her arms move from my shoulders, slidin' 'round my neck as her kiss answers me. Anya's lips part, and immediately, it's as if the radiance of her skin against mine is flowin' into me, scorchin' me. I groan because the intensity of it is unexpected. Her fingers tangle in my hair, causin' all sorts of things to happen inside me that I can hardly contain. At once the ache that I've had surroundin' my heart is soothed while the ache of desire builds and threatens to tear me apart.

Her fingertips slip to my cheeks, deepenin' the kiss as she holds my face in her hands. I pull her legs up to wrap them more firmly 'round my waist. Her dark wings push against the bookcase, pressing her tight against my chest.

Before I know that they're there, my hands grasp the back of her body armor, shreddin' it at the seams and pullin' the breastplate from her. She gasps as her white halter-top beneath it is exposed. Her eyes round in surprise.

"Sorry," I murmur, not meanin' it, "that was botherin' me." I fling the armor away to the floor. My lips search hers again as a sinister desire to figure out a way to get the rest of her armor from her grows.

Anya's eyes narrow again before her feet kick back against the wall, thrustin' hard while her wings spread wide. It catches me off guard and propels us backward. I crash into the spiral staircase behind us that leads up to the balcony. My wings take most of the shock as I come to rest on the steps. "Sorry," she says not meanin' it, "I'm not Evie." She hovers above me with a dangerous smile as she pins me down with her knees on my chest. "I'm not forgiveness and redemption. I'm violent retaliation and vengeance."

"So you're payback, huh?" I ask while I use my strength to grasp her shoulder and haul her beneath me so that I'm on top and she's pressed to the stairs. "That's good because I'm always lookin' for a return on my investment."

I think I've startled her, but I don't give her time to respond before I'm kissin' her again. Her arms travel up my arms and find their way behind my nape. As her fingers curl in my hair, it seems she does it more from instinct than for any other reason.

I try to beat down the lecherous need to growl as it builds in me. This attraction is so intense that I feel like I either have to get closer to her or smash somethin'. I rise from the stairs with Anya in my arms while I pull her legs around my waist. Backin' away from the stairs, I turn: *crash*. My wings sweep the lamp off the small table behind me; it shatters on the floor. I spare it only a cursory glance; my mouth never leaves Anya's.

Her hands clench in my hair. She growls against my lips, "*I* am not cocky. *You* are cocky," she nips my bottom lip.

"Ahh," I groan, wantin' her to stop, but when she does, I immediately want her to do it again.

Her hands leave my hair to touch my wings. She runs her fingernails over the spines of the feathers, *thick, thick, thick*, the sound is like a velvet warning, makin' some innate instinct within me thrill as my heart beats stronger in my chest.

My wings spread wide, like I'm about to fly. *Clang, smash*, Reed's art is swept from a shelf as my wing levels things as I pass them so that they find new positions on the floor. Anya's wings respond to mine, fluttering in a way that makes my fingers tighten against her skin, and even though I don't know what that means, it makes me feel like I might die soon if I don't have her. Then she gently strokes my wing; the muscles in my abdomen tighten. I hurry to the desk in front of us. Using my arm, I swipe it across the surface. A cascade of expensive artifacts and desk accessories strike the hardwood floor in a cavalcade of sound.

I feel like I'm between heaven and hell when I have to lift my mouth from hers as I rest her on the dark wood-grain surface of the desk. One hand slides down her side resting on the curve of her hip where her armor stops my descent. I growl in frustration, pullin' energy to me more from instinct then premeditation. Energy leaks out from my fingertips, spreadin' in burnin' embers of glowin' orange to turn the black armor to gray ash as it travels down her sides and over her thighs. The armor rapidly disappears from Anya as ash falls and floats away, leavin' just the soft, dark leggings behind that she must've had on beneath the armor.

A soft gasp comes from Anya as she looks down and sees the disintegration of her defensive combat attire. Lookin' up quickly with uncertainty in her eyes, a slow smile curls on my lips because I've managed to startle her again. I take control, raisin' my hand and swiftly sliding the ponytail holder from her hair, makin' the black waves spill 'round her shoulders as it flows down her back. I brush stray strands of it away from her soft skin. *Beautiful,* I think before I kiss the spot where her hair meets her temple only to discover that the scent of her hair compels the butterflies inside me to increase in force.

"Russell," Anya says before I can kiss her again, "wait." She presses her hands flat against my chest.

It takes me a second to understand what she just said because I'm wrapped up in the sexy way she said my name: in a raspy groan-like whisper.

My lips tease hers, "Hmm..." I murmur against them.

"Wait," she repeats as she tenses in my arms.

My brow furls. "Why do you have to know *that* word," I growl, lookin' in her eyes. "'Wait' is the worst word in the English language in a situation like this."

"You have to wait...this is confusing—you're not..." she manages to say before she looks away from my stare.

"I'm not what?" I ask her gently.

"You're not...you," she says with her eyes searchin' mine.

"I'm sorry?" I murmur with equal confusion. "I'm not me?"

She looks so lost before she glances away again. "You just ripped away my armor, like it was nothing, then you melted it."

"Is that a problem?" I ask. "We can get you another—"

"You ripped it off with your *bare* hands," she murmurs. "It's more..."

My eyebrows draw together in confusion as I try to make eye contact with her again. "More? What's more?" I ask.

"*You* are more!" she accuses, meeting my eyes.

My eyes narrow as I try to understand her. "I'm more? How am I more?" I ask.

She bites her lower lip for a moment before she says, "Look at you," she flicks her hand to indicate my chest, "you've never been this...this...big."

"Big," I say, my eyebrows raisin' in surprise.

"And strong," she adds. "We never had this attraction before," she says, lookin' at me uncertainly.

"The butterflies?" I ask and she nods.

Her fingertips trail over my abdomen for a second. It's makin' me want to growl again. My muscles tighten with the need to pull her to me. "And this—this is unreal," her tone is accusatory again.

"Unreal?" I ask, frownin'.

"It's like someone carved you from stone," she says with a frown. Her hand lifts and her fingertips skim over the feathers of my wings. I inhale a breath because her touch is incredible. "And you have wings—Seraphim wings."

"Is that bad?" I ask, hopin' she'll say "no."

"You outrank me," she admits.

"I do?" I ask, feelin' a surge of warmth in my belly that I try to hide from her. It makes me feel powerful and I like that. I have this overwhelmin' need to protect her and if she has to listen to me then that will help.

"Seraphim, Cherubim, Throne," she ticks off each rank using her fingers, "in that order," she admits with a scowl. "Right now I am Throne-Seraphim, equal to your rank. When you remove our binding, then I will be Throne only."

"I thought that bindings were permanent," I say with narrowin' eyes. The thought of her removin' my wings from her is makin' me want to crush somethin'.

"Normally, there are very few reasons for a binding to be revoked," she says. "One reason would be if there was a fall," she says. "If one angel were to fall from grace, a case could be made to remove the binding between them. In our case, you made it a stipulation of this mission."

"So right now, we're equal rank, but if I were to unbind you, I'll outrank you and you'll *have* to listen to me?" I ask for clarification.

"Grr," Anya gives a sexy growl with her eyebrows comin' together again, "you see! You are different now that you are part angel," she says. "*My* Russell would not want me to follow his *orders. My* Russell would want me to be his equal in all things!"

My eyebrows come together, too. "Well, that's great for *your* Russell. *Your* Russell got you in Paradise where it was safe. *This* Russell, me, *new* Russell," I retort, pointin' at my chest, "has you here on Earth where just 'bout everythin' 'round us is a threat."

"Maybe *I* don't like *new* Russell," Anya says with an incredibly sexy pout.

"Well, darlin', *new* Russell is the only one here at the moment," I say grimly. "So let me get this straight, we're equal right now because you have my wings, but if I take them off you, then I'll have authority over you?"

"Yes," she nods stiffly. "You outrank everyone here but Evie."

"You'd be disobeying an order if you tried to execute your plan without my permission?" I ask.

"*In theory?*" she counters.

"Yeah, in theory," I repeat.

"Yes," she says sullenly.

"Then I'm orderin' you to stay here while we take care of Brennus," I say, feelin' relief like I've never felt before.

Anya's scowl grows darker. "You can't *order* me. I still have your wings and you need a Virtue to remove them," she says, while stabbin' her finger at me. "Unless you can locate a Virtue in the next few hours, I'm going back to Ireland."

She wiggles out of my arms and climbs off the desk, straightening the little white halter-top that is hardly coverin' her because of the way it's almost entirely backless. I focus on the tight black leggings that accentuate her shape and I call myself every kind of idiot as I watch the sexy way she crosses the room and slams the library door closed behind her.

I shuffle over to the couch, fallin' onto it. I grab a pillow and pull it over my face. A few minutes later I hear the door to the library open up. I sit up, hopin' it's Anya, but instead, I see Red standin' by the door.

I frown at her and ask, "What?"

"We had a meeting," Red says in a quiet tone, lookin' really sad. "Anya has just as much to lose in this if Brennus succeeds as the rest of us. So, we've decided that she's part of the team, Russ. If she wants to come, she's in."

Fear and anger vie for supremacy within me. Anger wins within seconds. "I don't get a say in this?" I demand between my teeth.

"It would just make the vote five-to-one," Red replies, straightenin' her shoulders. "And I'm an equal rank to you."

"And there's nothin' I can say to change your mind?" I ask, pointin' accusingly at her.

Shakin' her head, Red murmurs, "No."

My eyes bore into Red's and I can tell that she's strugglin' not to look away from me. Quietly, I say, "Anythin' happens to her and I'll never forgive you."

Palin', Red breathes, "I know."

Evie

CHAPTER 25

Doubt The Stars

Slowly, I sink down on the large bed while my eyes touch upon the destruction in Reed's disheveled room. Ancient paintings and works of art lie like carcasses of dead flesh upon the floor along with shards of glass piled beneath the broken frames of the once elegant mirrors. Reed's clothing is shredded beyond recognition, strewn like kite tails under diamond shapes of broken plaster from the pock-marked walls.

My fingers tremble as they run over the slashes in the sheets and mattress. Reaching down, I numbly pick up a silken pillow from the floor, hugging it to me for comfort as the feathers flee from it.

The fellas had torn the house apart in their search for clues to find me months ago, but nowhere had they taken it to the extent as in this room. No, this bedroom was more than searched; it was destroyed.

My heart thumps wildly as I think, *Brennus did this. This is his hatred…and he has Reed…*

I bring the pillow to my nose, inhaling the faint scent of Reed on it and feeling a piercing pain in my heart.

Please be alive, I pray quietly for Reed, as I hug the pillow tight to me.

"Evie?" Anya's soft voice asks from the doorway of Reed's room.

Buns and Brownie just finished working on Anya. Clad in a milky-white dress that only reaches her mid-thigh, Anya is breath-taking. The dress belongs to Buns, but it fits Anya like it was made for her. Nearly backless, the gossamer material contrasts starkly with her ebony wings, setting them off perfectly. With her dark hair loose and flowing over her shoulders, she's stunning.

"You look…ready," I murmur, rising from the bed and letting the pillow slip from my fingers.

Anya runs her hands down the sides of her dress, saying, "This doesn't feel like a weapon. I would much prefer my quiver and bow."

"I know, right?" I ask her in rhetorical agreement. "I thought that Buns was mental when she first told me that there was strength in the feminine mystique. But she's right. Against the Gancanagh, beauty and appeal are powerful weapons. We need you alive. When they see you like this, they'll want to keep you around for as long as possible," I explain.

Tentatively, Anya reaches out and touches the black, silken material of my dress that pours over my skin and clings to me like liquid.

"What about you?" she asks me as her green eyes search mine. "Will this keep you alive?"

"I don't know what Brennus will do," I reply with a small quiver in my voice. "It could buy me some time, or it could work against me. I'm hoping that it will distract him from remembering that I didn't bring Russell."

At the mention of Russell's name, Anya stiffens. "Brennus will never have Russell. We will make sure of it."

"You love him," I state.

"Yes," she agrees.

"I love him, too," I admit.

"I know," she says gravely, taking my hand in hers. "They're waiting for us downstairs."

"You'll take care of him?" I ask, holding her hand tighter.

Anya's fair eyes show worry as she replies, "If I'm not able to, I know that you will."

My steps falter when I understand her meaning. "You have no plan B," I whisper, dragging my feet as we enter the hallway. "I'm right, aren't I? You don't expect to survive this."

"Shh," she whispers back. "Russell, will hear you." Anya's eyes narrow dangerously. When she sees me hesitate further, she adds defensively, "I have the right to protect my *aspire!*"

Knowing that she's right, I begin walking toward the stairway at the end of the hall. "You do," I agree, "but I've discovered that having a plan B is…helpful."

Anya is silent as we descend the stairs, and then she replies, "You can be in charge of my plan B, then."

"Not me," I whisper, approaching Reed's media room, "Russell will."

Russell's back stiffens the moment we enter the masculine enclave. The media room had been a mixture of something between a chic, modern Manhattan apartment and the Batcave. Now, it holds little appeal. Shelves that had held an array of sly and engaging high-tech hardware are now barren.

Leaning with *faux*-casual grace against the shattered, multi-touch, media table in the center of the room, Russell's chocolate-brown eyes rove over every inch of Anya next to me. The pitch-black body armor he's wearing is dripping with an array of weapons: knives, daggers, guns, and grenades. He isn't prepared to rely on magic to win; he's bringing an arsenal, too.

With every step Anya takes, Russell's gaze grows darker and his jaw tighter. "Ah, naw, Red!" Russell says with irritation in every word. "Why don't you just sprinkle some salt on her and ring the dinner bell?" His eyes don't meet mine, remaining exclusively on Anya, but I can see the worry in them anyway.

"I prefer to think of it as icing," Buns answers, joining us and coming to stand next to Russell.

Brownie stands next to Buns and winks at Anya when she says, "She looks fierce, right?"

Brownie is dressed in a curve-hugging, black sweater that reaches her mid-thigh, her inky leggings tucked into her sexy, black lace-up boots. A cowl can be drawn over her platinum hair and face to protect her from the toxic skin of the Gancanagh. Buns is similarly attired in a deep-gray ensemble. I'd much prefer that she and Buns wear body armor, but they thought it might tip-off the Seraphim to what we're doing.

Russell's mouth thins in disdain, just like a true Seraph's. "I'd like her to play hard-to-get, 'cuz right now, she looks like prey," he counters, keeping his expression the same.

"It's strategy, Russell," Zephyr advises from his position across the room where a door in the wall stands open, exposing Reed's secret cache of weapons. "She is nonthreatening in that attire."

Zee's body armor is strapped with two sheathed swords crisscross-ing his back in a sinister X. His eyes capture Russell's for a moment, but it's only a moment.

"Nonthreatenin'?" Russell murmurs. "In what sense?" he asks with his arms crossed over his chest.

"In the hack-and-slash genre," I reply softly, and receive a scath-ing look for opening my mouth.

"She looks like a walkin' disaster," Russell replies, pointing at Anya. "They'll all be salivatin' for her."

"Exactly, with each willing to turn on the others. The opportunity to have her for his own will be overwhelming," I explain, subsuming Russell's anger.

Instead of helping Russell, my words just make his expression grimmer. He turns stiffly away from us, concentrating on the closed portals resting on the large media table. The two avenues we have back into the Gancanagh estate are almost diametrically opposed in appearance. One portal is housed in an old, brown leather-bound book of poetry. The gilded-edged book is so old as to have been created before the advent of type setting. The other is concealed in the sleek contours of a highly customized laptop computer.

Zephyr's authoritative voice rings out as he asks, "Everyone has a personal portal?"

Buns and Brownie both nod, touching their masculine-looking wristwatches. Russell holds up his wrist with the same style of watch on it while Zephyr similarly displays his for us. The open ends of each of their personal portals are aligned as a menagerie of clocks along the shelf on the far wall. The dials of each clock spin at dizzying speeds so that once the wristwatch portal opens, the bearer will be sucked into it instantly and wind up back in this room.

When Zee's eyes shift to Anya, she nods, her fingertips lightly toying with the stunning diamond-encrusted locket that falls daringly between her breasts. The mate to her necklace is the matching silver compact with embedded diamonds on its open lid. It, too, rests on the shelf, right next to Russell's clock.

"I have mine," I murmur with a nod when Zephyr's eyes fall on me.

An ebony, oval-shaped onyx brooch has been secured to a silky, black ribbon and tied at my throat. The black stone, mounted to the pin, can be opened to reveal the portal. The matching onyx compact sits next to Anya's on the shelf.

Walking to the mantle, Zee picks up each compact, spinning them so that they turn in perpetual motion, hovering inches above the shelf where they had rested. Crossing back to us, Zephyr holds my gaze.

He gently touches my cheek, saying, "Live through this, Evie, and when it's done, we won't look back."

My eyes instantly grow hot with unshed tears, but I force them down. I can't control the goose bumps, however, as my entire body reacts to his words. I wonder feebly if he knows that I'd give my body, my soul, to be alone with Reed for just a few moments... however long it will take to change him back to what he had been.

All I can do is nod. I must not exude much confidence, because Russell grasps me by my upper arms. When his intense stare locks with mine, he begins to coach me.

"This is gonna be as simple as takin' the back roads home, Red," he says, trying to hide his dark unease with a winsome smile. "You know Brennus, just like you once knew every twist, bend, and crack in the pavement along that route. He's weaker than you, so I expect you to beat six shades of crap out of him. Do you hear me?" he asks.

I nod, unable to speak past the tightening in my throat.

He nods, too. "You're gonna make it. Now get amped up so we can get your boy back!" My eyes widen at his words and when he sees my surprise, his expression turns to one of true affection. He smoothes a strand of hair back from my face, saying, "I'd rather risk soundin' like a hypocrite than send you in there without a pep talk. You're goin' in regardless of what I say, so go knowin' that I won't bail on you...I got your back."

"I never thought you'd bail on me," I reply with the certainty of a thousand lifetimes.

Russell nearly crushes me then, hugging me to him with a strength that insinuates his fear louder than his anger had. "Don't let Brennus have Anya," he whispers in my ear. "She's not his."

"I know," I breathe in his ear. "She's yours."

"Remind her if she forgets," he responds while he tries to hide the unruly panic that's banking in his lovely brown eyes.

Slowly, Russell lets go of me and straightens. Without a word, he turns around and sweeps Anya into his arms, hugging her much like he had embraced me. "You can have whatever you want from me... just come back," he says against her hair.

Anya closes her eyes, like she's in pain. "You're impossible to fig-ure out," Anya replies in a soft tone.

"Naw, I'm simple. I'll show you when you get back," he promises before he kisses her.

I discreetly avert my eyes from them because it isn't a friendly peck on the cheek. Zephyr clears his throat not soon after and Russell releases a rather stunned-looking Anya.

"Are you ready, sweetie?" Buns asks Russell in a careful voice. Russell's jaw is too tight to answer her. His brow furrows, looking from Anya to me and then back again before he nods once.

Buns and Brownie stand in front of the table, near the antique book. They'll enter it first and then Anya and I will follow them. Russell and Zephyr will use the laptop portal to gain access to the estate. Reaching out, Buns takes Brownie's hand in hers. The look that passes between them is one of love that transcends mere friendship. They are sisters in the most important sense of the word. Buns glances at Zephyr and I have to bite my lip so I won't beg her to stay behind—for his sake. Zee's eyes are those of a man who has his back against the wall. He says something to her in Angel that makes her smile faintly at him, before giving him a coquettish wink.

Lifting the lid of the book, the room begins to swirl and distort. Buns and Brownie whirl away into a turning, twisting darkness beyond the empty pages. Zephyr closes the cover for a moment, allowing Anya and me to compose ourselves. Russell has the look of a boxer about to enter the ring. He can't help bouncing around, dodging unseen shadows that jab at him. Feeling Anya's fingers thread through mine, I lift my eyes to her face and find it ashen with fear.

Zephyr lifts the lid on the book just as Anya pleads softly, "Russell, don't let me fall—"

As we distort, Russell's urgent words follow us into the portal, "I'll be there to catch you—"

Traveling rapidly through tea stained-colored, parchment passages, covered on all sides by ancient, rune-like symbols, I'm ejected from the paper shroud much like a bookmark slipping from a text.

I land on my hands and knees in a patch of streaming sunlight from the long gallery of arrow-slit windows in the Archive room. Swallowing hard against the bile rising in my throat, I glance up to see Brownie's platinum hair spilling over Preben's arms wrapped around her.

Clasping the closed book-portal under her arm, Buns reaches down with her other hand to help me up. I give her a curious look while rising to my feet. She shrugs, saying, "Preben's happy to see her."

As I look past Preben's silvery hair, I see no less than two score of Power angels; they watch me with unwavering stares. I square my shoulders, adopting the stature of a leader. When Preben's gray eyes lock with mine, he eases Brownie to his side, holding her in place with his arm over her shoulder. "We are assembled," he says, and seeing the question in my eyes, he adds, "They are Prostat Powers—friends of Zephyr and Reed."

"I see," I reply, but then my brow wrinkles in concern. "You're a Dominion Power. Won't helping me go against the Seraphim's leadership?"

Preben smiles, saying, "It would, if I were still a part of Dominion. They have chosen to follow your father's leadership. But, I have since elevated in rank to Prostat Power. That makes me no longer beholden to Dominion."

My eyes widen as I point out, "You're still outranked though."

He smiles in amusement. "I am taking my direction from a Seraphim, am I not?" he asks me, while one silvery-blond eyebrow rises in question.

"So, I *am* a loop-hole," I breathe a shuddering breath.

"Your rank is open for interpretation," Preben agrees. "There has been no official ruling regarding your level or position among us, so should we choose to follow you, we will not be committing treason."

"Then, I thank you all for coming," I reply with a wry smile of my own.

"It is our honor to fight with you," Preben replies, inclining his head.

"I just want to make one thing very clear. No one kills Reed," I say in my most menacing tone. "Do you understand?" I ask him.

"Is that an order?" he counters in a calm tone.

"Yes," I reply.

"Then, it will be obeyed," he responds.

I blink, unable to believe that I'm not coming up against harrowing resistance. Feeling all of their eyes on me, I try to hide my bewilderment. Focusing on Anya, I see that she's watching me, too. Her skin has almost no color now and she holds her hands together in front of her in an effort to stop them from shaking. I claim one of Anya's hands, holding it tight in mine and squeezing it reassuringly. She gives me a fragile smile, but her green eyes betray her mounting anxiety that goes well beyond unease.

Preben breaks our silent communication as he says, "The Seraphim guard the doors to the Knight's Bar. They've surmised that should you return, it is where you'll go."

My brow wrinkles as I curse wordlessly in my mind.

"Sweetie," Buns smiles at me. "Brownie and I can take care of them."

"You have a plan?" I ask her in surprise as we huddle to discuss it.

An engagingly sly smile passes between Buns and Brownie, before Brownie intones, "It's a blend of the sophisticated and uncomplicated. We'll just pretend to stumble upon them."

"That's your plan?" I ask skeptically, thinking that they're going to get caught.

"Sweetie, they think Reapers are hare-brained," Buns explains. "We'll just prey upon their expectations."

"We'll lead them away," Brownie promises. "All you need to do is get in there." Remembering the dark energy surrounding the Knights Bar, hackle-like goose bumps rise beneath my skin. I force down the shiver that begs to run through me, managing a nod instead. "Alright then," Brownie nods back and we clasp each other in a group hug, like we used to do after a huddle in field hockey.

The male angels surrounding us wear slightly lecherous expressions when we straighten up. Still holding Anya's hand, I spy the suit of armor, the only decoration in the room. Leading her to it, I grasp the battleaxe clutched by the armor's silvery glove. Wrenching it away, I listen while the weapon hums its eerie music in soft vibrations.

Anya's skin prickles next to me as she surveys the wicked, serrated blade of the axehead. She asks, "Whose ax is that?"

"It was a gift," I reply while I tug at her hand, following Buns and Brownie out of the archive.

We split up, Brownie and Buns hurrying away to approach the hallway of the Knight's Bar at the opposite end from us. Preben and the Powers come with Anya and me, trailing us like silent shadows. Nearing the passage, I pause just before the archway. Preben produces a small mirror on an extendable pole, angling it so that we can observe the occupants of the corridor. Tau stands motionless in the center of the hall, directly across from the medieval armor sentinels that I had placed there to guard the doors. Seeing my father causes my stomach to clench in pain and my legs to go numb with fear. I try hard not to panic, but my labored breath sounds loud in my ears.

*He could stop me...*my mind booms, but I force myself to calm down and evaluate the situation.

Cole stands just beside Tau. He has adopted a casual slouch, leaning against the wall mired by silent, decaying watermarks. He's studying Xavier as the latter paces the floor between the empty alcoves, his supernatural speed causing him to resemble the elongated, crimson body of a Chinese, ceremonial dragon. Flanking them on either side are dozens of Dominion Powers. Low murmurs of Angelic conversation drifts to us in soothing, melodious rhythms. These conversations cease when Buns and Brownie's placid voices insert themselves between the harmonious strains.

I recognize Buns's loquacious resonance as she says, "Sweetie, I thought it was Truman Copote that said, 'when the going gets weird, the weird turn pro.'"

Appearing at the opposite entrance to the hallway, Brownie counters, "No, that was definitely Hunter S. Thompson..."

Brownie stumbles to a halt, much like a deer in headlights, while grasping Buns by the elbow. Buns's eyes fly wide with feigned shock worthy of an Oscar. Backing away, Buns mutters, "Uh oh…" before she turns on her heels and runs away in a blur of long, golden curls.

Xavier stills, his face brightening from a snarl to one of hope. Brownie begins to spew a delicious panoply of nasty words while she bolts in the opposite direction from that which Buns had taken. Xavier doesn't hesitate, but launches himself forward to pursue Buns with the intensity of a devoted lover. When several Powers follow him, I hold my breath and send up a silent prayer to Heaven that they won't harm her if they catch her.

Cole's dark, hazel eyes scan Tau's until he receives a quick nod from his auburn head. A fraction of a second after that, Cole is gone, following Brownie toward the North Tower. Only a handful of Powers remain behind with Tau to cover the Knight's Bar. Tau takes a couple of steps away from us, toward where the Reapers had shown themselves at the other end of the hallway. But he pauses, his back becoming rigid. He glances back over his shoulder toward where we're hidden just beyond the bend in the corridor. Preben quickly pulls the small mirror back behind the cover of the wall. Setting it down on the floor, he silently pulls his sword from its sheath, causing my eyes to narrow in panic.

Taking a deep breath, I go down on one knee, coaxing a shimmering clone to spill from me. Directing her forward, she strolls to access the corridor. I make her stop dead when Tau sees her. "Tau!" I project my voice, while my clone quails.

"Evie!" my name is torn from Tau like a desperate, involuntary appeal.

I give my father no time to work out my ruse before I make my clone run, tearing a path along our corridor away from us. Realizing that I have to hide my entire contingent and myself, I hold up my palm, expelling what little energy I've gathered in a soft burst. I only manage to erect a thin illusion of an empty hallway; it hovers like a soft cloud. Should Tau touch it, the illusion will disappear and he'll find me there before him.

When Tau breaches our corridor, he pauses. He turns in my direction instead of the direction my clone had run. He takes a couple of steps and then he pauses again. His storm-gray eyes hover above mine. Scrunching my eyes closed, I hold my breath, but not before inhaling the clean scent of my father within arm's-length of me. He turns away then and a soft breeze caresses my cheek as he disappears from the corridor in the opposite direction in pursuit of my clone. Opening my eyes, I don't expect the brutal pain that tears at my heart when I see that he's gone. It almost feels as if he has betrayed me again.

The few Dominion Powers that remain to guard the Knights Bar quickly scatter as I release several more clones, all of which escape in different directions. The corridor is clear, so I stand up, dropping the magical façade that shrouds us. The air feels heavier upon my skin the closer I get to the Knight's Bar. Approaching the medieval armor guards blocking the doors, I wave my hands in their direction, pushing them aside in a rattling clatter of metal against cold, gray stone.

Reaching the doors, Preben steps in front of me, holding up his hand to stop me from opening them. "Let us enter first, Evie," he states, pulling the bardiche from the handles of the doors.

He flings the doors wide, stirring the evil current of energy rushing by us into the room. A shiver shakes me as I ask Preben, "What do you see?"

He folds his beige, falcon-like wings behind him as he observes, "Bright light pouring in from glassless rosette windows, broken furniture, rusted human armor, chandeliers hanging askew."

The Prostat Power angels prowl in through the doors, disappearing from my sight. "Are they still there?" I ask Preben while my voice strains as I find it suddenly hard to breathe.

"Yes," he says, blinking in surprise. "Can't you see them?"

"No," I reply, in a clipped tone.

"What do you see?" he asks through narrowing eyes.

"Brennus," I whisper.

Just beyond the threshold, Brennus stands, watching me with a small tilt of his head. A slow smile stretches his full lips as he extends his hand to me. His lipid, light-green eyes beckon me to join him within. Dressed in a dark, elegant suit, he affects a poised demeanor, as if he had been expecting me at precisely this moment.

Abruptly, Preben slams the doors closed, pushing the bardiche through the handles again. His expression is grim when my eyes meet his in question. "You knew he was in there!" Preben accuses.

My brow darkens in confusion as I answer, "Uhh, yeah—"

"How am I to help you if he is beyond my reach?" Preben growls, showing his unease.

Anya pipes up, saying, "It will not be long. As soon as we go in, be prepared to fight." When she steps next to me, her skin is as pale as her gossamer gown. Fear makes her hands shake as she holds them together in a desperate attempt to get them to stop.

Her terror twists like a knife thrust in me. "You don't need to do this," I whisper to her. "Stay here with Preben!"

Shaking her head slowly, Anya's green eyes meet mine. "Don't underestimate me, Evie," she says in a voice that quivers. "You need me."

"You're afraid," I state, not like a question.

"Yes," she admits as her chin bobs. "I'm freaking out—the bad kind, but that's a small sacrifice for love."

Facing away from me, towards the doors, Anya takes a position between my arms. Pressing her wings in tight to her body, she makes me lift the battleaxe so that I grasp the shaft in both my hands with the handle resting against her abdomen. Glancing at me over her shoulder, she says, "Now, it looks like I'm your prisoner."

I breathe a heavy sigh, attempting to calm my lurching heart. "Open the doors, Preben," I order, meeting his eyes.

His jaw tightens as he struggles with his need to protect us, but he does what I ordered and pulls the bardiche from the handles. He swings the doors wide. Brennus is no longer near the threshold. He has moved back into the center of the room. The hazy veil that shrouds the magical realm distorts his image, making him waver like the smoke from a fired gun.

"Here we go," I breathe low into Anya's ear, while we both step forward, breaking the plane of the room.

Weightlessness captures me, and with it, a sense of floating in a soundless night sky. My hair spreads out around me, like in the ambient submersion of water, but my skin remains cool and dry. Abruptly that changes, replaced by the rush of tumbling and falling sideways.

In the next moment, Anya and I are sprawled upon the hard, flagstone floor of a very different Knight's Bar. In this realm, the kirk is twice as big and the proportions are entirely off. The vaulted ceiling is cavernous, lofting high above my head. The gothic chandeliers that levitate beneath the exposed beams are enormous, three times as big as the ones in the destroyed bar had been. The rosette windows are larger and different, too. They no longer contain shattered shards of colorful stained glass but now are covered in an inky, shifting film that projects a starry sky filled with an orbiting array of planets.

The armor lining the walls is no longer human either, but the collection of Faerie armor that had been stored within the Archive

Room. It shines like polished diamonds, reflecting against the dark, Celtic knots carved into the walls. And within every suit of armor, a Gancanagh soldier stares back at me with cold, dark eyes. They stand in divisions along the capricious room and arching galleries above.

Getting to my feet, I wait for Anya to rise next to me. Her hair, like mine, waves and floats, as if it's caught in a current of a magical pool. Seeing the intense fear in her eyes, I want to take her hand again, but I resist the impulse. Something slides quickly across my peripheral vision, drawing my gaze to it. Brennus moves with such speed, speed I can't remember him ever possessing, to stand just a few feet from me. Startled, my mouth opens a little, betraying my shock.

Without me seeing him do it, his finger reaches out and touches my chin, gently closing my parted lips. My nostrils flare in fear, while my eyes go wide. *He's hundreds of times faster than me!*

Seeming to read my mind, a smile spreads too quickly upon his lips; it doesn't develop, but is just there in a fraction of a second. "If dis were music, *mo chroí*," Brennus explains, "ye'd be playing in adagio...slow tempo. Ye didn't believe that I would let ye in here wi'out some kind of promise that I could control ye, did ye?" he asks me as his voice churns the air around me in pelting rhythms of ominous sound.

"Somehow I knew that you'd find a way to make me claw my way off your playground—" I begin, but I stop and wince as Brennus reaches out and squeezes my upper arm tight. It's a not so subtle signal for me to shut up.

His Cheshire-cat grin swims near my face as he exposes his sharp fangs that make my skin ache with the echoes of remembered pain.

"Shhh, *síorghrá*," he croons while he draws my face up to his chest; it presses against the heavy fabric of his dark suit jacket. Holding one hand to the back of my neck he strokes my hair with his other hand. "As bad as I like ye right now, 'tis worse wi'out ye. Do na make me kill ye."

I want to lift my cheek from him to scan the room for Reed, but I dare not move. "Who is dis ye've brought wi' ye?" Brennus asks in a brittle tone. His hand on my neck isn't allowing me to move, so I can't see Anya at all.

Heat spreads to my cheeks while my stomach twists. "A gift..." I utter feeling choked.

"Is it now?" Brennus asks with doubt in his tone. "'Tis said dat 'tis only for her own good dat da cat purrs. Whah about dis gift makes ye purr?"

"She's special," I reply.

"She's na da other. Ye believe dat I would take jus any *aingeal?*" he growls, his fingers thread into my hair, tipping my head to the side so that my neck is exposed. His lips move to my throat and I feel his fangs puncture the surface of my skin.

"No—" I exhale, but I can't say anymore because his hand tightens on my throat threateningly.

He doesn't drink, but pulls back a little to hover over the small holes on my neck that begin to well up with blood. He inhales the scent of it. "I told ye ta bring da other. Ye disobeyed me. If ye intend for me ta kill ye—ta send ye off ta some other place where ye'll be safe from me, dan ye're mistaken. I'll na let ye be destroyed. Ye need ta begin to hear me again, ta know dat I am yer king. Pain is a good teacher. A good thrashing will go a long way wi' ye." His hands shift to my bottom, rubbing it softly.

"No," I whisper.

"*Dún do chlab,*" Brennus says with menace, telling me to shut my gob as his hands squeeze me threateningly. His black hair has fallen over his forehead in disarray. "Ye will be punished, but dat will be later...in private. Ye're still me queen and da fellas need ta respect ye."

I shiver at what Brennus has planned for me. "And you're very sadistic and you'll enjoy it too much to do it now," I say in a low tone.

"Dere is dat too, *mo chroí,*" Brennus admits with a cunning smile. "I plan to enjoy every moment of it—of ye."

"If you do that, I'll hate you," I promise.

"When I do dat, I'll own ye," he replies. "But for now, dere is other pain ye need to learn." Before I can think, Brennus orders, "Kill dis *aingeal!*"

"*Tristitiae!*" I snarl blackly at Brennus.

Brennus holds up his hand, staying the handful of fellas who circle Anya with vicious smiles. "You said you wanted revenge! Well, I'm giving it to you!" I sneer. "If you kill her now, then you'll have to come up with another plan to get Russell because your last idea completely FAILED!"

In an instant, Brennus' cool fingers entwine in my hair at the back of my head, tilting my face up to his. My breath catches in my lungs as he half pulls half drags me over to face Anya. My hands reach out to his sleeve to steady myself as my feet stumble along.

Anya's eyes widen as I come to an abrupt halt in front of her. Brennus leans down and inhales the scent of my skin before his soft breath tickles me. "Ye must explain whah ye mean when ye say me plan failed, *mo chroí*," Brennus whispers in my ear.

Feeling like my knees might buckle from fear, I reach out to him, resting my hands on his shoulders for support. "*Tristitiae*," I whisper, "you told me once that it means sorrow—that it's my weakness."

"I recall," Brennus replies, while tracing a path over my jaw with his thumb.

"It's also Russell's weakness," I explain, feeling my heart pumping harder. "We're the same in that way."

"'Tis true," Brennus agrees with a small frown when he pulls his lips away from my neck.

"You were wrong to think that he would come with me—that he'd do anything for me," my voice wavers when his eyes bore into mine. To distract myself from my fear, I allow my fingers to travel up his neck to touch his cheek gently. "He wanted to save me, just like he saved me in the caves…"

Brennus' pupils darken, widening when his eyebrows narrow. "He tried to kill ye!" Brennus' voice is black with hatred.

"He's only interested in my soul. If I die, he'll see me again," I reply. My touch is light on his skin and his eyes seem to soften involuntarily. "But Anya is an angel, if she dies…" I shrug, "his *aspire* doesn't possess a soul or the will to resist you…" I trail off. I feel sick. Even as I've just saved Anya from being killed outright, I may have just submitted her to a far worse fate.

"Ye say dat she's da other's *aspire*?" Brennus smiles wickedly, glancing at Anya who has been watching us like a cornered rabbit. "Ahh, I remember ye," Brennus murmurs to Anya, "ye're da reason we had such problems in Poland. Ye threatened ta kill me queen."

Using my fingers, I turn Brennus' cheek, making him look at me again. "If you touch her," I caution, "Russell will have no reason to come to us."

"'Tis na true," Brennus says, stroking my cheek lovingly. "Dere is always revenge. He'll ache wi' a need ta kill me, should I turn his *aingeal* and his soul mate."

"True," I reply, dropping my eyes from his, "if you want to wait for him to make his move. Russell isn't stupid. If we were already turned, he'd take his time, plotting his revenge—making sure he found just the right opportunity to kill you. But if you want him to come now…" I let my words die.

"Ye've taught dis trough, have ye now?" Brennus asks me rhetorically, his lips brushing my forehead. "Finn would be proud o' ye, were he here." Brennus' lips move to kiss each of my eyelids tenderly.

"Where is Finn?" I whisper to him, closing my eyes tighter.

"He is securing our next home. He's determined ta help ye, *mo chroí*," Brennus says in an intimate tone, tracing his finger over my lower lip until my eyes flutter open and I look into his light green ones. "He believes dat we need ta be gentle wi' ye—coax ye into loving us again. He tinks dat if I makes ye feel safe, dat ye'll lay yer body down next ta mine and never leave me."

A tear slips over my cheek. Brennus catches it, crushing it between his fingertips. His voice turns cold and brittle as he says, "Finn is wrong. 'Tis strength dat ye respect, so whah I could na achieve wi' love, I'll get trough fear. I will keep ye dis time. Ye're moin."

"What are you going to do?" I ask with a catch in my voice.

"'Tis na whah I'm going ta do, but whah ye'll do," Brennus replies with cold calculation in his eyes. "Ye have ta make a choice now."

"What choice?" I ask, feeling a chill creep over my body.

"Ye knew dat I would na share ye—dat da very tought o' another touching ye provokes me ta da brink o' madness," he says, while his hands clamp my upper arms. "So ye may choose—do I end yer *aingeal* or do ye?"

"What?" Dizziness makes my hands crush the lovely lapels of his jacket as I hold on to them for support.

"Tink it over, Genevieve. Should ye make me kill him, I will do it slowly...torturously. He'll live for days knowing dat ye could've ended his pain so quickly—if ye had only loved him enough ta do it," Brennus whispers in my ear, his voice casting its shadow over my heart and blackening it.

My desperate fingers pull Brennus closer to me as words spill from me without forethought. "If I could fix you—cure you, Brennus, would you let Reed go?" I ask him pleadingly.

Brennus' hands cover mine, easing them off of him. He holds them in each of his while a sinister smile graces his beautiful mouth. "Cure me?" he asks in an amused tone. "Dere is nuting ailing me, Genevieve. I'm a god—whahever I want, I take."

"But, what if I could give you back all that you've lost—give you your wings back—make you alive again?" I press on, ignoring the coldness of his stare.

I don't see the slap that knocks me to the floor, but when I look up, Brennus is crouched in front of me with his face inches from mine. "Never make me any more promises ye can na keep," he states with cold fury.

"But, what if I can?" I croak, holding my hand to my cheek.

"Never speak of dat again," he says softly, "or ye'll spend da next tousand years in whahever dark hole I decide ta confine ye ta." He looks around warily at the fellas in the room to see if any one of them heard what I said. Several fellas closest to us look stunned.

In the next second, Brennus has pulled me to my feet. "Now," he says, "'tis time ta cut all da strings dat bind ye ta da *aingeal* one-by-one." My eyes fly to his face, seeing his eyebrow arch. "I've had many, many conversations wi' yer *aingeal* dese past days. 'Twas hard to keep from killing him when he gave me dis."

Reaching into his pocket, Brennus pulls out a folded scrap of paper that is worn and frayed around its edges. He holds it up for me, but he doesn't need to open it for me to know exactly what it contains. It's a piece of the note I had once left Reed, telling him that I love him with a verse from Shakespeare.

"When he's gone, 'twill be only me dat ye see," Brennus promises as he drops the note back into his pocket. "Bring me her *aingeal.*"

My eyes swiftly move around the room, up to the gallery tier just below the rosette windows, looking for Reed. The legions of silvery-clad Gancanagh, who thickly line the whimsical walls of the kirk, part. Reed emerges from the apse, walking like a man would who has been trapped in the desert for days without water. If I thought that I was prepared to see him, I was mistaken. It seems that my heart, which I thought to be entirely broken, can still be torn further.

As Reed stumbles forward, nausea chokes me, making it easier to hold myself in check and not run to him. Everywhere my eyes touch on his bare chest he is covered with puncture marks and trails of seeping blood. His once proud wings lay broken and limp against his shoulders; bare, featherless patches mar their elegant, charcoal lines. Deep bruises, in various stages of healing, discolor his face and arms.

Reed's green eyes don't meet mine, but stare with longing at Brennus while he approaches us, waiting for his master to notice him. The thrall is a noose around his neck, strangling him and his pain is mine. When Reed reaches us, he goes down on one knee in front of Brennus, bowing his head in supplication.

Brennus smiles at me nefariously, saying, "Ye see, *mo chroí,* yer lover is already dead...he jus refuses ta admit it."

Brennus reaches down and touches Reed's cheek, infusing his pained, feverous eyes with a dopey, contented pallor, making them dull and lack-luster. It's taking everything that I am to refrain from attacking Brennus. Dark rage burns within me, well beyond anything I've ever experienced. I begin struggling to gather energy to me, searching for it in the cracks and crevices between wood, bricks and mortar. It's flowing in an intricate dance just beyond the sphere of magic that is entrapping and shrouding me.

"Stand, *aingeal*," Brennus orders arrogantly. "See whom I brought for ye."

Reed stands immediately, and his eyes shift to mine. "Evie," Reed says, his voice is low and dull, a ghostly shadow of its former self.

"Dat's right, she's come ta take ye from me," he says coolly.

Reed's eyebrows pull together abruptly and he leans towards me in an aggressive posture, spreading his broken wings as wide as they'll go. "I do not wish to be parted from you," Reed replies with an air of menace in his tone while his predatory eyes scan me ruthlessly.

"She is jealous of whah we share, *aingeal*," Brennus lies. Reed growls at me, low and scary, causing the hair on the back of my neck to rise. "Ye'll need ta fight her if ye wish ta stay wi' me," Brennus explains in a tone that implies regret. "Ta prove ta da fellas dat ye should be da one ta remain wi' us."

A slow, cruel smile forms in the corners of Reed's perfect lips. "I am prepared to fight."

"I knew dat ye would be," Brennus smiles wickedly. "Ye need but choose a weapon," he commands, sweeping his hand toward a wall adorned with evil, hand-to-hand combat weapons.

Reed's head tilts to one side. He scans the array of wickedness, searching for the perfect weapon with which to kill me. I stand perfectly still, continuing to find and draw trickles of energy to me. But, it doesn't take Reed long to find what he's looking for, and moving with surprising speed, he plucks two short daggers from the wall.

Brennus' smile deepens, enjoying his game. Turning to me, he asks, "Which weapon will ye choose?"

I don't look toward the weapons wall, but lift my hand, murmuring soft words that strain to rhyme.

Anger enters Brennus' eyes when the front of his suit jacket tears open as the dull, steel blade of a letter opener he had hidden there emerges from his interior pocket. It comes to me, striking the palm of my hand as if I'm a high-powered magnet.

"There you are," I say to it softly.

Uncertainty enters Brennus' eyes as he notices that my hair is no longer hovering around me weightlessly. His eyes shoot immediately to the gallery above us. My eyes follow his and I spy a few familiar faces from the dozen or so youthful-looking undines lining the arching loft.

Safira stands out among them, her long, golden hair falling in waves around her, making her appear every inch the mermaid-like creature that she resembles. But, there are subtle differences in her appearance from when I had seen her last. Now, she has the dopey façade of one under the thrall of the Gancanagh. Her sisters, Marlowe and Kendall, don't look much better as they breathe heavily between their sharky teeth, trying to wrest the energy that I've stolen from them back again.

"Your undines are growing weak," I comment to Brennus. "Maybe you should feed them better."

Brennus regains his calm quickly, smiling back at me when my hair floats up from my shoulders, indicating that they've regained control of me once again.

"Dere is no need ta attend ta dem. I do na plan ta be here much longer. Once we've finished here, I will na need dem."

"They'll be so bummed," I reply, letting my eyes fall again on the wicked creatures who are creating this magical room that separates us from the angels. Brennus shrugs indifferently. "Why not just turn me now?" I ask out of curiosity, toying with the little letter opener in my hand. Memories of how I had thrust the tiny blade into Brennus' foot in my attempt to escape from him in Houghton flicker in my mind.

"Ye might enjoy killing yer *aingeal* after ye've been turned. Dis way, da pleasure is all moin," he says before he caresses my cheek.

A ghost of a smile touches my lips when my eyes find what I've been looking for in the gallery. The tall, silvery flash of Faerie armor, standing just below the rosette window, makes my heart swell with pride.

"You should leave this house of cards now, Brenn," I warn. "Before you're rendered irrelevant."

"Ye'd have me miss seeing ye kill da *aingeal?* I remember how ye sorted out Keegan down in da caves. 'Twas yer first kill...I would na dream of missing dis," he replies.

"Maybe he'll kill me," I murmur, trying to buy more time. "As you said, I'm playing in adagio. My speed will definitely be a factor. All of my movements are so much slower—it's like you've rendered me human again. Even Reed has quicker reflexes than me."

Brennus' eyes darken as he warns, "Do na tink dat I'll allow ye ta escape into a true death...dere will be suffering should ye try."

Brennus turns from me to Anya who hasn't moved from the spot where we'd fallen earlier. Several fellas still hover around her, displaying their fangs to increase her terror. Brennus brushes by them, coming closer to her. Fear pours from Anya; her eyes lurch from Brennus to me and then back to Brennus again.

"She is exquisite, *mo chroí*," Brennus says to me over his shoulder. "Perhaps I will share her with ye later…" He reaches out to her then, touching her cheek.

A soft sigh comes from Anya's lips as she relaxes in an instant, her eyes roving over Brennus like he is the most beautiful creature she has ever seen. Taking Anya by the hand, Brennus guides her away from me toward the apse where an elegant chair awaits him. When Brennus sits in it, he positions Anya to sit at his feet, her head resting lovingly against his knee while he strokes her long, dark hair like a favored pet.

Brennus waves his hand in the air, toward where Reed and I stand facing him. "Ye may begin," he says, like a king upon his throne.

The weightlessness that I've experienced since I entered this place immediately falls away. My hair no longer hovers, but lies placidly against my shoulders. I can suddenly move faster than slow motion, which is really fortunate because the moment that I realize this, Reed's dagger slashes through the air, cutting a long slice into my arm.

Feeling my skin burn as blood drips from the edge of his blade, I hear the room erupt with *click, click, click* as fangs engage. The Gancanagh have caught the scent.

I grip the letter opener more firmly in my hand as I try circling away from Reed while he assesses my every move. He stalks forward slowly, mirroring my steps as if he knows what I'll do as I do it. I back up and bump against an invisible wall the undines have created to keep me within the sphere of their control.

Momentarily distracted, I'm just able to spin away from Reed when his dagger slashes toward my neck. It cuts the air as it misses me, but the blade in his other hand doesn't; it leaves a small, painful cut on my cheek. Brennus hisses in anger. I ignore him, but Reed doesn't; he looks toward Brennus in question. The distraction is just what I've been hoping for. I reach my hand out to touch Reed's chest.

As my finger's graze Reed's skin, I whisper to him, "Doubt thou the stars are fire…" My hand glows as if it's being lit from within, drawing some of the poison from Reed's flesh. Something breaks within my wing, while I see his wing straighten.

Reed stumbles back from me, breaking the connection before I can bond to him fully. He's stunned, shaking his head, like he's shaking the cobwebs from it. I move to him again, saying softly, "Doubt that the sun doth move…" I rest my hand on his shoulder and see the bloody puncture wounds marring his skin close up and smooth over, leaving it flawless once again.

"Doubt truth to be a liar…" I fall against Reed. His arms encircle me, holding me to his chest. "But never doubt that I love…" My voice falters as blood oozes from the opening puncture wounds along my neck and chest. The strength drains from me as I gaze up at Reed's perfect green eyes.

And then, I hear Reed whisper near my ear, "But never doubt that I love…I love thee best, O most best, believe it," while clutching me tightly to him.

Russell

CHAPTER 26

Step Into The Ring

My stomach churns like it got pulled through the antique book portal along with Anya and Red. Holdin' the media table for support, that feelin' doesn't go away when Zee shuts their gateway to Ireland, closin' them off from me. My knuckles turn white as I crush the clear, glass surface causin' it to crack like expandin' ice. I can't even look at Zee, but watch the minutes tick by on my watch, waitin' for the time when I can follow them to Ireland using the other portal.

"Do not dwell on what could happen to them," Zephyr advises with a frown. "Think instead of all the problems that you plan to lay at Brennus' feet."

"There's room for all of that in my mind now," I reply wryly, easin' my hands off the table. "I can obsess on everythin' simultaneously, but it's the thoughts 'bout Anya that are rippin' my guts apart."

"Yes," Zee replies grimly, "I understand that problem...Buns is a force of nature."

"She is," I say with a reluctant smile, "you're kinda screwed, dude. She's definitely got her own ideas."

Zee grins, too. "Do not laugh too hard, playa, yours is a Throne... karma..." he says, noddin' his head before grimacin' and addin', "ouch."

My smile broadens involuntarily. "Zee, when did you become funny?" I ask.

"It is difficult to be funny in Human," he says, before lookin' at his watch and then graspin' the cover of the portal computer. "Learn my language and you will think I am hysterical." After a second he sobers and asks, "Are you ready to do this?"

I give him a look full of hubris, while sayin', "Shoot, I've already turned pro...this is like headin' back to the minors."

Zephyr flashes me an evil grin, "You are becoming more of an Angel every day."

He opens the laptop and immediately we swirl into the dark tunnel woven with coursin' blips of light and circuitry. In the next instant, I'm squeezed out of a CD slot and deposited into a supple, leather seat of a luxury automobile.

Lookin' 'round at the high-polished shine from the tortoise shell dashboard, my eyes widen at Zee in the driver's seat. "Do portals come standard on all Bentleys?" I ask, feelin' the perfection of the hand-stitchin' on the seam of my seat.

"No, this one is custom. Buns installed it before we had to leave," he states proudly, while touchin' the steerin' wheel in front of him as if it were a lover.

"Remind me to have her bling my ride when this is over," I say, assessin' the garage outside my window. It seems a shame to call it a garage, 'cuz it's more like a homage to luxury vehicles. I'd like to live here beneath the vaulted ceilin' with its ribs that turn into columns of support. "Where are we?" I ask.

"The carriage house—it's across the lawn from the kirk," he replies, depressin' a button. Immediately, the wooden garage door in front of the vehicle slides soundlessly sideways, allowin' bright sunlight to spill into the dim interior.

"Can I drive?" I ask after he orders the car to start with some kind of Faerie-soundin' word.

"No," he says with a smile, "I'm the driver."

"C'mon, Zee," I beg. "The only car I've ever had was the beater I bought when I turned sixteen."

"All the more reason for me to drive. You cannot handle her... she's European," he says with a smug smile, pullin' out of the garage and headin' down the gravel drive toward the estate. When he glances at me and sees my hostile look, he adds, "Do not be angry, I will buy you one when this is all over."

"I'm not angry," I say with a frown. "I'm concerned."

I point up ahead of us to Xavier standin' with his arms crossed beneath a rosette window of the kirk.

"How'd he know we'd be here?" I ask.

"He caught one of them," Zephyr replies, his face goin' ashen.

"Would he hurt them?" I ask as Zee drives the car recklessly now in the direction of Xavier.

"Would you if they could lead you to your love?" he counters. I growl in response.

Zephyr tears up the grass in deep chunks as we speed over the lawn. Xavier doesn't even flinch or move at all when Zee stops the car a mere inch from him. It's only when I fumble for the door handle that he shoots to my side of the car, rippin' off my door and pullin' me out like I stole it.

Without thinkin', I send a burst of energy at him, knockin' him away from me in a stunnin' flash of light. He is only on the ground for half a second before he is up and comin' at me again. But Tau lands in front of Xavier, holdin' him back from me.

"We need him!" Tau says fiercely to Xavier, who at once stops strugglin' against Tau. Evie's father immediately turns to me and says, "Evie went into the kirk with Anya, at which time they disappeared from the estate."

"They're still here," I reply gruffly, seein' the anxiety in his eyes that are just like Red's. "I'm here to help them."

"How do we assist you?" Tau asks with a taut expression.

"Ahh, you wanna help now?" I counter sarcastically. I glance at Zee who gives me a significant look. "You can start by bringin' us our Reapers," I sigh in a relentin' tone.

"Cole, retrieve them," he orders without takin' a breath. "What else?" he asks me succinctly.

"I don't know. I need to check it out," I say, brushin' past them and leapin' into the air. I fly to an enormous, flower-shaped window and hover there, tryin' to look beyond the dark, starry patina, cloudin' and distortin' the shiftin' details of the church below me. It's like tryin' to look through foggy water.

"She's not in there!" Xavier snarls next to me, jumpin' down my throat. "I've been through it—questioned all the Powers!"

I scowl back at him, "I'm fixin' to go off on you! Can you shut up for a second?" I ask before continuin' my recon.

"Do you see them?" Zee asks next to me.

"Yeah," I reply in a calmer tone. "They're alive." Then I have to clench my teeth as Brennus slaps Red and I see her sprawl on the ground.

"What happened?" Tau asks, his face turnin' red at my expression.

"He's just slapped Evie," I reply, not sugar-coatin' it. "She can't fight back—"

"Why? What's wrong with her?" Xavier demands with a tone of desperation that I've never heard from him.

"I don't know. She looks weird...slow," my eyes dart away from Evie as I evaluate the other elements of the chamber below.

"You have to go in there—kill him!" Xavier urges, proddin' me in the shoulder.

"I'm plannin' on goin' in there! Just give me a second to figure out how not to get killed when I do! There are hundreds of armed Gancanagh in there and a bunch of freaky-lookin' mermaids."

"Mermaids?" Tau asks softly, before his eyes snap to mine. "You mean undines?"

"They look like mermaids to me—they have gills," I touch the sides of my neck, "and long, flowing hair, barracuda teeth—"

"Undines," Tau growls, his face turnin' redder. "The innocent bound to the damned..."

"They don't look innocent...they look totally vicious," I chime in, pullin' my hand through my hair. "Okay," I say to Zee, "I gotta check the way in."

I approach the glassy film of the window; it resembles a perfect rendition of the night sky, but with planets in it that don't belong to this solar system...and it's orbiting like it's real. Tentatively, I touch my finger to the glass and it sinks right through it, tuggin' at me to follow it. I pull my hand back, feeling relief to see I still have my finger.

"Now, I just need to blend in," I mutter to no one in particular.

I fly down to the ground near the Bentley. Closin' my eyes I concentrate on my objective.

Xavier lands next to me, askin' in a derisive tone, "What are you doing?"

"Shh," I whisper, openin' my eyes, "I'm gettin' somethin'."

In a few seconds, a small smile creeps to my lips as I hear the sound like a couple of garbage can lids bein' clapped together. Along the low, gray fieldstone wall, Brennus' Faerie armor runs toward us. It doesn't stop when it nears me, but runs right into me, meltin' 'round me and coverin' me like a second skin.

"Wicked," I breathe, lookin' at my arms and chest protected by shiny, lightweight armor. "Finally, somethin' that fits." I smile.

"You look like a Faerie," Buns says next to me. She taps the shiny, silver helmet on my head lightly, addin', "I have to admit that Brennus has style."

"Buns," I say, glancin' at her and seein' bruises and swellin' 'round her mouth. A low growl comes from Zee as he engulfs her in his arms.

"I'm okay," she murmurs to Zephyr. He presses her closer to him. Zephyr's eyes pierce Xavier. "When this is over, I will find you."

"You would've done the same thing. I regret that it has come to this," Xavier says with little expression.

Zephyr's eyebrows narrow dangerously. "Still...hand on my heart we will meet."

"You are not where you belong," Xavier replies.

"I think you are mistaken, Seraph," Zephyr replies. "That is you. Evie has moved on."

"Then why does Evie need me more than ever?" Xavier counters Zephyr darkly, no longer unemotional.

I interrupt them to ask, "Buns, where's Brownie?"

Buns's bruised lips spread in a wide smile, "Oh, sweetie, Cole couldn't catch her. She's probably with Preben now."

"Good," I breathe. "Then, I don't have to worry 'bout her."

I begin murmurin' a spell and rhymin' 'the reekin' smell of rotten candy' with the phrase 'it'd come in handy'. Then, a scent weaves 'round me that'll guarantee that I blend in among the Gancanagh. Xavier takes a step back from me with his nose wrinklin'.

"Excellent," I inhale, smellin' the air 'round me and thinkin' that I got the odor just right.

Zephyr doesn't shy away from me. "You will need to pull your wings in immediately upon entering the kirk." Zephyr advises.

Lookin' over my shoulder, I see the bright crimson of my wings. "You're right," I nod. "I will."

"Then I will see you when you remove the haze," Zephyr says with no sign of doubt.

"Remember, you owe me a new car when this is over...so make sure you make it," I say gruffly.

"I remember," he replies stoically.

"Then, there's no sense in hangin' here any longer," I murmur. Buns gives me a quick hug before releasin' me. I smile at her and then look toward the rosette window above.

"I will reward you, should you save my daughter," Tau says next to me.

As I glance at Tau, I see somethin' in his eyes that makes my gut clench. Regret, sorrow, confusion—he's her dad. No doubt. "Don't worry," I assure him. "The Gancanagh can't stop me now. Just be ready."

I take off, leapin' into the air and flyin' back up to the window. Glancin' in, I see Reed kneelin' in front of Red and Brennus. My heart thumps in relief that he's alive. A grim smile touches my lips 'cuz every eye in the place is riveted on the scene playin' out on the flagstones below. I won't get a better opportunity to enter than this. Lowerin' the faceplate on my helmet, I whisper, "God, be with me."

Takin' a deep breath, I draw all the energy that I can hold to me. Then, I push my head through the cold window, feelin' it immediately pull me in. As I retract my wings, I lurch forward, shiftin' laterally, like I'm goin' sideways down an icy, flowin' river. In seconds, I land on top of a couple of armor-clad, stinky fellas stationed along the balcony below the window.

The sound of our armor clatterin' together would be deafenin', if I hadn't released some of the energy I'm holdin' to draw the sound back to me before anyone else can hear it. As I straighten, the two Gancanagh that I'm stompin' on move to attack me with soundless growls. I wave my hand in their direction, petrifying them where they stand. Rigid from my magic, only their eyes move.

Now, to collapse their infrastructure, I think as a bead of sweat slips down my face. Lookin' toward the choir-like loft, I find the undines who are concentratin' on the action below.

Following the blond fish-woman's gaze downward, I see Brennus standin' next to Anya. Reachin' his hand up to her, he touches her cheek. A torturous stab slicin' my heart makes it feel like somethin' in my chest is burnin'. I stop, unable to move as I clutch the railin' overlookin' the scene below. Brennus holds Anya's hand while he leads her to his throne, makin' her sit at his feet. Rage explodes inside of me.

Breathin' heavy, I hear Brennus say, "Ye may begin."

With those words, I'm released from my stupor. Clenchin' my jaw tight, I grasp the sword from the hand of the petrified Gancanagh next to me. Pulling it out of its sheath, it makes the most satisfyin' sound as it begins to sing for me. The sound of the Gancanagh's fangs engagin' speeds rapidly down the aisle of fellas linin' the upper gallery. They're reactin' to the smell of blood from Red as Reed cuts her. A growl escapes from me. In the next instant, every pale-white face in the upper balcony turns toward me in domino-like succession.

Softly, I hear my own voice say, "Here we go."

The gleam of brilliant-white fangs from the scores of fellas comin' at me makes my muscles tighten. The first fella to reach me raises his sword, hackin' at my chest while his mouth lunges for my exposed neck. I wince at the force of his sword's blade as it bounces off my armor breastplate, dentin' it. Filled with adrenaline, I bring my sword down on his neck, hackin' his head clean off his body. The next fella's cold stare bores into me as he winds his hand back, throwin' magic that's manifestin' into a shower of dagger-sharp, iron nails. Their ebony points crush the silver veneer as they spatter against my armor, soundin' like rain on a tin roof. Again, the magical armor holds solid.

I taste sweat and the acrid tang of fear when sprays of colorful light and fire come shootin' at me from all directions. Deafenin' explosions and sparks crackle, ignitin' the air in blindin' flashes. Usin' the energy I came in with, I manage to deflect other frightenin' lights that morph into the terrifyin' creatures resemblin' gray, lichen-covered gargoyles. Pushin' energy at the fire-spewin', stony reptiles, I turn them back on the fellas who created them. Horrifyin' shrieks tear from the mouth of one as it pounces on a fella's chest, rippin' through his armor and gorgin' on the dead flesh within it.

As I shift to face another Gancanagh soldier in the line, a sound like a choir of angels begins rainin' down on me. The harmonious chantin' makes my fingers tighten on my sword's hilt with calm and purpose. Lungin' at the fellas nearest me, the spray of coal-black blood drips from the edge of the sword. And as I hack at the undead in front of me, the soft, soothin' melody continues chantin', motivatin' me to keep movin' forward. Heads fallin' to the floor and rollin' away like wobbly, misshapen spheres, are as nothin' to me. Screamin', the crackin' of bone, the plastic smell of musty-sweet blood, isn't touchin' me in a visceral way. These are all just things in the way of my goal: Brennus—dead.

Before I know how I got here, I reach the choir loft. The sapphire eyes of the blond undine shift to me; her drugged stare shows little emotion as she jumps at me with her mouth wide, showin' all her sharp, barracuda teeth. Extendin' my hand to her, I lay it over her face. My hand glows with light and like a parishioner on a Sunday mornin' TV evangelist show, she falls over twitchin'. When her sisters run at me, they get the same shock. Then, everythin' 'round me begins meltin' away.

Lookin' over my shoulder at the scene below, Reed is holdin' Red in his arms as the room grows still. The air is stained with the shapes of the other kirk and standin' like waverin' watermarks 'round the space are the familiar faces of the angels I know. The two realities are beginning to blend into a single dimension.

"DA OTHER," Brennus calls to me in a satisfied tone.

His voice causes the hairs on my arms to rise. Seein' him still seated upon his throne, I gnash my teeth together as he deliberately reaches down to stroke Anya's hair. Graspin' the stone railin' of the choir loft, it's turnin' to nothin' in my hands 'cuz the magic that created it is slowly fadin'. My red wings unfurl from my back to spread out 'round me as I leap over the banister and glide effortlessly to the flagstone floor below.

My voice is little more than a snarl. "Your magic is gettin' thin, Brennus." I point out, stridin' toward him purposefully.

"'Tis na me magic," Brennus replies coolly. "'Tis the undines and I no longer need dem, since ye're here."

"Aren't you gonna run away now? Isn't that what you do when things fall apart?" I ask, spreadin' my arms out, indicatin' that the angels are comin' into sharper focus the closer I'm gettin' to him.

"We've jus been waiting for ye," he replies with a smug smile.

"You knew I was comin'?" I ask.

"I knew ye'd be here. I have whah ye can na exist wi'out," he replies.

"Russell," Evie gasps my name as I come within feet of her wrapped in Reed's arms. "Wait," she begs weakly. Bite marks cover nearly every inch of her exposed flesh. She's pulled tight against Reed's body as he's guardin' her from the fellas inchin' closer to them.

"Can't," I murmur. "He's got my girl."

"Yer girl…" Brennus smiles humorlessly. "'Tis na even da right species," he says condescendingly. "'Tis fortunate for ye dat I claimed ye," he whispers conspiratorially to Anya. "Dis boy-*aingeal* tinks ye're a girl."

Anya giggles, amused by his comment. "He's trying to shape me to fit his innocence," she says with a smile that can melt any heart.

"Whah did ye see in him?" Brennus asks Anya while he shakes his head in pity.

Anya's smile grows as she says, "He is made for love."

"Is he now?" Brennus asks in a thoughtful tone that makes my flesh crawl, 'cuz he's unafraid even with his world crumblin' 'round him.

"Russell, please stop!" Red pleads, makin' me hesitate as I glance at her again.

"Why?" I frown at her. "He couldn't touch me before—in the garden—"

"He was drunk on my blood then," Red replies, her eyes shiftin' to Brennus over Reed's shoulder. He's watchin' her like he'd like to bite her. "He's not now."

Glancin' past her, there are scores of fellas creepin' nearer to them. Reed growls low and menacingly at the cold freaks, causin' several to stop and take a step back. Feelin' pulled in two different directions at once, I glance from Red to Anya.

"I'll solve yer problem for ye, da other," Brennus says with a sneer. "Genevieve is moin. If ye still want dis one, den ye had best come and join me before I snap her neck." Brennus' fingers shift from Anya's hair to her throat, restin' idle on it. It would only take seconds for him to kill her. I feel frozen, not knowin' what to do as Anya smiles dopily at me.

Without my seein' him move, Reed is next to me, holdin' Evie in his arms. His back is to Brennus, watchin' our back. Reed whispers, "Can you heal Evie?"

I gaze at Red quickly, cringin' inwardly at the sight of her. Deep, bruisin' rings have formed under her eyes, makin' them appear sunken-in and her lips are blue from blood loss. Her black dress is wet with seepin' blood as it trails down her white arms to drip from her fingertips. The aroma of her is drivin' the Gancanagh nearest us almost mad. Feral whimpers are comin' from some of them as they're shakin', tryin' to keep themselves in check and not attack her.

"Yes," I breathe. "But then—"

"I'll get Anya for you. His magic is useless against me," Reed says so low and so fast that I barely understand him.

"No!" Red groans weakly, clutchin' him tighter. "Stay with me," she pleads in desperation.

"Always," Reed replies, squeezin' her tighter, too. "When he's gone. Here, Russell," Reed says, thrustin' Red into my arms. "He'll try to take her from you—don't let him." Reed plucks the letter opener out of Red's fist before spinnin' away in a blurry, charcoal-colored streak. The Gancanagh between Brennus and us start fallin' to the flagstone with arms hacked off, tendons sliced, and with bones left juttin' out of bloody flesh as Reed tears them to pieces.

Brennus' voice shatters the air as he roars, "KILL DA *AINGEAL!*"

I begin to understand in the next instant that Brennus has been waitin' for Reed to let Red go 'cuz he couldn't make Reed magically give Red to him. That, however, is not the case with me. Wrappin' my arms 'round Red, I see Brennus shoot to his feet, pullin' Anya up with him to press against his body like a shield as his hand extends in my direction. Immediately, Red and I are hit with a burst of energy that makes me almost deaf upon impact. Feelin' like my insides just got crushed, my feet leave the ground as I levitate twenty feet in the air with Red still clutched to me.

Red is slippin' through my arms, while I'm tryin' desperately to hold on to her. Releasin' energy that I've been drawin' to me, I'm just managin' to create a barrier between the Gancanagh and us. I use this energy to push Brennus back, but his magic is still gettin' through, tearin' at Red. Pain is twistin' her features as the agony of bein' stretched taut is showin' on her face. I can't throw any of my magic back at Brennus, 'cuz he's hidin' behind Anya. Strainin' and tryin' to keep Red in my arms, my wings beat frantically to hold us back from Brennus. Beads of sweat are runnin' down the sides of my face.

All 'round us, angels are comin' into sharper focus. Reed is nearin' Brennus as he's fightin' off swarms of Gancanagh. He's pilin' them up in mounds of discarded bodies while he's movin' almost soundlessly forward. Next to me, Zephyr's shape is comin' into focus—his sword is drawn and he's swingin' it at the Gancanagh I've been managin' to keep from Red and me with my magical wall of energy. His sword is just waftin' through 'em like vapor. I have to hold on a little longer, I think, pantin' desperately for air.

Then, I glance at Brennus. He smiles, showin' me his knife-sharp fangs. In the next moment, he lifts his wrist to his mouth, tearin' a brutal chunk out of his own flesh. Dark, wet blood seeps from his mouth and his smile grows. Liftin' his wrist to Anya's mouth, he presses it against her lips. As I watch horrified, Anya begins to drink Brennus' blood.

A sound of pure agony rips from me as my heart burns in my chest.

"Russell," Evie's voice penetrates the ragin' chaos swirlin' in my brain. I glance at her face so near to my own. "You have to let me go."

My eyes shift back to Anya, seein' her fingernails diggin' into Brennus' wrist while all the color is drainin' from her face. She looks like she's dyin'—her dull, dopey stare is rapidly bein' replaced by a feverish, tortured-look. "No!" I growl between my teeth.

"You can save her, Russell!" Evie says urgently. "Let me go!"

"I CAN'T!" I shout desperately.

"DO IT, RUSSELL!" Evie shouts back just as desperately. "YOU CAN STILL SAVE HER AND I CAN TAKE CARE OF MYSELF!" Shakin' my head, I close my eyes. When I open them in the next breath, Red's beautiful gray eyes stare into mine as she pleads, "She needs you Russell, please, you have to set me free!"

I stop strugglin' against Brennus' magic. Together, Evie and I hurdle towards Brennus and when we are in arm's-length of him, I let her go. Brennus drops Anya to catch Evie up in his arms. Instantly, he hugs Evie to him as a satisfied smile touches his bloody lips.

"*Mo chroí*," Brennus breathes with an enraptured smile. Then, in a blur of speed, Brennus pulls a compact from the pocket of his suit coat. As he flips open the lid, Evie and Brennus disappear from sight into the open portal. It drops to the ground by Anya as she falls.

Catchin' Anya before she hits the floor, I hold her cold body against mine. Shoutin' and screamin' echoes all 'round me while angels and Gancanagh are clashin' together in battle. We're back in the Knights Bar in Ireland. The undine magic that has kept us separated from it has dissolved away. Anya chokes and sputters as the poisoned blood she ingested is slowly workin' its way through her veins. I bring her cheek to mine, pressin' it against me and feelin' how cold she is already.

A whimper of pain is forced from between her icy-blue lips. "Russell," she whispers, her teeth chatterin' from the cold. "I'mm sssorry."

My throat constricts so I can't even speak. I brush her hair back from her face before I pull her closer to me as my jaw tightens. Then, bendin' down, I gently lay her on the cold, flagstone floor. Standin' and reachin' out, I grasp the first Gancanagh I can find. Rippin' him off his feet by his neck, I hold the front of his armor and tear it away from his chest. As he struggles to try to knock my hand from his throat, I slam him down on the floor next to Anya, petrifyin' him with magic so he can't move.

Breathin' heavily, more from emotion than from exertion, I place my hand on Anya as I hold the Gancanagh soldier down with the other one. When my eyes meet hers, I can't look away. My hand on Anya begins to heat up and glow, and then I whisper, "Hush now, darlin'. You never have to be sorry."

Evie

CHAPTER 27

Home

Softly falling snow drifts around me as my cheek lies against Brennus' chest. Holding me close to him, Brennus murmurs tender, unintelligible words to me. Sweeping his fingers gently over my forehead, he smoothes my hair away from it. After he shrugs off his jacket, he drapes it over my wings and shoulders as we stand on a sidewalk beneath the soft, yellowish pool of light from a black-iron lamp.

"'Tis okay, *mo chroí*," Brennus says softly. "Ye're home."

"Home?" I ask in a murmuring tone while lifting my head off of Brennus weakly. I gaze around; even in the dark, I see a distinctive clock tower rising starkly against the silent, starry sky.

"'Tis sorry I am dat I hit ye. Ye can never speak of healing any of us. 'Twill make some of the fellas desperate ta make ye try, and should ye fail, dey would go mad," Brennus says.

"But what if I could?" I ask him.

His expression turns pained. "Ye can na try. It would likely kill ye."

"You don't know that," I counter.

"I know enough ta know dat ye can na save me. 'Tis ye who needs saving," Brennus says, stroking my cheek. "I have a gift for ye."

"What can you possibly give me, Brennus, that would replace what you've stolen from me?" I ask, shivering in his arms.

"I have stolen nuting. I have replaced whah ye tink you need wi' whah I know ye need. I told ye once dat yer blood reveals all of yer secret desires. It told me dat dis is da place ye call home now...where ye long ta be. I've brought ye home."

"Crestwood," I whisper feebly, glancing around at the familiar building called Central Hall. The grounds are deserted. It must be really late.

"'Tis. We can live here for as long as ye desire. We will make it our home—together."

"This isn't my home without Reed. You know that—my blood must be screaming it," I say softly, taking a step back from Brennus. His coat falls from my wings to the carpet of snow.

Brennus' eyebrows draw together over his sea-foam green eyes. "All of dat will end soon. I promise ye. Ye'll no longer be tormented by yer need for da *aingeal*—"

"My need for him?" I ask, seeing his jaw grow tight.

"Da string dat binds ye both together. He told me of it—'tis a terrible pain for ye both. I will sever it. I know a way ta make it so dat ye no longer ache for him," Brennus replies with a pained expression as soft white snow clings to his beautiful, black hair.

"How?" I ask while I struggle to remain on my feet. Blood is still seeping from the bites covering my body that I took from Reed. Looking down at the snow beneath my feet, there is a speckled line of blood between us as it falls from my hands.

"Me blood will cure ye of it, *mo chroí*. 'Twill wipe away da desperate yearning dat ye feel for yer *aingeal*." As he says this, he lifts his wrist and shows me his pale skin that has already healed, but his blood still covers his once white shirtsleeve. "Der is a new life awaiting ye in death—no more pain, or bein' hunted by *aingeals*—dey'll all bow down ta ye."

"You're suffocating me. It'll only be a new life for my body, not my soul. You'll hand me over to Sheol and I'll only be an empty shape for you to love. I'd rather die!" I say, while lifting my chin and trying to straighten my shoulders.

"Would ye now?" he asks in a sad tone. "Look at yerself. I know how strong ye are, but whah will ye do when da hallucinations begin? 'Tis jus a matter of me openin' up me flesh and I can make dem all go away...'tis time—"

As if on cue, the clock tower tolls out the hour. BONG...BONG ...BONG...

"Let me give ye everyting, Genevieve," Brennus smiles lovingly at me, before he rips open both of his wrists, allowing his blood to flow. "*Táim i ngrá leat*," Brennus intones, telling me that he's in love with me. "Ye're me heart, me only love. Ye're moin," he says, while extending his wrists to me. He waits, unmoving, for me to come to him.

My trembling hands ball into fists as I try to resist the scent of his blood that floats in the air, surrounding me. It calls to me, like the aroma of baking bread to a starving person. My vision distorts as I look away from him, feeling desperate to stop the craving. The glowing lamppost near me begins to sway; it bends in my direction like a tree in the wind. Radiance from it brings hideous shadows swooping all around me. I shy away from it, unaware if it's a hallucination or Brennus' magic that's making it do that.

From the corner of my eye I catch sight of a blacked-winged creature as it dives past the lamppost; the ruffle of its leathery gargoyle wings makes the sound of a sheet billowing on a clothesline. My eyes widen in fear. "Brennus!" I gasp, feeling my chin beginning to tremble.

Brennus tracks the flight of the gargoyle-like phantom as it weaves a path around us. " Tis a *reconnoître*, dat ting ye see. Sheol searches for ye even now. Dey've sent out scouts ta all da corners of dis world," he says with a pitying-look. "'Twill na enter da light. 'Tis nocturnal; it can na abide it."

Trying to think of a spell, I focus it on the lamppost. Instantly the tall, tapering light brightens, while the black base sprouts legs. It pries itself from the ground with a shower of powerful sparks and the sizzle of electricity. It stumbles forward on squeaky, iron limbs while my wavering hand directs it toward Brennus and me. His smile deepens as he faces down my creation, unafraid.

"A light-pole craitur?" Brennus asks me, like he finds me amusing. "'Tis someting I've na seen before, but 'tis jus one, *mo chroí*. Ta survive, yer craitur will need an army." Brennus raises his hand toward the row of ironclad lampposts that line the sidewalk. A score of poles begin to struggle, unearthing themselves from the ground. Sparks shower down and the kinetic zing of electricity crackles in the air. Yellow light casts eerie glowing shadows on the sidewalk as they lurch forward, approaching the light-pole I had conjured.

Brennus' expression becomes soft. "Ye see…'tis just like ye: alone. Ye need an army ta protect ye. If na, den ye are jus an animal… trapped." I watch as Brennus' tall, sinister tapers near and surround us; they use their garish, illuminated heads to cast pools of light over the snowy courtyard. Beyond the glowing circles, shadowy figures of Gancanagh emerge from everywhere I look; their hisses of yearning when they catch my scent resonate in the air.

"Our army," Brennus says like an introduction while sweeping his hand and gesturing to the hordes of icy, undead Faeries. "'Twill make a fine nest. Dere are many advantages in Crestwood."

I choke, seeing their numbers; there are legions of them. I wonder briefly if I recognize any of them from my time among them or if he had brought them from somewhere else. In the next moment, elf darts erupt from the fellas, hitting the *reconnoître*, knocking it out of the sky. When if falls to the snowy ground, the fellas closest to it tear the beast to pieces.

"All dey need now is a queen. Dey, like me, jus want ta share deir existence wi' ye," Brennus admits in a low tone.

Panic, overwhelming and sickening, hits me. Remembering my personal portal, I touch my neck with my fingertips, expecting to feel the smooth, onyx pin at my throat. But, what I feel instead are slick trails of blood streaking it.

"Ye're looking for dis?" Brennus asks, holding up the black ribbon with the onyx portal attached to it. "Where does it lead?" Brennus asks with a sublime smile. "'Tis my guess dat 'tis somewhere nearby… at da *aingeal's* house, perhaps? 'Tis where he tought ye'd all go— should ye escape. He knows ye well…almost as well as me. Perhaps we'll go dere next…after ye join us…"

Black dread pounces on me, and without thinking, I lift my hand toward Brennus, sending out a pulse of white, hot energy. It hits him where he stands beneath a pool of light from the hovering lampposts, lifting him off his feet and sending him hurtling into the darkness beyond. He sprawls flat on the ground, coming to rest in a drift of snow.

"No one touches my family," I murmur.

Immediately, Brennus lifts up to his feet: not by bending in the way a human would, but by magically levitating up from the ground in one, fluid motion. Hisses resonate from the fellas, who inch toward me in anticipation of blood. A feral growl elicits from Brennus, staying the fellas from coming any nearer to me.

Brennus' eyes turn and lock on mine. "Ye understand nuting. Ye're so naive—'tis like speaking ta a child. Ye have no idea whah da *aingeals* are after, do ye?" he asks rhetorically. "Dey need ye to fall, Genevieve. Dey need ye to join da Fallen. Do ye na see dat?"

"What?" I cringe. "You're insane! Everyone has been trying to protect me—protect my soul from you."

"Dat is because dey have other plans for ye, Genevieve! Dey need ye to remain as ye are, a half-breed when ye fall. Dey can na afford ta have me separate yer soul from yer body. The Fallen are only interested in ye as ye are now. Yer soul is a prize, ta be sure, but it is na powerful wi'out yer *aingeal* body. I can only save da *aingeal* part of ye from Sheol. If dere was a way ta save yer soul as well, I'd do it," he says in a tense tone.

"You're talking about fallen angels—" I say

He cuts me off, "I'm speaking of divine *aingeals*, too!"

"Why would all of the angels want me to fall?" I ask, feeling sick with dread because I know Brennus. He believes what he's telling me.

"I have na been able ta discover da 'why.' Maybe da divine want ye ta get close ta someone in Sheol. One way ta do dat is ta fall from grace—become one of dem," Brennus says as his hands become fists. "Ye trust dem blindly, even after I told ye na ta!"

"I can't trust you, Brennus. You just want to control me," I retort, struggling to remember that he is truly my enemy.

"I do want ta control ye. Ye have no idea whah is comin'. 'Tis bigger dan ye. Ye balk at being me queen, but 'tis da only way I can see ta save ye," he says with an earnest expression. "'Tis as I said before. Da only ting dat ye respect is strength. So be it," he spits out. "I will show ye strength."

"Show me mercy, Brennus," I breathe. "Please...mercy..."

"Ye are achingly lovely, *mo chroí*," Brennus says as if he shares my pain. "Ye tink I want ta change ye? I'm more like me old self when I'm wi' ye—I'm like da being I was before Aodh changed me. Ye do someting ta me. I can remember whah it is to be good when ye are wi' me. I do na want ta lose any part of ye, but dis *is* mercy. Sheol will na get all of ye...because if dey do, dis world ends. Ye'll destroy dis world and every livin' ting in it. Come wi' me now. I'll protect ye. I won't change ye until it becomes absolutely necessary. Ye've me word."

Reed's unmistakable voice comes from behind me, saying, "*Go hIfreann leat*," the rough translation of which means: to hell with you, Brennus. Then, Reed's strong arms wrap around my waist, pulling me against him, beyond Brennus' reach.

"Reed," I breathe with churning emotions of relief and heart-stopping fear.

Holding me tight against his warm, bare chest, Reed's face bends near my ear. His soft breath stirs my hair as he whispers, "I want to kill him slowly, painfully, for you, love, but I don't think I'll be able to restrain myself. Will you forgive me if I do it quickly?" he asks.

My throat constricts. "Reed, wait, he has an army," I counter through trembling lips.

Reed's strong arms press me tighter to him as he says against my hair, "I promise you that he'll die before me. I need you to switch on, Evie, like you did in Torun," he murmurs against my hair. "Be ready to fight," he breathes in a low tone. Then, Reed shifts me behind him so that he stands between Brennus and me. Glancing over my shoulder, the fellas surrounding us are creeping closer, closing in.

"'Tis obscene da way ye managed ta escape me thrall, *aingeal*," Brennus says with a severe twist of his lips. "Genevieve is unpredictable—"

"She's unparalleled," Reed counters, his hand tensing on the small letter-opener in his hand, but otherwise he remains unmoving.

"SHE'S ALL I WANT," Brennus bellows, startling me with his unsuppressed rage.

In a soft tone, Reed states, "And she's the only thing I need. Should I fail to kill you, Brennus, she will finish you. Can you feel it, the lack of oxygen as she pulls energy to her? She's fierce," he says with a small smile touching his lips as he glances back at me.

Brennus loses his scowl. "I taught her dat," he says.

"And she learned it well—ask Lonan...oh wait, you can't. She turned him into ashes..." Reed replies.

Brennus smiles. "Why do ye na tell her whah is coming *aingeal?*" Brennus asks in a low tone.

"I don't know what's coming," Reed says with no inflection.

"Dat is na entirely true. Ye expect someting...remember, we discussed it?" he asks in a cajoling way.

"We discussed my deepest fears," Reed replies easily.

"Same ting," Brennus shrugs. "Whah ye fear most will come to pass. Why do ye na tell her dat ye fear dat she will fall—dat she's *meant* ta fall?" Brennus asks with scorn. "All da signs are dere. Her sire is a negotiator wi' Sheol. Her soul mate bond has been severed—dat can only happen if 'twas negotiated as part of a mission. She'd only do dat ta save her soul mate from *tristitiae*—sorrow as the result of her eventual fall. Ye found her alone—unprotected. Sheol was upon her—she barely escaped dem. She was like a sacrificial lamb. Ye fear dat she is a compromise from Heaven ta Hell."

"Heaven doesn't compromise," Reed states.

"Heaven already did! Look at her! She's an *aingeal* wi' a human soul. Dere has never been a greater compromise," Brennus argues as he gestures in my direction.

"Look again, Brennus. She's growing more powerful by the hour," Reed states, undaunted by what Brennus is revealing.

"She is weak—ye make her weak. Her blood spills from her wi' each passing moment. 'Twill na be long before she'll be too frail ta stand," Brennus replies, but his eyes are focusing on me.

Reed frowns, still standing motionless between Brennus and me. "Her only weakness is that she's young...she doesn't yet know what she's capable of, but I do. I've seen her potential and up to this point, she has been merciful. The time for mercy is over."

All around me, Gancanagh soldiers creep closer. They're waiting for Brennus' signal to attack. My heartbeat thumps painfully in my chest. Struggling to pull every ounce of energy out of the air, I feel the tug-of-war for it as the undead Faeries try to keep it from me. My chin trembles in fear and suppressed emotion as my breathing becomes labored.

"Ye can na win dis, *aingeal*," Brennus snarls.

"She loves me. I cannot lose," Reed says with a sublime smile.

"She's moin. I will kill for her. I will die for her," Brennus promises. He strips his shirt off slowly, revealing his pale chest that resembles carved, Grecian marble. Without looking away from Reed, Brennus extends his hand toward a Gancanagh soldier nearest to him. Immediately, the soldier relinquishes his knife to his *máistir*.

"Then, I accept your challenge and you can die for her. Here. Now." Reed says with a satisfied smile.

In the next instant, I can't breathe as Reed and Brennus both tense before rushing toward each other in the blinding speed of blurring shapes. Brennus raises his arm in a wide, arcing, sweep before bringing it down near Reed's neck. Reed bursts apart in the next instant, exploding into a swarm of bees that engulfs Brennus in a shroud of pestilence. The bees collect behind Brennus, morphing back into Reed as he plunges the letter opener into Brennus' back, wrenching it viciously down to carve a deep, bloody line into him. Then, Reed kicks Brennus forward, sending Brennus stumbling to remain on his feet.

The mass of fellas assembled around us begins to push forward, surging in to protect their king. With all my remaining strength, I create a magical barrier, surrounding Reed, Brennus, and me within it. As it pushes back the snarling horde, sweat forms on my brow. The Gancanagh nearest us throw elf darts that strike hard against the wall, making energy surge back into me and then pull it away as I try to maintain the invisible edifice. A shower of magical fire rains around us as other spells are being continually cast at us.

Brennus readjusts his knife, flicking it around in a circular motion against his palm. His eyes close briefly as his lips move in a silent spell. The next time the knife spins Brennus spins with it. He becomes a blurring whirl, as pieces of him break off, falling away to become several *Brenns* standing beneath the glow of the lampposts.

He cloned himself! I gasp, seeing Reed halt his forward progress, glancing around at each of the dozen dark-haired killers that resemble the Gancanagh leader.

Reed growls as his eyebrows slash together. His chin drops in a predatory stare while four exact copies of Brennus launch forward to attack him. Reed slashes the first, cutting a deep gash into his chest. The wounded *Brenn* is pulled backward into the Brennus standing at the back in the pool of light; his face is etched in pain before he's absorbed into the other, causing them to merge into a single being. A laceration breaks open on Brennus' chest; his face blanches as he touches his chest with the tips of his fingers, welding the injury closed with the light of magic.

I glance at all the *Brenns* one-by-one. *They're not magical clones. They're pieces of Brennus,* I surmise.

Vicious cuts break through Reed's defenses as the *Brenns* mob him from every angle. Reed's chest bleeds with jagged slashes, blood running from his perfect chest. Reed hacks three *Brenns* back at once, dispelling them from him. They weave a path back to Brennus, fitting back into him with devastating effects. Wounds appear, marring Brennus' abdomen and face.

In my distraction, my barrier falters, allowing a handful of Gancanagh soldiers to slip through it. I grunt, concentrating again and closing the gap. An agonizing stab of pain breaks in my chest as I see Reed get shot in the back by a gun-wielding fella. Reed cuts the arm off of a *Brenn* he's fighting while wrenching his knife blade from the hand before the appendage hits the ground. Never hesitating Reed pivots, throwing the knife at the fella who shot him; it slices the fella's head off. As the pieces of the destroyed *Brenn* collect and shift back to the original, the other *Brenns* hesitate.

Reed breaks free from the remaining *Brenns* attacking him and focuses on the fellas. In less time than it takes me to breathe in and out, the fellas in our sanctum are dead, strewn like dirty laundry upon the ground, killed by the letter opener in Reed's hand. I'm panting now as my entire body shakes with a need to give in to the pressure being exerted on it. A whimper escapes from between my parted lips and I close my eyes. I'm connecting to the energy flowing through the fellas on the other side of the barrier. They're trying to steal it from me, but it's as if the energy is magnetized, accruing in me as if by choice: choosing me, not them.

I groan as the flames inside me become excruciating. When I open my eyes, I glance at Brennus, only two *Brenns* remain, the rest have been reconnected with Brennus. He's a mess, his body a roadmap of abuse. He's bent over, holding his bloody abdomen, but he's also healing quickly. Brennus' eyes meet mine and he tries to hide his pain from me as he calls the remaining *Brenns* back to him. In that moment, his pain makes mine more intense and I cry out.

"Evie?" Reed says, turning his full attention to me.

"Burning," I say desperately, feeling a tear trickle down my cheek. Reed moves to my side, but as he extends his hand to me he winces as heat and energy flow in a current into him, but he doesn't let me go, instead, he picks me up in his arms.

"Reed, run," I warn him, "I'll open up a gap and you can fly—"

"I'm not leaving you," he growls.

"Something's happening to me," I groan.

In the same moment, the magical wall I created to hold everything back slips nearer to us, caving in as it draws closer. Soon it will no longer exist. I try to hold it, but the energy I'm using to create it wants to swirl into me instead.

"Ye have ta let go of da energy, *mo chroí.*" Brennus says in a harsh tone. He doubles over in pain, unable to move toward me. "'Twill kill ye if ye do na!"

I shake my head as suffering contorts my face. Hostile soldiers lurch in our direction when the curtain that keeps them back hops forward a few feet. Anticipation at getting to Reed shines in their eyes like lust. Hands splay, aching to touch Reed with their toxic skin, and fangs extend with resonating *clicks.* They're primed to tear him apart; he won't escape again.

Reed's fingers are tender on my brow, brushing my hair from my face. "Let go, Evie," Reed whispers to me.

"I can't," I say through gritted teeth. "They'll kill you!"

"Whatever happens, love, we'll be together," he says in a gentle way. "Let go."

With most of my remaining strength, I open a gap in the barrier above us, enough for him to fly up and pass through. "It's open—please go—you have to get away from me. Something's wrong with me," I whisper. Reed shakes his head no. "Please—" I beg him.

"Not without you. Never without you," he says. He looks into my eyes and mouths silently, "I love you." Then, his lips lower to mine and I have no choice. I let go.

Reed

CHAPTER 28

Crestwood

God, please protect her...

Rippling, white light rolls outward from Evie in a fiery shockwave. The blinding energy impacts me; it pulsates throughout my body and I feel as if I've been set aflame. My jaw clenches in an effort to retain the air within my lungs and my arms close tighter around Evie to keep her with me, but I'm not strong enough. When I'm torn from her, I'm blown within the undulating energy, tumbling in the chaos of the inferno. The deafening euphony of thunder eulogizes silence, leaving my eardrums muffled when its noise is spent. Within seconds, I come to rest on a patch of charred earth.

*Evie...*My fingers twitch on the smoldering ground.

*Breathe...*with effort I manage to expand my collapsed lungs. The sound of my gasping inhales are almost inaudible to me. The aching-tear of scorched membrane within my lungs makes me want to rebel against my need for oxygen. I stamp down the desire I have to hold my breath and I force myself to inhale again.

The sweet smell of crackling flesh hangs in the air. Soon, however, that scent is replaced by a burnt odor of skin. I lie on the ground in confusion until something soft touches my cheek. Opening my eyes, I brush away a gray flake of ash only to have it replaced by several flakes that drift down like falling snow from the sky.

Evie...

The light around me has extinguished; the lampposts have all fallen over in inanimate heaps of melted iron. The ground surrounding me is a large, blackened circle reaching out in at least a fifty-meter radius. Blinking, I try to clear away the soot from my eyes.

Evie...Evie...

I attempt to sit up; my eyes close involuntarily and I slouch to the ground once more. The pain is nearly insuperable. Dead, blackened skin hangs from my arms in places; new flesh is rapidly forming beneath, but it's pink and tender, barely covering muscle.

Pain is ephemeral...control it...GET UP...

My arms must have somehow protected my face because my skin is intact there; it's just my arms, legs, chest, and abdomen that are in the process of healing.

EVIE...

I move my head, searching for my angel. Dark shadows sprawl out on the ground and it takes me moments to recognize what they are: they're the ashen silhouette remains of the Gancanagh soldiers. The fellas have disintegrated into embers, blanketing the once snow-covered ground with their essence.

FIND EVIE...GET UP! EVIE...

Ignoring the agony it takes to bend forward, I get to my knees. I hang my head as I compartmentalize the pain. My hands draw into fists. I push up to my feet and feel my wings unfurl to balance and stabilize me. I begin to shake: the result of trauma. I ignore that, too.

Where are you now...be here...please...be here...Evie...

A soft luminescence draws my eyes to it. Brennus stirs to life on the ground several yards from me. His skin is glowing, lighting the very air and pushing back the shadows. He brings his radiant hands near his face, examining them like he's never seen them before. Something moves behind his back, and as he seems to feel it, he shifts, peering over his shoulder. Brennus' wings knit out behind him; the rapid meshing of their velvety-texture wefts in spiraling, symphonic patterns as they reach to points above his head. At the conclusion of their regeneration, they float for just a moment, entirely white and resplendent. His skin glimmers golden, taking on the healthy veneer of a faerie. But in moments, dark splotches appear at the tips of Brennus' white wings, running like dye down them until they turn as ebony as his hair. His skin pales a bit too, it doesn't revert to the stark pallor of a Gancanagh, but neither does it retain its faerie-like glow.

As the shimmer of Brennus' skin dims, he casts his hands in small circles while his lips move silently. Orbs of light float up above us, illuminating the ruined lawn of Central Hall. Ashes continue to float down and it would be beautiful if it weren't repulsive.

Tear his ears from him and push them down his throat. Pluck out his eyes from their sockets. Crush his cranium between my fists...no, that death is too expeditious...he must suffer...why didn't Brennus die along with his soldiers...

I take a step in his direction. Butterflies flutter in my abdomen; I lose my breath.

Evie...

I pause and scan the terrain. Lying still and broken on the ground in the spot where we'd last been together, I find my love. Her dark-feathered wings are a stark contrast to her pale skin as they fan out, framing her. I can detect no movement coming from her and since I cannot hear her heartbeat, I cannot ascertain if she lives. The acrid taste of fear burns my throat as I immediately change direction to go to her. My muscles feel like inflexible wires as I force my knees to bend, limping forward. I stretch out my wings, they lift me off the ground easily and I fly to her, touching down on the ground by her feet. I sink to my knees by her side before I gather her to me in my arms. Her cheek rests against my neck and I blanch at how cold it is.

She's not breathing...

My lips move near her ear and I can hardly speak past the tightening in my throat as I whisper, "Evie, don't go. Stay with me. I'm lost here without you..." I glance up at the sky, seeing the moon shine white with indifference against the night. "Don't take her from me... please," I manage to say, as my jaw grows taut, "and if that is too much to ask, then...take me, too. Forever is too long..."

I feel her breath stir against my skin. The blood from her bite wounds pulses from her and smears on my chest. *She's alive...*

"That's it, love," I say coaxingly, fighting the need to crush her to me. "Breathe."

"She is bleeding out," Brennus' deep voice states beside me. It sounds as desolate as the burnt, leafless trees behind him.

Kill him. A low growl rips from me as I pull Evie closer to protect her from him.

"She's dying!" Brennus says in an urgent tone I can barely hear. He kneels down beside us with an anxious expression. "Give her ta me."

"Attempt to take her from me and you die now. I will never let you change her," I growl.

Brennus scowls as he reaches his long, white hand out. He brushes his fingers against my cheek. "Give Genevieve ta me," he orders in an even tone.

"Never. Going. To. Happen," I growl back between clenched teeth as I snatch Evie back further from him.

Brennus' eyes widen as he states, "Ye're na enthralled."

"No," I reply as it registers in my mind that either Brennus has lost his ability to enthrall his victims, or I have become immune to it...

or both. I draw back my fist and punch him in the face, knocking him back from Evie. With one eye still closed, Brennus shakes his head, a bit stunned before he rubs his chin ruefully. Then, both eyes open and narrow as he studies me.

"Ye'll let her die?" he asks in an angry tone. His black moth-like wings move then, extending in agitation. The glow from the hovering orbs above reflects on his wings and casts garish shadows behind him.

"I will save her soul from you—from Sheol," I murmur, feeling panicked at my own words. *Can I save more than her soul? Can I save her life?* Overwhelming sorrow crushes my heart and I can hardly breathe.

"She's moin," Brennus hisses with venom as his face coils, ready to strike. "Ye can na keep me from her." His lips move silently, as he casts his hands in my direction.

My arms open involuntarily when a powerful force seizes me. The air is quickly being drawn out of my lungs as I feel a force shoving me back. Evie begins slipping from my arms. Her hair slides over my palms like unraveling kite strings. My empty hands feel frozen when she's no longer in them. When she is in Brennus' arms, he holds her to him, kissing her temple. In the same instant, I'm magically thrown back away from them. Losing her again is suffocating me; the loss of her is excruciating.

I come to rest on the ground several yards away from them. My eyes narrow and I growl, getting to my feet immediately. Brennus gently strokes Evie's hair back from her forehead. I launch at Brennus, but he raises his hand. I'm knocked back again, coming to rest on the charred earth once more. When I rise, I come up short, my wings stretch out at full extension as I'm levitated off the ground and held in stasis as if I'm a specimen pinned to a matte.

Brennus smiles tauntingly. "She has changed me, *aingeal.* Her blood is in me veins and it has protected me from her most lethal weapon— her incendiary nature. 'Tis da only way ye survived as well. Ye have her blood in ye. I feel her power within me. Da energy she has released has rendered me stronger...she gave me a power-up. Me magic works on ye now," Brennus finishes with a hint of awe in his tone.

"You're becoming alive?" I ask, trying to distract him from Evie.

Brennus frowns. "I felt alive...for a moment, but it did na last."

Find a way to break his spell then reach inside him and pull out his spine. Crush him...

I soften my face, making it expressionless. "She can try again—" I say urgently, trying to find the persuasive argument that will stop him from sharing his blood with her.

His lips twist in desperation. "She can na if she dies!" Brennus growls.

"BRENNUS!" I shout in frustration.

"I'll save her, *aingeal*. I'll make her strong again," Brennus says. *Click*, his fangs engage and he uses them to tear open his flesh. He lets his dark blood well up.

I pull with all my strength against the force that holds me aloft. Pain doesn't deter me; it makes all of this more real. It increases my determination to get to her. "You'll lose what you love the most! She won't be the same without her soul! You'll destroy the only part of her that truly loves you..."

He holds his bleeding wrist above Evie's lips, but he pauses. I see him stiffen and I hold my breath. His hand begins to tremble as his jaw tightens.

Convince him not to kill her. In a soft tone I say, "You will have a lovely shell of her, but her soul will no longer be yours. She will belong to Sheol for eternity..."

A groan filled with agony comes from Brennus. His wrist twitches and I flinch like a knife cut. After a moment, he drops his bloody wrist from Evie and clutches her limp form to him.

"Why can I na do it?" Brennus spits out in torment. "Why can I na turn her?"

Relief makes my neck bend and my head hang forward. "You love her soul—willing or not. Her soul has been rooting for you—for your redemption."

"Dere is no redemption for me, ye know dat," Brennus says the first thing that I can agree to.

"I know," I say without hesitation.

"She does na accept dat," he says.

"No," I agree.

"I can na let her go," Brennus says, waveringly. "She has ta stay on dis side of eternity. Immortality is a curse wi'out her..."

My eyes flare wide as fear explodes in me that he will change his mind again. I struggle for a way to save my angel. *Brennus is the only other being to share my fears of immortality after her loss...*

"Give her back to me and I will take her to Russell—the other," I say urgently. Brennus' response is to clutch her tighter. "He can save her—it's the only way!"

"Da other," Brennus murmurs. Pure malice etches his face for a moment as he battles himself. He's struggling over the extreme torture of losing her again: handing her back to me. I have no altruistic feelings for him, even having felt the same when I had to leave Evie with him.

He must die...soon. My need to crush him is a palatable thing.

"Russell is exactly like her—she healed me, he can heal her." I wait, unable to breathe. I watch Evie's face: her eyes remain closed, her brow unfurled. Blood drips openly from her wounds, like the ticking of time. *Tick, tick, tick...*

"He's weak," Brennus says dismissively.

I shake my head. "Russell's strong—that's why you wanted her to deliver him to you. He'll save her," I state with absolute certainty. "He'll make her stronger. She'll be able to defeat Sheol. If you let Sheol have Evie's soul now, then it's over—her innocence will be tied to the damned. One day you may have to look upon her soul—when it again comes in search of the body from which you separated it. She'll bring all of the Fallen with her." I taste bile on my tongue as I show him the future I fear the most. "You now have the means to keep her with you without turning her. Your magic is immense. You'll find a way to have her without losing her soul once she's healed."

Brennus falters, his eyebrows knitting together. "I'll na lose any part of her ta dem," Brennus says in a tormented voice. He strokes her wing lovingly. Then he bends close to her and whispers, "Ye're me only love...so ye can na die. I'll come for ye, *mo chroí*, after da other makes ye well again. Do na get comfortable wi' da *aingeal*...he's na for ye. I'm still yer king."

He waves his white hand and removes the invisible force that holds me aloft and I instantly fall to the ground. I'm next to them in a second, extending my arms to take Evie back from his. Gingerly, Brennus relinquishes her to me. Immediately, something eases in my chest, an ache around my heart is soothed for a moment. Brennus' face becomes ashen, more from her loss than from his undeath. Pain shines in his eyes. The orbs of light above us dim, like I've taken his power from him, too.

Yes. Suffer.

Brennus swallows hard. "Find da other quickly," he orders. He pulls an ebony brooch pinned to a black ribbon from a pocket. "Dis will bring ye ta him...if he still lives. 'Tis da portal she had wi' her. Dis will lead ta where dey planned ta meet."

When he hands me the brooch, he grimaces with anguish and balls his hands into fists. "Do na let her die or I will kill ye slowly. I'll be around ta collect her soon."

I don't assuage his fear. "I'll end you when you come," I promise him.

His smile is sinister. "Ye'll try," he says as I open the portal and Evie and I begin to distort.

A pull begins in the pit of my stomach, interrupting for a moment the flutter of butterflies that I have there. I jerk forward with Evie pressed to me and we surge and contort to fit into the portal. Once inside, dark walls swirl by silently. The ebony stone is lined with veins of mother-of-pearl; it shimmers like the inside of a seashell. Brighter light appears ahead and I instinctively protect Evie's body with my own as we near the threshold. Emerging from the portal, Evie and I spill out upon the floor of the media room. I flinch as my new skin breaks open in places and begins to bleed. The *pop* in my ears is my auditory canals adjusting to the pressure in the room and everything is incredibly loud once more.

Anya gasps from her seat on the wide leather sofa; the soft blanket around her shoulders slips from her as her hand comes up to cover her parted lips. Russell, seated next to her, has his elbows resting on his thighs with his head cradled in both of his hands. He looks up when I try to rise from the floor with Evie's still body resting against my chest.

Russell leaps to his feet, yelling, "ZEE!"

My cheek rests against the hardwood as I orient myself. Tremors of pounding feet coming toward me vibrate the floor. Evie's head is pressed tightly to my chest; I would pull her inside of me and have my heart beat for us both if I could. Russell looks confused as he stands over me. He doesn't know where it's okay to touch me to help me to rise.

Never having been much acquainted with the word "help" I'm unable to say it even now. I do what I always do when the day has shown me its worst: I make do. I manage to stagger to my feet with Evie in my arms, but I do it clumsily.

Buns, standing at the window, takes a step back from us in shock. Her hand reaches for the silken drapery as she steadies herself. Evie and I must look frightening to her and the irony in that hits me: she is a Reaper who now fears our deaths. We must resemble the dead. My skin is red and raw, peeling off of me in places where it's regenerating. My wings are molting, shedding charred feathers as new ones replace them. Evie is so pale and blood-soaked that it appears that there can be no way that she still lives. But she does. I can finally hear her heart beating...*th-thump...thump...th-thump... thump*...it's very faint, but it's there. It falls between the cracks in my heart, helping me to control my panic as that raging fear tries to control me.

"EVIE!" Russell howls next to us. "ZEE, THEY'RE HERE!" I know his shout is from fear rather than to necessitate the presence of

Zephyr, since a whisper would suffice to get Zee's attention wherever he is in the house.

Zephyr enters the media room on the tread of panther feet, silent. With him, clutched in one glove-covered fist, is a flailing Gancanagh soldier. He is no threat to Zee, having had his arms cut off at the elbows, but Zee is taking every precaution with him anyway. He must have tried to touch Zee otherwise Zephyr would have left him intact. The Gancanagh's death-white, twisted face changes as he catches the scent of blood pouring from Evie; it turns hungry with yearning eyes as his fangs gleam under the soft lighting in the room. I feel nothing for him, the evil soul-skinner—the animated corpse. He would destroy Evie in seconds if he were to be turned free. He can end now.

Like the scent of rain, the shift in the air alerts me to the storm coming. Russell is pulling energy to him and I wait for the ripple of thunder to roll silent as the lightning from his hands already begins to warm.

"Put her down over there, Reed!" Russell indicates the wide, cracked media table in the middle of the room.

I feel a soft touch on my elbow as Brownie materializes next to me. She puts her other hand on my wing, gently urging me forward to the table as her lips curl in a smile of encouragement, but her eyes are glassy with unmitigated fear.

My tread is centipede-like, as my will to move must wait for my body to comply. I lurch forward but seem to get nowhere. A chair falls to the floor as I bump into it. Buns's eyes widen from her position across the room at my uncharacteristic lack of fluidity. In the next second, Buns touches my other elbow, helping to guide me to the table. When we reach it, I place Evie upon the surface as gently as I can. I stroke her tangled hair away from her pale face. Her eyelids never move.

Crouching down close to her ear, I want to beg her for her forgiveness for all that she's been through—for this. Instead, I whisper, "I'm lost without you, Evie. I'm only found in your eyes." Something in my heart squeezes painfully.

*Do I pray for her life or for mine? They're one in the same...Be this soul in Thine hands...*I stop, unable to pray for her ascension. *I cannot let her go,* I think in agony. I try again, *May this soul in Thine hands be with me...always...*

Zephyr slams the Gancanagh down next to Evie on the table. The soldier's neck thrusts and rears forward, his fangs snapping at her in his desire for her blood as she remains just out of his reach. Russell's hand covers the Gancanagh's chest and he simultaneously motions Zephyr to step away from them. Zephyr glances toward me, his jaw clenches at his inability to help further. Like me, there is nothing else he can do.

"Reed," Russell casts me a meaningful look; he needs me to back away from Evie so that he can lay his hand on her.

Tearing myself away from her now is nearly impossible. I feel like she'll ascend if I'm not touching her and the guilt of wanting her to stay with me is crushing. My throat tightens and it's almost impossible to speak, but I force myself to whisper, "The most fortunate day of my life," my voice falters and I have to pause before continuing, "was when I stumbled across you, Evie. I need you to stay with me... please...I will love you every day until my last. I promise you that I will." Then I do the hardest thing I've ever done in my life: I let go of her.

The fear that has been at a manageable level oxidizes: it turns rancid. I quietly shake, rooted to the floor, unable to move. Russell's fingers begin to glow with the gold, diamond-fire light of raw energy. In moments, Russell's hand fuses to Evie while his other hand does the same to the Gancanagh. Russell's face contorts in pain, like a pianist with his hands upon ivory keys as he pounds out an exquisite melody.

Evie's face is placid, and its lack of any expression of pain causes sweat to form on my brow. I fear that she's already dead, even when I can still feel her. Bite marks slowly recede on her pale skin, as they break open on Russell's neck and forearms. Russell's wounds only last for moments before they heal, but the Gancanagh thrashing on the table begins to bleed in earnest, black blood oozing from his undead flesh. And then, what I've been waiting for happens.

"Gah ah," Evie arches her back in agony while inhaling an enormous gasp of air. Her eyes open wide as her hands come up to clutch Russell's hand on her chest, attempting to knock it away, but she's weak. Russell's eyes connect with Evie's and he grits his teeth, silently communicating that he feels her pain. Next to them, the Gancanagh's eyes grow black and bow out like an albino frog. His eyes burst and black blood runs from them while dust billows up in a black cloud from his mouth. It smells like the smoke from a peat fire.

The light from Russell's hands slowly dies and he sags against the table as he moves them to help prop himself up. When he looks up at Evie again, she begins to cry. "NOOO! REEEED!" A wailing scream rips from Evie. "REED! RUN!" She struggles to move as gasping screams fly from her. Her elbows flail, trying to move her to a sitting position, but she's too weak.

"Red!" Russell says wearily. His strength is gone; it took most of what he had to heal her. His brown eyes connect with her lovely gray ones.

"No, Russell, Nooo!" She wails again. Her hand reaches up to cover his mouth as her own mouth takes on the shape of agony. "I killed him, Russell! I killed Reed!" Evie cries like I've never heard her cry before—not even for her uncle. This is excruciating, unconcealed terror wrapped in guilt. This isn't the heartbreak of loss; it's the sickness of tragedy and sorrow. *Tristitiae.*

I have to move because it's too painful not to. I force myself forward into Evie's line of sight. Her breath catches in mid-sob when she sees me, but tears continue to run unchecked from her eyes.

"Reed," she whispers, her torment interrupted by the thread of hope as her eyes rove over me, taking in my torched skin. Her fingers reach out to touch my chest, but she hesitates. She bites her lip and her fingers tremble because she doesn't know where she can touch me without hurting me. I reach out and take her hand in mine, bringing it to my cheek. When I lay her hand upon my face, I close my eyes in relief.

I exalt in the language that comes naturally to me—Angel.

I hear Evie choke, trying to stifle another sob. My eyes open and I reach for her, taking her in my arms. I pick her up and hug her to me. Her arms slip around my nape as her cheek rests against my neck. She's crying again, huge wracking sobs. I glance at Russell who's watching us as he leans exhaustedly against the table.

"Thank you, Russell," I say.

Russell shrugs. "For what? Oh, that? Pshh, that was nothin'," he says with a slow smile full of hubris, but his eyes tell another story.

I frown. "Whatever you have left, Russell, you have to direct it out to protect the house," I say in a low, deadly serious tone.

Russell immediately straightens, becoming fully alert once more. "Why?" he asks with dread in his voice.

"Because if you don't, Brennus will try to kill us all," I reply, unable to say it any plainer. "Everyone but Evie."

Zephyr's voice breaks the silence that hangs in the air. "He lives?" he asks.

My jaw clenches and I can hardly speak. "He's more powerful than he was before—his magic works on me now. Evie's blood protected him and when she annihilated his soldiers with energy...it changed him. Can you protect us, Russell?" I ask him pointedly.

Russell says in a hoarse whisper, "I can. I'll shield the house now. Nothing will get in."

Shock and haunting stares meet my glance as I look around the room at each of the members of my family: Buns, Brownie, Zephyr, Russell, and Anya. I know they want an explanation, but I just can't give that to them now. Instead, I turn away from them and leave the room with Evie in my arms. I make my way slowly to the stairs in the foyer and climb them.

When we reach my room, I hesitate at the threshold. It's been destroyed. I should have some emotion for what I'm seeing, but I don't; it's the smallest of trespasses in all of this. Turning, I move on to the bedroom that Evie once occupied. I walk through it to the attached bathroom, closing the door behind us.

Cold water falls like rain from the ceiling mounted showerhead when I turn it on. I don't bother to try to take our clothes off, I only wait a moment until it becomes warm and then I enter the glass enclosure with Evie in my arms. Water beats down on us causing the ashes in our hair to make dark trails of black tears on our cheeks. The soot mixes with blood to form swirling patterns as it washes away into the drain.

After a few minutes, I sink to the wet floor and lean against the tiled wall with Evie on my lap. Gently, I stroke her wing. The water soothes my skin, helping me to heal. I flex my hand, watching the raw hue fade to a normal, healthy tone.

"I thought I killed you," Evie whispers. She hasn't lifted her forehead from the hollow of my throat.

"Not today," my abraded voice whispers in return. I squeeze her reassuringly. "Today, you saved me."

"He didn't die?" she asks without breathing.

"No, he didn't," I answer.

"Then he'll come for me," her tone holds no hint of doubt.

"He'll try," I murmur. I won't deceive her.

Evie stirs in my arms; her chin tilts up and brushes against my cheek. Butterflies stir too, increasing at her simple touch. My fingers tighten on her hip as I react to the attraction between us. Her heart begins to sing to me, the Siren's song that's calling me to shipwreck. I go to it willingly. When her lips meet mine, I know I'm lost, I'm found—I'm home.

Something between a groan and a growl comes from me as she shifts in my arms, straddling my hips. The black silk of her dress rides up her thighs as my hands caress her bare skin. She presses herself to me and the feeling of silk touching my chest is a thousand times more exquisite since being healed. My hand slowly moves up her, past the perfect curve of her hip, up her back to her shoulder. Water continues to pour on us as I slip the dark strap of her dress away from her.

When my mouth touches her shoulder, her hands slip into my hair and tighten. It does something to me. I reach up and grasp her dress, rending it in half and pulling it from her. The only thing that comes between us now are what's left of my jeans and a flimsy, lacy square of material that attempts to pass as her undergarment. I correct that with a soft tug to the delicate fabric that clings to her hips. Evie's sultry red wings spread wide as the lace square falls away from her and is tossed to the corner of the shower.

She reaches down and pops the button on my ragged denim. As I stand up with her in my arms, the heavy, water-drenched fabric shrugs from my hips. I hold Evie as her lissome legs wrap around my waist. Her wet skin against mine is more sensual than the silk of her dress had been. The muscles in my abdomen tighten as my need for her grows.

Her wings flutter and another deep growl is torn from me. My wings respond, spreading out to full extension as I press her against the tiled wall. Delicate fingertips softly toy with the waistband of my underwear before she gives them a tug and it becomes a nonissue. My hands cup her perfect bottom, and then my heart nearly explodes when she moves her hands to mine, squeezing it.

I have to kiss her again; I start with her lips. When I taste her on my tongue, I want more. I need more. Tugging on her bottom lip with mine elicits a soft groan of pleasure from her. I live in the sound of it.

When our bodies fit together, like pieces falling into place, I'm nearly undone by it and by her eyes. They narrow and her forehead leans forward to rest against mine. Through her eyes, I can almost see inside her soul. That's where I long to be: centered near her soul, wedged between it and her heart. Her angelic body and heart are mine, have always been mine, but Russell was right when he said her soul loves him and now there is a piece of her heart that loves Brennus. I want it all; I understand that now. The battle for her entire heart *and* her soul starts now.

I begin my seduction as I pull my lips from hers. My assault on her soul is a slow rhythm that increases with her heartbeat. Trailing kisses over her neck, my lips come to rest on my wings imprinted on her chest. *They're still there. My aspire.* A small smile forms for the first time. I press my lips to the symbol branded on her, speaking to her kittenish soul in Angel. I know that Evie doesn't understand that language yet, but her soul knows it for its own. I tell her soul that I love her—that I will wait for her to love me the way that I love her.

I lose myself in her: her scent, her touch, and the taste of her. I will never get enough. There will never be enough. Goose bumps break out on her arms, even with the heat between us. When Evie cries out, it's my name on her lips; it's in the only language I care about: hers.

My self-control reaches its limit. I gather up her heavy wet hair at the base of her nape in my hand, pulling her lips from me so that her eyes are forced to look into mine. "Evie, I—I can't be gentle," I growl between my clenched teeth.

Her nails dig into my back. "I don't care how you touch me, just touch me."

My stomach clenches with the rush that only she gives me. I thrust her back against the wall. The tiles crack behind her wings, spidering and falling in pieces to the shower floor. Her thighs squeeze me tighter, drawing me nearer to her while her teeth gently rake my shoulder.

"I thought I lost you," she murmurs close to my ear as she raises her head.

"Never," I promise. Her flat belly rubs against mine while the sultry scent from her wet hair drives me on. "I'll always find the thread that binds me to you."

"Reed," my name is a plea on her lips.

My head swims with desire for her and I'm unable to come up for air. "I love you," I murmur, and being most assuredly unable to speak further, we both fall silent, allowing our bodies to communicate the rest of what is in our hearts.

Evie

CHAPTER 29

Grace

My hair lies across Reed's shoulder like a mantle; the strands shine with brassy fire on his perfect skin. The rising sun touches the rumpled white sheets of our bed, turning them golden. I haven't slept. I can't close my eyes because the war is just outside our door; it wages on. I know that now. Killers will call on me. I can't hold back their shadows from falling upon us.

"You have to sleep, Evie," Reed says, softly touching my hair as his thigh moves against mine. Its weight is comforting as he pulls me tighter against his body. We'd made love all night, not like we had in the shower, but slowly, a rediscovery of each other—a gentle exploration to assure each other that we'd survived.

"I can't..." I trail off.

"Why not?" Reed prompts me.

"They're out there," I say quietly. Goose bumps rise on my body; I suppress the need that I have to shudder. "Brennus, the Fallen, scary monsters I don't even know about yet..."

Reed feels my reaction and his hands smooth over my arms, rubbing them reassuringly. "Yes, they are out there somewhere. But you can't fight the next battle until it comes. You have to recognize the moments of grace and live in them. Fighting the invisible enemy will only lead to exhaustion. This moment is a gift of peace. Take it."

"What if I can't stop them?" I ask in a shallow voice.

Reed is quiet for a moment as he traces the line of my arm to my shoulder. "You are an extraordinary being, Evie. But, even in that, you're not God. If you accept that, then the regret over your inability to control the outcome of any of this is easier to bear."

I roll over and straddle his hips, looking down at him. His hand comes up to cup my cheek and I turn my lips to it and kiss his palm.

Reed uses his thumb to trace my lips. I part them, lightly nipping his thumb. He watches me with an unwavering stare as I lightly flick my tongue over the tip of it.

"The things that you can do to me with just a simple touch," Reed murmurs. "Come to think of it, you can do the same without even touching me. It can just be the scent of your hair as you walk near me, or the elegant lift of your eyebrow when you ask a question. I have to constantly restrain myself from pulling you to me and tearing your clothes from you."

"I'm at a distinct disadvantage now," I say, looking down at myself. "No clothes."

"Then I must press my advantage," he smiles, sitting up and allowing just about every single inch of our bodies to touch. I melt against him. As our bodies mesh as one, I know that this is the heaven I want to fight for: the one in my arms.

In the quiet afterward, I lie in Reed's arms waiting for my heartbeat to come slowly down. I wonder if anything will ever be normal again. A small fire burns in the grate, warming the room against the frost covering the windowpanes.

I breathe Reed in. My cheek rests in the hollow of his chest; his fingers stroke the arch of my lower back, following the line downward. There are no bruises upon his skin. His scars are all healed—all the ones I can see, but below the surface, fresh abrasions reside. He spent days with Brennus. He'd been abused; how badly, I don't know. It comes to me now that this is how Reed must have felt when I was with Brennus and he couldn't find me. He had to bear that pain for months. I only had a taste; his captivity lasted days. *What is the extent of the devastation?*

I turn my lips to his chest, pressing them to him. I want to be the shelter from the storm for him, but I'm the storm. I have a tangled crown upon my brow, an unwilling queen. I'm a tragedy in the making. The phantom ribbon binding my heart to Reed's violently rejects such thoughts; it tightens painfully. I'll fight anyone who tries to keep us apart, anyone who tries to hurt him again. *But, what if it's me who hurts him again?*

"Reed...are you...did they—"

"I don't want to speak of it. It's over," Reed says, picking up my hand and bringing my fingers to his lips. He kisses them, his lips sliding lower, kissing my wrist. It causes a shiver to pass through me.

"How can you not?" I ask, but I know it's possible to be hurt and then not want to talk about it.

"I should say that I never dwell on it. When certain outcomes are anticipated, it's not overly surprising when it comes to fruition. I was prepared to die. It was a blessing that I did not."

"Don't do that," I say in a hushed tone. Lifting his lips from me, Reed stops kissing me to raise his eyebrow in question. "Don't die for me."

"I could say the same words to you, but I know you won't listen, just as I won't listen. I swore to protect you with my body. I broke that vow."

"You didn't—"

"I did, Evie," he says in a pain-filled tone. "You should never have done what you did. I could've killed you."

"Then I would've died with you," I murmur.

Reed's response is a deep growl of frustration before he says, "How did you even come to be in the Knights Bar? Why didn't your father protect you?"

"He wasn't interested in saving you, Reed. He wouldn't have been able to get you away from Brennus. I had to go!"

"Did he try to stop you?"

"Yes," I answer.

"And you defied him?" Reed says in a concerned tone.

"He's lucky that's all I did to him," I reply as my eyebrows draw together. "Xavier drugged me and tied me up. It was Anya who freed me. You're here with me now because your family loves you: Zee, Buns, Brownie, Russell, and Anya."

"And you," he adds in a soft tone.

"And me. I'm your family, your *aspire*," I say in a quiet voice. "I have to protect you. You're mine."

"And you're mine," he says.

"I am," I agree in all seriousness.

"Do you trust me?" he asks me evenly. His green eyes, fringed by the dark, masculine lashes, bore into mine."

"Do I trust you? Reed, you're the *only* one I trust." I sit up to face him. I kneel in front of him on the bed.

He nods once, and then gets to his feet and drags the sheet with him to wrap around his hips. He moves toward the bedroom door and slips out. I have a need to follow him; it's more than an impulse, it's bone-deep panic to protect him. I make myself stay where I am. He returns in moments, allowing my heartbeat to come down to an acceptable level. In his hand, he has a simple, medieval dagger. He crawls back on the bed and kneels in front of me.

Reed holds the sharp end of the blade in his closed fist nonthreateningly between us, like a cross. He speaks in Angel, his sexy voice clear and unfaltering. Then he pauses. He switches to English and says, "Genevieve Ava Claremont, with my blood, I pledge my fidelity, my loyalty, and my allegiance to you, and only you, under God."

With his free hand, he grasps the hilt of the dagger, dragging the blade over the closed fist that clutches it. When his hand begins to bleed, he opens his palm showing the cut; its rusty scent fills the air between us. He lays the dagger aside and reaches his uncut hand to pluck a silky, gray feather from his wing. He dips the spine of the feather in his blood before he reaches over, inserting his feather among the crimson ones on my wing.

Reed leans forward, resting his forehead in the hollow of my breast while his arms wrap around my waist. I pull him closer, my hands entwining in his hair. His wings are magnificent, stretching out around us.

"Reed?" I ask, wondering what just happened.

Hearing the question in my voice, Reed says, "Now your father can't come between us, Evie. I swore my allegiance to you. You are my authority. The only one above you for me is God. You were created Seraphim—my natural leader. Only a direct messenger from God can break it now."

"What?" I say, my mouth becoming dry.

"I knew it could come to this. There will be a struggle for power. Your father is a leader. He will fight you for control of you—of the army that will come to align with you."

"Align with me?"

"Divine angels have scattered the world over, they'll come and decide who they'll follow."

"I don't want to lead them."

"You have no choice unless you want to be at Tau's mercy. He may not allow us to remain together. We have to find a way to get him to align with you without giving up your power. And you *will* have an army, whether you want it or not."

"Here, give me the knife—I'll swear my allegiance to you—"

"You can't, love," he says, pulling back to look into my eyes. "It has to be you who leads, but you're not alone."

"I'm afraid," I whisper.

"Don't be afraid," he murmurs, wrapping me tighter in his arms. "We're together. I'll be with you. Anything that I have is yours. I'll fight for you and with you until my last breath. I'll never again break my vow to protect you. Whatever comes, we face it together—as one."

"As one," I agree. There are no more words between us. We seal our promises with our bodies.

⌒〇

Hunger is the one thing that finally drives Reed and me from our room. Wrapped in a towel, I let Reed lead me by the hand down the hall to his room. Rifling through his closet, he hands me one of his button down shirts. It's the best option because the Gancanagh have taken every scrap of clothing that once belonged to me. They probably have it in Ireland...I falter...*no, the Gancanagh don't have it now. I slaughtered so many of them...my father is in Ireland and he has everything that once belonged to me.* My hands shake in fear, remembering what it is I can do with them. They're capable of incinerating everything I see.

Reed notices my hands. He takes one in his own, bringing my fingers to his lips and kissing them. I get lost in his gaze; it warms me, abating the chilling dread. When he lets go of my hand, his fingers go to the buttons of my shirt, buttoning them for me so I don't have to awkwardly try to do it myself. When he's finished, he drags on his own jeans. He draws in his wings, pulling a white cotton t-shirt over his head. It falls like water over his rippling muscles that are like weathered sand, causing me to frown as I lose sight of them.

I lightly grasp the bottom of his t-shirt, lifting it so that I can see the contours of his abdomen. Leaning forward, I press a kiss to the hollow of his chest and then another one, lower on his torso. The shirt in my hand rips as Reed's wings push out again from his back, leaving the white fabric slack in my hand. I let the cotton slip from my fingers to the floor.

Reed's fingers grasp the hair at the base of my neck, angling my face up so that he can press his lips to mine. His kisses are crushing, making my knees weak. I have to lean into him for support. Letting go of my hair, Reed's hands move to my collar, pulling the fabric apart so that the buttons he just closed suddenly pop off the shirt and fall to the floor in a soft twinkling of sound. His hands part the shirt and then run with a sultry heat over my skin. I make a soft sound that is somewhere between a groan and a squeak.

"I missed that sound," Reed says against my skin as he kisses my throat, making me shiver.

"Hmmm?" I murmur, half in question and half in pleasure.

"The little noises you make—I especially like that one," he says. He kisses the round edge of my shoulder. His teeth graze my skin, and I inhale a small gasp. "I like that one, too," he growls. "There are several more I need to hear before we can leave the closet," he says. Reed pulls me with him to the floor; he elicits an array of other intimate sounds from me that I didn't know I make.

❧

Dressed in another one of Reed's shirts and a pair of his boxers, I hold his hand as I trail him to the kitchen. Pool balls striking each other make me glance into the Billiards Room as Reed leads me by it. Zephyr is hunched over the table about to take a shot and Russell is leaning against his pool stick. They both look over at the doorway as we slip by. I also don't fail to notice the huge claymores resting within their reach, leaning against the wood-trim wainscot of the wall. Seeing the swords, I cringe and become alert. They're expecting something, too. It makes my hand tighten in Reed's.

In the kitchen, Reed and I go to the refrigerator. Buns and Brownie must've stocked it when they'd arrived. I doubt Zephyr is letting them near the foyer, let alone past it to get outside. Russell has created a barrier around the house; I can feel his magic there. He's protecting us.

Reed opens the freezer and smiles. He reaches in and pulls out the family-size box of mac and cheese, lifting his eyebrow as he holds it up to show me. A blush stains my cheeks as I smile at him and nod. I take it from him and unwrap it. I turn away, setting it on the counter before I prepare the oven. Reed's arms slip around my waist from behind, pulling my back against him and kissing my hair tenderly. His hand slips upward, tracing the line of my breast. I shiver.

"What's for supper?" Russell asks, strolling into the kitchen with Zephyr right behind him. They have their swords with them, which they discretely lean against the other side of the counter out of my view.

I stiffen and look up to see Russell's brown eyes assessing me from head to toe. My hair is tousled, hanging loose down my back. I self-consciously drag my fingers through it to try to smooth it.

"Don't, Red," Russell says as if reading my mind. "You'd win the sexy bed-head contest the way it is."

"Thanks," I reply as my cheeks redden. "We're making dinner. You in?"

"In," he says without reservation "You okay?"

"I'm..." I falter, "alive."

"That's half the battle...stayin' alive," he says, watching for my reaction.

"What's the other half," I ask sadly.

He shrugs. "Kickin' some ass," he replies, trying his hardest to lessen the weight of everything that's happened.

"Thanks for taking care of the first part for me," I try to smile while winding my finger in the air, but I know it's not reaching my eyes.

"I couldn't let you off that easily. I still need you," he admits, lowering his chin.

I shake my head. "You don't need me. You're as strong as I am...stronger."

"I do need you," he murmurs. "You're my best friend...and Zee gives the worst relationship advice ever. Anya still isn't talkin' to me."

A reluctant smile forms on my lips. "She'll come around. How could she not?" I ask, meaning every word.

Russell rubs the stubble on his chin thoughtfully. But, his eyes narrow in concentration when Zephyr says to Reed, "Brennus lives?"

They'd been staring at each other, assessing each other's state of being. Reed's expression of calm doesn't change as he says, "For the moment."

"I thought I would have to hunt you," Zephyr says in a quiet tone. "I do not think I could have killed you."

"If it ever comes to that, I would be grateful it was you," Reed replies.

"And, I, you," Zephyr agrees.

Reed shrugs off his shirt, allowing his wings to unfold from his back. As they spread wide, I watch Zephyr do the same, tugging off his t-shirt and expanding his light brown wings. Reed reaches out and pulls a feather off of Zephyr's wing. Zephyr mimics the same action, pulling off a feather of Reed's wing. Reed tucks Zephyr's feather in his wing where his other has gone missing. Zephyr does the same.

"What was that?" Russell asks, looking from Reed to Zephyr.

"A promise," Zephyr says, and then adds, "to my brother."

Brownie and Buns breeze into the kitchen with Anya.

"Something smells wonderful," Buns says. "I'll set the table. Brownie, get the glasses." As Buns passes on her way to the mahogany cabinets, her hand touches my shoulder, squeezing it lightly.

Her attempt to be normal isn't lost on me. I straighten my shoulders. I feel Reed's fingertips touch my inner elbow, they slide down my arm, causing my whole body to attune to him. His fingers cross my palm and thread with mine. He gives my hand a gentle squeeze. I let go of him and say, "I'll check the oven. It should be almost ready."

"Are you hungry, Anya," Russell asks Anya as she hovers in the doorway, looking unsure. He walks to the table and holds out a chair for her by the snapping fire in the fireplace. Anya nods, walking further into the kitchen to the table, allowing Russell to seat her.

Gathering the food, Buns, Brownie, and I bring it to the table while Reed and Zephyr open a couple bottles of wine and fill our glasses. We each take a seat except for Reed. Reed remains standing and says something in Angel. I gather that it is their version of a prayer by the devout expressions on the faces of the angels. Reed switches to English as he lifts his wineglass, "To my family, no matter what the future holds for us, may we always find our way back to each other."

"To family," each of us says in turn before drinking. Reed takes his seat next to mine and finds my hand beneath the table. His simple touch relaxes me and I settle back to enjoy this respite with my family, this moment of grace.

Glossary

Aingeal – angel (Gaelic/Irish)
Aspire – angel significant other, similar to a human husband or wife (Angel)
A-tkel-el-ini – troublemaker (Navajo)
Banjax – destroy (Gaelic/Irish)
Be-al-doh-tso-lani al-tah-je-jay – many big guns (Navajo)
Cogadh – war (Gaelic/Irish)
Da-de-yah – depart (Navajo)
Dún do chlab – shut your gob (mouth) (Gaelic/Irish)
Gdzie poszedł – where did he go (Polish)
Go hIfreann leat – Go to hell (Gaelic/Irish)
Grá mo chroí – love of my heart (Gaelic/Irish)
Ifrit – shapeshifting demon who hunts divine angels (Angel)
Iniqui – demons who reside in the corpses of other beings, especially humans (Faerie)
Ji-din-nes-chanh – retreat (Navajo)
Khac-da – ambush (Navajo)
Leh-chi lit – red smoke (Navajo)
Lei-cha-ih-yil-knee-ih il-day – army arrive (Navajo)
Máistir – master (Gaelic/Irish)
Mo chroí –my heart (Gaelic/Irish)
Mo shíorghrá – my eternal love (Gaelic/Irish)
Na-dzah – return (Navajo)
Na-ne-klah – difficult (Navajo)
Ne-ol – storm (Navajo)
Nevarache - lizard-like creature with black scales, yellow eyes, and long talon-like claws (Faerie)
Nil-ta – stubborn (Navajo)
O-zhi – miss (Navajo)
Pocałuj mnie w dupe – kiss my ass (Polish)
Póg mo thóin – kiss my ass (Gaelic/Irish)
Reconnoître – black-winged nocturnal demon from Sheol who scouts and hunts prey – a messenger (Faerie)

Riser – demon from Sheol that resembles an enormous greyhound dog until it consumes blood, and then it changes by rising into a vicious beast (Angel)

Sclábhaí – slave (Gaelic/Irish)

Síorghrá - eternal love (Gaelic/Irish)

Sláinte – cheers (Gaelic/Irish)

Táim i ngrá leat – I'm in love with you (Gaelic/Irish)

Tkin – ice (Navajo)

Tkoh – water (Navajo)

To-altseh-hogan – temporary camp (Navajo)

Toh-bah-ha-zsid – afraid (Navajo)

To-ho-ne – suffer (Navajo)

Tristitiae – sorrow (Latin)

Tso – big (Navajo)

Tuigim – I understand (Gaelic/Irish)

Twoja matka to bajki – Your mother is a faerie (Polish)

Wans – human women (Gaelic/Irish)

Werree – demons who steal body parts of other creatures to wear over their own shadowy figures (Faerie)

Yah-a-da-hal-yon-ih – take care of (Navajo)

Acknowledgements

Thank you, God, for the many blessings You have given me.

Thank you to my mother, Gloria Lutz, for all of her hard work and dedication copyediting the entire Premonition series.

To my husband, Tom, thank you for putting up with my writer's uniform and the general disarray! I love you.

To Max & Jack, you're my loves. Always.

To Aprille, I love you, sis.

To all of you who continue to read my stories, I'm extremely grateful for your love and support. Thank you!

To my Indie Hellcats: Georgia Cates, Shelly Crane, Rachel Higginson, Angeline Kace, Michelle Leighton, Samantha Young, and Quinn Loftis, thank you for helping me navigate the publishing world and for being a bevy of information on all things called life. You all have such style and grace. I'm fortunate to walk among you.

To the amazing Celeste Harrington of The Book Hookup who gave me my first interview ever. I'm really grateful and honored by you! And to all of the sublime women who gave me my first podcast review at The Book Hookup: Celeste Harrington, Christina Gaillard, Ana Hayes, Jag, and Amy Conner! I love you guys! Thank you (flaily arms for Christina). And for Ana, maybe the only person on Team Russell, you make me smile with every single one of your tweets.

SupaGurl. You. Are. Awesome. It was a perfect day when you came into my life. I hope you stay forever.

To Janet Wallace, for allowing me to be a part of UtopYa Con 2012. It brought the best people into my life. Thank you for your brilliance.

To Volatastic Phil, Ben has nothing on you. You're a poet.

To Rob Guthrie, thank you for your friendship.

To all of the amazing book bloggers who take a chance on authors every day, I thank you from the bottom of my heart. Your love of books is awe-inspiring. I'm truly grateful to you.

Coming Soon
Iniquity
The Premonition Series Volume 5

CHAPTER 1

My Heart
Without You

Soft whispering touches cascade against my cheek, so light that they're almost a shadow against my eyelashes. I stir in bed, stretching my arm to Reed, searching for my angel even in my half-conscious state. My arms come up empty as my fingertips touch damp earth. I open my eyes to the hazy sense of wrongness. My fingers trip over the silky softness of my feathers. The acrid smell of smoke is all around me as my head lies against the grassy ground. Above me, angels are flying, moving chaotically across the sky.

Fire rains across the dusky skyline, turning what is left of the blue filament to red and orange as giant rockets burst and riot. The explosions make the ground tremble beneath me. There is a pain in my belly; fear twists it. A shrill roar causes all the hairs on my body to stand up at once. I've never heard its like and I dread seeing what is capable of making such a sound.

As I sit up, my head throbs painfully. Using my trembling hands, I rest my head in them, hoping that the world will stop spinning. From the corner of my eye, I see an armored Power angel flying low to the ground near me. His forward trajectory switches in the sky as a hulking Seraph broadsides him. They rapidly lose altitude, plummeting towards me.

When the angels tumble to the ground only a few feet away, my hands go up to cover my head and I brace myself for their impact. Rather than being crushed by them, I'm scooped up and thrown over someone's shoulder. My cheek rests against his strong, blood-colored wing. Yelling in Angel echoes in the air as carnage from the war waging around me litters the ground.

"Mo chroí," the soft voice echoes in my skull like it's being amplified.

No longer slung over an angel's shoulder, I awake in my bed, but I'm not in my room in Crestwood. The bed is in the middle of the battlefield I'd just awoken to. A thin, white sheet barely covers me as I sit up against the pillows with a jerk.

I feel Brennus in my bones before I ever see him. I breathe him in; his exotic scent makes my skin dance to touch him. I could paint him red and he wouldn't be anymore startling to me. Brennus' black, velvety wings float around him as dark as a shadow in the night. They're nearly as black as his hair.

His iridescent green eyes drink in every inch of me. I clutch the stark white sheet to my breasts to cover them, only to find as I look down that it's nearly translucent. I push my long auburn hair over my shoulders to cover them.

"Ach, Genevieve, have I na told ye before dat yer attempts to hide yer beauty from me are made in vain? Ye only succeed in looking more seductive."

"Where are we?" *I ask, moistening my lips that have suddenly gone dry. I'm still in my bed, but I'm far from my room.*

"Ye tell me, 'tis yer dream," *Brennus smiles nefariously as I gaze around in trepidation.* "As soon as I entered dis nightmare, it began to crash down around me—Heaven is secretive, but I was able ta discern enough."

"What did you see?" *I ask him.*

I shiver and he smiles. "'Tis na a pleasant future. Welcome ta da new age, eh? 'Twould appear dat tomorrow has been cancelled." *Brennus lifts his eyebrow, looking around as the dreamscape surrounding us is changing, turning from catastrophic destruction to a haze and blur of shapes. Dust swirls in the wasteland.*

"How did you enter my dream?" *I ask, deciding to focus on the least scary of everything I'm seeing around me.*

"I was worried dat da other wouldna be able ta save ye. I have been to da aingeal house, but dere are layers of magic surrounding it. I couldn't be certain it was yer magic. Da other has a similar scent ta his spells."

"Magic has a scent?" *I ask.*

"It does," *he nods.* "Yers is exotic—intoxicating."

"You didn't know I survived?" *I cringe inwardly. He's been here at the house studying us.*

"I have been going out of me mind wi' worry over it. Me yearning for ye was so strong dat I had ta find a way ta quench it. I retrieved one of da perfume bottles ye gave ta me."

"The ones with my blood?" *I ask with my heart skipping a beat.*

"The moment I tasted ye on me tongue, I felt ye. I lay down and shut me eyes and tought o' ye. I tought of da way ye smile, da way ye walk, da turn yer eyebrow takes when ye're angry. It made me heart ache. I was afraid ye died. Dere was a pull within me...here," *he says, indicating his heart as he lays his hand over it, "...and I followed it...ta ye—ta dis place." He opens looking around at the contours of my dreamscape. "Me heart aches without ye."*

I'm an idiot, I think. I gave him a gift that provides him a means to reach me—to get inside my head—my dreams.

"It's a cruel world, Brennus. Imagine how my heart felt when you tried to kill me," I murmur, watching him warily as he turns toward me and smiles again.

"'Tis a violent world, Genevieve. Dat's why I'm here. I've found out a few tings. Tings ye need ta know."

"Oh?" I ask, stalling for time so I can try to figure out how to wake up from this nightmare. I pinch my arm hard, but nothing happens except now my arm hurts.

"Have ye na learned yet dat 'tis us against dem?" he asks me earnestly.

My mouth hangs open until I snap it closed. "No," I say heatedly. "I thought it was me against you."

Brennus frowns, "'Tis na. We're on the same side. Ye're me queen."

"I'm not your queen! You tried to kill me. I'm divorcing you or dethroning you—whatever! We're done!"

"Ye really hurt me. No one has hurt me like dat—ever," Brennus says as he draws nearer. His skin is a softer color; it's not just the lighting. His bare chest is like that of an angel's. It's almost like he burns brighter now. His wings move with an elegance that would be hard to copy. He notices me staring at them. A crooked smile crosses his lips as he says, "But, den, ye gave me back me wings... dey're na da same color as was born ta me—dey once were white."

"Do they work? Can you use them?" I ask, biting my lower lip lightly because I have an impulse to go to him and pet his wings to see if they're soft like velvet—black velvet.

"Oh, dey work grand," he says, "dey're stronger dan me old ones. Finn is jealous."

"Finn...he's alive?" I ask, and something within me exalts knowing that I didn't kill Finn when I'd unleashed my wrath of energy against Brennus and his soldiers.

"He was na among dem," he says, seeing my relief and trying to suppress a smile. "He is yet undead and more dan a wee bit angry wi' me, truth be told. He blames me for losin' ye again. He tinks dis is all me fault."

"It's not your fault. I just love someone else," I breathe.

"Ye love me, too—ye love me da most," he says.

"I don't—"

"Ye do love me da most. Ye have ta fight it, shift it ta hate because ye fear it," he says. "Ye only hate me because I will na play by yer rules. I make ye abide moin."

"I hate you for what you did to Reed," I snarl.

"I let him live," he says with his jaw clenched. "He'll na be so fortunate should he try ta come between us again."

"I love—"

"Ye just met him first. But ye'll need a god o' war if ye intend ta survive and so ye've made one. Me. Ye made me stronger wi' new found power."

"That was an accident, Brennus. I was trying to kill you, like I killed all of your men," I point out.

"Den we're even and so we can begin again—and ye only emptied da cradle. Dat was but a few of me newest warriors ye ended, na even close ta all o' dem. Ye can na drown da fire wi'out me. Ye feel it now? 'Tis na cold between ye and me. 'Tis fire."

He's right; the closer he gets to me, the warmer it becomes between us. He sits on the sheet as I draw up my legs away from him. The bed sags under his weight. He's really here in my dream. He has a physical presence; he's not just a ghostly shape, but is as real as I am.

Barely breathing, I watch him reach for my sheet, tugging it lightly so that I have to clutch it to keep myself covered. The supple fabric trails over my flesh anyway, feeding his hungry eyes. I pull harder on it, but Brennus flicks his hands and my arms splay wide and are tied behind me to the headboard of the bed.

My eyes narrow as I glare at him, feeling the sheet slip lower on my breasts as I struggle against the binding on my wrists.

Brennus' eyes go from sultry to frustrated when he pulls the sheet lower only to find me fully clothed in a baggy t-shirt and jeans, brought about by my hastily cast spell. I smirk at him when he looks into my eyes. I rub my wrist that I unbound using my own magic.

"Dat's no fun, Genevieve," Brennus says with another smile. He flicks his hand at me and when I look down at myself I'm attired in a silky black corset pulled tight enough to crack my ribs. Skimpy black panties and black-gartered stockings complete the ensemble.

He reaches for me, but I growl and flick my hand at him. He is thrust backward to the wooden poster of the bed. His hands are bound behind him and a metal manacle around his throat keeps his head from turning away from me.

"Is that fun?" I ask, getting up off the bed and approaching him with my hands on my corseted hips.

"Honestly?" he asks me with a raise of his eyebrow. "'Tis, mo chroí." Then he smiles his wicked smile that seems to touch me everywhere. I conjure a black trench coat and hastily tie the belt at my waist.

I turn away from him, not wanting him to see how he affects me; the ache to touch him is there, just under the surface. Brennus' arms slip around my *waist from behind, startling me, not only because he freed himself from my spell, but also because his arms are warm against me, not cold. They cause a riot inside of me.*

"Brennus," his name falls from my lips in surprise.

"Do na fight me, Genevieve. I have someting important ta tell ye and it can na wait."

I allow him to hug me as I grow still. "What do you need to tell me?" I ask in a whisper. I know him, he's calm on the outside, but his voice betrays something...it sounds like concern...deep concern.

"I was wrong about ye," he brushes my hair away from my neck, breathing in the scent of it.

"This is bad. You rarely admit to being wrong."

"And ye're very stubborn. Ye rarely relent ta listen ta yer demon, unless ye need him...and ye do," he says, running his fingertips over the curve of my throat.

"You're my demon?" I ask.

"I am," he affirms. "Yers and no other's."

"You keep shifting on me, demon, and I can't keep you happy," I wait for him to coil in retort, but he doesn't. "You're ruthless."

"Yer love is ruthless," he breathes against my cheek. "Hush, now. We can argue about it later. I was wrong ta tink ye're like Persephone," he admits as he explains. "Dat portrait blinded me ta whah ye are. Dere is another name dat suits ye better." He turns me around so that he can look into my eyes. His green eyes shine with ancient fire. "Ye've begun a havoc in Sheol. 'Tis yer face," he uses his thumb to rub my cheek tenderly. "Beauty wi' grace. 'Tis a face worthy of launching a tousand ships. Ye're na Persephone atall ta da ones dat hunt ye now...ye're Helen."

"What?" my voice shakes as I whisper.

"'Twas Finn who learned da truth—Molly really. She has developed a taste for Fallen. She attracts dem with a certain skill, 'tis her air of innocence dat draws dem in. 'Tis like milk and honey ta dem. She stumbled across quite an interesting bird."

"Interesting how?" I ask.

"One dat knew a great deal about ye," he says. "'Twas Finn dat made him elaborate on whah he knew."

"Which is?" I murmur, feeling all the blood draining away from my cheeks.

"We were wrong when we tought dat ye're da only hybrid human-angel..."

"I know I'm not the only one—there's Russell..." I trail off as he slowly shakes his head at me.

"I'm na speaking of da other. Sheol has found a way ta create deir own version of yer kind...and dey want ye ta meet him. Ye're very special, Genevieve, special in that ye're still the only one—da only female."

"How can you be sure your source wasn't lying?" The need to deny what he's telling me is so strong that I can taste the fear on my tongue.

"Our source was interrogated by Finn. He told Finn anyting he wanted ta know just for the pleasure of his touch."

"What does this mean?" I ask as my hands rest against his chest for support. I feel like my legs might give out on me at any moment. "What do they want?"

"Yer enemies, da Fallen, have decided dat ye're worth a war. Dey're gathering da means ta wage dat war. Every demon is now deciding whether dey'll play a part."

"And what part do you intend to play?" I ask.

His neck bends and his lips hover inches from mine. "The part that allows us ta survive, of course. Da Fallen would like ta introduce ye ta deir spawn. Dat does na fit inta me plans."

"What if the price becomes too high," I wonder aloud, "for yer plans?"

"Ye have me marrow in yer bones, mo chroí. And I've yers. I will lay down me life ta protect ye," he promises. "We have ta strike a truce. I can na fight ye and dem, too."

"I don't trust you. There can be no truce."

"I'll love ye in yer dreams until ye do," he says in a husky voice. "'Tis yers ta decide. Do I have ye in da day or in da night? Da choice is yers, but either way, I will have ye."

Brennus lowers his head then, kissing me roughly and causing an ache for him to spread inside of me. His hands entwine in my hair, keeping my lips to his. I shiver at the craving for him he generates with his intoxicating kisses. Stroking my hair, he murmurs against my lips, "I love ye, Genevieve. I'll protect ye from yer nightmares."

My twisting sense of fate abruptly ends when Reed's voice whispers, "Evie," breaking the fever growing within me.

"Evie...love?" Reed says again, less distant. My eyes fly open to find Reed reclining next to me on our bed in our room. "Good morning," he murmurs brushing his lips to mine, but it's not Reed that I taste on my tongue...it's Brennus.

About The Author

I live in Michigan with my husband and our two sons. My family is very supportive of my writing. When I'm writing, they often bring me the take-out menu so that I can call and order them dinner. They listen patiently when I talk about my characters like they're real. They rarely roll their eyes when I tell them I'll only be a second while I finish writing a chapter...and then they take off their coats. They ask me how the story is going when I surface after living for hours in a world of my own making. They have learned to accept my "writing uniform" consisting of a slightly unflattering pink fleece jacket, t-shirt, and black yoga pants. And they smile at my nerdy bookishness whenever I try to explain urban fantasy to them. In short, they get me, so they are perfect and I am blessed. Please visit me at my website: http://www.amyabartol.com

Please enjoy an exclusive excerpt from Shelly Crane's YA novel, Devour. It's available now for purchase through Amazon and Barnes & Noble.

There's a game you play. The one where you guess what the shapes and objects the clouds have made above you. Today there was a lady with a long witchy nose, a rabbit, a sailboat. Everyone's perception is different; we all see different things. I personally think you see what you want to see.

I was solely entranced in my gazing. The sun was bright behind me as I lay in the grass, my head on my jacket. My insanely dark black hair was long and almost too warm as it fanned around my head and caught the sunlight. The small hill on the edge of the park was the perfect spying spot. Spying on clouds, on people, on squirrels, but I was alone. Alone here and alone in life. My family used to come here together, but no more. My sister was gone, joined the Navy and would be gone for four years. She couldn't handle the fact that our parents died and decided to fulfill my dad's wish for us to be in the armed forces.

The burglary, and the burglar who took their lives, was something we all wished to forget. Even the Montana police hastened the investigation because things like that just didn't happen in our town. But there I was, stuck in my last year at high school, living with my Pastor's family as a temporary custody home until I graduated and went off to college. I was as alone as I could be.

The sun so bright behind me made the shadow that was suddenly loomed over me startling.

I looked up to see a guy standing by my head looking down at me. He had a little smile, almost wistful, on his lips as he cocked his head to the side. I sat up and twisted to see him better. His eyes were a freakishly bright violet. I'd never seen a guy with purple eyes - well, I'd never seen anyone with purple eyes. It was a rare thing, I guess, but now looking at them like that, they almost seemed natural.

He was wearing a deep green button up shirt with the sleeves rolled up and jeans with a small tear in the knee. Aviator sunglasses hung from his collar. His hair was as black as mine and close cropped. His hands were in his pockets and he continued to stare at me until I spoke.

"Hi."

"Hello, there," he finally said, his voice deep and lilting with a small accent that I couldn't place.

"Can I...help you with something?" I asked since he continued to gaze at me unabashedly.

"Nope. Just enjoying the view," he said and then smiled slightly as he turned to look up at the clouds and then back down to me. "There always seems to be a rabbit and an old lady doesn't there."

"How did you know I was..."

"I guessed. Why else would you be laying here, alone, looking at the clouds?"

I laughed nervously and twisted the ring on my finger; my nervous tick.

"Are you new here? I haven't seen you around. Big Timber is a small town so, you kinda know everyone whether you want to or not."

He laughed and it was delicious and rich making my stomach flip. I frowned. I had a boyfriend. What was wrong with me?

"Yeah, I'm new. Just moved stateside from Zimbabwe. My parents were teachers at one of the schools there. I'm Elijah Thames, but everyone calls me Eli," he said and knelt down in front of me, sticking out his hand in greeting.

"Clara Hopkins."

I took his hand, almost expecting something to happen when our skin met. Though his hand was warm and rugged, it was just a normal handshake.

"Nice to meet you, Clara Hopkins."

"You too, Eli. You came at the perfect time I guess. Second semester starts tomorrow so we all get new classes. It won't just be you getting a new schedule."

"That's nice, I guess. I'm pretty used to being the new kid though."

"Are your parents missionaries or something?"

"Of sorts," he said vaguely and stood. "So, what's there to do in this town on a Sunday afternoon?"

"You're looking at it," I said through a giggle. "This is about it, I'm afraid. There is an old theater in town but it only plays one movie at a time and there's a club here, but I've never been to it. We usually just hang out at the burger place."

"Who's we?"

"What?"

"You said 'we hang out'. Who's we?"

"Oh. My friends and I. My boyfriend," I said and was shocked at how reluctant I was to tell him that.

"Ah, I see. I should have known it wouldn't be that easy, huh?"

"What wouldn't?" I asked though I felt the blush creeping up, knowing exactly what he meant.

He just smiled.

"Well, can I walk you home at least? It'll be getting dark soon."

"Um...sure, I guess." I took the hand he offered and then picked my brown corduroy jacket up, slipping it back on. "So, do you always walk up to strange girls in the park and start conversations?"

"Nah," he said slyly and bumped my shoulder. "They didn't have parks in Zimbabwe."

I burst out laughing and was intrigued by how comfortable we seemed to be together already.

"Where do you live?" I asked him as we hopped onto the sidewalk.

"We bought a place on Buxton."

"The bed and breakfast?"

"Yeah. My parents are all about trying something new."

"Wow. Well, it's a nice house. I've always loved that place."

"It's nice and big. Too big but I guess once you get a house full of guests it won't be big enough. I made my room the basement though, so that should help with the privacy."

"The basement? Won't that be cold and muggy and...creepy?"

"You watch a lot of scary movies, do you?" he said in amusement.

"Maybe I do," I spouted playfully. "I'm sure it's nice enough anyway. But you know, it could be the attic," I said and shivered in mock horror.

"Oh, attic's are *way* creepy."

We laughed and it resounded in the quiet darkening street.

He seemed to know right where he was going so I just walked beside him and let him lead us. Buxton was only a few blocks away from the city park and I lived beside the church near there.

We walked and talked for about a block before trouble turned the corner.

My boyfriend, Tate, was coming down the street in his big 4x4 truck. He was on the wrestling team, the town's pride. He was really good to me, very attentive, and while I enjoyed spending time with him, I wasn't in love with him. And he was a very jealous guy. All he ever talked about was us going to college together next year, but I didn't want to go to college. I wanted to go on a mission trip or maybe apply to a Music or Art school. If my parents were alive, they'd be so disappointed. My dad dreamed of his alma mater and the Army and my mom wanted me to marry right away and find a man to take care of me. Both of those dreams were nil.

But Tate was a sweet guy. Even though he was popular, he was pretty nice to everyone...except guys who tried to talk to me. He once almost pummeled my science lab partner when he stopped me in the hall to get my notes.

Apparently, his mom cheated on his dad all the time and his dad had no inclination to do anything about it. The whole town knew about it but they held a position of status and prime real estate in the town so no one cared, essentially. But Tate had always cared.

"Oh boy," I mumbled.

"What? What's wrong?"

"Nothing's wrong, just my boyfriend. Just don't listen to anything he says for the next five minutes, ok? I'm sorry ahead of time."

"Ok," he said, dragging it out in apprehension.

Tate stopped the truck and I saw it overcome him. His fingers turned white on the steering wheel, his lips grim in a tight line. He opened the door and closed it gently, too gently to be considered normal. It was a façade.

"Hey, Tate. Were you coming to see me?"

"You weren't at home. I was headed to the park to give you a ride...but I see you don't need one what with prince charming walking you home and all," he sneered, glaring daggers at Eli.

"Tate, this is Eli. He's new here and lives near me. We were walking home together, talking about school tomorrow."

"Uhuh."

"Tate," I chided and went to give him a kiss on the cheek. I felt his skin, hot and angry on my lips before I pulled back. He flicked his eyes to me once before looking back to Eli. "Tate, this is ridiculous," I whispered to him. "Why don't you trust me?"

"It's other guys I don't trust!" he yelled, making me jump. "You have no idea what guys are thinking about."

I took a deep confused breath. He'd never been that vehement before. I glanced over at Eli to apologize but he looked strange. Almost like he was...in ecstasy. His mouth was slightly open and his eyes hooded as he watched me. His breathing was heavy. I squinted at him and he seemed to snap out of it.

"Come on, man," he said to Tate. "Really, it was nothing. She was just telling me about classes changing and all since I just moved here. She told me she had a boyfriend within the first two minutes of talking to her."

Tate looked at me, his eyes softening a little. I looked at him pleadingly. He took a hesitant step towards me and when he saw I made no move to step away he caved and pulled me to him.

"I'm sorry, Clara, you know how I get. I can't... It's dumb, I know. I'm really sorry." He pulled back to look at me. "I didn't mean to be like that."

"I know you didn't," I said softly and him being the blonde, beefy guy he was who stood right at my height level, put his forehead to mine.

"How do you even put up with me?" he whispered.

"I don't know," I said jokingly, "you're pretty cute. I guess it makes up for it."

"Pretty cute?" he joked and suddenly dropped to one knee and in his best English white knight accent began to beg. "Oh, please, my darling. My love. Forgive me and my assness!"

This was the Tate I knew and cared about. He was fun, playful and not afraid to make a fool of himself.

I laughed and bowed a little.

"You're forgiven. Now. Tate, this is Eli Thames. Eli, this is Tate Richman. He's captain of our wrestling team and his dad's the mayor," I said proudly.

"Hi," Eli said cautiously and stuck his hand out.

Tate stood and took the hand offered.

"Hey, man. Sorry. I'm can be a bit of an ass when it comes to this girl. I'm sure you can understand," he said with a wry smile.

"Understood." Eli looked back to me and smiled a little sadly. "Well, I guess I'll see you guys tomorrow."

"You can have lunch with us tomorrow," I threw out. "I'm not sure if I'll see you before then, but we eat at the long table right in the middle of the cafeteria."

"Ok. Thanks."

"See ya, man," Tate said and waited for Eli to turn, then pulled me to him, snuggling into my neck. "Oh my gosh, Clara, you smell like something I very much want to eat."

I giggled and pushed him back a little.

"You think you're getting off that easy, buster?"

"What do I owe you this time?" he asked amused and touched his tongue to his lip to think. "Diaper duty? Because if that's it, it was nice knowing you."

"Hey!" I yelled playfully and smacked his chest. "No. Mrs. Ruth has the kids tonight, but you do have to take me home and...watch the last Vampire Diaries I DVRed."

"Ah, Clara," he groaned. "Anything but that."

"Come on, it's not that bad."

"It's torture," he said pointedly and then smiled. "But for you I'd do just about anything."

"I know," I agreed and I did. Tate had reasons to be the way he was and the way he normally treated me would put the Salvatore brothers to shame. But for some reason, I just couldn't move past the feeling that he was just some guy I liked, had feelings for, but knew it wasn't going anywhere. "Come on."

He helped me into the truck and drove the short distance to the Parish. Once we stopped in front of the house, I started to get out but he stopped me.

"Wait. Before we enter the no-touch zone..."

He pulled me to him across the seat and kissed me. Tate was usually a gentleman and knew how far I was willing to let him go. Sometimes he casually tried to push the envelope; he was a guy after all. This was apparently going to be one of those times.

His hand gripped my leg, as if to tug me into his lap. I let him. He seemed fueled by that and as his hands on my hips pulled me closer to him. I heard him groan a little. It rumbled through me and made my heart beat a little faster. I knew it was only torture to do this. I'd never let him do anything more than this. We were both virgins, though I was happier about it than he was. But sometimes, I just needed to feel the glue to the envelope strain a little.

I let him kiss me for a good while, just like that. I ran my fingers through his hair. It'd been a year since we started dating. We'd both always gone to the same school together, always lived in this town. We hung out with the same friends but he'd never seemed interested in me before and I never thought about him that way. I'd been on a few dates with other guys but never really dated anyone exclusively. Then one day, he met me at my locker, alone. It was odd because usually there was a group waiting there for me. As I made my way to him, he smiled bashfully.

"Hey."

"Hey," I had said cheerfully ignorant.

"How was Spanish? I have that next semester."

"Brutal."

"I was afraid of that. So, um...there's this movie playing at the Cineplex, Adam Sandler is in it. Looks pretty good. I was wondering if you wanted to go tonight?"

"Sure. Who else is going?"

"Just you. And me."

"Oh," I had said and even I heard the odd note to my voice. He mistook that as reluctance.

"It's ok if you don't want to go, I just figured it might be fun. It's ok," he had said and started to walk away.

"No, wait. I didn't say I didn't want to go."

"Do you want to?" he'd asked and came to stand closer than he'd ever stood before.

I remembered my pulse had suddenly jumped and I noticed how green his eyes really were for the first time.

"Yeah. I do."

His smile was genuine and a little surprised.

"Great. I'll pick you up at five thirty. We can get something to eat first if you want."

"Yeah. Sure."

He'd walked backwards, grinning, away from me. That night he'd picked me up and we had fun, lots of fun. When he dropped me off I couldn't help but ask why he was all of a sudden interested.

"I can't say it was all of a sudden," he'd answered. "I just wasn't sure if you'd want to and I didn't want things to be weird so I just watched you. But you never looked at me different...so I took a shot." Then he touched my cheek, his thumb sweeping across my cheek bone. "I'm glad I did."

"Me too."

Then he had kissed me and I felt something in me burn, like slow lava. We'd stood there on my parents porch and kissed slowly and gently for a good while before my dad turned the light off and on, making us laugh.

Two months later, when my parents died, he was there for me like no one else. He was the first person to meet me at the hospital waiting room. He held me - just held me - for hours in those uncomfortable chairs as I bawled my eyes out. My sister had been gone on a skiing trip with friends and wasn't there yet. I had been to a movie with my friend who moved to another town, Addison, and found my parents when she dropped me off. Tate stayed with me all night. Took me home, held me as I finally fell asleep on the couch. I don't know what I would have done without him.

And now as he ravished my mouth with skill and restraint I was still thankful for him but, I didn't love him. He had never said the words to me and I wasn't sure what I'd say if he did. I couldn't lie.

"Mmm, Clara, you are driving me every kind of crazy," he spoke huskily against my lips.

"Then maybe we should stop."

"No. No, don't stop," he said and took my lips again.

"Tate," I whispered. "You're not making this easy."

"Then give in to me," he suggested and I could hear the smile in his voice.

"Tate," I chided.

"Ok, ok." He blew a long breath. "It should be illegal for you to look the way you do and me not be able to have you."

"That's so cheesy," I said through a smile.

"I know," he laughed. "Alright, fine. Vampire Diaries in the preacher's house it is."

"Thank you," I said and pressed one last kiss to his lips before climbing out of the truck.

We spent the night like we spent a lot of nights; watching television on my bed, with the door open and a clear view of us from the door. I was allowed to lay by him but there was no kissing in the house. The preacher, Pastor Paul, was very lenient with me but there were certain rules of conduct, especially with Tate, that he was strict about. Despite us being young and all, we were both kind of home bodies. I'd rather sit and watch a movie at home with him than go out with a whole bunch of people. Our friends and I usually had to work pretty hard to get Tate to go out somewhere. He much preferred to be alone with me.

I was back, laying in the grass in the park. It all looked so real. The sun was bright and gorgeous behind me as it cast sparkles on the lake. A perfect day. I saw a shadow over me. At first I thought it was Tate but this person was taller and leaner and I felt something coming from him. Like I could feel his interest in me like a tangible thing. He knelt down beside me and I sat up. His face was covered in shadow from the halo of sun around his head. He reached out and touched my face. I gasped at the pleasure his touch elicited from my skin, goose bumps spread widely and I tingled all over. A response I'd never felt before, not even with Tate.

He moved in to kiss me and I was helpless to stop him. His lips almost touched mine. I felt the heat from his breath and a tremor ran through me. I suddenly felt afraid for no apparent reason at all and he moaned, seeming to enjoy my reaction. He pulled me to him and I whimpered as my terror spiked and he continued to hold me to him, like I was something he couldn't live without.

I jolted me eyes open with a start. What was that? I wasn't even asleep yet. Too many vampire shows for me...

The next morning I woke feeling a little strange. The first face I saw was Eli's and I immediately felt guilty. Tate was good to me, though he had his flaws like everyone else. He was very desirable; a hot commodity at our school, and I was lucky he wanted to date me. At least that's what everyone told me. It couldn't be that he was lucky to be with me.

So I threw on my school uniform. Most people hated them, but I loved them for some reason that escaped me. It was a typical uniform; red and black plaid skirt, white collar shirt and a vest that matched the skirt. No knee highs though, thank goodness. We were instructed to wear black ballet flats. After I fixed my hair and threw in some earrings, I made my way downstairs.

After helping Mrs. Ruth with all the babies breakfast - she had five kids under the age of five, the latest being twins who were only four months old - I rushed off to school, a little later than I'd wanted. I came through the gray concrete halls of our prison looking high school looking for Eli. I had wanted to get there before homeroom bell to make sure he found his class easily, but the bell was about to ring. Dang, I was going to be late. The church and the parish were across the street from the school. They shared a parking lot in fact, so I never got a ride with Tate; I didn't need one.

I ran to my new home room just as the last bell rang. I slid into the first empty seat I saw by the door. I noticed Tate across the room, looking at me with amused eyes. He made kiss lips at me as we both turned to face forward.

After the bell rang, we made our way to the hall. I waited for Tate and he studiously threw his arm around my shoulder and kissed my temple.

We walked to my locker and there was Eli. At first I thought he was waiting for me there and wondered what Tate would do, but I saw him reaching into the locker next to mine. He was now my neighbor.

"Hey, Eli," I said.

He looked surprised to see someone knowing his name and almost dropped his books, catching them very cutely in a jumble before they hit the floor and stuffing them in his locker.

"Oh. Hey, guys," he said in that low rumbling voice of his.

"Who do you have for homeroom?"

"Mr. Winepeeno?" he tried and Tate and I both laughed.

"It's Winepegofski. I know, it's an impossible name. I think he's from Russia or Poland or something."

Someone called my name and I looked up to see Ashley. I waved and turned back to Eli.

"A Polish guy teaches U.S. History?" Eli asked with a smirk.

"Welcome to America, Mr. Zimbabwe."

He laughed and leaned on his shoulder against his locker. I looked up to Tate to see him no longer smiling. He was looking between us with a slight frown gracing his brow.

"Tate, who do you have next?" I asked, trying to include him.

"Bishop. Shop," he spouted shortly.

"Ugh, well, we definitely won't share that class. I have Menendez."

"Me too," chimed Eli.

"Huh," Tate said, clearly annoyed. "I'm out. Gonna be late and Bishop will ride me all year."

"Tate," I called and grabbed his arm. "I'll see you at lunch, ok?"

"Ok," he said tightly.

"Hey," I pulled him to look at me and saw a couple freshman giggling at us from across the hall. I ignored them. "I'll miss you," I said to appease him. "It's too bad we don't have anymore classes together."

"Yeah, I'm sure you'll really miss me with Zimbabwe over there," he said low where Eli couldn't hear us.

"I will. He doesn't watch vamp shows with me and follow silly rules at the house I live at. He doesn't know exactly where to find me when he comes to see me and I'm not home. He's just a guy, Tate."

He laughed a small breathy laugh.

"Ok," he conceded. "You better miss me," he joked and poked a finger at my chest gently.

"I already do," I said and accepted his kiss. He usually didn't kiss me on the lips in school, but right then he was letting me have it. I felt his hand on my lower back, pressing me closer. In the distance I heard a whistle from someone and I pulled back to breath. "Wow."

He chuckled.

"I can definitely deal with wow."

"Bye."

"Bye, babe."

I watched him walk away as he bumped fist with someone and they started to jog across the campus.

Then I turned to see Eli still standing there, with a wry look on his handsome face. The fluorescent lights made his hair even blacker. He looked almost ethereal like that. Today he'd worn his hair spiked to the side and I noticed he had his right eyebrow pierced with a small silver rod. I hadn't seen that last night. He was wearing the same jeans as before but with a Queen 1986 Tour shirt. It was his first day, so he didn't have his uniform yet. It always made the new kids stick out like sore thumbs.

"Hey, sorry. I told you he's...I don't know. And I'm sorry about last night too."

"No worries. It's not your fault. So," he grabbed a black messenger bag from his locker and threw it over his shoulder, "can I walk with you to our next class or will I get my spleen removed for it?"

"Ha ha. Yes, walk with me. It's way over on the other side of the gym, so we better get going."

We walked and I saw he was getting quite a lot of attention. I even got the stink eye from a couple of girls and I couldn't help but laugh. He was definitely cute with a bad boy thing going that made me cringe with the cliché of it. He wasn't hot in the traditional sense, I guess. He was a little rugged and jagged, but he was extremely nice and not cocky so that added to his appeal.

"Hi, Clara!" Sarah called as she passed.

"Hey."

"Who's this?" she said and walked backwards beside us to eye him appreciatively.

"This is Eli. He's new."

"Oooh. New meat. I'm Sarah. I'm single by choice, a Pisces, and I'm on the spirit squad with Clara. I'm also free this Saturday."

Eli chuckled and it had the same effect on Sarah as it had on me yesterday. She looked about to jump him right there in the hall, so I saved her some embarrassment.

"Sarah, we're late. You can ogle him at lunch, ok?"

"Ok. Bye, babe! Bye, Eli," she sang his name and flounced away.

"She eats lunch with you?"

"Afraid so. You may as well get used to it now. We hardly ever get new kids at our school and the girls I hang out with are...forward when it comes to guys. You can back out now and I wouldn't blame you."

"No. No, I like a challenge." I looked at him sideways to see him smiling in his profile. "So the spirit squad? I didn't peg you as a cheerleader."

"You pegged right. I'm not," I laughed. "Spirit squad decorates for games and sells tickets and ribbons and stuff. We try to pep people up for events."

"I see. Sounds interesting. And cheerleaders can't do this?"

"Not when they're too busy *getting* busy in the bathroom before the games."

He laughed and I looked at him with a smile. He was so different somehow.

While gazing at him I forgot to watch where I was going and plowed right into a freshman, but he may as well have been Andre' the Giant. He was huge and the fact that I was a girl apparently had no effect on him.

"Watch it," he growled.

"Sorry."

"Why don't you just take your," he slapped my butt hard, "pretty little pampered spirit squad butt back to where you belong and get out of my way."

"Whoa, pal," Eli said and pulled me behind him. I was surprised by it but grateful. "Don't talk to her like that and don't *ever* touch her again."

By this point there was an eager crowd with the word fight dancing in their eyes.

"Who are you, Pippy?" Everyone laughed and snickered. "If I were you I'd watch it. You're not making a very good first impression at this school. First, you're hanging out with spoiled ice queen over here, and now you're messing with me. I'd just go around me and pretend you never got in my way if I were you."

"Sure. I'll do that after you apologize," Eli said calmly.

"I don't apologize to brats who get everything they want. She should apologize for bumping me."

"I did," I mumbled at the same time that Eli said, "She did."

"Whatever-"

"Get to class!" Mr. Brank called from his classroom and everyone scattered. "Now."

"Later, Pippy," the big freshman jerk called. "Later, spoiled brat."

We started to walk and heard the bell. We were still a couple hallways away from class and I saw no point in rushing now.

"Thank you," I said after some time. "I have no idea who he was but he apparently knows me."

"I don't think he does if he thinks you're a pampered spoiled brat."

"You don't know me," I said but thought it sounded defensive so I added jokingly, "I could be a horrible drama queen who stomps freshman under my leather stiletto boots."

"I highly doubt that," he rebuted and looked at my feet, then dragged his gaze back up to my eyes. "Besides, I don't see any stilettos."

I realized we'd stopped in the hall and were now just standing there, looking at each other.

"Thanks. Really. You didn't have to do that. Now you've already made an enemy and it's the first day."

"Yeah, but I made a friend too."

Gosh, his eyes were so breathtaking. It made me feel like I had Jell-O knees looking at him. His face changed and he cocked his head a little before opening his mouth slightly. He looked surprised this time though. He had that same look before, last night, when Tate and I had been fighting; like he was in ecstasy.

"What is it?" I asked.

He shook his head and smiled sheepishly at me.

"Sorry. You're just...um. We better get to class."

"Yeah," I said nodding.

We walked into Menendez's class well after the bell, everyone turning to look and see the new guy. I saw a couple people I sat with at lunch in this class too and dreaded the conversation I knew would take place later as we took the only two seats left; the two sitting right next to each other in the back.

End of Preview
You may find ways to purchase Devour as well as more of Shelly's other books and information at her website
www.shellycrane.blogspot.com

Made in the USA
Lexington, KY
04 December 2012